THE TEXAS PAN AMERICAN SERIES

Recollections
of Things to Come

(LOS RECUERDOS DEL PORVENIR)

By ELENA GARRO

TRANSLATED BY RUTH L. C. SIMMS

Drawings by Alberto Beltrán

UNIVERSITY OF TEXAS PRESS AUSTIN & LONDON

The Texas Pan American Series is published with the assistance of a revolving fund established by the Pan American Sulphur Company and other friends of Latin America in Texas. Publication of this book was assisted also by a grant from the Rockefeller Foundation through the Latin American translation program of the Association of American University Presses.

Introduction

ELENA GARRO'S FIRST NOVEL, *Recollections of Things to Come*
(*Los recuerdos del porvenir*), appeared in 1963 and was awarded
the important Xavier Villaurrutia Prize for that year. With action occurring in the 1920's, the novel depicts life in the small
Mexican town of Ixtepec during the grim days of the Cristero
rebellion. The town tells its own story against a variegated back-
ground of political change, religious persecution, and social unrest. Miss Garro is a masterly storyteller. Writing in a style that
is more akin to poetry than to prose, she constructs a plot of dramatic intensity and suspense.

Yet this is a book that does not depend for its effectiveness on
narrative continuity. It is a book of episodes, one that leaves with
the reader a series of vivid impressions. The colors are bright, the
smells are pungent, the many characters clearly drawn in a few
bold strokes.

We glimpse intimate scenes of the "passionate and secret" life
of those who dwell in the Hotel Jardín: General Francisco Rosas,
morbidly obsessed by jealousy; the beautiful, impassive Julia
Andrade; the other officers and their mistresses. We see Luchi's
squalid bawdyhouse and its slatternly occupants, and in their
midst the incongruous presence of the irrational Juan Cariño, who
decries the lack of reason of those about him and extols the value
of words, the tools of rationality. We attend the gatherings at the
home of don Joaquín and doña Matilde Meléndez, where the
members of their social circle exchange inconsequential conversation and sip cool drinks on nights of oppressive heat. We ob-
serve the snobbery, greed, and selfishness of the wealthy Goríbars.
In sharp contrast are the abnegation and integrity of such strong,
humble characters as the faithful retainer Félix, the old servant

woman Gregoria, and the young manservant Cástulo, in whose nature any malice or self-seeking has no place.

Interspersed with the major episodes there are subordinate incidents of great power and poignancy, such as the humiliation of don Ramón Martínez at Pando's cantina, the rehearsals for the play and the magic wrought by the rediscovery of illusion, the people's reaction to the closing of the church, the general exaltation accompanying the preparations for doña Carmen's party, and the abortive escape attempt of the mistresses.

But the reality the author imparts to the novel stems not from the outer world of objects and events, the world of clock time, but rather from the skillful mingling of introspective revery with the dramatic episodes. Sporadically, attention is focused on the inner world of the personages, on what they retain in the depths of the soul, as a means of character delineation. For the protagonists, memories are a refuge, an almost mystical experience, by which they defeat mutability and escape from the calamitous times in which they live, from the violence and cruelty that surround them. The memories from the past, mingled in the present with intimations of the future, thus become the only reality, and time, losing its validity, is refuted.

Martín Moncada's desire to free himself from the shackles of mechanical time is symbolized each night at nine when his servant Félix, "obeying an old custom of the house," stops the clocks. The family then enters "a new time." And Moncada also eschews the "anecdotic time" of the calendar which would deprive him of the "other time" within him, that of his "unlived memory." If he is a failure by worldly standards, it is merely that he cannot accord importance to the things of the real world—the world that others call real—preferring instead to find refuge in his own world of fantasy.

And doña Matilde never quite understands this eccentricity of her brother's until, when the grotesqueness of events has become overwhelming, she grasps the meaning as if by intuition and acknowledges that don Martín has been right in wanting to live "outside of time."

For Isabel and her brothers, who feel a deep mutual kinship for one another and a sense of alienation from those around them, adulthood is resignation to humdrum existence. The past beckons themselves in the world." Their youthful resolve to leave Ixtepec to them alluringly, and returns them to the pristine days of their childhood, "when the three shared the infinite surprise of finding is realized at last as, departing by separate routes, they are united in an identical destiny.

Before our eyes, other characters are stripped down to their memories, to what they retain that sets them apart, differentiates them from all the others. And the reason for the General's obsessive jealousy of Julia is precisely this: her memories—of other times, of other men—will always stand as barricades he can never penetrate, a part of her innermost being he can never possess.

And when time stops dead to permit Julia and Felipe Hurtado to flee from Ixtepec, the fantasy world is made dramatically concrete, clock time is tangibly shown up as the illusion it is.

The book fascinates us, down to the final gruesome episode. In *Recollections of Things to Come*, Miss Garro ensnares us in a shimmering web of pathos and passion, of love and death, that we are not likely to forget easily.

Elena Garro was born in Puebla, Mexico, on December 11, 1920. She studied at the National Autonomous University of Mexico. For a time she arranged choreographies for the Theater of the University, and later served as a journalist in Mexico and the United States. Miss Garro's marriage to the famous Mexican poet and essayist Octavio Paz subsequently ended in divorce.

In 1954 she began to write for films. She achieved her first fame as a Mexican playwright of note in 1957 with three one-act plays which were presented by the Poesía en Voz Alta drama group. The following year these works were published, along with several other one-act plays by Miss Garro, in a single volume entitled *Un hogar sólido* (A Solid House). Critics hailed the author's dramatic originality and poetic sensitivity. Other plays followed, establishing further her reputation as a writer of importance.

The year after her brilliant debut in the novel with *Los recuerdos del porvenir*, Miss Garro gave additional proof of her versatility with a successful volume of eleven short stories, *La semana de colores* (Week of Colors). This collection revealed the contrast between fantasy and reality, the powerful imagination, and the deep human sympathy that have come to be her trademarks.

Miss Garro's stories and plays have been published in reviews in Mexico as well as abroad, where they have been translated into English, French, German and Swedish. She has traveled extensively throughout Europe and the Far East and has spent considerable time in France.

RUTH L. C. SIMMS

PART ONE

ONE

Here I sit on what looks like a stone. Only my memory knows what it holds. I see it and I remember, and as water flows into water, so I, melancholically, come to find myself in its image, covered with dust, surrounded by grass, self-contained and condemned to memory and its variegated mirror. I see it, I see myself, and I am transfigured into a multitude of colors and times. I am and I was in many eyes. I am only memory and the memory that one has of me.

From this height I contemplate myself: vast, lying in a dry valley. I am surrounded by spiny mountains and yellow plains inhabited by coyotes. My houses are squat, white-painted, and their roofs appear to be sun-baked or water-shimmering, depending on whether it is the dry or the rainy season. There are days like today when remembering makes me sad. I wish I had no memory, or that I could change myself into pious dust to escape the penalty of seeing myself.

I knew other times: I was founded, besieged, conquered, and decked out to receive armies. I knew the unutterable joy of war, which creates disorder and unforeseen adventure. Then they left me undisturbed for a long time. One day new warriors appeared

3

who robbed me and changed my position. Because there was a time when I was in a green and luminous valley, of easy cultivation, until another army with drums and young generals came to take me as trophy to a highland where there was much water, and I learned of waterfalls and rains in abundance. I was there for several years. When the Revolution was in its final agony, a last army, encircled with defeat, left me abandoned in this dry place. Many of my houses were set on fire, after their owners had first been shot to death.

I still remember the hallucinated horses crossing my streets and my plazas, and the terrified shouts of the women who were snatched up by the riders and carried away on horseback. When they were gone and the flames had turned to ashes, the shy young girls began to come out by the curbs of the wells, pale and angry because they had not taken part in the disorder.

My people are brown-skinned. They wear clothing of coarse white cotton and on their feet the leather thong sandals called huaraches. For adornment they wear gold necklaces or tie a pink silk handkerchief at their throat. They move slowly, speak little, and look at the sky. In the afternoons, at sunset, they sing.

On Saturdays the church courtyard, planted with almond trees, is filled with people buying and selling. Shining in the sunlight are the colored drinks, the bright ribbons, the gold beads, and the pink or blue cloth. The air is heavy with the mingled odors of meat frying, bags of charcoal still smelling of wood, mouths drooling alcohol, and burro dung. At night, firecrackers and fights explode: machetes glitter by the piles of maize and the oil lamps. Very early on Monday morning the noisy invaders go away, leaving me some dead bodies that are picked up by the municipal government. And this has been going on for as long as I can remember.

My main streets converge on a plaza planted with tamarinds. One street continues and descends until it passes out of sight on the way to Cocula; far from the center of town the pavement ends; as the street slopes downward, the houses rise on high banks along each side.

On this street there is a large stone house with a square porch and a garden filled with plants and dust. Time does not pass there: the air stood still after so many tears were shed. The day they came to take away Señora de Moncada's body, someone—I do not remember who—closed the front door and dismissed the servants. Since then the magnolias have bloomed with no one to see them, and weeds have covered the stones of the patio; spiders take long walks across the pictures and the piano. It has been a long time now since the palm trees died, and since any voice rang out under the colonnades of the porch. Bats make nests in the golden garlands of the mirrors, and Rome and Carthage, side by side, are still laden with ripe fruit that will fall from its own weight. Nothing but silence and oblivion. And yet in memory there is a garden illuminated by the sun, radiant with birds, populated by running and shouting. A smoky kitchen set up in the purple shadow of the jacarandas, a table where the servants of the Moncada family eat breakfast.

The shout pierces the morning: "I'll sprinkle salt on you!"

"If I were the señora, I would have those trees cut down," says Félix, the oldest of the servants.

Nicolás Moncada, standing on the highest branch of Rome, watches his sister Isabel straddling a fork of Carthage; she is studying her hands. The girl knows that Rome will be conquered by silence.

"I'll cut off your children's heads!"

Patches of sky filter through the boughs of Carthage. Nicolás descends from the tree, goes to the kitchen to get a hatchet, and comes running back to his sister's tree. Isabel contemplates the scene from above and swings slowly from branch to branch until she reaches the ground; then she stares at Nicolás and he, not knowing what to do, stands there with the weapon in his hand. Juan, the smallest of the three children, bursts into tears.

"Nico, don't cut off her head!"

Isabel moves away slowly, walks across the garden and disappears.

"Mamá, have you seen Isabel?"

"Leave her alone, she's a very bad girl!"

"She disappeared! She has magic powers."

"She's hiding, silly."

"No, Mamá, she has magic powers," Nicolás repeats.

I know that all this took place before the time of General Francisco Rosas and before the event that saddens me now by this apparent stone. And as the memory contains all times and their order is unpredictable, I am now in the presence of the geometry of lights that invented this illusory hill like a premonition of my birth. A luminous point determines a valley. That geometric instant is joined to the moment of this stone, and from the superimposition of spaces that form the imaginary world, memory returns those days to me intact; and now Isabel is here again, dancing with her brother Nicolás on the porch, which is lighted by orange-colored lanterns, whirling round and round with her curls in disarray and a dazzled smile on her lips. A group of young girls in light dresses surrounds them. Her mother looks at her reproachfully. In the kitchen the servants are drinking alcohol.

"They'll come to no good end," the people sitting by the fireplace declare sententiously.

"Isabel! Who are you dancing for? You look like a crazy woman!"

T W O

When General Francisco Rosas came to impose order, I was overcome by fear and I forgot the art of fiestas. My people no longer danced in the presence of those alien, taciturn soldiers. The lamps were extinguished at ten o'clock and the night became dark and terrible.

General Francisco Rosas, chief of the garrison of the plaza, was sad. He walked through my streets striking his leather boots with a riding whip, spoke to no one and glanced at us coldly in the manner of a stranger. He was tall and violent. His sallow look betrayed the tigers within him. He was accompanied by his deputy, Colonel Justo Corona, a sullen man like himself who wore a red scarf knotted about his neck and a Texas hat slanted over one eye. People said they were from the north. Each of them carried two pistols. The General's were decorated, in little gold letters enlaced with eagles and doves, with the words *Los ojos que te vieron* and *La Consentida*.

Their presence was not to our liking. They were government men who had come by force and were remaining by force. They were part of the same army that had left me forgotten in this place with no rain and no hope. Because of them the Zapatistas had gone away to an unknown location, and since that time we had been waiting for them to appear with their clamor of horses, their drums and smoking torches. In those days we still believed in the night startled by singing and the joyous awakening of their return. That luminous night remained intact in time, the soldiers had cheated us out of it, but the most innocent gesture or an unexpected word could make it a reality. And so we went on waiting in silence. In the waiting I was sad, under the watchful eye of those grim men who kept the trees supplied with hanged men. Fear was everywhere. Even the General's footstep filled us with dread. The drunkards were sad too, and from time to time gave vent to their grief with a long, broken scream that echoed in the fading light of late afternoon. In the dark their drunkenness would end in death. A circle was closing in on me. Perhaps this oppression had its start in my abandonment and the strange sensation that I had lost my destiny. The days weighed on me, and I was uneasy and anxious as I waited for the miracle.

The General too, incapable of creating his days, lived outside of time, with no past and no future. To forget his illusory present, he organized serenades to Julia, his mistress, and wandered about in the night, followed by his aides and the military band. I kept silent, behind closed balconies, as the chief passed with his retinue of songs and bullets. Early the next morning some men were hanging from the trees by the road to Cocula. We saw them as we passed, pretending not to see, each with a scrap of tongue showing, head drooping limply, and long, spindly legs. They were cattle thieves or rebels, the military dispatches said.

"More sins for Julia," Dorotea said to herself as she passed by the trees very early to get her glass of milk fresh from the cow. "God have mercy on their souls!" she added, looking at the hanged men, who were barefoot and clothed in coarse white cotton, seemingly indifferent to Dorotea's pity.

"The Kingdom of Heaven will belong to the poor in spirit," the old woman remembered, and Glory, resplendent with golden rays and snow-white clouds, appeared before her eyes. She had only to stretch out her hand to touch that pure moment. But Dorotea took care not to do it; she knew that a minuscule fraction of time contained the enormous abyss of her sins and separated her from the eternal present. The Indians hanging from the trees were obeying a perfect order and were now in the time she would never reach.

"They are there because they are poor."

She saw her words slip from her tongue and go to the feet of the hanged men without touching them. Her death would never be like theirs. "Not all men attain the perfection of dying; there are the dead and there are the corpses, and I shall be a corpse," she said to herself sadly; the dead one was a barefoot self, a pure act that reaches the realm of Glory; the corpse lives on, nourished by inheritances, profits, and revenue. Dorotea had no one to whom she could tell her thoughts, because she lived alone in a house that was almost in ruins, behind the walls of doña Matilde's house. Her parents had owned the Alhaja and Encontrada mines in Tetela. When they died, Dorotea sold her big house and bought the one that had belonged to the Cortina family, where she lived until the day of her death. Now that she was alone in the world, she spent her time making lace for the altar, embroidering gowns for the Infant Jesus, and soliciting jewels for the Madonna.

"What a good person she is," we all said.

When there were feast days, Dorotea and doña Matilde took charge of dressing the statues. The two women worked reverently in the church. Don Roque, the sacristan, brought down the saints and then respectfully left them alone.

"We want to see the Virgin naked!" Isabel and her brothers shouted as they came running into the church. Taken by surprise, the women quickly covered the statues.

"Why, children, your eyes must not see these things!"

"Go along, now!" their Aunt Matilde urged.

"Aunt, please, just once!"

Dorotea fought to keep from laughing at the children's impetuous curiosity. What a pity that it would have been a sacrilege to laugh!

9

"Come over to my house; I'll tell you a story and you'll see why curious folks don't live long," Dorotea promised.

The old lady and the Moncada family had always been friends. The children cleaned her garden, brought down her honeycombs, and cut the shoots of her bougainvillea vines and her magnolia blossoms, because Dorotea, when her money was gone, replaced her gold with flowers and spent her days weaving garlands to decorate the altars. In those days, Dorotea was already so old that she forgot what she had left on the stove and her tacos had a burnt taste. When Isabel, Nicolás, and Juan came to visit her, they would cry, "Something's burning!"

"Oh, really? Since the Zapatistas burned my house, my beans have been burned too," she replied without getting up from her low chair.

"But you are a Zapatista," the children said, laughing.

"They were very poor and we hid our food and money from them. That is why God sent us Rosas, so we would miss them. You have to be poor to understand the poor," she said, gazing down at her flowers.

The children drew closer to kiss her and she looked at them with amazement, as if they changed so much from one day to the next that she could scarcely recognize them.

"How you are growing! Better behave now! Don't let yourselves be carried away by the devil's tail!"

The children laughed, showing their even white teeth.

"Doro, will you let me see your room?" Isabel asked.

The walls of the only room Dorotea used were decorated with fans that had belonged to her mother. There were also holy statues and the scent of candlewick and burned wax. Isabel never ceased to be fascinated by that room, which was always kept in semidarkness. She liked to study the fans with their miniature landscapes illuminated by moonlight, the dark terraces where tiny, wanton lovers embraced. They were pictures of the minutiae of an unreal, diminutive love, preserved in those mementos kept in the darkness. Through the years she spent much time gazing at these intricate and changeless scenes. The other rooms were

10

black walls through which furtive cats wandered and the shoots of the blue bellflowers forced their way.

"Nicolás, when I am very old, I'll have a room like this!"

"Quiet, young lady! You're not likely to live alone! And when you marry, you're to have the fans you like the best."

Nicolás looked dejected, his black hair and eyes seemed disturbed.

"Are you going to get married, Isabel?"

Nicolás watched Isabel go out of Dorotea's room with her face transfigured, lost in a world unknown to him. She was betraying him, leaving him alone, breaking the bond that had united them throughout their lives. And he knew that they had to be together: they would run away from Ixtepec. The roads with their aureole of shining dust were waiting, and the field lay ahead for the battle to be won. Which one? They had to find it so the opportunity would not slip through their fingers. After that they would be with the heroes who were calling them from a glorious world of trumpets. They, the Moncadas, would not die in their beds, in the sweat of damp sheets, clinging to life like leeches. The noise in the street was calling them. The distant clamor of the Revolution was so close to them that by merely opening the door of their house they could enter the startled days of a few years before.

"I would rather die in the street or in a tavern fight," Nicolás said bitterly.

"You're always talking about your death, child," Dorotea replied.

Nicolás, who was busy looking at his sister, did not answer. It was true that she had changed; his words had no effect on her. Isabel was planning to go away, but not with him. "What will her husband be like?" he asked himself with astonishment. Isabel was wondering the same thing.

"Nico, do you think he has been born yet?"

"Don't be silly!" he exclaimed. His sister irritated him.

"He must be somewhere at this very moment," she replied without altering her expression. And she went to seek him in unknown places and found a figure that overshadowed her and

11

passed without looking in her direction. "No, I don't think I'll marry . . ."

"Don't imagine things that don't exist, or you'll come to no good end," the old woman advised when the children were about to leave.

"Doro, the only thing that's worth imagining is what doesn't exist," Isabel replied, standing by the front door.

"What do you mean by that nonsense?"

"That you must imagine the angels," the girl yelled and kissed the old lady, who stood pensively at the door watching the last three friends she had in the world walk away down the stony street.

THREE

"I don't know what to do with you ..."

Don Martín Moncada interrupted his reading and gave his children a puzzled look. His words drifted down in the study at that peaceful hour and were lost without an echo in the corners of the room. The children, bending over the checkerboard, did not move. For some time now their father had been repeating the same words. The circles of light distributed in the room remained intact. From time to time the faint tap of a checker being moved on the board opened and closed a tiny door through which it escaped, overwhelmed. Doña Ana let her book fall, delicately raised the wick of the lamp, and exclaimed in answer to her husband's words, "It is difficult to have children! They are different people ..."

Nicolás moved a checker on the black and white board, Isabel leaned forward to study the play, and Juan clicked his tongue several times to ward off an argument between the two grownups. The clock in its mahogany case hammered out the seconds.

"What a lot of noise you make at night!" don Martín said, looking at it sternly, shaking his finger menacingly.

"It's nine o'clock," Félix said from his corner; obeying an old

13

custom of the house, he got up from his stool, went to the clock, opened the little glass door, and unhooked the pendulum. The clock became silent. Félix put the piece of metal on his employer's desk and went back to his place.

"You won't run for us any more today," Martín remarked, eyeing the motionless hands on the white porcelain face.

Without the ticking, the room and its occupants entered a new and melancholy time where gestures and voices moved in the past. Doña Ana, her husband, the children, and Félix were changed into memories of themselves without a future, lost in a yellow, individual light that separated them from reality to make them only personages of memory. That is how I see them now, each bending over his circle of light, engrossed in forgetfulness, outside of themselves and outside of the feeling of sorrow that came over me at night when the houses closed their blinds.

"The future! The future! What is the future?" Martín Moncada exclaimed impatiently.

Félix moved his head, and his wife and children remained silent. When he thought of the future an avalanche of days pressed tightly together came hurtling down on him and his house and his children. For him, days did not count in the same way they counted for others. He never said to himself, "Monday I shall do such-and-such a thing," because between that Monday and him was a multitude of unlived memories which separated him from the need to do "such-and-such a thing that Monday." He struggled with various memories, and the memory of what had happened was the only thing that was unreal to him. As a boy he had spent long hours remembering what he had never seen or heard. The presence of a bougainvillea in the patio of his house surprised him more than the news that there were countries covered with snow. He remembered snow as a form of silence. Sitting under the bougainvillea he felt possessed by a white mystery, as certain to his dark eyes as the roof of his house.

"What are you thinking about, Martín?" his mother asked, astonished at his attitude of concentration.

14

"I am remembering snow," he replied from his five-year-old memory. As he grew older, his memory reflected shadows and colors of the unlived past which blended with future images and acts, and Martín Moncada always lived between those two lights, which in him became one. That morning his mother began to laugh without any regard for the memories that stirred deep within him as, incredulous, he contemplated the violence of the bougainvillea. There were odors, unknown in Ixtepec, which he alone perceived. If the servant girls lighted the stove in the kitchen, the aroma of burning torch pine added visions of pine trees to his other recollections; and the smell of a cold, resinous wind rose through his body, leaving its imprint on his memory. Surprised, he looked around and found himself near the warm hearth, breathing an air that was heavy with swampy odors from the garden. And the strange impression of not knowing where he was, of being in a hostile place, caused him not to recognize the voices and faces of his nursemaids. The bougainvillea flaming through the open kitchen door filled him with terror and he began to cry, feeling that he was lost in an unfamiliar place.

"Don't cry, Martín, don't cry!" the servant girls chided, their dark braids close to his face. And he, more alone than ever among those strange faces, cried more bitterly than before.

"I wonder what's wrong with him," the servants said, turning away. And gradually he recognized himself as Martín, sitting on a wicker chair and waiting for breakfast in the kitchen of his house.

After dinner, when Félix stopped the clocks, he let his unlived memory run freely. The calendar also imprisoned him in an anecdotic time and deprived him of the other time that lived within him. In that time one Monday was all Mondays, words became magic, people changed into incorporeal personages, and landscapes were transmuted into colors. He liked holidays. The people wandered about the plaza, bewitched by the forgotten memory of the fiesta; from that forgetting came the sadness of those days.

"Some day we shall remember, we shall remember," he said to himself with the certainty that the origin of the fiesta, like all man's acts, existed intact in time and that only an effort, a desire to see, was necessary in order to read in time the history of time.

"Today I went to see Dr. Arrieta and spoke to him about the boys," he heard Félix say.

"The doctor?" Martín Moncada asked. What would he do without Félix? Félix was his day-to-day memory. "What are we going to do today?" "What page of my book was I on last night?" "When did Justino die?" Félix remembered everything that he, Martín, forgot and answered his questions without making any mistakes. He was Martín's alter ego and the only person in whose presence he did not feel strange and who did not seem strange to him. His parents had been enigmas. He found it incredible, not that they had died, but that they had been born on a date so close to the date of his own birth, and yet more remote in his memory than the birth date of Cyrus or Cleopatra. It astonished him that they had not always been in the world. As a small boy, when they read him the Sacred History and introduced him to Moses, Isaac, and the Red Sea, it seemed that only his parents could be compared to the mystery of the Prophets. That sensation of antiquity was the reason for the respect he had felt for them. When he was very small, when his father bounced him on his knee, it made him uneasy to hear the other's heartbeat, and the memory of an infinite sadness, the stubborn memory of man's fragility, even before they had told him of death, left him overcome by grief, unable to speak.

"Say something, don't be silly," they begged. And he did not find the unknown word that would express his profound sadness. Compassion abolished the remote time that his parents represented, made him careful with his fellow men, and took from him the last vestige of efficiency. That was why he was ruined. His various occupations provided barely enough to live on.

"I explained the state of our accounts and he agreed to give the boys work in his mines," Félix concluded.

16

The oil lamps sputtered and gave off a black smoke. It was time to fill them again. The young people were still at the checkerboard. "Don't worry, Papá, we're going away from Ixtepec," said Nicolás, smiling.

"Thus we shall find out if they are tigers with teeth or without teeth, because there are very few lambs," Félix replied from his corner.

"I wish Isabel would get married," the mother said.

"I am not going to get married," the daughter answered.

Isabel disliked having differences made between her and her brothers. The idea that a woman's only future was matrimony she found humiliating. For them to speak of marriage as a solution made her feel like a commodity that had to be sold at any price.

"If the girl goes and they stay, this house won't be the same," Félix said. "It would be better for the three of them to go away, as Master Nicolás said." He could not bear the thought of Miss Isabel's going away with a stranger.

I still hear Félix's words spinning between the walls of the living room, clinging to ears that no longer exist and repeating themselves in time for me alone.

"I don't know, I don't know what I'm going to do with you," Martín Moncada repeated.

"We're tired," Félix explained, and disappeared, to return a few minutes later carrying a tray with six glasses and a pitcher of water flavored with tamarind. The young people gulped down their refreshment. At that time of night the temperature dropped and the perfume of night and the scent of jasmine flooded the house with coolness.

"It may be good for the children," Félix added when he picked up the empty glasses. Don Martín acknowledged the words with a grateful look.

Later, when he was in bed, a doubt tormented him: would sending his sons to the mines be a violation of their will? "God will give the answer in due course," he told himself anxiously.

17

He was unable to sleep. Strange presences surrounded his house, as if a curse put on him and his family many centuries ago had begun to take effect that night. He tried to remember the harm that threatened his children and he only managed to elicit the terror he experienced every Good Friday. He tried to pray and he found himself alone and powerless to exorcise the menacing darkness.

F O U R _____

I remember when Juan and Nicolás left for the mines of Tetela.
The preparations went on for a whole month. Blandina, the
seamstress, arrived one morning armed with her glasses and sewing basket. Her dark face and small body hesitated for a few
moments before entering the sewing room.

"I don't like walls; I have to see leaves in order to sew," she
said gravely, and refused to enter the room.

Félix and Rutilio moved the Singer and the work table out to
the porch.

"Do you like it here, doña Blandina?"

The seamstress sat down unhurriedly, adjusted her glasses,
bowed her head, and pretended to work; then she looked up in
dismay.

"No, no, no! Over there, by the tulips. These ferns are very
interesting!"

The servants put the sewing machine and the table in front of
the tulip beds. Blandina tilted her head.

"Too bright! Too bright!" she said with irritation.

Félix and Rutilio became impatient with the woman.

"If you don't mind, I'd rather be near the magnolias," she said sweetly, and walked over to the trees with her mincing step, but once there she looked disappointed and said, "They're too solemn and they make me sad."

The whole morning passed and Blandina did not find a suitable place to work. At noon she sat down to lunch meditating soberly on her problem. She ate without seeing, as detached and motionless as an idol. Félix waited on her.

"Don't look at me like that, don Félix! Put yourself in my unfortunate position, to put scissors to expensive cloth hemmed in by walls and disagreeable furniture! I don't feel at home!"

In the afternoon, Blandina felt "at home" in one corner of the porch.

"From here I see nothing but foliage; everything else is lost in the greenery." And with a smile she began to work.

Doña Ana came to keep her company, and from Blandina's fingers began to emerge shirts, mosquito nets, trousers, pillow cases, sheets. For several weeks she sewed energetically until seven each night. Señora Moncada marked the clothing with her children's initials. From time to time the seamstress looked up from her work.

"It's Julia's fault that the children are going so far away to face the dangers of men and the temptations of the devil all alone!"

In those days, it was Julia who determined all our destinies, and we blamed her for the smallest of our misfortunes. Ensconced in her beauty, she seemed unaware of our existence.

Tetela was in the mountains, just a four-hour ride from Ixtepec, and nevertheless the distance in time was enormous. Tetela belonged to the past, it was abandoned. All that was left was the gilded prestige of its name vibrating in the memory like a timbrel and the charred remains of some palaces. During the Revolution the owners of the mines disappeared, and the very poor people who lived there left the shafts. A few families engaged in pottery-making remained. On Saturdays very early we saw them coming, barefoot and ragged, to sell their wares in the market of Ixtepec. The road that crossed the sierra to reach the mines passed groups of peasants who were consumed by hunger and malignant fevers. Almost all of them had joined the Zapatista rebellion and had returned home after a few brief years of fighting, their numbers decimated and their poverty unchanged, to occupy their place in the past.

The countryside made the mestizos afraid. It was their creation, the image of their plunder. They had established the violence and they felt they were in a hostile land, surrounded by ghosts. The reign of terror they established had left them impoverished. That was the cause of my deterioration.

"If only we could exterminate all of the Indians! They are the disgrace of Mexico!"

The Indians remained silent. The mestizos, before leaving Ixtepec, armed themselves with food, medicine, clothing, and "pistols, good pistols, you Indian bastards!" When they gathered together, they looked at one another with distrust, they felt they were without a country and without a culture, leaning on some artificial forms that were nourished only by ill-gotten gain. It was their fault that my time stood still.

"You have to keep a tight rein on the Indians, you know," Tomás Segovia recommended to the Moncadas at one of the gatherings held to bid farewell to the young men. Segovia had grown accustomed to the pedantry of his pharmacy and he prescribed advice in the same tone of voice he used for prescribing remedies. "One pill every two hours, you know."

"They are so treacherous," sighed doña Elvira, the widow of don Justino Montúfar.

"Indians all look alike—that's why they're dangerous," added Tomás Segovia, smiling.

"It used to be easier to fight them: they had more respect for us," doña Elvira replied. "What would my poor father say—may he rest in peace!—if he could see these Indian uprisings? He was always so respectable."

"Be tougher with them. Don't be so gentle. Keep your pistol handy," Segovia insisted.

Félix, sitting on his stool, listened to them without flinching.

"For us, the Indians, the time to be silent is infinite," and he refrained from speaking. Nicolás looked at him and stirred nervously in his chair. The words of his family's friends embarrassed him.

"Don't talk like that! We're all part Indian!"

"I don't have a single drop of Indian blood!" the widow exclaimed in a choked voice.

The violence that blows over my stones and my people hovered under the chairs, and the air turned viscous. The guests smiled hypocritically. Conchita, the daughter of Elvira Montúfar, looked at Nicolás with admiration.

"How wonderful to be a man and to be able to say what one thinks!" she said to herself melancholically. She herself never took part in the conversation. She sat shyly and heard the words fall, enduring them stoically as one endures a heavy rainstorm.

The conversation became difficult.

"Did you know that Julia ordered a tiara?" Tomás asked, grinning to conceal the anger caused by Nicolás Moncada's words.

"A tiara?" cried the widow with surprise.

The mention of Julia's name dissipated the scabrous topic of the Indians, and the conversation became animated. Félix had not stopped the clocks; their small hands picked up the words that came from the lips of doña Elvira and Tomás Segovia and changed them into an army of spiders that wove together and then unraveled useless syllables. Alien to the sound they made, they snatched excitedly at the name of Julia, the love object of Ixtepec.

The tolling of church bells was heard in the distance. The living room clock repeated the sound in a softer tone, and the visitors scurried away with the speed of insects.

Tomás Segovia escorted doña Elvira and Conchita home through my dark streets. The widow took advantage of the shadows to speak of the pharmacist's favorite subject: poetry.

"And tell me, how is poetry these days?"

"Forgotten by everyone, doña Elvira," the man replied bitterly. "Only I, from time to time, devote a few hours to it. This is a country of illiterates."

"Who does he think he is?" the woman thought angrily, and was silent.

When they reached the Montúfar home, Segovia gallantly waited until the women had bolted and latched the door; then he went back down the lonely street. He thought of Isabel and her profile of a young boy. "She's shy," he said to console himself for the girl's indifference, and inadvertently rhymed "shy stand" with "high hand," and then "shy-standed" with "high-handed," and suddenly in the nocturnal solitude of the street his life appeared to him like an enormous storehouse of adjectives. Surprised, he walked faster; his feet were marking syllables too. "I'm writing too much," he thought nervously, and when he reached his house he wrote the first two lines of the first quatrain of a sonnet.

"You should pay a bit more attention to Segovia and not waste your time on Nicolás!" exclaimed Elvira Montúfar, sitting in front of her mirror.

Conchita did not answer; she knew that her mother spoke for the simple pleasure of speaking. Silence frightened her, reminded her of the unhappy years she had spent with her husband. The widow had no memory of how she had looked in that dark period of her life. "How strange, I don't know what I looked like when I was a married woman," she confided to her friends.

"Child, don't look at yourself in the mirror any more," the grown-ups ordered when she was small, but she was unable to resist: her own image was her way of recognizing the world. Because of it she knew the days of mourning and the festal days, loves and the dates of the calendar. At the mirror she learned words and laughter. When she married, Justino monopolized the words and the mirrors and she endured some silent and obliterated years in which she moved about like a blind woman, not understanding what was happening around her. The only memory she had of those years was that she had no memory.

She was not the one who had gone through that time of fear and silence. Now, although she urged her daughter to get married, she was happy to see that Conchita paid no attention to her. "Not all women can enjoy the decency of being widows," she said to herself in secret.

"I'm warning you that if you don't get a move on, you're going to be an old maid."

Conchita heard her mother's reproach and quietly placed the pan of water under doña Elvira's bed to drive away the spirit of the "Evil One." Then she put the *Magnífica* and the rosary between the pillowcases. Since childhood, Elvira had taken precautions before going to bed; her sleeping face frightened her.

"I don't know how I look with my eyes closed," and she hid her head under the sheets to keep others from seeing her unknown face, which made her feel defenseless.

"How tiresome to live in a country of Indians! They take advantage of sleep to harm us," she said, embarrassed that her daughter, at that time of night, was occupied with such duties instead of going to bed. She brushed her hair vigorously and looked at herself in the mirror with astonishment.

"My God! Do I look like that? Am I that old woman in the mirror? Is this how people see me? I'll never go out again, I don't want people to take pity on me!"

"Don't say such a thing, Mamá."

"Thank God your poor father is dead. Imagine how surprised he would be if he could see me now. And you, what are you waiting for? Why don't you get married? Segovia is the best catch in Ixtepec. I know he's a poor man! How tired I am of hearing it all the time! But—is this really me?" she repeated, fascinated by her face, which was making grimaces in the mirror.

Conchita took advantage of her mother's astonishment to go to her room. She wanted to be alone to let her mind ruminate on Nicolás. In the coolness of her room she could see the young man's face, recapture his laughter. What a pity that she never dared to say a word! On the other hand, her mother talked too

24

much, broke the enchantment. Tomás Segovia as a husband! Unthinkable! When Segovia spoke, Conchita's ears filled with glue. She saw his hair and felt she had been smeared with grease.

"If my mother mentions his name tomorrow, I'll have a tantrum." Her tantrums frightened doña Elvira. She smiled with malice and settled her head comfortably. She kept Nicolás' laughter under her pillow.

"Now I really want them to go to Tetela!" Isabel shouted angrily when visitors came to the house. But as soon as her brothers went away, she was sorry for her words. Without them the house became an empty shell; it was like a strange house, and the voices of her parents and the servants were like strangers' voices. She detached herself from them, moved backward to change herself into a point lost in space, and was filled with fear. There were two Isabels, one who wandered through the rooms and the patios, and the other who lived in a distant sphere, fixed in space. Superstitiously she touched objects to communicate with the apparent world and picked up a book or a saltcellar as a support to keep from falling into the void. Thus she established a magical flux between the real Isabel and the unreal one, and felt consoled.

"Pray, be virtuous!" they said, and she repeated the magic formulas of prayer until they broke up into words with no meaning. Between the power of the prayer and the words that expressed it there was the same distance as that between the two Isabels: and it came between her and the Ave Marias. The Isabel who was suspended could detach herself at any moment, traverse space like a meteor, and fall into an unknown time. Her mother did not know how to handle her. "She is my daughter Isabel," she repeated, looking with incredulity at the tall, questioning figure of the young girl.

"Sometimes paper beckons to us . . ."

Her daughter looked at her with surprise and she blushed. She meant that during the night she had thought of a letter that would annihilate the distance separating herself from the young girl, and in the morning, faced with the insolent whiteness of the paper, the nocturnal phrases had evaporated like garden mist, leaving her only some useless words.

"And last night I was so intelligent!" she sighed.

"At night we are all intelligent, and when morning comes we find we are fools," said Martín Moncada, looking at the motionless hands of the clock.

His wife returned to her reading. Martín heard her turn a page and looked at her in his usual way: he saw her as a strange, delightful being who shared her life with him but jealously guarded a secret that could not be revealed. He was grateful for her presence. He would never know with whom she had lived, but he did not need to know; it was enough to know that she had lived with someone. Then he looked at Isabel, submerged in an armchair, her gaze fixed on the flame of the lamp; his daughter was an unknown quantity too. Ana said, "Children are different people," astonished that her children were not herself. Isabel's anguish now reached him unequivocally. His wife and Félix, obstinate and quiet by their lamps, seemed to be unaware of the danger: Isabel was capable of changing into a shooting star, of running away and falling into space without leaving a visible trace, in this world where only the grossness of objects takes shape. "A meteor is the furious will to flee," he said to himself, and remembered the strangeness of those burned-out masses, flaming in their own anger and doomed to a more dismal prison than the one they had escaped from. "The will to separate oneself from the Absolute is hell."

Isabel rose from her armchair; she found it offensive; not only the paper but the whole house beckoned. She said good night and left the room.

"They have been gone for seven months now."

She was forgetting that her brothers sometimes came to Ixtepec, spent a few days with her, and then returned to the mines of Tetela.

"Tomorrow I'll ask my father to bring them," and she pulled

26

the sheet over her head to keep from seeing the warm darkness and the shadows that fused and broke into myriad dark spots, making a noise that was deafening.

Nicolás also languished, away from his sister. As he traveled back to Ixtepec, crossing the dry, barren mountain range, the stones multiplied under his horse's hoofs and the enormous mountains blocked his way. He rode on in silence. He felt that only his will could force open the road in that labyrinth of stone. Without the help of his imagination he would never reach his house, would be imprisoned in the walls of stone that were beckoning to him maleficently. Juan rode beside him, happy to be returning to the light of his room, the warmth of his father's eyes, and the ascetic hand of Félix.

"It's good to be going home again."

"One of these days, I won't be going home any more," Nicolás promised bitterly. He did not want to admit that each time he went back he was afraid of being confronted with the news of his sister's marriage and that this inadmissible fear tormented him. And he thought that his father had sent them to the mines not because of increasing poverty but to force his sister to accept a husband.

"Isabel is a traitor and my father is infamous . . ."

"Do you remember when you drowned me in the pool? I feel the same way now, with this dark night on my back," Juan replied, alarmed by his brother's words.

Nicolás smiled; he and his sister had thrown Juan into a pool of deep water and then had fought to save him. They rescued him, risking their own lives in the process, and came back to town carrying the "drowned boy" over their shoulders, looking at people from the depths of their secret heroism. That happened when the three shared the infinite surprise of finding themselves in the world. At that time even their mother's thimble shone with a different light as it darted to and fro constructing bees and daisies. Some of those days were singled out and stamped for all time on the memory, suspended from a special air. Then the world turned opaque, lost its penetrating odors, the light softened, each day became the same as the one before it, and people acquired the stature of dwarfs. There were still some places untouched by time, like the charcoal bin with its black light. Years before, sitting on piles of charcoal, they heard, trembling, the crack of rifles as the Zapatistas entered the town. Félix took them there during the invasion. Where did the Zapatistas go when they left Ixtepec? They went to green fields, to water, to eat green corn and whoop with laughter after romping with the people for several hours. Now no one came to brighten the days. Time was the shadow of Francisco Rosas. There was nothing but disillusionment in the whole country. The people were trying to adapt their lives to the General's whims. Isabel was trying to adapt too, to find a husband and a comfortable chair in which to rock away her boredom.

The brothers reached Ixtepec very late that night. Isabel helped them to dismount. Their parents were waiting in the dining room, where Félix served a home-cooked supper that made them forget the blue tortillas and stale cheese of Tetela. Leaning over the table, the brothers and sister surveyed each other, getting acquainted all over again. Nicolás' words were meant just for Isabel. Don Martín heard them from a distance.

"You don't have to go back to the mines if you don't want to," the father said softly.

"Martín, you're up in the clouds! You know we need that money," his wife replied, dumbfounded.

He did not answer. "Martín, you're up in the clouds!" was a sentence they repeated whenever he made a mistake. But was it not a more serious mistake to violate his sons' will than to lose a little money? He did not understand the opacity of a world that had money for the sun in its sky. "Poverty is my vocation," he would say to excuse his progressive insolvency. A man's life seemed unbearably short to spend it amassing wealth. He felt asphyxiated by the "opaque bodies," as he called the people who formed Ixtepec's society: they were wasting away in unimportant interests, forgetting that they were mortal; their error was the result of fear. He knew that the future was a swift retrogression toward death, and death the perfect state, the precious moment in which man fully recuperates his other memory. And so he forgot the memory of "Monday I shall do such-and-such a thing," and looked at efficient people with amazement. But the "immortals" seemed contented in their error, and sometimes he thought that he was the only one who was moving backward toward that astonishing encounter.

The night slid ceaselessly through the open door that led to the garden. Insects and dark scents settled in the room. A mysterious river flowed implacably, and connected the Moncadas' dining room with the heart of the remotest stars. Félix removed the plates and folded the tablecloth. The absurdity of eating and conversing descended on the inhabitants of the house and left them quiescent before an indescribable present.

"I don't fit in this body!" Nicolás exclaimed, overcome, and he covered his face with his hands as if he were going to cry.

"We're tired," Félix said from his stool.

For a few seconds the whole house zoomed through the sky, became part of the Milky Way, and then fell back without a sound into the spot it now occupies. Isabel felt the jolt of the fall, jumped up from her chair, looked at her brothers, and felt safe; she remembered that she was in Ixtepec and that an unexpected gesture could return us to the lost order.

"Today they blew up the train. Perhaps they're coming . . ."

The others looked at her sleepily and the moths continued their dusty flight around the lamps.

FIVE

The train from Mexico City arrived each evening at six. We waited for the papers with news from the city, as if that would put an end to the spell of quietness into which we had fallen. But we only saw the photographs of those who had been executed. During that time of firing squads we thought that nothing would save us. Thick walls, gratuitous gunfire, ropes for hanging appeared all over the country. This multiplication of horrors reduced us to dust and heat until six o'clock the following evening. Some days the train did not arrive and rumors circulated, "They're coming now!" But the next day the train arrived with its news and night fell over me, irrevocably.

From her bed, doña Ana heard the sounds of the night and felt asphyxiated by the quiet that guarded the doors and windows of her house. Her son's voice came to her: "I don't fit in this body." She remembered the turbulence of her own childhood in the north. Her house with the mahogany doors that opened and closed for her brothers; their sonorous, savage names repeated in the upper rooms where the smell of wood smoke lingered in wintertime. She saw the snow accumulate on the windowsills and heard the music of polkas in the cold, drafty hall.

Wildcats came down from the mountains and the servants went out to hunt them, howling with laughter and consuming quantities of sotol. In the kitchen they roasted meat and passed the pine nuts around, and the sound of voices flooded the house with strident words. The premonition of joy destroyed the petrified days one by one. The Revolution broke out one morning and the door of time opened for us. In that instant of splendor her brothers went to the Sierra de Chihuahua and then came home again, entering the house noisily in their boots and army hats. They were followed by officers, and in the street the soldiers were singing "La Adelita."

> If Adelita went off with another
> I'd follow where'er she might be.
> On land by a troop train, no other,
> By warship if she went by sea . . .

Before they were twenty-five, her brothers were dying, one after the other, in Chihuahua, in Torreón, in Zacatecas; and all that Francisca, their mother, had left were pictures of them, and of herself and their sisters dressed in mourning clothes. Later the battles won by the Revolution were undone by Carranza's treacherous hands, and the assassins came to dispute the spoils, playing dominoes in the brothels they opened. A dismal silence spread from north to south, and time turned to stone again.

"Oh, if only we could sing 'La Adelita' again!" the señora said to herself, and was glad that they had blown up the train from Mexico City. "These are the things that make you want to go on living." Perhaps the miracle that would change the bloody fate hanging over us could still happen.

That afternoon the train announced its arrival with a long, triumphant toot. Many years have passed, not one Moncada is left, only I remain as a witness of their downfall to hear the train from Mexico City arrive each evening at six.

"If we just had a good earthquake!" doña Ana exclaimed, angrily jabbing her needle into her embroidery. Like the rest of

31

us, she longed for a catastrophe. Her daughter heard the train whistling and kept silent. The señora went to the balcony to spy from behind the curtains on General Francisco Rosas, who was on his way to Pando's cantina to get drunk.

"How young he is! He's not even thirty! And already so many misfortunes!" she added sympathetically, watching the tall, erect General, who passed without looking to the left or the right.

An aura of coolness came from the cantina. The dice rattled in the shaker and rolled on the table, and money changed hands. The General, a good gambler who was protected by luck, was winning. When he won, he let himself go and drank to excess. And when he was drunk he became dangerous. His aides tried desperately to win, and when they saw that he went on winning they exchanged uneasy glances.

"Have a little game with the General, Lieutenant Colonel Cruz!"

The Lieutenant Colonel smiled and came over to win one from General Francisco Rosas. He was the only one who could beat the General easily. Colonel Justo Corona, standing behind his chief, observed the game with a sharp eye. Pando, the barman, watched the men closely; he knew by their facial expressions when the climate was getting dangerous.

"Get out—the General's winning!"

And the other people in the bar slipped away unobtrusively.

"If he's winning, it's because Julia doesn't love him; that's why he's in such a rage," we said exultantly, and outside we uttered shouts that could be heard in the bar and made the officers angry.

Much later, the hoofbeats of Rosas' horse shattered the night. We heard him going up and down the streets, moving through the dark town, lost in his misery.

"What's he looking for at this time of night?"

"He's trying to get up his nerve before he goes to see her."

He was still on his horse when he entered the Hotel Jardín and went to the room of Julia, his mistress.

SIX _____

One evening a stranger got off the train. He was wearing a dark cashmere suit and a traveling cap and he carried a small suitcase. Standing on the platform of broken bricks he seemed unsure of his destination. He looked around as if he were asking himself, "What is this?" He stood there for a few minutes, watching bales of maguey fiber being unloaded from the cars. He was the only traveler. The porters and don Justo, the stationmaster, looked at him with amazement. The young man seemed aware of the curiosity he was causing, and reluctantly moved across the platform to the dirt road. Then he crossed the road and continued straight ahead until he came to the river, which was almost dry. He waded through it and went to the entrance to Ixtepec. From there, as if he knew the shortest route, he entered the town before don Justo's surprised eyes. The stranger seemed to be smiling to himself. He passed the house of the Catalán family, and don Pedro, nicknamed "La Alcancía" because of the gash in his cheek left by a bullet, watched him while unloading tins of lard at the door of his grocery. Toñita, his wife, was curious and came to the door.

"Who's that?" she inquired without expecting an answer.

33

"Looks like an inspector," her husband replied suspiciously.

"He's not an inspector!" Toñita said with assurance. "He's something else, something we haven't seen around here!"

The stranger continued on his way. His eyes rested softly on the roofs and the trees. He seemed not to notice the curiosity he was causing. He turned at the corner of Melchor Ocampo Street. Behind their screens, the Señoritas Martínez greeted his presence with shouting. Don Ramón, their father, had great plans: automobiles would replace the horse-drawn carriages that had gone back and forth under the tamarinds in the plaza for fifty years; electricity would be installed and the streets would be paved. He discussed these plans with his daughters as he sat on a wicker chair while doña María, his wife, made coconut candy with pine nuts, sweets of egg yolk, and other confections to sell to the merchants in the marketplace. Hearing his daughters' shouts, Señor Martínez went to the balcony. All he could see was the stranger's back.

"A modern man, a man of action!" he exclaimed enthusiastically. And he made a mental note to enlist the stranger's support for the improvements he was planning. Too bad that the Military Commander, as he called the General, was so reactionary.

There was no doubt, the newcomer was a stranger. Neither I nor the oldest person in Ixtepec remembered having seen him before. And yet he seemed to know the layout of my streets very well, because he came straight to the door of the Hotel Jardín. Don Pepe Ocampo, the proprietor, showed him to a large room with a tiled floor, green plants, a white metal double bed and mosquito netting. The stranger seemed to like it. Don Pepe was always talkative and polite, and the presence of a new guest stimulated him.

"It's been a long time since anyone passed through our town! That is, anyone from such a distance. The Indians don't count: they sleep in doorways or in the church courtyard. Traveling salesmen used to come, with their suitcases full of novelties. Are you one of them, by any chance?"

34

The stranger shook his head.

"You see, Sir, what a state I'm in as a result of this political situation! Ixtepec used to have many tourists, business was very good and the hotel was always filled. You should have seen it, with little tables set up on the porch, and people eating and talking until very late at night. Life was worth living in those days! Now I have almost no one. Well, no one except General Rosas, Colonel Corona, a few less important officers—and their mistresses."

He said the last word in a very low voice, drawing closer to the stranger, who smiled. The young man took two cigarettes and offered one to the hotelkeeper. As it was learned much later, don Pepe noticed that he had picked them out of thin air. He had simply stretched out his hand and the cigarettes, already lighted, appeared. But at that moment don Pepe was in no condition to be surprised by anything, and the occurrence seemed natural. He looked at the young man's eyes—they were deep and there were rivers and sheep bleating sadly in their depths. The two men smoked in silence, and then went out to the porch, which was full of moist ferns. They heard the crickets chirping.

Beautiful Julia, the General's mistress, wrapped in a bright pink negligee, with her hair hanging loose and several strands caught in her golden earrings, dozed in her hammock nearby. As if she sensed the alien presence, she opened her eyes and looked at the stranger sleepily, with curiosity. She did not seem startled, but she was adept at concealing her feelings. Since the evening when I saw her get off the troop train, she had impressed me as a dangerous woman. There had never been anyone like her in Ixtepec. Her manner, her way of talking, walking, and looking at men, everything about Julia was different! I can still see her walking up and down the platform, sniffing the air as if she found everything insignificant. If a person saw her once, he had a hard time forgetting her, so I do not know whether the stranger had already met her; the fact is that he did not seem surprised by the encounter or by her beauty. He walked over to her and talked for a long time, leaning toward the pretty girl.

35

Don Pepe never was able to remember what he had heard. Julia, lying in the hammock with her robe partly open and her hair in disorder, listened to the stranger.

Neither she nor don Pepe seemed to be aware of the danger. The General might come and take them by surprise at any moment. He was always so jealous at the thought that another man might talk to his mistress, look at her teeth and see the pink tip of her tongue when she smiled. And therefore whenever the General arrived, don Pepe hurried out to meet him, to say that Señorita Julia had not spoken to anyone.

At night Julia wore a pink silk dress covered with white beads, put on her gold necklaces and bracelets, and went for a walk around the plaza with the anguished General. She looked like a tall flower brightening the night, and it was impossible not to stare at her. The men sitting on benches or strolling about in groups glanced at her with longing. More than once the General lashed out with his whip at those who dared to look at her, and more than once he slapped Julia's face when she looked back at them. But Julia seemed unafraid and indifferent to his anger. It was rumored that she had been brought from a faraway place, no one was certain where, and that she had been loved by many men.

Life in the Hotel Jardín was passionate and secret. People peeked through the balconies trying to see something of those loves and those women, all of whom were beautiful and flamboyant, all mistresses of the officers.

Out in the street, passersby could hear the laughter of Rosa and Rafaela, the twins, who belonged to Lieutenant Colonel Cruz. They were from the north, and voluble, and when they were angry they threw their shoes into the street. When they were happy they put red tulips in their hair, wore their green dresses, and sauntered about, inviting glances. They were both tall and strong, and in the afternoon they sat on their balcony eating fruit and regaling the townspeople with smiles. They always left their blinds open and generously shared their intimacy with the street.

People could see them lying there together on the bed with its white lace spread, showing their shapely legs, on either side of Lieutenant Colonel Cruz, who caressed their thighs and smiled with bleary eyes. Cruz was a good-natured fellow and was equally indulgent with them both.

"Life consists of women and pleasure! How can I deprive them of what they ask for when they don't deprive me of anything!" And he laughed, opening his mouth wide and showing the white teeth of a young cannibal.

The grey horses with identical white markings on their heads, his gift to the sisters, had long been a cause for wonder in Ixtepec. The Lieutenant Colonel had looked all through Sonora to find two animals that were so much alike.

"All we have to gratify are our desires! A desire that isn't gratified can kill you. This is what my girls wanted and I gave it to them!"

Antonia was a blonde, melancholy girl from the coast, with a penchant for weeping. Colonel Justo Corona, her lover, gave her presents and serenades, but nothing could console her and rumor had it that she was terrified during the night. She was the youngest of the mistresses and never went out alone. "She's so young!" the women of Ixtepec would say, shocked, when Antonia came to the serenade on Thursdays and Sundays, pale and frightened, on Colonel Corona's arm.

Luisa belonged to Captain Flores, and because of her bad temper she was feared by her lover and the other guests at the hotel. She was much older than the Captain, very short, with blue eyes and dark hair; her dresses were cut to show her unfettered breasts. At night Julia heard her fighting with Flores and running up and down the hall stamping her feet.

"There goes that bitch in heat! I don't know what Flores sees in her!" the General said with disgust. He sensed Luisa's hatred for Julia and he in turn found his aide's mistress hateful.

"You've ruined my life, you animal!" Luisa yelled, her shrieks piercing the walls of the hotel.

"My God, when life is so short, why spend it like that?" Cruz said.

"She's always jealous," the twins replied, stretching lazily on the bed.

Antonia shuddered. Justo Corona drank a glass of cognac.

"And you—what do you say? Did I ruin your life too?"

The silent Antonia burrowed deeper into the bed. Francisco Rosas smoked until the shouting had stopped. Lying flat on his back he peered at Julia, who lay beside him unabashed. "If only she would complain, just once," he thought, "it would be a relief." It depressed him to see her always so listless, so indifferent. Her reaction was the same if he came or did not come for many days: Julia's face and voice did not change. He drank to get up his courage with her. At midnight, as he approached the hotel, a thrill that was always new overpowered him. With misty eyes, riding his horse, he reached her room.

"Julia, are you coming with me?"

His voice changed when he was with her. He spoke very softly because her presence sapped his strength. He gazed into her eyes, tried to find what she was hiding behind her eyelids, beyond herself. His mistress evaded his eyes, tilted her head and smiled, looked down at her naked shoulders, and withdrew into a distant world, noiseless, ghost-like.

"Come, Julia!" the General begged, vanquished, and she, half dressed and still smiling, mounted her lover's horse. The two went galloping through my moony streets to Las Cañas, the place of water. The General's aides, also on horseback, followed at a distance. Ixtepec heard Julia's laughter at midnight, but did not have a right to see her like that, riding by in the moonlight with her taciturn lover.

At the hotel the other women waited for the men to return. In her nightgown, with a lamp in one hand and a cigarette in the other, Luisa went into the hall to knock at the doors of the other rooms.

"Open up, Rafaela!"

"Leave us alone and go to sleep!" the twins answered.

38

"They've taken Julia out and they won't be back until daybreak," Luisa whispered through a crack in the door.

"Who cares? Go to sleep."

"I don't know what's wrong with me; my stomach feels cold."

"Well, go find Antonia, she's a night owl like you," the sisters replied sleepily.

Antonia heard the conversation from the next room and pretended to be asleep. Finally she heard Rafaela lighting the lamp and she hid under the warm sheets, her eyes wide open, lost in that strange darkness.

"What is Papá doing now, I wonder? He's probably still looking for me . . ." Five months had passed since Colonel Corona had abducted her from her home on the coast.

Luisa knocked at the door. Antonia put her hand over her mouth to stifle a scream.

"Come and join the girls. What are you doing in there all alone?"

Antonia did not answer. It reminded her of how they had knocked at the door of her house that night. "Antonia, go and see who's knocking at this time of night," her father said. She opened the door and saw a pair of flashing eyes, felt someone throw a blanket over her head, wrap her up in it, and carry her out of the house. There seemed to be many men. She could hear their voices. "Hand her here, quick!" She was passed from one to another, put up on a horse. Through the blanket she felt the heat of the animal's body and the body of the man who held her. They galloped away at breakneck speed. She was suffocating under the blanket, just as she was now, with Luisa calling to her, and she covered her head with the sheets without knowing why. Fear had paralyzed her. She did not dare to make any movement that would enable her to get some air.

The man reined in his horse. "We can't carry her covered up all night, she'll suffocate."

"But the Colonel said he wanted us to bring her like this," the others answered.

"When we're almost there, we'll cover her up again," said the

39

voice of the man who was carrying her. And without dismounting he loosened the blanket and uncovered her face.

Antonia found herself looking at a pair of young eyes that viewed her with curiosity.

"She's a blonde!" said the astonished man, and the curiosity in his eyes changed to longing.

"Of course! Her father is the Spaniard Paredes," the other voices replied.

Captain Damián Álvarez held her tight. "Don't be so frightened, nothing's going to happen to you. We're going to take you to Colonel Justo Corona."

Antonia began to tremble. The man held her close. When day broke they arrived in Texmelucan, where the Colonel was waiting.

"Don't take me to him. Let me stay with you," she begged.

The Captain did not reply. He lowered his eyes, not wanting to look into hers.

"Don't take me to him."

Álvarez held her close, without speaking, and kissed her.

"Please—let me stay with you!" Antonia sobbed.

And instead of answering he covered her face with the blanket and brought her to Corona without saying a word. Through the blanket she could perceive the smell of stale alcohol.

"Everyone get out!" the Colonel ordered. Captain Álvarez' footsteps faded away. The smell became unbearable. She had never been so afraid, not even on the night when she heard the question, "Antonia, have you seen the Güero Mónico yet?"

On the dark porch of her house, which was filled with branches and shadows, some strange girls thrust their curious faces at her and waited for her answer with anxious eyes.

"No."

"Ha, ha, ha," they laughed malevolently. "You'll see when the moon comes down and bites you between the legs. You'll see the blood spurt out!"

Antonia was terrified, unable to move, trapped between thick shadows of branches reflected on the whitewashed walls.

40

"The Güero Mónico comes every month!" And the girls ran away laughing.

She had never been so frightened until she found herself in a blanket alone with Colonel Justo Corona. He lowered the blanket, and his small dark eyes, those of a stranger, came closer and closer as he hunted for her lips. Antonia tossed and turned on the bed, covered with perspiration. "Where is the breeze from the sea? I can't breathe in this valley . . ." She heard voices in the next room.

"Go and get the blonde. I know she must be crying."

"I don't want to. You know how she screams when anyone knocks at her door."

Luisa sat there smoking nervously, looking at the two sisters, who lay on the same bed half naked, their breasts tender and their skin, smooth as a pine nut, beautiful. Their sleepy eyes and their mouths, childlike at that hour, betrayed their wish that Luisa would go back to her room.

"Why is she like that?" Rosa asked, referring to Antonia.

"I don't know. I keep telling her to calm down and act like she's getting used to it when he makes love to her. If she did, he wouldn't bother her so much," Rafaela said thoughtfully.

"Anyway, the bad time soon passes, and then you even get to like it," Rosa added.

"You said it!" Rafaela exclaimed, and as if she found this idea stimulating she leaped out of bed and reached for the basket of fruit.

"Let's have some fruit while we wait for those . . ."

"What would they say if we went on a spree?" Luisa said, nibbling on an orange.

"They don't go on sprees. They can't leave the General. Don't you see how he is? That mean Julia—she'll come to a bad end!"

Luisa stiffened with anger. "I wish he'd kill her! Then we'd be better off."

"Be quiet, don't say such a thing!"

Luisa felt alone in the midst of her friends and thought bitterly that she was different from them. "I left my children to go with

41

him. I sacrificed everything. I'm not like you two. You came just for the fun of it. I had a house of my own. But Julia is a whore and if you don't believe me, ask Father Beltrán."

"O.K., O.K., but we're all in the same boat," Rafaela said.

"Not me!" Luisa replied, stretching to her full height.

"Go on! Are you his legal wife?" Rosa said cheerfully.

"I made a mistake and I did it for love. I lost my head. And this man isn't worth it!"

"He must be worth something. He has very nice eyes, and when we were swimming I noticed that he has good shoulders."

Luisa looked at Rafaela with rancor. It was true that all of them were whores. In her imagination she saw her lover's shoulders covering Rafaela's. She felt insecure with these women gorging on fruit. They looked stupid, sitting almost naked on the messy bed. She wanted to leave, and peered through the crack in the door: it was getting light. Julia would not be long in returning to the hotel with her lover and his men.

During the day the women, deprived of the officers' company, arranged their hair, rocked in their hammocks, ate with no appetite, and waited for the night, full of promises, to come. Sometimes in the afternoon they went riding: Rosa and Rafaela on their grey horses, Julia on her sorrel, all three of them laughing, with their breasts flying like birds, their gold trinkets, their silver spurs. The whips they carried were for flicking off the hats of men who did not uncover their heads as they passed. Their lovers followed after them. Ixtepec, fascinated, watched them pass. The girls looked down at us superciliously and disappeared in a cloud of dust, swaying to the rhythm of their horses' rumps.

These outings displeased Luisa. She did not know how to ride, and seeing Flores in the group caused her to weep bitter tears. She sat on her balcony and tried to attract the attention of the men passing below. She flaunted her naked shoulders, smoked, and glanced about seductively. A drunken soldier stopped.

"How much, girlie?"

"Come on in!"

The man entered the hotel and Luisa called to the soldiers who were shining the officers' boots near the fountain.

"Tie him up and beat him!" she ordered. The soldiers exchanged glances. Luisa was furious and her shouts caused don Pepe Ocampo to come running.

"For God's sake, Luisa, be quiet!"

"Beat him or I'll have the General shoot him!"

Seeing the futility of his request, don Pepe covered his face with his hands. The sight of blood sickened him. Shaking with fright he saw them tie the man to a post and heard the blows strike the victim's body. Then he saw the soldiers throw the bleeding man into the street. The hotelkeeper felt sick and went to his room. That night he told Captain Flores about the scene. The young officer bit his lip and asked for a separate room. When his aides went to get the Captain's clothes, Luisa came out of the room crying. "He locked himself in his room and she spent the whole night outside his door, moaning," don Pepe told the people of Ixtepec later.

SEVEN _____

The stranger, who did not know about this secret and passionate life, was still talking to Julia when the General arrived at the Hotel Jardín. Gossips said later that when the General saw him bending over her, he struck the stranger with his whip while calling don Pepe a pimp. Julia was horrified and ran into the street. The General ran after her and together they returned to the hotel and went to their room.

"Why were you afraid, Julia?"

The General moved closer to his mistress and took her face in his hands to look into her eyes. It was the first time that one of his rages had frightened Julia. The girl smiled and offered him her lips. She would never tell Rosas why the purple welt on the stranger's face had frightened her.

"Julia, why were you afraid?" the General insisted, but like a cat she hid her face on her lover's chest and kissed his throat.

"Tell me who he is, Julia."

The girl broke away from her lover's arms and without saying a word lay down on the bed and closed her eyes. The General

44

studied her for a long time. The first orange shadows of night came in through the blinds. In the sun's last rays Julia's feet took on an ephemeral and translucid life, and seemed to exist apart from the body wrapped in the pink robe. The afternoon heat accumulated in the corners was reflected in the bureau mirror. A vase of hyacinths was smothering in its perfume, heavy aromas came from the garden, and a fine dry dust filtered in from the street. Francisco Rosas tiptoed out of the room. The silence of his beloved had got the better of him. He carefully closed the door and angrily called to don Pepe Ocampo. That day my fate was sealed.

The stranger received the blows on his face and without a word picked up his suitcase and walked slowly out of the hotel. I saw him standing impassively in the doorway. Then he walked down the street, came to the corner, and turned in the direction of Guerrero Street. He walked along the narrow sidewalk, not looking to left or to right, apparently lost in thought. He ran into Juan Cariño, who always left the house of the tarts at that hour for his daily walk. The stranger was not surprised by his morning coat or the presidential sash he wore across his chest. Juan Cariño stopped.

"Do you come from far away?"

"From Mexico City, Señor," the stranger replied courteously.

"Mr. President," Juan corrected gravely.

"Excuse me, Mr. President," the stranger quickly agreed.

"Come to see me tomorrow at the executive offices. The young ladies in charge of my appointments will take care of you."

Of all the madmen I have had, Juan Cariño was the best. I do not remember that he ever committed a discourteous or a wicked act. He was gentle and polite. If the nasty boys in the street threw stones at his top hat and knocked it in the dirt, Juan Cariño would quietly pick it up and continue his evening walk with dignity. He gave alms to the poor and visited the sick. He made civic speeches and pasted notices on the walls. How different he was from Hupa! That one was shameless! He would lie down for whole days at a time, scratching his lice and scaring the passersby. Or he would suddenly appear as they were turning a corner, and would dig his long black fingernails into their arms, grunting: "Hupa! Hupa!" He deserved the violent death that came to him: some children found him lying in a ditch; his head had been crushed by rocks and his chest carefully tattooed by a razor. He was demented.

Juan Cariño always lived in the house of the tarts. On the walls of his room were pictures of his heroes: Hidalgo, Morelos, Juárez. When the girls told him to put his picture up alongside theirs, Juan Cariño would get angry.

"No great man has had a statue made of himself during his lifetime. Caligula was the only one who did that!"

The girls were impressed by that name and kept still. If there were quarrels between them and the soldiers who visited them, Juan Cariño intervened very politely.

"Girls, let's have some order! What will these strangers think?"

The day they slashed La Pípila to death with a razor, Juan Cariño arranged the funeral service with great pomp and presided over the burial, which featured music and firecrackers. Behind the blue coffin walked the girls with painted faces, short purple skirts, run-down heels, and black stockings.

"All occupations are equally honorable," said Mr. President, standing by the open grave.

The funeral procession returned and the house was closed during the nine days of prayer. Juan Cariño was in mourning for a whole year.

That evening he tried to help the stranger. The latter thanked him for the offer and continued on his way. Juan Cariño reflected for a few moments and hurried to catch up with him.

"Young man, be sure to come tomorrow. We're going through hard times, we're occupied by the enemy, and we can't do everything we'd like to do. But anyway, something will be done for you."

46

"Thank you! Thank you very much, Mr. President!"

They bowed to each other and parted. The stranger turned down several of my streets and returned to the main plaza. Half-heartedly he sat down on a bench. It was growing dark. Sitting there, he looked like a motherless child. At least that was how don Joaquín explained it to doña Matilde when he brought the stranger home.

Don Joaquín owned the largest house in Ixtepec; its patios and gardens covered almost two blocks. The first garden, of leafy trees, was shaded with dense foliage. No sound could reach that place situated in the middle of the house and surrounded by porches, walls, and roofs. Its stone paths were bordered by giant ferns that flourished in the protection of the shade. On the right, the living room of a four-room pavilion opened onto this garden, which was called the garden of ferns. The windows of the other rooms faced the rear garden, called the garden of little animals. The living room walls, painted with murals, were a prolongation of the park, depicting dense thickets and red-coated hunters with horns, who pursued the deer and rabbits that fled before them into the underbrush. Isabel, Juan, and Nicolás had spent many hours studying that miniature hunting scene during their child-hood.

"Aunt, what country is this?"

"England."

"Have you ever been in England?"

"I?" And doña Matilde began to laugh mysteriously. Now that the children were grown, the pavilion was closed and the family had forgotten about "England."

The darkness and the silence were making inroads throughout the house. In the rooms with stone walls a pitiless and rustic order reigned. The blinds were always closed and the starched curtains drawn. The house had a rhythmical, exact life. Don Joaquín bought only the things that were necessary to improve its strange, solitary operation. Something inside of him needed that repetition of solitude and silence. His room was small; it had scarcely enough room for the bed and no balcony facing the street; an open peephole near the ceiling was the only exit to the outside. A white wooden dressing table with a shiny porcelain pitcher and wash basin bore out that austerity, strangely belied by the scent of fine soap and perfumed shaving lotions and creams in containers with French labels. The room joined that of doña Matilde, his wife.

In her youth doña Matilde had been gay and spirited, quite unlike her brother Martín. The years of married life, the silence and solitude of her house, had turned her into a pleasant, gentle old lady. She lost her ease in dealing with people, and an almost adolescent shyness caused her to blush and giggle whenever she was with strangers.

"I don't know my way any more, except around the house," she told her niece and nephews when they insisted that she go out. If someone died, she did not go to the funeral. She could not understand why the face of a dead friend made her laugh.

"My goodness, Ana, do you think the Olvera family can ever forgive me for laughing at the face of their dead father?"

"Yes, of course, they've already forgotten that," her sister-in-law replied.

"I'm terribly sorry about it."

But in spite of her regrets, she could not think of the sad face of a dead man dressed in black, with a black tie and black shoes, without laughing.

"But really! Dressing a poor corpse so elegantly!"

The unexpected arrival of her husband, accompanied by the stranger, upset her and gave her a sudden feeling that she was going to be sick to her stomach: as if all her solitude and the order that took so many years to establish had been shattered.

"The young man is our guest for as long as he wants to stay," don Joaquín announced, ignoring the displeasure in his wife's eyes. After exchanging her first words with the stranger, she promptly forgot her irritation. She was used to seeing her husband arrive with all kinds of animals, but this was the first time

48

he had brought a man. She went to the kitchen to tell the servants that there was a guest, although she would have preferred to say, "We have another animal." Then she went with her husband and the stranger to the pavilion. She wanted him to be removed from her intimacy.

"Here in 'England' you will feel more independent."

And she looked at the young man shyly. Tefa, the servant girl, opened the doors of the hunting room and those of the bedrooms and lighted the lamps. The stranger seemed to like the place. Doña Matilde, with Tefa's help, selected the largest bedroom, made the bed, opened the window that faced the garden of little animals, and gave her guest various instructions on how to close the mosquito netting to keep the bats out, although they were harmless.

The young man introduced himself as Felipe Hurtado and put his suitcase on a little table. The servant girl put fresh water in the pitcher, brought several cakes of French soap, and put clean towels on the bathroom shelves.

During dinner the señora fell in love with her guest's smile. Afterward, when he had gone back to the pavilion and she and her husband were alone, don Joaquín described the scene at the Hotel Jardín. Don Pepe Ocampo had told him about it when he passed the hotel.

"Now we've made the General our enemy!"

"That man can't do whatever he damn pleases."

"But he does!" she answered sweetly.

Very early the stranger woke up with a start. Cats were swarming over his bed; his host had forgotten to tell him that hundreds of them lived in the garden of little animals. Ravenous at that hour, they came to get the milk and meat the servants put out for them. Hurtado did not know what was happening. The cats came and went through his open window while quacking ducks approached along the stone pathways of the garden; there were also deer, goats, dogs and rabbits. The stranger could not get over his amazement. He was filled with a mixture of tenderness and irony; he realized that the animals were being given shelter as he was.

Much later he decided to leave his room. The sun was high and could scarcely be seen through the dense foliage. He walked gingerly between the plants and ferns, moved a stone, and saw beneath it a creature that made him step back with repugnance.

"It's a scorpion," said Tefa, who was studying him from a distance.

"Oh! Hello," the stranger said courteously.

"Kill it! They're bad. I guess you don't have them in your part of the country, because you don't seem to be familiar with them," the servant said maliciously.

"No, I'm from a cold region."

A mist rose from the garden. The plants gave off dank, penetrating odors. The large fleshy leaves with stalks full of water remained upright despite the intense heat. The clumps of banana plants were filled with strange noises, the earth was black and humid, the fountain disported its greenish water while decaying leaves and huge drowned butterflies floated on the surface. It too exuded a putrid, swampy odor. The garden, which was black and luminous at night, filled with mysterious leaves and flowers perceived by the intensity of their perfume, was infested by day with odors and presences that were a threat to the stranger's nose. He felt nauseated.

"What time does the señor return?"

"He doesn't go out," the servant answered facetiously.

"Oh, I thought he went to work."

"He does—over there." And the woman moved her head to indicate an open door in the wall that led to the garden of little animals.

"Perhaps I'd better not disturb him."

Tefa did not answer. The stranger could feel the woman's hostility. Then suddenly he seemed to remember something.

"Tell me, where does Mr. President live?"

"Juan Cariño? On Alarcón, near the edge of town, on the way

50

to Las Cruces," she answered, surprised. She wanted to ask questions but the young man's detachment restrained her.

"I'm going to see him. I'll be back at dinner time," he said simply.

And Felipe Hurtado walked toward the gate. Tefa watched him go and had the impression that although he was stepping on the plants his footsteps did not leave any mark.

"I wonder where he's from! I wish the Señor wouldn't go around picking up tramps!" She ran to tell the other servants, who were eating lunch in the kitchen.

"Do you know what he did at the hotel?" asked Tacha, the chambermaid. "He tried to get involved with Julia and the General almost killed him, as well as her—and don Pepe, too."

"I don't think he's used to the good life. When I went to make his bed today, he had already made it and was reading a red book."

"You see? Guess how he spent the night!"

"Do you know where he went just now?" Tefa asked, and as the others looked at her questioningly she announced in a triumphant voice: "To the house of the tarts!"

"Go on! He's a little early!" Cástulo said, smiling.

"I say that something bad has brought him to Ixtepec," Tefa added with firm conviction.

"Behind a man you'll always find a woman," Cástulo said with dignity.

Felipe Hurtado, oblivious to the gossip, walked across the town and passed by the hotel. Don Pepe, who saw him coming from a distance, hurried to the door and peered after him curiously.

"Impudent fellow! We haven't recovered from the incident yet, and he comes around again!" he said to himself bitterly. And as it happened, the General had come out of his room the night before to question him. Don Pepe had never seen him so saturnine.

"Who is that man?"

Don Pepe, confused by the General's cold stare, did not know what to say because, in fact, he did not know who the stranger was.

"I don't know, General—a stranger looking for a room. I didn't have time to ask any questions because you came immediately after he did."

"And what right do you have to dare to rent rooms without my permission?" Rosas asked, disregarding the fact that don Pepe Ocampo was the owner of the Hotel Jardín.

"No, General, I didn't plan to rent him one. I was telling him there was nothing available when you came . . ."

Luisa, lying in her hammock, was paying close attention to the conversation.

"General, he talked to Julia for over an hour." This was her way of getting back at Julia and don Pepe.

Francisco Rosas did not look in her direction.

"I heard them talking about Colima," she added maliciously.

"Colima!" Rosas repeated sullenly. He did not want to listen to her. Without further ado he went back to his room.

Don Pepe looked at Luisa with loathing. She continued to swing in her hammock, and then she too went to her room. The hotelkeeper moved stealthily to the door of the lovers' room and tried to overhear their conversation.

"Tell me, Julia, why were you afraid?"

"I don't know," she replied quietly.

"Tell me the truth, Julia. Who is he?"

"I don't know . . ."

Don Pepe could see her, curled up like a cat, resting her head on the importunate General's shoulder as she looked up at him with her almond eyes.

"She's a bad one! I'd beat the truth out of her!" the old man thought.

The arrival of Lieutenant Colonel Cruz made him quickly abandon his position and his musings.

"Eavesdropping, eh?" the officer said, laughing.

"It's nothing to laugh about . . ." And the frightened old man told his story.

Lieutenant Colonel Cruz seemed worried.

"Oh, that Julia!" he said, having lost his desire to laugh.

Francisco Rosas left his room. He was pale, and went out without calling his friends. He came back before midnight, drunk.

"Julia, let's go to Las Cañas."

"I don't want to."

It was the first time that Julia had refused to do her lover's bidding. The General hurled the vase of hyacinths at the bureau mirror, shattering it. The girl covered her eyes.

"What have you done? That's bad luck!"

The other guests at the hotel heard the crash and were alarmed.

"My God, can't we have any peace?" Rafaelita wailed.

"I want to go home!" Antonia screamed, and Colonel Justo Corona put his hand over her mouth.

Felipe Hurtado arrived at the house he was looking for. He knew it was the right one because it stood out from the others like an image reflected in a broken mirror. Its walls were in a ruinous state and loomed enormous at the end of a street that turned into rubble.

"There he is!" shouted some children who watched him with interest.

The stranger observed the faded door and the niche with a statue of St. Anthony the Wanderer. He rang the bell.

"Come in, the door's open," said a weary voice.

Hurtado pushed the door and found himself in an entrance hall with a stone floor; it led to a room that served as a parlor. Red velvet armchairs, dirty paper flowers, tables and a cloudy mirror were its furnishings. There were cigarette butts and bottles littering the floor, which was painted red. Taconitos, in her underwear, disheveled and wearing shoes with crooked heels, greeted him.

"You're out begging rather early," the woman said, with a smile that revealed a shiny gold tooth.

"Excuse me, I was looking for Mr. President."

"You're a stranger, aren't you? Well, I might as well tell you that you have to have an appointment." And the woman went away, still smiling.

Mr. President did not keep him waiting. He cordially offered the stranger a chair and sat down beside him. Luchi appeared with a metal tray and two small cups.

"Are you Julia's friend? Better be careful," Luchi warned, laughing saucily.

"Friend?" Hurtado murmured.

Juan Cariño, seeing the stranger's embarrassment, drew himself up, coughed, and spoke. "We have been occupied and can not expect anything good from the invaders. The Chamber of Commerce, the Municipal Presidency, and the Police Department are under their control. My government and I have no protection. That is why you must watch your step."

"Keep your ass out of it or we'll have to pay," Luchi interrupted.

"What kind of talk is that, girl?" Mr. President protested, embarrassed. After a painful silence he added, "There are times when desire leads a man to folly. Without exaggerating, we can say that Julia has driven General Rosas crazy."

"Do you plan to stay around here long?" Luchi asked.

"I don't know."

"Well, don't stay around *her* very long."

"Follow Luchi's advice. You will learn that every time he has a falling-out with Señorita Julia, he imprisons and hangs our people. Fortunately, his persecutions have not yet affected the dictionary."

"Mr. President likes dictionaries," Luchi hastened to add.

"And why shouldn't I, since they contain all the wisdom of mankind? Where would we be without dictionaries? I can't imagine. The language we speak would be unintelligible without them. *Them*! What does *them* mean? Nothing. Just a sound. But if we consult the dictionary we find: 'Them, third person plural.' "

The stranger laughed. Mr. President liked his laugh, and leaning back comfortably in his shabby chair he took several spoonfuls of sugar and stirred his coffee slowly. He was happy: he had misled the stranger, because although what he had said was true, the important thing was what he had not said—that words were dangerous because they had an existence of their own and the defense of dictionaries prevented unimaginable catastrophes. Words had to remain secret. If men knew of their existence, their own wickedness would drive them to say them and release them into the world. Ignorant people already knew too many words and used them to make others suffer. His secret mission was to wander through my streets and pick up the evil words spoken during the day. He slyly seized them one by one and hid them under his top hat. Some were very perverse; they fled and forced him to run for several blocks before they let themselves be caught. A butterfly net would have been most useful, but it would have aroused suspicion because of its size. Some days his harvest was so large that the words did not fit under his hat, and he had to go out several times before he finished his task. Returning home, he went to his room to reduce the words to letters and preserve them once again in the dictionary, which they never should have left in the first place. The terrible thing was that as soon as a bad word found the route of an evil tongue it always escaped, and so his work was never-ending.

He searched every day for the words "to hang" and "to torture," and when they got away from him he arrived home in despair, did not eat, and stayed awake all night long. He knew that in the morning there would be more bodies hanging by the road to Cocula, and he felt that he was responsible. He looked kindly at the stranger, who was, he felt certain when they met the day before, a person he could trust. Juan Cariño had invited him to the Executive Offices to initiate him into the mysteries of

55

his power. "When I die, someone else will have to inherit my mission. Otherwise, what will become of this town?" First he would have to know if his heir had a pure heart.

"*Metamorphosis!* What would *metamorphosis* be without the dictionary? A jumble of little black letters." And he studied the effect of the word on the stranger, whose face turned into the face of a ten-year-old boy. "And what would *confetti* be?"

The word caused a carnival to light up in Felipe Hurtado's eyes, and Juan Cariño was transported with delight.

Luchi could listen to him for hours. "What a pity! If he weren't crazy, he'd be very powerful, and the world would be as bright as the Wheel of Fortune," and Luchi was sad that Juan Cariño lived in the whorehouse. She wanted to find the moment when Juan Cariño had become Mr. President, but she could not find the line that separated the two persons; the crack through which the world's happiness escaped; the error that produced the little man in the brothel who had no hope of recovering his brilliant destiny.

"Perhaps one night he dreamed that he was the President and he has never awakened from that dream, even though his eyes are open," the girl thought, remembering her own dreams and her strange behavior in them. That was why she served him many cups of coffee and treated him solicitously, as one treats a sleepwalker.

"If one day he were to awaken . . ." and she scrutinized Mr. President's eyes, thinking she could find in them the astonishing world of dreams: the spirals to the sky, the words spinning alone like threats, the trees planted in the wind, the blue seas on the housetops. And did she not fly in her dreams? She flew over streets that flew after *her*, while down below some phrases were waiting. If she happened to wake up in the middle of that dream, she would believe forever in the existence of her wings and people would taunt her. "Look at Luchi. She's crazy. She thinks she's a bird." That was why she kept watching Juan Cariño, to see if she could make him wake up.

"When you want to spend a few minutes on the words, come

and see me: from this moment on I am placing my dictionaries at your disposal," Luchi heard him say.

"I promise that your invitation will not be forgotten," the stranger replied, smiling.

"I even have three volumes of the dictionary of the English language. I haven't been able to get hold of all of them. It's most unfortunate!" And Juan Cariño lapsed into a great sadness. Who could be using those books? No wonder there was so much unhappiness in the world!

Luchi left the room and came back a few minutes later with a dictionary that had an orange binding and gold letters. Juan Cariño took the book reverently and began to introduce his friend to his favorite words. He repeated them, dividing the words into syllables so that their power would fall on Ixtepec and free it from the power of words spoken in the street or in the office of Francisco Rosas. Suddenly he stopped and looked at his friend.

"I suppose you go to mass."

"Yes . . . on Sundays."

"You must be sure to join in saying the words of the prayers. They are so beautiful."

And Juan Cariño began to recite the litanies.

"It's after one-thirty and the fire hasn't been started yet," Taconitos announced, poking her tousled head through the door.

"One-thirty?" Juan Cariño asked, interrupting his prayer. He wanted to forget the woman's strident voice, which brought him back to his wretched life in the house of dirty walls and beds.

"One-thirty!" the woman repeated and then disappeared.

"She's a freethinker. They're the ones who have made the world so horrible," Juan Cariño said angrily. He got up and stood close to Felipe Hurtado. "Keep my secret. The General's greed is insatiable. He is a freethinker who pursues beauty and mystery. He is capable of adopting any measures to persecute the dictionary and would bring about a catastrophe. Men would be lost in a disorderly language and the world would collapse in a heap of ashes."

"We would be like dogs," Luchi explained.

57

"Even worse than that, because dogs have organized their barking, although we can't understand it. Do you know what a free-thinker is? A man who has rejected thought." And Mr. President escorted his visitor to the door. "My warmest regards to doña Matilde and don Joaquín, but I'm very sorry they never honor me with a visit."

Juan Cariño stood pensively on the doorstep, waving goodbye to the stranger, who walked away in the radiance of early afternoon. Then he closed the door sadly, returned to the dirty little room, and sat down on the same chair he had occupied before. He tried not to see the cigarette butts and the filth.

"Mr. President, the little bird of glory sang to us! I'll bring your tacos soon," Luchi said, trying to cheer him. The other women were just beginning to get out of bed.

In those days I was so miserable that my hours accumulated shapelessly and my memory was transformed into sensations. Unhappiness, like physical pain, equalizes the minutes. All days seem like the same day, acts become the same act, and all persons are a single useless person. The world loses its variety, light is annihilated, and miracles are abolished. The inertia of those repeated days kept me quiet as I contemplated the vain flight of my hours and waited for the miracle that persisted in not happening. The future was the repetition of the past. Motionless, I let myself be consumed by the thirst that rankled at my corners. To disperse the petrified days all I had was the ineffectual illusion of violence, and cruelty was practiced furiously on the women, stray dogs, and Indians. We lived in a quiet time and the people, like the actors in a tragedy, were caught in that arrested moment. It was in vain that they performed acts which were more and more bloody. We had abolished time.

News of the stranger's arrival coursed through the morning with the speed of joy. Although this had not happened in many years, time whirled through my streets, causing lights and reflections on the stones and the leaves of the trees; the almond trees were filled with birds, the sun rose with delight in the

58

mountains, and in the kitchens the servant girls chattered noisily about his coming. The scent of orange tea permeated the rooms to awaken the ladies from their foolish dreams. The stranger's unexpected presence broke the silence. He was the messenger, the one who was uncontaminated by the misfortune.

"Conchita! Conchita! Matilde has a man from Mexico City! Go and visit her!" doña Elvira shrieked when her maid told her the news, and then she leaped out of bed. She wanted to be early for seven o'clock mass so she would be the first one to have news of the stranger. Who was he? What was he like? What did he want? Why had he come? She dressed quickly and studied herself calmly in the mirror. Her face revealed nothing.

"What a good color I have! What a pity your poor father can't see me now! He'd be envious, he was always so sallow!"

Conchita, standing by the dressing table, waited patiently for her mother to finish admiring herself.

"There he is! There he is, spying on me from inside the mirror, angry to see me a widow and still young! I'm leaving now, Justino Montúfar." And she stuck out her tongue at her husband's image in the mirror.

"He's trapped in there because he looked at himself too much," she said to herself on the way to church. "I never knew a more conceited man!" And she recalled with irritation the carefully ironed cuffs of his shirts, the perfection of his ties, the strips of cloth to reinforce his trousers. When he died she did not want to dress him: "Just a shroud!" she begged her friends, weeping, glad to deprive him of the whims that had tyrannized her for so many years. "This will teach him!" she said to herself while her friends shrouded the body in an ordinary sheet: at that moment she was in control of her will again, and she imposed it vengefully on the dead man, who, pale and shrunken, seemed to be trembling with rage.

"How late Matilde is! Old women are so slow!" she exclaimed outside the church, annoyed that her friend had not yet arrived. She showed her displeasure by stamping her foot impatiently. Conchita lowered her eyes. She felt that her mother's words and actions were attracting the glances of the others who were waiting, although they concealed their own impatience.

"She may not come. She's such a show-off! Poor boy, he doesn't know what a madhouse he's living in!"

Conchita signaled to her to be quiet.

"Why are you signaling like that? We all know that Joaquín is crazy. He thinks he's the king of the animals . . ." and she burst out laughing at her witticism.

She was unable to continue her speech because she saw doña Lola Goríbar coming with Rodolfo, her son.

"Here comes that fat pig," she said with irritation.

Doña Lola almost never went out. Perhaps that was why she was monstrously overweight. She suffered from fear, but her fear was not the same as ours. "If a person had no money, no one would want to help him," she said anxiously, staying close to her high cabinets where the gold pieces were stacked in neat, equal piles. On Saturdays and Sundays the servants heard her, locked in her room, counting the coins. The rest of the week she patrolled her house ferociously. "We never know what God has in store for us," and this thought terrified her. There was a chance that God might want to make her poor; and to guard against the divine will, she accumulated more and more wealth. She was a very good Catholic; she had a chapel in her house and heard mass there. She always spoke of the "holy fear of God," and we all knew that the "holy fear" referred only to money. "Don't trust anyone, don't trust anyone," she whispered in Rodolfo's ear. We were astonished to see her coming, leaning on her son's arm. "They're looking at us," the mother said in a low voice. We admired the young man's gabardine suit and the diamond brooch that sparkled on doña Lola's bosom. He bought his clothes in Mexico City and the servants said he had more than a thousand ties. On the other hand, his mother always wore the same black dress, which was beginning to turn green at the seams.

Señora Montúfar went to greet them, and doña Lola eyed Conchita with distrust: the young girl looked dangerous. Rodolfo tried not to see her. "I don't want to raise her hopes. You never know about women: they try to compromise a man on the slightest pretext."

Doña Lola Goríbar was afraid that the stranger had some bad intention that might jeopardize her son's peace of mind. "I say it's not fair, it's not fair! Rodolfito has so many troubles now!"

"Don't worry about me, Mamacita."

With resignation doña Elvira followed the dialogue between mother and son. Señora Goríbar felt an unbounded admiration for Rodolfo: thanks to him her lands had been returned to her and the government had paid her for the damage done by the Zapatistas. It was therefore only fair that she should express her gratitude in public. That was the least she could do.

"He is so good, Elvira!" and doña Lola touched her diamond brooch.

Señora Montúfar leaned forward to admire the jewel. "Justino was also a very good son," she thought with irony.

Rodolfo made frequent trips to Mexico City and when he returned to Ixtepec he went to the Military Command to talk with General Francisco Rosas.

"Now the boundaries have been changed," we said when we saw him emerge smiling from the General's office.

And as it happened, after each trip Rodolfo, assisted by his gunmen from Tabasco, moved the boundary lines of his ranches and acquired peons, huts, and lands for nothing. Under one of the almond trees in the courtyard, waiting for seven o'clock mass, was Ignacio, whose sister, Agustina, ran the bakery. He looked at doña Lola's son for a long time; then he approached politely and asked if they could have a few words together in private. It was rumored that Ignacio was an advocate of agrarian reform. The truth was that he had fought in Zapata's ranks and now lived the life of an ordinary, barefooted peasant. His trousers of coarse cotton and his palm hat were consumed by sun and wear.

"Look, don Rodolfo, you'd better leave the boundaries alone. The land reformers say they're going to kill you."

Rodolfo smiled and turned away. Ignacio, mortified, retreated and contemplated Rodolfo Goríbar's slight figure from a distance.

Goríbar did not even look at him again. How many times had he been threatened? He felt safe. The slightest scratch to his person would cost the lives of dozens of agrarian reformers. The government had promised him that, and had authorized him to appropriate the lands he wanted. He had the General's support. Each time he enlarged his holdings, General Francisco Rosas received from Goríbar's hands a large sum of money, which was then converted into jewels for Julia.

"Do you see how a woman can dominate a man? That brazen hussy is ruining us!"

Rodolfo kissed his mother to comfort her for the indignities she was forced to suffer because of Julia's shameless conduct. And to make amends, he also gave jewels—to his mother.

"He pays, and the Indians won't work," he heard her say. He came closer to her; her voice mitigated the harshness of Ignacio's words. He felt that he and his mother were united by a tender and unique love. His happiest moments came at night when both were in bed in adjoining rooms and carried on secret, passionate conversations through the open door. Since boyhood he had been the consolation of his mother, who was the victim of an unhappy marriage. His father's death had only emphasized the delights of the exclusive love they shared. To doña Lola he was still a small, frightened boy who was hungry for caresses, and she lavished her affection on him.

"The secret of pleasing a man is soft soap and good cooking," she said with malice, and astutely kept a watchful eye on her son's whims and meals. When he was a small boy and bumped into a chair or a table, she had the maids whip the furniture to show him that it was guilty, not he. "Rodolfito is always right," she said seriously, and justified even the least of his temper tantrums.

"You don't know, Elvira, how happy I am to have a son like Rodolfito. I don't believe he'll ever marry. No woman would understand him the way his mother does."

Doña Elvira did not have time to answer. She was distracted by the arrival of doña Matilde.

"Did you see? Did you see how insolent she is?" asked doña Lola, referring to Conchita, as soon as the young girl and her mother had gone.

"Yes, Mamá, but don't worry."

"The look she gave you!"

Doña Matilde crossed the courtyard with her gay, mincing step. She was late because she had stopped to talk to Joaquín about their guest, and her haste to arrive before mass ended had made her breathless. When she saw her friends waiting she tried to keep from laughing. "They're so curious—I'll have to invite them over!"

That night at don Joaquín's house they took the chairs out on the porch, lighted the lamps, and prepared trays of cool drinks and candies. It was so long since a social gathering had been held in Ixtepec that the whole house took on a festive air, but no sooner had the guests assembled than the merriment evaporated, leaving the friends intimidated by the stranger's presence. Stiffly they uttered brief greetings and then sat in silence contemplating the night. A blazing heat hovered over the garden, the ferns grew preternaturally large in the shadows, and the obtuse shapes of the mountains that surround me settled over the rooftops and oppressed the night. The ladies were still: their lives, their loves, their useless beds filed by, deformed by darkness and the quiescent heat.

To forget the oddity of being in the presence of those strange faces, Felipe Hurtado concentrated on the lugubrious rhythm of the swaying fans. Isabel and Conchita, condemned to a life of gradual deterioration within the walls of their houses, picked halfheartedly at the confections, dripping with warm honey, for which they had no appetite. Tomás Segovia, stringing together brilliant phrases like beads, was unnerved by his friends' silence and, losing the thread, glumly saw his utterances rolling on the floor until they were lost under the chairs. Sitting apart from the others, Martín Moncada contemplated the night. He heard some of Segovia's words.

"He's very eccentric," doña Elvira whispered in the stranger's ear. The dull gathering prompted her to make confidences. Hurtado looked surprised, and the widow waved her hand to indicate Martín Moncada's voluntary isolation. She wanted to tell him what she thought of her friend, but she was afraid that Ana would hear.

"He was a supporter of Madero," she said in a low voice, by way of explanation.

The stranger smiled, not knowing what to say.

"Our troubles began with Madero," she said, sighing perfidiously. She knew that an argument would bring the dying conversation back to life.

"The forerunner of Francisco Rosas is Francisco Madero," said Tomás Segovia sententiously.

The figure of General Rosas appeared in the dark center of the garden and came up to the forlorn group on doña Matilde's porch. "He is the only one who has a right to live," they said to themselves bitterly, and felt they were caught in an invisible web that left them without money, without love, without a future.

"He is a tyrant!"

"You don't have to tell our guest—he saw it with his own eyes!"

"Since the General has been here, he has done nothing but commit crimes and crimes and more crimes." There was ambiguity in Segovia's voice: he almost seemed to be envying Rosas, whose job it was to hang agrarian reformers instead of sitting on the porch of a mediocre house saying useless words. "He must go through some terrible moments," he said to himself, feeling an intense emotion. "The Romans didn't have the ridiculous concept of mercy either, least of all toward those they conquered, and the Indians are the conquered ones here." In his mind's eye he formed the sign of death with his thumb, as he had seen in illustrations in his Roman history book. "We are a people of slaves with a handful of patricians," and he placed himself with the patricians to the right of Francisco Rosas.

"Since we assassinated Madero we have had a long night of

64

expiation," Martín Moncada exclaimed, still with his back to the group.

His friends looked at him virulently. Hadn't Madero been a traitor to his own people? He belonged to a wealthy creole family, and yet he headed the rebellion of the Indians. His death was not only just but necessary. He was to blame for the anarchy that prevailed in the country. The years of civil war that followed his death had been atrocious for the mestizos who resisted the hordes of Indians fighting for rights and lands that did not belong to them. But when Venustiano Carranza betrayed the victorious Revolution and took the power into his own hands, the moneyed classes had some relief. Then, with the assassination of Emiliano Zapata, Francisco Villa, and Felipe Ángeles, they felt safe. But the generals who betrayed the Revolution installed a tyrannical and voracious government that shared the wealth and privileges only with their former enemies and accomplices in the betrayal: the big landholders of the days of Porfirio Díaz.

"Martín, how can you talk like that? Do you really think we deserve Rosas?" doña Elvira Montúfar asked. Her friend's words made her ashamed.

"Not only Rosas but Rodolfito Goríbar and his thugs from Tabasco. You accuse Rosas, forgetting that his accomplice is even more bloodthirsty. But, after all, it was a follower of Porfirio Díaz who gave Victoriano Huerta the money to assassinate Madero."

The others were silent. They were really surprised at the bloody friendship between the Catholic followers of Porfirio Díaz, known as the Porfiristas, and the atheistic revolutionaries. The two groups were linked by greed and the shameful origin of the mestizo. They had inaugurated an era of barbarism unprecedented in my memory.

"I don't think they paid to have Madero assassinated," the widow said uncertainly.

"Elvira dear, Luján paid Huerta six million pesos," Moncada said hotly.

"You're right, Martín, and we're going to see worse things yet.

65

Why do you think Rodolfito brought those gunmen from Tabasco? To hunt stray dogs?" Saying this, don Joaquín shuddered, remembering the many starving, mangy dogs that roamed through my stone streets, plagued by thirst, miserable pariahs like the millions of Indians who had been stripped of their possessions and brutalized by the government.

"Gunmen!" That was still a new word, and it left us stunned. The gunmen were a new class that came into being when the perfidious Revolution merged with the movement of Porfirio Díaz. Stuffed into expensive gabardine suits, wearing dark glasses and soft felt hats, they performed the macabre task of making men vanish only to reappear as mutilated corpses. The generals called this kind of legerdemain "Building a country," and the Porfiristas called it "Divine Justice." Both expressions meant dirty business and brutal plunder.

"Things would have been better with Zapata. At least he was from the south," doña Matilde sighed.

"Zapata?" doña Elvira exclaimed. Her friends had either gone mad or were making fun of her in front of the stranger. She recalled how relieved everyone had been when they learned that Emiliano Zapata had been assassinated. For many nights afterward they seemed to hear the sound of his body falling in the courtyard of the Chinameca plantation and they could sleep in peace again.

"Matilde is talking like a government general," Segovia said with an amused air, and he thought of the new official language in which the words "justice," "Zapata," "Indian," and "agrarian reform" served to facilitate the plundering of lands and the assassination of peasants.

"It's true! Did you know that the government is going to erect a statue of him?" doña Elvira asked happily.

"So no one will say they aren't revolutionaries! There's no question about it, the only good Indian is a dead Indian!" the pharmacist said, remembering the words that had guided the dictatorship of Porfirio Díaz, and applying them now, maliciously, to the use that was being made of the name of the assassi-

66

nated Indian, Emiliano Zapata. The others celebrated Segovia's cleverness with hearty laughter.

"I think that's a stupid joke," Martín Moncada said.

"Don't be angry, don Martín," Segovia begged.

"It's all very sad."

"Of course, the only one who always stands to win is Julia," the pharmacist replied bitterly.

"Yes, that woman is responsible," Señora Montúfar exclaimed.

"Don't they know in Mexico City what's going on around here?" doña Matilde asked slyly to exorcise Julia's ghost.

"Isn't there a theater in Ixtepec?" the stranger asked, answering her question with another question.

"Theater? Doesn't this woman give us enough histrionics?" Conchita's mother replied, startled, looking at the stranger with astonishment.

"That's too bad!" he said calmly.

The others stared at one another without knowing what to say.

"People are happier when they have a theater. It provides a little illusion and that's what Ixtepec needs: illusion!"

"Illusion!" the host repeated gloomily. And the dark lonely night enveloped them with sadness. Nostalgically, they searched for something indistinct, something they could not quite give shape to, needing it in order to get through the innumerable days that spread before them like an enormous panorama of old newspapers in which news of crimes, weddings, and advertisements are mixed together in hit-or-miss fashion with no regard for their relative importance, like facts devoid of meaning, outside of time, beyond memory.

Fatigue descended on the women, and the men looked at each other inanely. In the garden the insects were destroying each other in the invisible and active struggle that fills the earth with sounds.

"The rats are making holes in my kitchen," doña Elvira Montúfar thought, and stood up to go.

The others did likewise, and together they went out into the night. Felipe Hurtado offered to escort them home. The group moved thoughtfully through my silent streets. They were busy avoiding the ruts and the uneven terrain, and scarcely spoke. When they arrived at the deserted plaza they saw light coming through the blinds of Julia's balcony.

"They're in there!" doña Elvira said spitefully.

What were they doing? The image of an alien joy left them dejected. Perhaps Francisco Rosas was right. Perhaps Julia's smiling face was the only thing that could dissipate the days of newsprint and replace them with days of sunshine and tears. Uncertainly they moved away from that special balcony and lost themselves in the dark streets, searching for the doors of their houses through which they came and went each identical day.

When he returned, Felipe Hurtado stopped outside the balcony of the love object of Ixtepec. Then he crossed the street and sat down on a bench in the plaza, where he could watch Julia's window. With his head in his hands he abandoned himself to infinitely sad thoughts as he waited for the dawn.

In the morning, his hosts looked at him with surprise. Although they did not dare, they wanted to tell him that they had waited all night for him to return, afraid that some misfortune had befallen him. He simply appeared, gentle and meek, like a cat; his friends accepted his presence and were grateful.

EIGHT

Which tongue first uttered the words that were to make my luck take a turn for the worse? Many years have passed, and I do not yet know. I can still see Felipe Hurtado pursued by those words as if he were pursued, day and night, by a small and dangerous animal: "He came for her." In Ixtepec there was no other "her" but Julia. "He came for her," said don Ramón's daughters when they saw the stranger's tall figure from their balcony. Their father went to meet him, displaying warmth and concern, and tried to induce him to talk of private matters.

"Do you plan to stay with us long?" Señor Martínez asked, avidly scrutinizing the stranger's eyes.

"I'm not sure. It depends."

"But, really, a young man must have some idea . . . Perhaps my indiscretion disturbs you," he hastened to add when he saw the other's cool reaction to his words.

"No. Why should it? On the contrary, I appreciate your interest," the stranger replied.

"The first time I saw you, I thought you belonged to that group of dynamic young men who are looking for employment—something brilliant, productive . . ."

"Employment?" Felipe Hurtado asked, as if such an idea had never crossed his mind. "No, I never thought of such a thing!" he added, laughing.

"Well, my friend, just imagine, that Catalán thought you were an inspector. I assured him that nothing was more unlikely than that!"

Felipe Hurtado laughed heartily.

"An inspector!" he said, as if he found don Pedro Catalán's idea amusing.

"He's an old busybody!" don Ramón said to excuse his curiosity and find a way to continue the conversation, but Felipe Hurtado made it clear that he was leaving and don Ramón had no choice but to let him go.

"I'm certain now! I'm absolutely sure!" don Ramón shouted triumphantly as he entered his house. His daughters hurried to his side. "This young man who calls himself Felipe Hurtado 'came for her,' " the old man assured them.

The women felt sorry for the stranger as he passed, and repeated the words that followed him through my streets. He seemed oblivious to the phrase that went from mouth to mouth, and walked calmly to the open country, where the sun beats down relentlessly, the ground bristles with thorns, and snakes sleep among the rocks. Mule-drivers found him by the Naranjo River, walking or sitting on a boulder, with a book in his hand and his face afflicted by a sorrow we had not observed in him before.

On the way back he passed the Hotel Jardín. Julia was at the window. No one ever saw them say hello. They just looked at each other. Expressionless, she watched him disappear under the portico. Passersby exchanged glances, gesturing maliciously to say, "He came for her."

And it was clear that something was happening. After the stranger's arrival, Rosas acted worse than ever. It seemed that someone had whispered to him the words that were meant for all ears except his, and he lived tormented by doubt.

With malice and jocularity we watched those passionate and

70

dangerous relations, and finally concluded: He is going to kill her. Secretly we found the idea exhilarating, and when we saw Julia in church with the black shawl draped around her neck to reveal her exquisite bosom, we looked at each other and mutely raised a chorus of reproaches. The General waited uneasily outside. He never went to mass, not caring to mingle with pious women and sanctimonious men. Standing under an almond tree, he smoked nervously, and his aides waited with him. The mistresses were devout and went to mass regularly. Rosas' surly expression caused us to give him a wide berth as we left. We saw him from a distance and prudently made our exit.

"That woman has no fear of God!"

Women dressed in mourning left in little groups, looking greedily at Julia, who walked away leaning on her lover's arm.

"We should complain to Father Beltrán—she shouldn't be allowed in church," said María's daughter, Charito, who was head of the Ixtepec school.

"Everyone has a right to God!" Ana Moncada protested.

"But don't you realize, Ana, what a bad example she is to the young girls? And besides, she's offensive to virtuous women."

Julia left the church grounds with her lover without hearing the hostile comments. Isolated, out of her element, she was cut off from my voices, my streets, my trees, my people. Her dark eyes showed traces of cities and towers, distant and strange. Rosas steered her along at a good clip to protect her from the envious glances that followed her tall, pensive figure.

"I want to walk," the young girl said, smiling to excuse her whim.

"Walk?" Francisco Rosas asked, looking over his shoulder at the girl. Julia displayed her imperturbable profile. The General studied the line of her forehead. What was she thinking about? Why did she want to walk? She was usually so indolent. He remembered a name, and turned toward the hotel.

"Tell me, Julia, why do you want to walk?"

Rodolfo Goríbar, accompanied by two of his gunmen from Tabasco, was waiting at the door of the hotel. When he caught sight of the General he went to meet him, knowing that with Julia there he would be unwelcome.

"General," he called timidly.

Rosas looked at him as if he were a total stranger.

"May I have a word with you, General?"

"See me later," Rosas replied, not looking in his direction, and went into the hotel with Julia.

Rodolfo Goríbar walked back to his friends.

"Let's wait," and he paced back and forth in front of the hotel. He knew from experience that the General would not take long. He would concede all deaths when he was angry with Julia. Rodolfito smiled blissfully.

"Indian bastards!"

His men stared at him, spat out of the corners of their mouths, pulled their hats to one side. They could wait for hours. Time passed quickly when the prey was certain, and their chief's placid expression assured them of that.

"Just a matter of hours," they said.

Julia fell in a heap on the bed and turned her face away. Francisco Rosas, not knowing what to do or say, went to the window. His eyes, deadened by the fear that the girl's tedium caused him to feel, looked directly into the torrent of sunshine streaming through the blinds. He wanted to cry. He could not understand her. Why did she insist on living in a different world? No word, no gesture could extricate her from the streets and days that were part of her former life. He felt like the victim of a curse that over-powered both his will and Julia's. How could he abolish the past? That shining past in which the luminous Julia floated in mis-shapen rooms, jumbled beds, and nameless cities. That memory was not his and he was the one who had to put up with it like a permanent and badly-drawn hell. In those alien and incomplete memories there were eyes and hands that looked at Julia and touched her and then took her to places where he himself got lost trying to find her. "Her memory is pleasure," he said to himself bitterly, and heard Julia get up from the bed, call the maid, and

72

order a hot bath. He heard her moving about behind him, looking for perfume bottles, selecting soap, towels.

"I'm going to take a bath," the girl whispered and left the room.

Rosas felt very lonely. Without Julia the room was dismantled, it had no air, no future. He turned and saw the impression of her body on the bed and felt he was spinning in a vacuum. He had no memory. Before Julia entered it, his life was a long night through which he went galloping across the mountains of Chihuahua. It was the time of the Revolution, but he was not seeking the same thing his companions, followers of Villa, were after; instead he longed for something ardent and perfect. He wanted to escape from the mountain night, where his only consolation was to look at the stars. He betrayed Villa and went with Carranza, and his nights were still the same as ever. Nor was power what he was seeking. The day he met Julia he had the impression of touching a star from the sierra sky, of crossing its luminous circles and reaching the girl's intact body, and he forgot everything but Julia's splendor. But she did not forget and in her memory continued the repetition of gestures, voices, streets, and men that preceded him. When he was with her he felt like a lonely warrior in the presence of a besieged city with its invisible inhabitants eating, fornicating, thinking, remembering, and he was outside of the walls that guarded Julia's inner world. His rages, his fits, and his tears were to no avail: the city remained intact.

"Memory is the curse of man," he said to himself, and pounded his hand on the wall until he injured it. And that gesture—would it not endure in time forever? Again and again, as he spoke to his friends, Julia would stroll by, naked, in his imagination. He followed her, saw her eyes and her neck moving in the humid world of gazelles, and heard his subordinates talking about card games and money. "Memory is invisible," he thought bitterly. The memory of Julia came to him even when he was the one who carried her sleeping body through the streets of Ixtepec. That was his irremediable sadness: not to be able to see what went on

73

inside of her. Right now, as he suffered from the dry rays of the sunshine, she was playing with water, forgetful of Francisco Rosas, who suffered because she did not forget. She was probably splashing in the water, remembering other baths and other men who waited avidly for her to finish. He saw himself in many men asking her with no hope of a reply, "What are you thinking of, my love?"

He smelled her perfume and heard her approaching, walking barefooted on the red tiled floor. And he heard her walking in many other similar rooms, leaving damp tracks that quickly evanesced in airy wisps. Julia entered many rooms and many men heard her coming and breathed her scent of vanilla, which rose in spirals to an invisible, lost world.

"Julia!" he called without turning.

The girl came up to him. Francisco Rosas felt the approach of the vast world concealed by her forehead, which was like a high wall that separated her from him. "In her inner mind she is deceiving me," he said to himself, and saw her galloping through unknown countrysides, dancing in dark small-town saloons, entering enormous beds accompanied by faceless men.

"Julia, is there a part of your body that no one has kissed?" he asked without turning around, surprised by his words. The girl drew closer to him and remained silent.

"Julia, I've never kissed anyone but you," he said humbly.

"Neither have I," and her lie grazed the nape of his neck.

Along with memories of Julia, Francisco Rosas pictured Felipe Hurtado's gentle face in the sunshine that poured in through the blinds. Without a word he left the room and called for don Pepe Ocampo.

"Señorita Julia's windows are not to be opened!"

He went out to search with his yellow glances for the stranger. Rodolfito Goríbar came to meet him. The General went on walking. The younger man signaled to his men and the three followed at a safe distance. Seeing the General pass, people smiled maliciously. "What is Rosas looking for?"

74

He returned to the hotel very late. His eyes were red, his face sunburned, and his lips dried by dust. Julia was waiting with a smile playing about her lips. The man threw himself on the bed and stared at the dark beams on the ceiling, persecuted by memories that martyrized him because they were imperfect. "If only I could remember," he repeated to himself with a desiccated will that filled his head with dust, "but I don't remember faces."

Julia moved closer and leaned over his hot face. "You've had too much sun," she said, touching his forehead.

Francisco Rosas did not answer. At some time in the past Julia had made the same gesture, perhaps it was not even to him she was doing it now, and he, Rosas, saw her caressing an unknown man in her memory.

"Is it my forehead you are touching?"

Julia took her hand away as if it had been burned. Frightened, she put it on her breast. Some memories that Rosas glimpsed fleetingly in her eyes disappeared behind her lids. Sitting quietly in the perfumed room, which was the same room they shared every night, Julia seemed like the same Julia, and nevertheless he, Rosas, was another man with a different body and face. He stood up and went to her. He would be the other man, he would kiss her as they had kissed her in the past.

"Go, Julia, go with anyone. What does it matter if Francisco Rosas is so unhappy?"

In the morning the servants brought the news: five men had been hanged from the mango trees along the road to Cocula and one of them was Ignacio, the brother of Agustina, who ran the bakery. She was arranging for permission to take her brother's body and none of us had sweet rolls for breakfast.

"Poor men, maybe they didn't want to give up their land!" doña Matilde explained to the stranger without wanting to say what she really thought. This time one of her friends was involved and she preferred to keep quiet. She was mortified.

Felipe Hurtado did not know what to say. It was the first time since his arrival that there had been deaths in Ixtepec. He looked at the table set for breakfast, poured himself a cup of hot coffee, and tried to smile. Doña Matilde had nothing more to say.

"It's Julia! She's to blame for everything that happens to us! How long will this go on? Well, I'm not going to eat breakfast!" doña Elvira screamed, violently pushing away the coffeepot that Inés had just put on the table. Conchita poured herself a cup and looked at her mother. How could she be annoyed because there were no sweet rolls when poor Ignacio was hanging in the sun, dead and wretched after an even more wretched life? Since she was a small girl she had seen him padding through town in bare feet, dressed in his old suit of patched cotton. How many times had he spoken to her? She seemed to hear his voice—"Good day, Señorita Conchita"—and felt she was going to cry.

"If you cry, I'll cry too," doña Elvira threatened, aware that her daughter was fighting to hold back the tears. She casually poured a cup of coffee and drank it slowly, lost in thoughts that were troubling her for the first time. "Poor Ignacio! Poor Indians! Maybe they aren't as bad as we think!" The mother and daughter sat across the table from each other, not knowing what to say. Before them was a long, tiresome day, one of those days, so frequent in Ixtepec, populated by deaths and sinister omens.

Doña Lola Goríbar got up early and painstakingly checked the order of her house. She was uneasy. Her son was sleeping peacefully, oblivious of the fact that this was a dangerous day. She watched him for a long time and felt powerless to escape from the shock of knowing that this was a hostile world. "My God! My God! Why do people treat us so badly?" and she looked at her son with commiseration. Since girlhood she had felt this threat: people had ill will toward her. As far back as she could remember, there was a distance that separated her from games and later left her alone at parties. The envy in others' eyes had opened that breach between her and the world. Gradually this envy, which sorely tormented her, had forced her to withdraw from her friends and to lead a lonely, ordered life. When her son was born, she was plagued by fear and tried to protect him from the evil that afflicted her and that seemed to be hereditary— Rodolfito aroused the same envy that she had aroused in Ixtepec. Experience taught her that she could do nothing to combat that misfortune, nothing but proceed with the utmost caution. "Don't forget, my son, he who gives willingly gives twice." But Rodolfo was an innocent, he slept like a baby, cut off from the town's machinations. At that very moment, tongues and eyes were already pointing menacingly at their house. Thoughtfully, the mother went out to call the servants, eyeing them shrewdly.

"Don't make any noise. Master Rodolfito came in very late. He needs his sleep, he's very tired."

The servants listened sullenly and went away without answering. Doña Lola watched them make their exit among the garden plants. It was clear that they hated her. When hatred hovered over her house, she exercised her power willingly. She went to the dining room to wait for her fragrant hot chocolate.

"There aren't any sweet rolls, Señora."

"I know, the just have to pay for the sinners," and she sipped her cup of chocolate, complacently watching the servant girl tiptoeing back and forth.

In the kitchen the other maids were breakfasting on black coffee and tortillas with salt.

"It was that mamma's boy. He took advantage of Rosas' jealousy."

"He'll come to no good end."

They were sad and forsaken by fortune, their bare feet lacerated from constant exposure to stones. They would willingly have left doña Lola Goríbar's house, but the hunger they suffered in the countryside forced them to remain in her kitchen.

"Don't say it in front of the girl!" Ana Moncada shouted when she heard the news of Ignacio's death. Her husband listened to the news sadly and looked at the luminous blue morning that settled on the plants. Many years before, his mother had shouted the same thing: "Don't say it in front of the boy!" Why were the maids forbidden to say that Sarita had died that morning? That day he had no difficulty in remembering the church and the white cloth that covered Sarita's head. He remembered her kneeling at the altar and he remembered her white satin shoes with yellow soles. The maids had kept quiet as they did now at Ana's insistence, and his mother peeped into the pot of chocolate and sniffed its fragrance with delight. Without a word he had gone out of the kitchen, passed through the outer door, which was open at that hour, and walked down the street. It was the first time he had gone out alone. The dead girl's windows beckoned to him urgently. He saw himself walking on the stone pavement with his five-year-old body. He was stopped by the petrified air that enshrouds the homes of the dead. He climbed up the wall until he could reach the iron bars on the window, and looked inside the house. He recognized the skirt and the white shoes pointing motionless at the window through which he was spying. Sarita was alone and dead. Surprised, not at death, but because it was Sarita who had died, he lowered himself to the sidewalk and went home feeling dejected.

"Where were you?" his parents, his sister Matilde, and the servants yelled.

He did not answer. Alone, he began that day overwhelmed by unlived memories. At night, in his bed, he remembered his own death. He saw it many times having already occurred in the past, and many times in the future having not yet occurred. But it was curious that in the past it was he, Martín, who had died; and in the future it was a strange person who was dying. And while he, lying in bed in his room, envisaged his two deaths, the reality of his small bed, his five-year-old body, and his room assumed an unimportant dimension. With the morning sun, the dark beams on the ceiling returned him to a banal present that was in the hands of his nursemaids. Since that night his future had been mixed with a past that had not occurred and the unreality of each day.

He looked at the clock, whose pendulum wearily marked the

seconds, and its swaying motion reminded him of Ignacio swinging in the permanent time of the morning.

"Did they take him down yet?"

"No, Señor," Félix replied diffidently. He did not want anyone to guess the grief he felt for his people: "We the poor are a burden."

"We'll go and make arrangements for them to be returned," Martín said, convinced that he was living an unknown morning, and without knowing which bodies he was claiming nor where they were to be brought down.

"They may give them to you, Señor. They always have more respect for those who are well dressed," Félix said, knowing how it was with the barefoot ones.

"Girls! Girls! Get up, for God's sake!" Juan Cariño shouted when he heard about the death of Ignacio and his four friends. The girls heard him and went on sleeping. Mr. President rapped with his knuckles on the women's doors; never had he felt so out of sorts. The previous day he had seen Rodolfo Goríbar and his gunmen following the General on his disorderly ramble through town. "This fellow is out for blood," he said to himself, and he in turn had followed Rodolfo all day long. He did not see him talk to the General, and at night, when Francisco Rosas entered the bar, he lost track of Goríbar and his henchmen and calmly returned home. In a dream, something told him that Rodolfito was waiting in the shadows for the drunken General to come out of the bar. Now he felt he could never forgive himself for having been so careless.

He knocked at the women's doors again but they were still sleeping.

"Girls, five agrarian reformers have been assassinated! Let's go to the Military Command!"

"Mr. President, they'll laugh at us. It's no use to protest," Luchi said.

"No use? You fool! If everyone had thought as you do, we'd still be in the Stone Age," Juan Cariño replied gravely. The words

"Stone Age" made him shudder, and he hoped they had the same effect on the others. He looked closely at the girls and repeated dismally, "That's a fact: in the Stone Age!"

The frightened women kept still and prepared to obey his orders. He rummaged through his clothing until he found a black band, which he carefully sewed to the lapel of his frock coat. He felt sad. He was growing old and his powers were diminishing. He closed himself up in the little room with his dictionaries. He would go to the Command armed with words that could destroy Francisco Rosas' power and Rodolfo's. The girls would help him.

"This is all you have to do: just repeat after me whatever I say to the General."

"Very well, but remember, Mr. President, that we don't have permission to walk through the main part of town."

"Bah! Nonsense!"

Around five o'clock that afternoon Juan Cariño paraded through my streets followed by the tarts, who hung their heads in shame and tried to cover their faces with their black scarves. People were amazed, and asked questions.

"Where are you going?"

"To the Military Command. Would you like to join this demonstration?"

We laughed and answered Juan Cariño's invitation with coarse words. He tried to snatch them out of the air. After meditating all day, he was sure that his curse would annihilate Francisco Rosas. From then on he would fight violence with violence. He did not want to go on contemplating the martyrdom of the innocent. He arrived at the Military Command and the soldiers looked at him jubilantly.

"Hey! What's going on? Are you moving in here? That'll be very handy!"

The women did not answer. Mortified, they followed Mr. President, who strode confidently into the General's anteroom. Captain Flores, who was in charge of the office, stared at him with amazement.

"What do you want, Mr. President?" he asked, wide-eyed.

80

"Kindly announce my visit. I have come on behalf of the five victims."

Captain Flores did not know what to say. Juan Cariño had taken him by surprise. Fascinated by the madman's eyes, he rose and disappeared through the door that led to General Rosas' office.

"Sit down, and don't forget to repeat after me whatever I say to that man."

The girls sat in the empty chairs and waited quietly. Juan Cariño repeated the curses under his breath. He wanted to charge them with power so that when he actually uttered them they would burst out with the violence of a shot. The girls' voices would help. An hour went by, then another, and the church clock struck 8 P.M. Juan Cariño, bewildered, went to the door through which Captain Flores had disappeared, listened for a few seconds, and knocked. No sign of life came from the other side. The madman waited for a few moments, then knocked again. The same silence answered him. He was frightened. Perhaps the very violence of his curses, even before they were pronounced, had had the desired effect and Francisco Rosas, Captain Flores, and Rodolfo Goríbar were lying there, dead. He pushed open the door, wanting to find out for sure: no one was there.

"It's a trick!" he shouted, suddenly infuriated, and he began to scream and babble incoherently as if he had lost all control. The frightened girls tried to calm him. Some soldiers appeared.

"What's all this commotion? Get out!"

"Where is Francisco Rosas hiding?"

"Oh, dear, I'm so scared!" said one of the soldiers, imitating a woman's voice.

"Get out! The General left a long time ago! Get out or you'll all be arrested!"

And the soldiers removed Juan Cariño and the girls from the office by force. When they were outside, the women with their scarves torn and he without his top hat, he threatened, "Tell that assassin never to set foot in the presidential offices again!"

"Well, what do you know! The whores are on strike!"

The soldiers burst out laughing as Juan Cariño searched for his battered hat on the cobblestones. He returned home and locked the door.

"The assassins will not enter this place again until they wash away their crimes."

The girls agreed to his wishes. Late that night some soldiers and officers pounded on the door. Luchi did not condescend to open it.

The voice that tells secrets went from mouth to mouth and accused Rodolfo Goríbar of the murder of Ignacio and his friends. Perhaps acts are written in the air and we read them there with eyes we do not know we have. We passed doña Lola's house many times. "Here sleeps the assassin," said the light that surrounded it, and through the walls we could see him waking up very late and his mother bringing him a tray of food.

"Do you feel well, my son?" Doña Lola bent down and observed him anxiously.

"Now he is eating," we said, seeing what was happening in the house. We did not take our eyes away from his room, and his friends in their houses watched doña Lola come and go as she brought him croquettes, salads, and soups.

In the morning, Martín Moncada waited for several hours before Rosas gave the order to lower the bodies of the hanged men. That afternoon, while Juan Cariño waited in the Military Command, don Martín, accompanied by Dr. Arrieta, Félix, and some soldiers, went to the road to Cocula, and at 7 P.M. he came to Agustina's house with the five mutilated bodies.

"Oh, Señor, I don't know why they did this," Agustina sobbed, dry-eyed.

From that moment on, Rodolfo Goríbar, Ixtepec's most faithful son, inspired fear. The town tried not to think of him, tried to forget his mother's obesity and her grotesque words, and sought refuge in reading.

At nightfall a sudden fear took possession of my people. Seized with panic, doña Elvira shrieked, "Let's go see Matilde!"

She did not want to be alone. Arriving at don Joaquín's house, she found herself with the friends whose custom it was to assemble on the porch, looking at each other in amazement, not knowing what to do or say. No one dared to utter Rodolfito's name. Now and then, a "Poor Ignacio" would escape from their lips. Nor did they speak of the sight of Juan Cariño followed by the tarts. In silence they sipped their cool drinks and pushed their chairs together to close the circle so they would feel less lonely in the inhospitable night. Ignacio had to be covered with earth so that his mutilated body would never frighten them again. And what if someone else were really to blame? It was hard for them to believe that Rodolfito was the guilty one. Doña Elvira stirred uneasily in her chair. She wanted to talk, to break the silence that accused them before Felipe Hurtado.

"They say she's driving him crazy," the widow said, and she blushed slightly as she changed the subject to Julia, who was the real culprit.

The maids at the Hotel Jardín left their gossip in the kitchen and from there it moved on to tables and gatherings. Her friends looked at her with approval, encouraging her to tell what she knew about Julia's responsibility in the death of Ignacio.

"Did you see the General's face this morning?"

"Yes, he looked very haggard."

"Just imagine, last night he came back to the hotel around midnight, no doubt after hanging that poor Ignacio—may God pardon his sins—and around 3 A.M. he woke don Pepe out of a sound sleep and made him serve a special meal because Julia was hungry."

"I wonder what those two do at that time of night. Keeping watch like souls in purgatory!" doña Carmen Arrieta exclaimed.

"It's their remorse that keeps them awake," doña Matilde hazarded innocently.

"For God's sake, Matilde, those women always have bad habits!"

The men listened thoughtfully. Isabel felt strange among these people she had known since childhood. She moved closer to Hurtado. She trusted him, and with her brothers away she felt more attached to him than to her Ixtepec friends.

"He only takes her out to escort her to mass. Didn't you notice that she didn't come out on the balcony today?"

"That's true. And what are the other women doing?"

"Well, what do you think? You know—when the boss is sad, the servants pretend to be, too."

Doña Carmen interrupted to say that each day the train from Mexico City was filled with presents for Julia. And she described in detail the clothes, jewels, and exquisite foods the General gave his mistress. The others listened openmouthed.

"That's where the town's money goes!" the doctor remarked.

"He keeps her covered with gold!"

"We fought the Revolution for women like that!" the doctor exclaimed.

"You people didn't fight the Revolution. It's natural that you have none of the spoils now," Isabel ventured, blushing.

"The spoils!" Dr. Arrieta repeated, piqued.

"Doctor, Isabel was thinking of a lesson in Roman history," Tomás Segovia interposed.

Isabel looked at him angrily. Felipe Hurtado stood up, took her arm, and steered her away from the group. Together they went out to the garden and disappeared among the ferns. Conchita looked after them with longing. She too was bored by the same words repeated month after month. Her mother leaned close to doña Carmen's ear and whispered, "She sleeps in the nude!"

"What did you say?"

"That Julia sleeps in the nude."

The doctor's wife took it on herself to transmit this valuable piece of information to her neighbor. When Isabel and Hurtado returned, Tomás passed the secret along to the stranger, who turned to the young girl.

84

"There are times when one is superfluous in this world," he said under his breath.

"I have always been superfluous," Isabel replied.

The night wore on with difficulty, carrying the crimes of the day on its back. The garden was beginning to be scorched by the excess of sun and lack of rain, and the guests—after the flurry caused by Julia's name had died down—returned to their gloomy thoughts. They strained to see the ferns, still humid despite the drought. The intense heat of that year and Rodolfito's crime made them uneasy. They thought once again, "If Julia has another fight with the General, we'll be in for it," and they did it to exculpate Goríbar. Julia had to be the precious creature who would absorb our guilt. And now I wonder if she knew what she meant to us. Did she know that she was also our destiny? Perhaps, because from time to time she looked at us kindly.

NINE

Several days passed and the figure of Ignacio as I see it now, suspended from the uppermost branch of a tree, breaking the morning light as a ray of sunshine shatters the light in a mirror, gradually departed from us. We never spoke of him again. After all, his death only meant that there was one less Indian. We did not even remember the names of his four friends. We knew that before long other anonymous Indians would occupy their places in the trees. Only Juan Cariño persisted in not crossing my streets: locked in his room, he refused to look at me. Without his walks, the evenings were not the same, and my sidewalks were full of fruit husks, peanut shells, and ugly words.

Luchi's house was still closed when the Moncada boys returned to town. Their arrival filled us with excitement. They walked about gaily, and as they crossed my streets they left laughter and shouting everywhere. Felipe Hurtado accompanied them.

"They seem like brothers," Matilde said as she watched them laughing and talking, all chattering at once.

"Isabel, don't interrupt!" Nicolás yelled, as he in turn interrupted his sister.

The young girl answered the rebuke with a hearty laugh which the others found contagious. It was Sunday and there was a gathering at doña Matilde's. Trays of cold drinks and sweets circulated freely, and the guests, in their best clothing, talked about the latest news and the political situation.

"Calles is going to try to get reelected," someone said almost frivolously.

"That's unconstitutional," the doctor interposed.

"Effective suffrage, no reelection!" Tomás Segovia remarked pedantically, glancing at Isabel. She paid no attention to him and went on laughing with Hurtado and her brothers. Conchita and the pharmacist tried to catch some random words from that gay conversation which seemed likely to last all night.

"Oh, I think they're talking about the lovers," Segovia said, making what he thought was a sophisticated gesture.

The young people and Hurtado looked at him uncomprehendingly.

"Who?"

"Do you know what that woman did last night?" doña Elvira asked, overjoyed that she had a chance to talk about Julia again.

"What did she do?" doña Carmen asked.

"She got drunk," Conchita's mother said smugly.

"Oh, let her alone," Nicolás said impatiently.

The ladies protested. How could Nicolás dare to say such a thing when she did not let us alone? We lived in a state of perpetual unrest as a result of her whims.

"She is so pretty that any of our men would gladly change places with the General."

A storm of feminine protests greeted Nicolás' words.

"You've seen her at close range, Señor Hurtado. Is she really as pretty as they say?" doña Elvira asked, annoyed.

Hurtado thought for a minute. Then, looking into the widow's eyes and weighing his words carefully, he declared, "Señora, I have never seen a more beautiful woman than Julia Andrade."

He paused. Silence greeted his words. No one dared to ask him how and when he had learned her full name, because in Ixtepec we knew her only as Julia. The conversation became strained after the stranger's involuntary admission. His friends felt that they had inadvertently induced him to say something he should not have said.

"Why is everyone so sad?" Nicolás said, trying to enliven the group.

"Sad?" the others asked, surprised.

They could hear the military band playing marches in the plaza.

"Let's go to the serenade," Juan Moncada proposed.

"Then we can see Julia." And Nicolás rose, encouraging the others to follow.

When they reached the plaza, the serenade was well under way. Installed in the bandstand, the military band filled the air with lilting marches. The men walked to the left, the women to the right. They would circle like that for three hours, glancing at each other as they passed. Isabel and Conchita separated from the young men. The ladies, accompanied by the doctor, sat down on a bench.

The officers, each escorting his mistress, were the only ones who broke the pattern. The women were attired as usual, with their light dresses, lustrous hair, and gold jewelry. They seemed to belong to another world. Julia's presence filled the hot night air with foreboding. Her pale pink dress announced her nocturnal beauty from afar. Indifferent, with just the hint of a smile on her lips, she walked at the side of Francisco Rosas, the watchful.

"He's jealous!" we said maliciously.

The General seemed uneasy: with his yellow eyes full of dark images, he stood very erect and tried to conceal his anxiety and to find the source of the danger that threatened him. Hurtado's arrival at the plaza with the Moncada family startled him. Julia did not alter her expression. She moved among the people like a somnambulist, dazzling us with her translucent skin, her dark hair, holding her fan of finest straw in the shape of a transparent, bloodless heart. She took several turns around the plaza and then went to sit on her accustomed bench, forming an island of light.

In the center of this magic circle, surrounded by the mistresses and escorted by uniformed men, Julia seemed to be caught in a last, melancholy splendor. The branches cast flickering blue shadows on her face. Someone brought drinks from Pando's cantina. The General leaned forward to serve her.

The uneasy men walking round and round the plaza hurried to come to the place where Julia was. They could not lose her: they had only to follow the aura of vanilla that clung to her. Vainly they censured her from a distance, because once in her presence they could not escape her mysterious attraction. When Felipe Hurtado passed he lowered his eyes as if it pained him to look at her. He scarcely replied to the words of his friends.

On nights when Julia did not leave the hotel, the plaza languished. The men waited until very late, and when they were convinced that she was not going to come, they returned home feeling cheated.

That was one of the last nights we ever saw her. She was sad. She had lost weight; her nose looked sharper, paler. She gave an impression of sorrow and detachment. Submissively she let her lover take charge and arrange the straws so she could drink her beverage. Melancholically she waved her straw fan and looked at Francisco Rosas.

"I wonder why she doesn't love him," Isabel mused, watching the couple from a distance.

"Who knows?" Conchita replied, seeking out Nicolás with her eyes; he in turn was spying on Julia from a corner of the park, apparently trying to capture her transparent image for all time. Conchita blushed. Like all of the young girls in Ixtepec, she secretly envied Julia. She approached her with something akin to fear, feeling herself ugly and stupid, knowing that Julia's radiance diminished her own beauty. Despite her humiliation, fascinated by love, she came close to her superstitiously, hoping that some of the beauty would rub off on her.

"I wish I were Julia!" Isabel exclaimed vehemently.

"Don't be crude!" Conchita replied, shocked by her friend's

words, although she too had wished the same thing many times.

Doña Ana Moncada observed the love object with delight, sharing her children's unreserved admiration.

"You can't deny that she has something," she said to her friend.

Señora Montúfar looked at her reproachfully. "Ana, don't say such a thing! All she has is vice."

"No, no. She's not only pretty, she has something else."

Doña Elvira grew angry. Her eyes sought out her daughter and her hands signaled her to come. The young girls came to their mothers.

"Sit down and don't look at that woman any more!" Conchita's mother ordered.

"But Elvira, we all see her. She's so pretty!"

"At night, all painted up, she isn't bad, but you should see her when she wakes up with all her vices showing."

"Julia's beauty has nothing to do with the clock," Hurtado said, having joined the group. For several days he had seemed to be exasperated. He observed the love object from a distance, watching her consume her drink, outlined against a tree, under the close vigil of Francisco Rosas, and his face darkened.

"You're in love with Julia," Nicolás said in a low voice.

As if someone had suddenly said something intolerable, Felipe Hurtado left the group and strode out of the square without a word. Nicolás watched him go. He looked at doña Elvira bitterly and remembered Julia sitting on the hotel balcony with her face washed and her skin as fresh as a piece of fruit. Doña Elvira's anger was natural. For him, as for Hurtado and all Ixtepec, Julia was the personification of love. Before he went to sleep he often thought indignantly of the general who possessed that woman so unlike other women, so unreal. Hurtado's departure, provoked by his words and doña Elvira's, seemed to prove he was right. He looked obliquely at his mother's friend. "She is old and ugly," Nicolás thought virulently, taking his irritation at the stranger's sudden departure out on her.

Julia's sadness seemed to infect the whole group and spread

90

through the square. The branches cast black lace shadows that wrote maleficent signs on the officers' faces, suddenly grown sad.

Groups of men in white, leaning against the trunks of the tamarinds, uttered prolonged "ays" that lacerated the night. There is nothing easier for my people than that quick show of grief. Despite the trumpets and cymbals that made a golden explosion of sound in the bandstand, the music swirled about in pathetic spirals.

The General stood up and turned to Julia and the two left the circle of friends. We saw them go away, cross the street, enter the hotel. A different light enveloped them. It was as if we could see that Julia had alienated herself from him forever.

Before the concert ended the General came out again. He was very pale and went directly to Pando's cantina without stopping at the plaza.

"He came in drunk and they were awake all night long," don Pepe whispered to the curious the next day. "The more he loves her, the more aloof she becomes. Nothing pleases her, neither the jewels nor the delicacies. She's inaccessible. I've seen the boredom in her eyes when he comes close to her. And I've seen him sitting on the edge of the bed, watching her sleep."

"Do you love me, Julia?"

Standing by his mistress, with his coat open and his eyes downcast, the General asked the question a thousand times. She turned her melancholy eyes to him and smiled.

"Yes, I love you very much."

"But don't say it like that."

"How do you want me to say it?" she asked with the same indifference.

"I don't know, but not like that."

A silence fell between them. Still motionless, Julia went on smiling. The General, on the other hand, trying to find something that would amuse her, paced back and forth.

"Would you like to go riding?" he asked, thinking that it had been a long time since they had taken the horses out at night, and longing for a gallop through the open country.

"If you wish."

"What do *you* want, Julia? What would please you? Ask me for something!"

"Nothing, nothing at all. I'm just fine."

And she huddled silently on a corner of the bed. He wanted to ask her to tell him what was in her memory, but he did not dare. He was afraid of what she would say.

"Do you know that I live just for you?" he confessed humbly.

"I know." And Julia made a face to cheer him.

"Would you die with me, Julia?"

"Why not?"

The General left the room without saying a word. He was going to have a drink. Then he would have more courage to talk to her. As he went out he said to don Pepe, "See that the señorita does not leave her room or talk to anyone."

The instructions to don Pepe became more and more strict.

"The señorita's balcony is not to be opened!"

Julia's balcony was closed for a time, and she did not come out to the serenades on Thursdays and Sundays. We waited for her in the plaza in vain.

T E N

"Something is going to happen," the people said.

"Yes, it's too hot!" others answered.

Was it the drought of that year that cast my people into such anxiety, or was it the overlong wait? In the past few days the mango trees on the way to Cocula had had several corpses dangling from their branches. There was no use asking the reason for those deaths. Julia knew the answer, and she refused to tell.

No one looked at the General when he walked through the streets. His aides seemed worried and scarcely dared to speak to him. Don Pepe accompanied him to the door of the hotel and nervously watched him go away. Then, sitting on his wicker chair, he guarded the entrance and refused to give out any information.

"Yes, something is going to happen! Keep moving, keep moving—no questions," he replied to the curious who came to ask for news.

"Something is going to happen," Luchi said to herself out loud when Damián Álvarez left her room. She would have been happy if her words had caused a catastrophe, but instead they left the dirty walls of her room intact. She wrung her hands and tossed and turned uneasily on her messy bed. The sunshine streamed radiantly through the window and the wretched house seemed unbearable. "I'm tired, something has to happen," she repeated, and then stopped thinking, afraid of encountering the waiting day.

"And what if today is the day?" She covered her face. She did not want to remember how La Pípila's life had ended. "The knife stabbed the wrong body," they had said in front of the murdered woman, and from that moment on an unexpressed fear took possession of her and forced her to submit to others' wills for fear of provoking the crime that is only a stone's throw from all of us. She sat down on the bed and examined her fragile skin and her unsteady bones. She compared the softness of her knees with the solidity of the bars of her iron bedstead and felt a tender pity for herself.

"And Damián keeps inciting them to kill him!" She remembered the young man in his nakedness and the tears he shed over Antonia, Justo Corona's mistress, and felt sure she would never see him again. She scarcely knew the young girl. Once or twice she had seen the blond hair and the indistinct blur of her face from a distance. Antonia did not know that Damián Álvarez was weeping because he had not taken her away with him the night they brought her to Colonel Corona. The only one in Ixtepec who knew it was she, Luchi. Álvarez had told her this when they were in bed together, and had explained how he wanted to take the girl away from the Hotel Jardín.

"Don't try such a thing, you'd be killed," Luchi told him, afraid for Damián's fragile body.

"She's dead!" the soldier had said years before when she entered La Pípila's room. And he raised one of the dead girl's hands and incredulously let it fall back limply on the bloody breast. "I didn't know she would be so still," he added, staring at Luchi with childlike eyes. She looked at him, naked and terrified by his crime, she looked at the dead girl's skin and saw that it was identical to the man's, and left the room deep in thought. It did not

94

occur to her to call the authorities; the knowledge that a knife could leave her in that frightening quietude was conducive to melancholy. Damián Álvarez, like all of the men who slept with her, searched for another woman's body, and they eyed her with rancor for having deceived them.

"We whores were born without a mate," Luchi said to herself when they talked to her of "the other woman," and the naked men turned into the same man, while her own body, the room, and the words disappeared and all that was left for her was the fear of the unknown. Her acts took place in a vacuum and the men who slept with her were no one. "What am I doing here with you?" the officer had said and had turned his back on her. "You're here because you're looking for your misfortune." In the night, Álvarez tried to start fights with the drunks in the brothel and the frightened Flores brought him to Luchi's bed to avoid trouble. The woman's words released Damián's pent-up tears. "She asked me to take her away with me three times." She let him weep, sat up in bed and smoked one cigarette after another, while Damián Álvarez went on crying for Justo Corona's mistress. "If you take her out of the hotel you'll pay for it with your life. You'd be better off to leave Ixtepec."

Damián looked at her angrily. "What do you know about love, you slut!" And he went out, slamming the door. The room was perfectly still, illuminated by sunshine that detached the pieces of furniture from the walls and made them dance in the air.

"What if today is the day?" Luchi repeated to herself, and covered her face with the sheet to drive away the vertigo she always felt in the glare of noonday.

Juan Cariño knocked at the door and Luchi quickly slipped on her dress. It was most unusual for him to come to the women's rooms.

"Come in, Mr. President."

"Young Álvarez is looking for trouble. Something is going to happen."

"Do you think so, Mr. President?" she asked dejectedly.

And meanwhile, through my high blue cloudless skies, large

flocks of buzzards that had an eye on the hanged men by the road to Cocula swooped down in ever-narrowing circles.

"Something is going to happen!" repeated the group of friends assembled at doña Matilde's. They were tired and did not feel like talking. The night lay before them, long and tedious like every other night. The heat mounted to the stars and descended to the branches of the trees, the air did not move, and the conversation, which remained in an invariable time, repeated only the images of Julia and Francisco Rosas.

"And those two, in their room at the hotel!"

Elvira Montúfar was full of bitterness because the lovers still refused to share their secret with us. They ignored us, they were out of our reach, and words returned their distant shadows to us pulverized. They were alone and did not look for company. They were driven by a suicidal arrogance and we, merciless, minutely examined the fragments of their gestures that filtered through the walls of the Hotel Jardín.

"We're going to see them dead!" doña Carmen said sententiously.

Hearing her, Isabel remembered the nocturnal steps and the guarded whistle that accompanied them. She was an innocent, and awoke with a start at the noise that came from the street and echoed loudly as if someone were walking in church with a heavy step.

"Nico! I'm afraid!" and she and her brothers heard those evil steps grow fainter as the street became quiet again.

"Who is out walking at this time of night?" asked Juanito anxiously.

"It's death, Nico, out searching for someone."

"Shhhh! Don't mention it by name. Don't let it hear us talking," Nicolás replied, terror-stricken beneath the sheets.

"There goes Federico," they heard their mother say from the next room.

"Someone's probably having a baby and Arístides is out," their father's voice answered.

96

"But how can that boy take such a risk?" their mother asked in a very low voice.

"He's whistling because he's afraid," don Martín answered.

The children listened to the strange conversation. Later they looked at Federico, not knowing what he was searching for at midnight as he whistled to drive away his fear.

"Isabel, what does Federico look for when the doctor goes out?"

"I don't know."

"You know everything."

"Yes, but I don't know what Federico looks for."

And now doña Carmen, cooling herself with her Japanese fan, was waiting for the death of Julia and Francisco Rosas.

"The maids told me that there were three poor Indians hanging from the mango trees this morning," Señora Montúfar said, sipping her drink of Jamaica water.

"How awful!"

Isabel remembered the story of an Indian named Sebastián.

"Don't ever tell lies if you don't want to end up like the Indian Sebastián," Dorotea had told them one afternoon when they were children.

"What happened to Sebastián?" they asked apprehensively.

"Sebastián was the Montúfar family's overseer. He was a good man, but one day the money was stolen from the safe and don Justino called him in.

" 'All right, Sebastián, give me the money,' he said.

" 'I didn't take anything, boss.'

"Sebastián was like any other Indian: stubborn and deceitful. Don Justino, who was honest and inflexible, got angry.

" 'All right, Sebastián, you've worked with me for many years and I've always felt I could trust you. Tell me where you hid the money.'

" 'I didn't take anything, boss,' the Indian repeated.

" 'I'll give you five minutes to think about it. Don't you know that it's a sin to steal, but it's a bigger sin to lie?'

" 'But I didn't take anything, boss.'

"And don Justino, angered by Sebastián's stubbornness, had him whipped until he confessed. The next day was Elvira's name day and we went to congratulate her. And what did we see when we reached her house? Elvira was beside herself, because the servants had left on account of Sebastián's death.

" 'Just look at what happened to that stubborn Indian!'

"And she took us to the yard to show us Sebastián's body lying on the stones, waiting for his relatives to come and bury him."

"Poor Sebastián!" the children had shouted, frightened by Dorotea's story.

"See where lying gets you? It tries the patience of the just." Doña Elvira had forgotten Sebastián and now she took pity on the Indians who had been hanged by Francisco Rosas.

"It's natural for them to hang people now if you used to do it," Nicolás said.

"For God's sake, Nico, let's not start that again!" the doctor exclaimed impatiently. Then, to soften his remark, he added, "We're a young country in turmoil, and all this is temporary. This heat makes people excited. It's like this every year. The sun drives us mad."

The visitors fanned themselves: the doctor's words seemed to intensify the heat that settled on the garden. Silently they breathed the heavy perfumes of the night and sat quietly in their Austrian chairs, staring pensively at their cool, brightly-colored drinks.

"Where's Hurtado?" Isabel asked, breaking the silence. The guest had not put in an appearance, and although the question was on the tip of everyone's tongue, no one had dared to ask it.

"Where's Hurtado?" the girl repeated.

As if her words had unleashed a mysterious force, a flash of lightning crossed the sky and alarmed the whole town: it was the first one of the year. The friends stood up to examine the dark sky. There was a second flash.

"It's going to rain!" they shouted jubilantly. Two more flashes followed. The first outsized, heavy drops fell. Isabel held out her hand.

98

"It's raining!" she exclaimed joyfully and looked eagerly at the garden lashed by the sudden wind that brings storms in my country. In a few minutes the swirling water stripped the leaves from the jacarandas and the acacias. The tall papaya trees bowed under the rain. Birds' nests fell to the ground from the uppermost branches of the palm trees. The wind went whistling across the roofs, opening a passage between the raindrops and carrying with it green branches and maddened birds.

Doña Matilde's guests remained silent. Above the roofs, through the open sky of the garden, they could see the distant church tower as it swallowed the lightning bolts one after another.

"Who invented the lightning rod?" Isabel asked nervously. From an early age she had asked the same question whenever it rained.

They had answered her question many times and she always forgot the answer, and now, terrified by the storm, she repeated the query again, looking in bewilderment at the savage spectacle. The wind blew her black curls over her eyes and mouth. Laughingly, she pushed them away.

"Tonight," she said, shouting to make herself heard, "we'll sleep under blankets! It's going to be cold!" The suddenness of the storm made her forget Hurtado.

"Poor thing, here he comes!" shouted doña Matilde, pointing toward the garden.

Hurtado was walking along the stone pathway that connected the pavilion with the house. Advancing against the wind, bending down to avoid being struck by branches, with his hair and his dark suit whipped by the wind, and carrying a lighted oil lamp, he was a curious sight. Fascinated, they watched him as he approached, pushing his way through the rain and the gusts of wind.

"He must have felt very lonely," doña Matilde said solicitously.

Smiling, Hurtado joined the group. He put the lamp on a table and blew it out.

99

"What a wind! I thought it was going to carry me to the treetops of the next country!"

Much later, when Hurtado was no longer with us, doña Matilde's guests asked how he had passed through the storm with
the lamp still lighted and his clothes and hair dry. But that night
they found it natural that his light was still burning when he
took cover.

Isabel clapped her hands joyfully; Juan and Nicolás chortled
and stamped their feet. Without knowing why, Hurtado burst
into hearty laughter.

"We must do something to celebrate! Our luck has changed!"
Isabel shouted.

"Yes! We must do something!" her brothers chorused.

Nicolás took his harmonica out of his trouser pocket and
played a gay march while he spun round and round in a solo
dance. Isabel hurled herself on Juan, and the three danced to
the rhythm of the music and the rain, with their usual ease in
improvising merriment.

Suddenly Isabel stopped.

"Let's give a play!" she said, remembering Hurtado's words
about the theater and illusion.

He looked at her enthusiastically and said, "Yes, let's give
a play!"

And without listening to the objections of the elders, the
young man ran into the garden, followed by Nicolás. The two
came back with hair dripping wet and their faces washed by the
rain. Under one arm, wrapped in a blanket, the stranger carried
a book which he showed to his friends. He leafed through it slowly while the others looked on with curiosity. Isabel read over his
shoulder.

"This is our play."

"Read it out loud!" Nicolás begged.

"Yes! Yes!" the others urged.

Felipe Hurtado laughed and began to read. The streams of
water dripping from the roof provided an accompaniment for
his voice. The words flowed like magic, miraculous as the rain.

100

The brothers and sister listened to him spellbound. It was very late, and the rain had not yet begun to diminish, when they left for home. Hurtado accompanied them. They had much to say to each other that night, when they shared poetry for the first time.

But the rain did not produce such rapture in all parts of the town. It took the customers in Pando's cantina by surprise and left them quiet and isolated. This was the soldiers' place and they had not waited eagerly for rain. For them it did not mean crops or well-being, and so they could not share with us this blessing that filled us with joy.

Accompanied by his retinue, the General occupied his usual seat. His eyes were sad and from time to time he looked absently toward the street, bending down to look through the open door at the black sky embossed with lightning flashes, forgetting the dice in the shaker.

At the next table, Damián Álvarez and Lieutenant Flores drank alone and listened sadly to the sound of the falling rain.

"God knows what people think about when it rains," Flores remarked.

"I know what *I* think," Damián Álvarez replied.

"Well, keep it quiet!" his friend advised.

"I seem to attract death," Damián said morosely.

"I know, I know."

"No, you don't know. I'm a coward."

Flores poured his friend a drink to quiet him, but Álvarez went on talking.

"See them? They're there and I'm here!" And Álvarez pointed to the place where the General, the Colonel and the Lieutenant Colonel were sitting.

"We'd better be going," Flores urged nervously.

"I'll go when I'm good and ready. Have a drink with the unlucky guy!"

No one was paying any attention to the conversation or to Damián Álvarez's misery. Everyone went on watching the rain, each absorbed in his own thoughts. The cantina was filled with

101

that melancholy nostalgia that is only produced by rain, and the atmosphere was calm and almost silent. Don Ramón Martínez, stranded by the storm, was playing a game of dominoes and did not want to go out in the rain. He did not usually remain in the cantina when the General arrived with his men, but this time the fear of getting soaked detained him. From time to time Señor Martínez glanced furtively at the officers.

"The sky changes from night to day. And so does a man's luck." Thus spoke the taciturn and undulating voice of the General.

But his luck did not change; it was still linked to Julia's. At that moment she was losing herself in other rains. "I like to be kissed when it rains," she had said to him one stormy night.

She didn't say, "I like you to kiss me." Julia never gives herself...

"Very true, General." Lieutenant Colonel Cruz's reply bore out his thoughts: "Very true that Julia never gave herself." She escaped from him shining and liquid, like a drop of mercury, and slipped away into nameless places, accompanied by hostile shadows.

"I had no idea I'd end up in this town!"

Colonel Justo Corona looked at his chief, squinting to show pock-marked eyelids.

Julia didn't walk in this town. She didn't touch the ground. She wandered around, lost in the streets of other towns that had no hours, no smells, no nights: only a bright powdery substance into which she disappeared each time it touched the transparent streak of her pink dress.

"I lost!" Corona said in a low voice.

"It's no use to win. I always knew it, since the time I crossed the sierra and was overtaken by night, up there in the north." Francisco Rosas said these last words with misgiving, as if it pained him to speak of his country while in the south, which he had never loved.

"How far away the north is now!" The Lieutenant Colonel was also homesick for the apple trees and the cold wind.

102

Julia, like an icy rose, gyrated before Francisco Rosas' eyes, then vanished in the frigid wind of the sierra and reappeared floating above the tops of the pinyon trees. She smiled at him through the hail that hid her face and her frosty dress. Rosas was not able to reach her, nor could he touch the cold sound of her footsteps as she crossed the frozen sierra.

"Up north we're different. Since childhood we've known what life is and what we want out of it. That's why we're open and aboveboard. But the people around here are dishonest, sneaky. You never know how you stand with them."

Thus Colonel Justo Corona judged us with rancor.

"It seems that they're happy when others suffer," Rosas said.

"But they're paying for it," Corona added gloomily.

"Up north we don't like to see a man suffer, we're goodhearted. Aren't we, General?" Cruz's voice was conciliatory.

His chief did not hear him. Plunged into his melancholy silence, the sound of the words transported him to Julia and her remote world. He studied the rain and tried to see it through her eyes, and said to himself bitterly, "It will always rain for her tonight." Then he added out loud, "When is this rain going to stop!" He pounded his fist on the table.

His companions looked outside uneasily, as if the storm's violence were aimed at them.

"Let's do something—I can't stand this deadly stillness!" Rosas drawled his words, lengthening the vowels and brusquely clipping off the endings, in the manner of the speech of northern Mexico.

His friends looked at each other nervously, without knowing what to say or what to suggest.

"I wish this damn rain would end!" And the General turned around and discovered don Ramón, who was bending down to avoid being recognized.

"Look at him! Why is he bending down like that?" he asked angrily.

The others turned to look at don Ramón Martínez.

"Because of what we were saying. Because these people are

103

only good for talking behind your back and don't like to show their faces," Corona replied.

A gust of damp wind blew in, bringing with it the smell of leaves and fields, which blended with the coolness of the alcohol. The General poured himself some brandy and drank it in one gulp.

"Bring him over here. Let's invite him to have a drink!" he said, bleary-eyed.

The Lieutenant Colonel went to don Ramón's table. As soon as the latter saw him, he started to take leave of his friends.

"The General asks you to join him."

"Thanks very much, but I was just leaving. I have to get home."

"But you wouldn't want to offend us," Cruz said gravely.

The old man, not knowing what to do, stood up. Cruz took his arm and escorted him to the General's table. The other people in the bar watched the frightened old man as he let himself be led away without saying a word.

"Señor Martínez, please sit down," General Rosas said politely.

Don Ramón felt reassured. After all, there was nothing so bad about getting to know these unsociable people a little. Perhaps he might convince them that he was a person of some importance. His ideas about improvements for the town came to him in a rush. This was his opportunity, and he made up his mind he would talk seriously to the officers. He drank the first few drinks and then made a frontal attack on his favorite subject: progress.

The General listened, paying close attention, and responded with affirmative signs while filling the glasses as soon as they were emptied.

"We need a man of integrity! Someone who will understand our age of motors, factory whistles, great laboring masses, great ideas and great revolutions. Someone like you, General!" said don Ramón, who was now quite drunk. He was tired of waiting for the coming of the great leader who would bring progress to the backward town that was Ixtepec. And then Ixtepec would be an example to the rest of the feudal, stupid country, which was

104

not part of the modern history he read about in the papers. Industry, strikes, and European wars filled him with scorn for our familiar, petty problems.

"We have never suffered a crisis! Germany is passing through a very serious crisis at the present time. We only have uprisings of the hungry and the lazy. We don't like to work, and work is the source of all progress. That is why we need a leader like you, General."

"Oh! Someone like me—who will make you work?" the General replied slowly.

"Exactly!" the old man said.

"Well, I'm glad to know that."

"For our country to be a great power, we need men like you."

The General appeared to be getting bored with his guest's foolish chatter. "Stop making speeches and get to work!" Francisco Rosas broke in abruptly.

"But General, I was explaining my ideas . . ."

"Those aren't ideas. Pando, bring me a broom, my friend here wants to work," the General shouted.

"General, I was talking about something else."

"Pando, a broom!" Rosas ordered again.

Pando brought a broom and gave it to Francisco Rosas. The General put it in don Ramón's hands and he, not knowing what to do but intimidated by the General's look, stood up and smiled.

"Sweep the tavern," Rosas ordered.

Don Ramón took a few steps and the officers, sitting at the tables, looked at him jubilantly. Señor Martínez began to sweep, and his obedience increased the officers' amusement. The rain outside played a chorus for the men's laughter. Only the General remained serious, aloof, drinking his brandy and paying no attention to don Ramón. The officers threw corks and lighted cigarettes at the old man's head and he, frightened, tried to duck them by twirling around on his broom. Some of the men stood up and poured beer on the floor, broke bottles, threw plates and scraps of food, and dumped out the contents of ashtrays.

"Hey, ragman!" they yelled.

Pando did not budge. He did not approve of their actions. With his elbows on the bar he watched Señor Martínez sweeping his tavern, and he felt the old man's humiliation intensely. Frowning, he waited for the joke to end. But the others went on making a new mess wherever the old man had finished cleaning.

"I'm taking her out of the hotel right now!"

The voice of Álvarez could be heard above the clamor. Captain Flores, very pale, rose and tried to drag his friend out of the tavern.

"Leave me alone, damn you!"

Francisco Rosas looked up and, without batting an eyelash, watched the two officers struggling.

"You're drunk, you don't know what you're saying!"

"I'm saying that I'm taking her out of the hotel right now! Damn sons of bitches!" And Damián Álvarez staggered grimly toward his superiors' table.

The other officers forgot about don Ramón, and once again the rhythmical beating of the rain on the roof was heard. Captain Flores held Damián, and by pushing and shoving managed to get him outside. The insults and shouts of the drunken officer arguing with his friend at the door reached Francisco Rosas' table. Whom did Damián Álvarez want to take away from the hotel? The aides, very pale, stole glances at the General. With his eyes at a squint, he went on drinking his brandy. The scent of vanilla floated in, and the invisible presence of Julia, a stranger to Damián Álvarez, settled like discord in the center of the tavern.

Don Ramón took advantage of the silence, put down the broom, and with tear-filled eyes disappeared through the door to the men's room.

All that was heard from the street was the insistent sound of the rain. Where had Damián Álvarez gone? The officers imagined they could hear his unsteady footsteps walking toward Julia, and they looked at their chief without speaking. Francisco Rosas had a few more drinks. He seemed very relaxed when he said good night to his aides and left the cantina. He did not seem to want

106

company, so his friends made no move to join him when he went out into the night. Soon the place was empty and Pando went to call the old man, who was still sobbing in the men's room.

"He's not human!"

"Don't worry, don Ramón, it was just a joke," Pando said, embarrassed by the old man's tears. But it would not be easy for Señor Martínez to forget the indignity.

The Moncadas and Hurtado were crossing the square with rain-drenched faces when they tripped over the body of Captain Damián Álvarez in the middle of the street. His uniform was soaking wet and his hair, stirred by the water that had been falling on him for fully thirty minutes, moved strangely.

ELEVEN

A radiant new day dawned. The leaves, revived by the rain, shone in all hues of green. From the country came the smell of fresh earth and from the humid forests poured a mist charged with perfumes. The river, swollen after so many months of drought, moved along its yellow bed carrying broken branches and drowned animals. Through the cool morning air the rumor spread: "The General killed Captain Álvarez last night." Some had heard a shout ring out through the rain: "Turn around, Damián Álvarez, I don't want to kill you from behind!" But no one could swear that it was Rosas' voice.

"I don't know anything about it," said don Pepe Ocampo. "He came in drunk and kicked open the door to his room. Then he seemed to be crying . . . but I'm not sure of anything. It was very late and I don't know if I heard him . . . I could have been dreaming."

We did not know who picked up Damián's body, because when dawn came it was already lying in the Military Command. We passed the building and the balconies of the hotel, but we could not hear anything. The secret was kept in both places and the only thing we found out was what we already knew: that

Damián Álvarez had died that night near the entrance to the Hotel Jardín. On orders from Rosas, the officers, wearing black bands on their sleeves, stood guard by his body.

Around four that afternoon Rodolfito Goríbar crossed the town with his gunmen and entered the Command headquarters. He was wearing black and had come to pay his respects.

"It should have been you instead!" we said as he passed. "Bad weeds never die!" we answered ourselves, seeing how easily he entered the place to which we were denied access. After Ignacio's death, his delicate figure had rarely been seen on my streets. He had not moved the boundary marks again. Perhaps he was afraid, and preferred to hide near his mother. When it grew dark, the prayers for the repose of Captain Álvarez's soul began in doña Lola's chapel. The rosary was led by Señora Goríbar with her son, the gunmen, and the servants responding. We were not invited.

In the hotel the lovers' voices were not heard and the doors of their room were not opened. It seemed that they too had died. When night came, Francisco Rosas, very pale, came to stand guard by the officer's body. The twins took advantage of his absence to go to Antonia's room.

"Poor guy, to die at twenty-three!"

Antonia looked at them apprehensively. It seemed incredible that the warm memory of Damián's body was now just a memory and that no one, ever again, would feel the warmth she had felt all one night.

"And why did it happen?" the young girl asked timidly.

"Don't you know either?" the sisters said in bewilderment.

"No . . . I don't know," Antonia murmured. And in truth she did not know.

The three girls were deep in thought, trying to find the reason for the death of Damián Álvarez.

"It was because of Julia," Luisa said from the door, but neither she nor the others believed her words. The Captain's enigmatic death cast a shadow over those rooms where the women lived like recluses.

At dawn the officers returned to change clothes and shave. They looked saturnine. They drank hot coffee and then went back to the Military Command, where Damián Álvarez was waiting, his uniform pierced by bullets and still damp from the rain that accompanied him when he died. The burial took place very early, and that Monday remained in my memory as "the Monday they buried Damián Álvarez." People paid their respects to him and his name was on everyone's lips.

After a few days we began to forget the one who had died for Antonia, the daughter of the Spaniard Paredes. Justo Corona did not forget. He threw his pistol into the river and never told anyone what he did the night of Damián's death, when he returned to the hotel at daybreak.

We did not see the rain again. A whitish, burning heat devoured the woodland plants and made the sky invisible. The gardens and men's heads were consumed by the heat.

"You know that when the heat rises like this, misfortunes occur," don Ramón said to keep from going out of his house. He thought that time would erase his humiliation, and to save face, at least in his own home, he added, "Those shots were meant for me! I could see clearly that Rosas was going to kill me, but my courage and undeniable astuteness saved me from that unpleasant situation. The General is a primitive man who is unable to cope with intelligence."

"And now you see, that poor Damián Álvarez received the death that was intended for you," his wife replied sympathetically.

"We must go to Mexico City to give thanks to the Virgin of Guadalupe, who enlightened my dear Papá in those hours of danger," his daughters added, full of admiration for their father's bravery.

Don Ramón listened without hearing. He felt alone and terrified. He remembered the group of young men who laughed while he swept the cantina, and a strange heat burned his ears. "Everyone must have heard about it," he said to himself bitterly, and cursed the town and the people he knew who had witnessed his humiliation. "This town should be burned, razed, until not a single stone is left standing!" he said indignantly while rancor gnawed at his hours of sleep and his meals and his weeks and his house crumbled to pieces because of the tongues that made facetious remarks about his adventure.

"Well, Francisco Rosas finally did a good thing! He made Ramón Martínez work!"

Those were also bitter days for me. What a curious thing is memory, which reproduces, as it does now, sorrows now passed, pleasant days we shall not see again, faces that are gone and preserved in an expression they perhaps never knew they made, words of which not even an echo still remains. On his first night in Ixtepec, Felipe Hurtado had said to his hosts: "What Ixtepec needs is illusion." His friends did not understand, but his words were still written in my memory as if they had been engraved in an incandescent vapor that appeared and disappeared according to my state of mind. In those days, life was tarnished and no one lived except through the General and his beloved.

We had renounced illusion.

Where was my sky, of ever-changing colors and clouds? Where was the splendor of the valley, yellow as a topaz? No one took the trouble to look at the blazing orange sun that fell behind the blue mountains. People spoke of the heat as they would speak of a curse and forgot that the beauty of the burning air cast steaming faces and trees in a very pure, deep mirror. The young girls did not know that the light reflected in their eyes was the same as the motionless light of August. But I saw myself as a jewel. The stones acquired different shapes and sizes and I would have been impoverished if a single one had changed its place. The street corners turned to silver and gold. The columns of the houses grew larger in the evening air and then became thin to the point of unreality in the light of dawn. The trees changed shape. Men's steps wrested sounds from the stones, and the streets were filled with drumbeats.

And what is there to say of the church? The courtyard grew and its walls did not touch the ground. The mermaid on the

111

weathervane pointed to the sea with her silver tail, nostalgic for water. The singing of cicadas flooded the valley, rose from the reeds, sprang up by the still fountains; only the cicadas thanked the sun for moving so high overhead. No one looked at the iridescent lizards. All my splendor fell on ignorance, on a refusal to look at me, on a voluntary forgetfulness. And meanwhile my illusory and changing beauty was consumed and reborn like a salamander in the flames. Clouds of yellow butterflies crossed the gardens in vain; no one appreciated the sudden sight of them. Francisco Rosas' shadow covered my skies, dimmed the brilliance of my evenings, inhabited my street corners, and found its way into conversations. Perhaps the only one who appreciated me was Felipe Hurtado and the only one, too, who suffered because of the inertia into which my people had fallen. Perhaps that was why, with Isabel's help, he contrived the dramatic work. Don Joaquín was won over by his faith in illusion, and let him use the pavilion to present a play.

In it, Isabel ceased to be her usual self and was transformed into a young foreign girl. He was the unexpected traveler, and the words were luminous shapes that appeared and disappeared with the magnificence of fireworks.

Juan and Nicolás worked on the scenery. The pavilion, its windows opening on the garden of ferns, gave the impression of being much larger than it was. Ana Moncada brought her chairs for the audience to sit in, and she and her husband made the costumes. Conchita would wear white; Isabel red.

"It is the moon, the selfsame moon which rises on stage at this moment," Hurtado recited, half seriously, half joking.

They plunged into the task with enthusiasm and rehearsed the verses over and over again. In Ixtepec, word spread about the magic theater at doña Matilde's house. Isabel and Conchita, enraptured by their own beauty, walked through my streets like two more reflected images in the lavish August spectacle. "Something is happening," the young people said to each other without knowing what it was. Juan and Nicolás made scepters and swords and tried on the blue capes they would wear in the play.

112

The set was almost finished. The moment they mounted the steps to the stage, the young people entered a different world in which they danced and spoke differently, too. The words acquired mysterious vistas and, as in fairy tales, they felt that flowers, stars and fierce animals sprouted from their lips. The stage consisted of some roughly nailed boards and yet for them it was the whole world with its infinite variations. All Nicolás had to say was, "By this furious sea . . ." and from a hidden corner of the stage the sea rose with its huge waves and white foam and a strange breeze blew, flooding the room with salt and iodine.

"I always *did* want to see the ocean!" Isabel shouted when her brother finished the speech.

Everyone laughed. Doña Ana Moncada was happy; when her children came on stage a new light illuminated their eyes. For the first time she saw them as they were, and in the imaginary world they had longed for since childhood.

"You were right. We needed some illusion in Ixtepec," and she too laughed. Then she became thoughtful and listened to Hurtado, who was uttering a lament on stage. Suddenly his borrowed words no longer alluded to the love affair in the play, but sounded instead as if they were the General's words to Julia.

"It's all so sad!" Isabel interrupted.

Felipe Hurtado stopped talking and they all came out of the world of illusion. Her remark brought them back to the pathetic figure of the General and to the undaunted Julia, hidden behind her eyelashes. "Look at me, Julia," people said he begged. And Julia peered out of her almond eyes and gave him an expressionless stare.

Isabel broke the silence. She began to speak slowly, but before finishing the sentence she stopped and looked at her brothers with alarm.

Now, after many years, I see them all as they were that night. Isabel in the middle of the stage; Hurtado beside her, as if he were stunned by a sudden painful memory; Nicolás and Juan, with questioning eyes, ready to come on stage; Conchita sitting between the mother and the aunt, toying with a fine cord and

113

waiting to be called. Moving through the house I find the colored bows, the basted capes, Isabel's cloak, in doña Matilde's parlor. Returning to the pavilion, I hear Isabel's words, which caused her to stop short, still floating on the air: "Look at me before I am turned to stone!"

Those words opened a dark, unbridgeable chasm. They still echo in the pavilion, and that moment of surprise persists like the premonition of an unforeseen destiny. The brothers and sister looked into each other's eyes as if they saw themselves as children racing off on runaway mares near the cemetery walls when they were united by a secret, invisible fire. There was something infinitely pathetic in their eyes. They had always seemed somehow better suited for death. That was why since childhood they had acted as if they were immortal.

"What is it?" their mother asked, alarmed by the sudden silence and her children's look of somnambulists.

"Nothing! I had a horrible thought," Isabel replied. And she looked at her brothers, who had not moved and still riveted their eyes on her.

"A witch just passed with her procession," doña Matilde said, making the sign of the cross.

"She put a spell on us," the young girl answered in a lifeless voice.

Then they went on practicing until very late.

T W E L V E ⎯⎯⎯⎯⎯⎯⎯⎯⎯⎯⎯⎯

The enchantment was broken, and for the first time we had something to do, something to think about other than unhappiness. The magic that invaded doña Matilde's pavilion overwhelmed Ixtepec in a few days. My people spoke of the "Theater" with surprise, they counted the days until the opening, and wondered why we had deprived ourselves of this diversion in the past.

"Every city has theaters that stay open every day," doña Carmen said candidly.

"You're right, Carmen, I don't know why it didn't occur to us to organize one. We've lived like cannibals! Do you know that cannibals do exist? How horrible! Today I read in the newspaper about the explorers who ate each other at the North Pole. People say it was because they were cold! That's just an excuse. Then, because we're hot—we may eat each other one of these days. Did you read about it, Conchita?" Doña Elvira, back from the rehearsals, spoke gaily as she sat at her dressing table mirror.

"No, Mamá, I didn't read it."

"Read it, see if the same thing occurs to you." And doña Elvira, daydreaming, paused with her comb in hand, looking with approval at her round, chubby arm.

"The flesh of blondes must be very sugary. I think it must taste rather like custard . . ."

"Mamá!"

"What does Tomás Segovia taste like? He's a brunet, you know. Have you noticed that he doesn't come to the rehearsals? He's jealous of Hurtado because he never thought of organizing a theater group of his own." And eager to encounter new trivial dreams, doña Elvira fell asleep without a thought of Julia.

It was very pleasant to know that we could be something more than spectators of the violent life of the soldiers, and almost without being aware of it we turned from the hotel balconies to doña Matilde's. Those were halcyon days. The invaders became more tranquil, too. Damián Álvarez's mysterious death helped to appease the jealousy of Francisco Rosas. Only Julia went on being imperturbable, enveloped in her sadness.

The sight of Julia at the serenade, after an absence of several Sundays, brought us back at once to the days before the play. We forgot everything when we saw her enter the square. She was wearing one of her pale pink dresses, adorned with tiny translucent rhinestones that sparkled like drops of water, with her jewels entwined about her throat and her dark hair fluttering like airy feathers on the nape of her neck. She walked around the square several times, leaning lightly on the arm of her lover, who escorted her respectfully, as if she were the embodiment of night's unutterable beauty. Her impassive face revealed nothing. People moved aside to let them pass, and she advanced like an incandescent sailboat, breaking the shadows of the trees. Francisco Rosas took her to their usual bench. The other mistresses surrounded her, chattering gaily. She scarcely answered. Without moving, she scrutinized the square. Standing behind her, the General bent down toward Rafaela, who shouted to make herself heard above the music.

"How happy I am! The bad days are over now!" And she bent superstitiously to touch the wood of her heel with crossed fingers.

116

Rosas smiled.

"The world is so beautiful!" the twin continued, seeing the success of her first sally. "How beautiful it is to be in love, don't you agree?"

Francisco Rosas nodded and offered her a cigarette. The girl accepted it with aplomb and pressed his hand in a gesture of complicity. Her sister also turned toward the General with a generous smile. Francisco Rosas was pleased. He patted their cheeks and ordered drinks for everyone. Only Luisa seemed angry at Rosas' obvious happiness, and when he offered her a drink she refused it and turned to look at the passersby.

"No, thanks, I'm not thirsty."

With Julia present, the square was filled with lights and voices. The women walked around chatting audibly; the men passed at close range, not daring to look at her, breathing in the heady scent of jasmine that penetrated the night. And she, Julia, for whom was she waiting? For whom was she saving that almost imperceptible smile? She studied the square guardedly. She was looking for someone and did not take part in her friends' conversation. She was there for perhaps half an hour when, feeling thwarted, she asked to go back to the hotel. Francisco Rosas bowed and lightly touched her hair with his fingertips. He seemed to acquiesce willingly.

"But you just got here!" the twins said.

"I'm going," Julia replied. She rose and turned to whisper something to Rosas.

"Stay a little longer!"

"Spoilsport!"

"Let her go, she must have her reasons!" Luisa said.

"I'm sleepy," Julia replied. Her mind was made up, and she prepared to leave her friends.

At that moment a noisy group crossed the street and entered the plaza: it was the Moncadas. Laughing with their ringing and contagious laughter, they were accompanied by Hurtado and Conchita. I remember Nicolás' words: "Isabel, a peso for a horse-laugh!" and he showed his sister, who laughed easily, a silver

117

coin that she won at once, throwing her head back and showing her even white teeth.

Julia hesitated and did not finish her leave-taking. Rafaela noticed her confusion and invited her to sit down.

"Stay a while! Look, those people just came."

"I wonder what they're talking about, laughing like that," her sister said.

"Guess! There are times when I'd like to get to know some of these people," Rafaela replied.

Julia took advantage of the sisters' conversation and sat down again, feigning indifference.

The newcomers passed, and Hurtado slackened his pace and stopped laughing. It seemed that Julia had not looked in his direction. The General's face, serene only moments before, was distorted.

Lieutenant Colonel Cruz spoke: "And why do you want to get acquainted with some dopey kids and a no-good bum?" He said the last word scornfully, looking at the General out of the corner of his eye, so his chief would realize how insignificant the stranger was.

"Well, I don't know . . ." said Rafaelita, who did not have the slightest interest in knowing them.

"Julia knows one of them," Luisa said maliciously.

Her words caused a silence among the officers. The women remained in suspense and the men stared at the treetops. The music was loud and the whole square seemed to revolve around Julia, who looked quiet and pale. The General leaned down to speak to her.

"Let's go, Julia."

Julia, motionless, held her fan and looked into space.

Rafaela, frightened, urged, "Stay a little longer! It's such a hot night that it's good to be outdoors."

"Don't you hear, Julia? You always have to go against the General's will," Luisa said, bending close to Rosas' mistress.

Julia ignored her words. She did not move, she seemed to be made of glass, the slightest movement could break her into a

118

thousand pieces. The General took her by the arm and savagely forced her to get up. Julia did not resist.

"Good night," Rosas said, trembling with rage. Without further ado he crossed the square and went across the street with the young girl in tow.

"He's going to beat her!"

"Yes! He's going to beat her!" Antonia repeated, looking at Colonel Justo Corona in terror. With arms crossed, he remained impassive. On his sleeve was the black band that Rosas had ordered them all, including himself, to wear in mourning for the death of Damián Álvarez.

"She's very remiss. She deserves to be whipped a few times and then given her sugar, like a fine mare."

"I hope he gives her a good one and knocks out some of her meanness!" And Luisa's blue eyes turned white.

Her lover, Captain Flores, stood up. "I'm going, I have guard duty." He left the plaza and walked to Luchi's house.

"Luchi, are you jealous of Julia?"

Luchi thought for a few minutes, then said, "Why do you ask?"

"I want to know why women don't like her."

"Maybe it's because none of us are loved the way she is," Luchi replied honestly, and then put her arms around his neck.

The maids at the hotel said that when the General came back he beat his mistress "without mercy." From the hall they heard the sound of the whip striking her body and the broken voice of the man, who seemed to be grumbling. No one heard Julia make a sound. Then the General went to look for Gregoria, the old kitchen worker, who knew of many remedies.

"I don't want Dr. Arrieta to come. You must go and help Señorita Julia." Francisco Rosas' voice was unsteady.

At eleven o'clock at night the old woman left the hotel and went home to get some herbs. When she returned and knocked at the door to the lovers' room, the General went out and disappeared in the garden. Gregoria prepared poultices and cleansing waters, and used them to soothe the bloody skin of the one who was loved most in all Ixtepec. Then she also made an infusion that would diminish Rosas' ardor. The girl seemed not to hear the old woman's advice.

"Now, Señorita Julia, put this in the drink he takes before he gets in bed with you. But don't tell him I gave you the herb, or he'll kill me."

Julia, lying in bed with her eyes closed, did not answer. Gregoria tried to comfort her.

"You'll see, my dear. With God's help, he's going to stop loving you. When a man gets like this, a woman pays for it with her life. But God will make things better, even before you're well again. You'll see."

Julia remained very quiet during the treatment. She trembled and took small sips of brandy to regain her strength. A mauve welt on her cheek enhanced her pallor.

"Swear that you'll give him this remedy, Señorita Julia! He's bewitched."

The girl continued to tremble.

"And tell me—pardon my curiosity—what herb did you give him in your region to make him like this?" the woman asked.

"None, Gregoria."

"You mean, he simply began to love you like this?"

"Yes, Gregoria."

It was late when the General returned to the room, looked at Julia lying on the bed, came up to her and caressed her hair with his fingertips. The girl did not move and her lover sat down in a chair, sobbing. She let him weep.

"I'm going now, Señorita Julia," Gregoria said, feeling inhibited.

The lovers did not answer.

"I'm leaving your drink, Señorita Julia. Give the General some too, it will do him good, he looks very tired," the old woman added with a meaningful wink.

Julia remained silent. With his head in his hands, the General did not even say good night.

THIRTEEN _____

From here I can see Gregoria's house, and it seems to me that it is that same night and she is coming home, opening her door and crossing herself before entering. Inside are her pots, which had been oil cans, filled with geraniums and tulips. In her garden grow the herbs to make one forget, fall in love, escape from anger or from an enemy. It was not that Gregoria was a witch. No, she was not like Nieves, who gave me a bad reputation. From near and far they came to see her, brought her pieces of clothing, locks of hair and photographs of the ones who were to be bewitched. How many years had it been since the day when Marta, the girl from the coast, arrived in Ixtepec with Juan Urquizo? She brought him there so that Nieves would give him a love potion. The years came and went. Marta died in her land, we found out from Juan Urquizo, who, with the foolish expression that Nieves had given him, passed on foot through Ixtepec on his way to Mexico City. After that he appeared in my streets twice a year: once when he went to Mexico City and again when he returned. The purpose of his travels was to be on the coast on the anniversary of Marta's death. He took six months going and six months coming back, always on foot. When we saw him returning we knew that a whole year had passed. He lived at peace, unaware of his misfortune. He had been a merchant, he had had mules loaded with goods, and when the people saw him with tattered sandals, torn clothing, skin blackened by the sun, and his eyes bluer than ever, they were sorry for him. No one knew his family, because Juan Urquizo was from Spain. When he passed through Ixtepec, don Joaquín let him stay at his house, had soap and towels put in the red brick bathroom, and gave him clean clothes. Juan Urquizo accepted the charity gratefully. He stayed in the town for a night and a day, and early the next morning set out on the road to Mexico City or the road to the coast, depending on whether he was coming or going.

"Stay here and rest for a few days, don Juan," doña Matilde urged.

Juan Urquizo could not agree to rest.

"You're very kind, doña Matilde, but I can't fail Marta. If I lose a day, I won't reach the coast by November 14. Don't you know, doña Matilde, about the misfortune that has befallen me? Marta died on that date and I can't leave her alone. It's the only day when I can talk to her. Do you remember her, doña Matilde?"

And Juan Urquizo went on sobbing until doña Matilde, who knew what we all knew, said, "Don't cry, Juan. November 14 will soon be here."

Fifteen years ago he stopped making his circular journey. Some say he died on the plains near Tiztla. He was so old then that all he had left were a few white hairs, and surely that day the sun must have beat down intensely.

We never knew if Julia gave the drink to the General. She was reserved and always seemed like a stranger, not giving herself to us, wrapped in her smile, which kept changing as her luck changed. And each day was the same as the one before it. The people ate at 12:30, and at 3 P.M. few dared to cross my streets. The townspeople took siestas in their hammocks and waited for the heat to subside. The gardens and the plaza exploded in a fine

122

dust that clung to everything and made it impossible to breathe. The dogs lying in the shadow of the almond trees in the church courtyard scarcely opened their eyes, the fires in the stoves went out and were not lighted again until six in the evening. The Selims, a Turkish family who ran the clothing store called "The New Elegance," napped behind the counter with their scissors on their chests. Their children brought them little cups of very black coffee. "Very good for the heat. Over in their land this helped to relieve fatigue and suffocation."

In the plaza, Andrés took refuge under his candy stand and brandished a pink feather duster to drive away the wasps and flies that swarmed greedily around his coconut candy.

"I don't care what happens to that damn whore Julia. The others, those twins, are the good ones. That lucky Lieutenant Colonel, to find two pretty women and both at the same time!" he said. And when Rosa and Rafaela bought candy from him, Andrés made the price so low he almost gave it away.

Nearby, chained to the trunk of a tamarind tree, Lucero, his eagle, kept his fierce eye trained on the stinking chunks of raw meat that his master gave him.

"And where did you catch him?" the twins asked, always frightened by the bird's strength.

"Very high, girls, very high, where you find everything good."

Juana, who sold cool, brightly-colored drinks, her pink fingers soaked with lemon juice, stopped insulting the waifs who came to get her wares, and dozed with half-closed eyelids.

Javier left his heaps of baskets, pushed his straw hat down over his face, and, lying on his palm mat, peered out at the legs of the few women who happened to pass his stand.

The coachmen sitting in their boxes were still, and all that was heard was the stamping of the horses as they shook off the flies. The afternoons were the same. Dr. Arrieta was the only one who continued to move about, summoned by the fevers that abound in Ixtepec in the season of heat and drought.

It was on such an afternoon that Julia went out of the Hotel Jardín. The mistresses were taking a siesta. The drawn blinds made one think of naked arms and damp hair. Don Pepe Ocampo tried to stop her.

"Please, Señorita Julia, don't go out!"

"I'll go if I want to!" Julia said scornfully.

"The General will be here soon. Don't believe what he said. I'm sure he'll be back before he said he would."

"Well, keep him talking for a while."

"Señorita Julia!" the old man begged, darting back and forth in front of the door to keep her from going out.

Julia eyed him coldly and waited until the old man had stopped his antics.

"Have pity on me. I can't let you go out, think of the consequences if he finds out."

"Don't tell him. I'll be right back," and Julia pushed don Pepe out of her way and left the hotel. She was wearing no makeup, her hair was well brushed, and her lips were only slightly pink. Her presence on the sidewalk caused the merchants in the plaza to jump to their feet.

"Look who's coming!" Andrés exclaimed with amazement.

"And she's alone!" Javier replied, coming out from under his hat.

"What's she up to, that daring girl? She'll come to no good end." And Juana, openmouthed, stared at Julia as she walked by in her light cotton dress.

Her pale face still bore the dark trace of the welt she had received several nights before. In the sunlight she looked more fragile. She crossed the plaza and turned down Correo Street.

"She's going to his house."

"I told you he came for her."

"Such a pretty woman! Too bad we won't be seeing her around here much longer!" And Javier tilted his hat to one side.

"She's out for her last walk," Juana concluded.

The coachmen, from their boxes, kept giving news of the route the young girl was taking. Julia walked briskly, balancing on her high heels; she was not wearing stockings.

"She passed Pastrana's house."

124

Julia's figure grew smaller and finally disappeared in the tortuosity of the street. She passed the Montúfars' house, crossed over to the other side of the street, and stopped at don Joaquín's door. She knocked several times and waited quietly. No one expected a visitor. The knocking was lost in the density of the garden. After a long wait, Tefa opened the door.

"Is the señora in?" Julia asked in her distinctive voice.

"Just a moment," Tefa said, startled by the sight of the young girl.

Julia waited outside, under the sun's rays, not daring to enter. Tefa returned, breathless from her haste.

"Please come in, Señorita."

Julia entered the house, looking in all directions with her almond eyes; she was searching for someone hidden in the shadows. Doña Matilde appeared in the hall. She was frightened; her eyelids were swollen by sleep and one cheek was red with the marks of the lace on her pillow. Julia was bewildered, as if her visit suddenly had no purpose.

"Excuse me, Señora, excuse me, please! I am Julia Andrade."

"I've already had the pleasure . . . that is, I know you from a distance," doña Matilde said, confused.

She motioned to Julia to follow her through the dark hallway. The two women advanced with an air of mystery. Their steps made a hollow sound on the red tiled floor. "What has this girl come for? I hope this won't end badly!" doña Matilde was saying to herself, while Julia was forgetting the words she had prepared to explain her situation. "I won't say anything . . . I can't," Julia repeated to herself when they reached the door to the parlor. They entered the cool, high-ceilinged room solemnly. Rarely used was that parlor inhabited by porcelain shepherds keeping watch over black console tables and Pompeian women reclining on glazed jars, their hair crowned with roses and tame golden tigers at their feet. There were fans, mirrors, bouquets of flowers, and, dominating the room, a sculptured image of the Sacred Heart with lighted candles. On a chair were the costumes of Isabel and Conchita, ready to be worn. Doña Matilde picked them up.

"Excuse me, these are the costumes for the play." And she smiled, mortified by the word. What would her visitor think? Theatrical costumes in a decent house! "My niece and nephews are going to give a play for us, the family . . ."

The two women sat down and looked at each other, disconcerted. Julia, blushing, tried to smile, stared at the señora and then at her fingertips. She could not speak. Doña Matilde, in turn, did not know what to say and waited uneasily for her visitor to speak first. They remained thus for several minutes, scarcely daring to look at each other, smiling furtively, both of them timid and nervous.

"Señora, tell Felipe that he must go away. The General went to Tuxpan today and won't be back until very late. That's why I came to warn him."

At first doña Matilde did not know what the girl was talking about. Then she remembered that Felipe was the first name of her guest, and she sat there openmouthed, overcome by a jumble of confused thoughts. "Why must Felipe go away? Why did Julia come to warn him?"

"He's going to kill him," Julia whispered, bringing the words close to doña Matilde's ear.

The señora gave the girl a frightened look. It would have been better, she thought, if Julia had never appeared at her door, and now that she was inside of the house she wanted her to go away at once. But how could she tell her? As she looked at the girl she thought that she would be the first person the General would kill, for having betrayed him.

"What about you?" she asked.

"I? He'll never find out," Julia said without conviction.

"Someone will surely tell him." And the señora thought that perhaps she was seeing Julia for the last time. She stared at her, fascinated. "Will he be capable of doing anything to her?" She felt that she was in the presence of a being whose very frailty was imbued with violence, a being who had entered her home like a harbinger of disaster. The girl's unreal presence was more dangerous than an army. The señora examined her fragile collarbone, her delicate bosom revealed by the low-cut pink muslin dress, her hands resting on her lap. The flickering candles cast an orange glow on her golden skin. Julia's eyes grew larger as they filled with tears, and a damp smile spread on her lips. A violent blast of hail blew through the room.

"May I see him?"

Julia's voice reached doña Matilde from the center of a storm that started in the young girl's luminous body. Her brilliant image split and fell in glass splinters. The señora felt dizzy.

"Just for a few minutes," Julia's voice insisted, coming closer to doña Matilde's ear.

Icy winds blew and the hailstones vanished. The señora watched her sitting very still, with her hands clasped on her lap, her eyes as dark and alert as a gazelle's. Felipe Hurtado appeared in the doorway. Julia stood up and went to meet him, walking very slowly, and together they disappeared down the hall. Doña Matilde began to cry. Tears were the only possible outlet for the surprise of that afternoon and the visions caused by Julia's presence. Or perhaps she felt that now she had grown very old.

Julia and Hurtado walked across the garden and entered the stranger's room. They walked fast, arm in arm, looking at the ferns, as if they belonged to another order. The servants were spying on them from a distance.

"Julia came!"

"Don Cástulo was right: behind a man you'll always find a woman." And they searched in the air for the bright traces that had brought Felipe Hurtado to Ixtepec.

The servants, grouped beneath the arch that led to the kitchen, stared at the closed pavilion. Inside were the lovers. What were they saying to one another? The pavilion had entered a great stillness, the garden was quiet too, and the blessing of dreams came to the kitchen. The church tower struck five, the sky began to change color, and the branches of the trees became darker. The birds made no sound and the first perfumes of twilight permeated the house. Time passed, and the pavilion continued to be still.

"They'll pay for this with their lives."

The servants were sad to see the light spot of Julia's dress reappear in the garden. Felipe Hurtado walked beside her. The lovers were imperturbable, their faces at peace.

"Too bad! Too bad!"

The couple returned to the room where doña Matilde still waited motionless. Seeing them, she became panic-stricken. It was as if she had forgotten they existed.

"My dear! Why did you come?"

"To tell him he must go away."

"Yes, yes, he must go away. I'll make preparations for his trip right now."

The señora went to give orders to the maids. "I have so much to do, so much to do," she repeated, staring at her hands as she stood in the hall.

Her first impression when Hurtado arrived was that the stranger had come to alter the implacable order of her household, as a tiny grain of sand placed in a clock's mechanism causes imperceptible and fatal changes in the seconds. Now, on that afternoon which slid away among the trees of the garden, her hours and her gestures, reckoned in advance, broke into pieces and fell at her feet in the haphazard disorder produced by catastrophes. "What must I do?" Her words lacked meaning; her whole life, composed of nothings, appeared to her like a broken machine. "My brother Martín is right to live outside of time," she said to herself without understanding what she was saying. All her calculations had been in vain. The servants awaited her orders.

"We have to make preparations for the young man's journey," she said, not knowing what journey she was talking about or what sort of preparations had to be made.

"Did Joaquín come yet?"

"No, Señora."

"Why is he out at this hour?"

It seemed to her then that the invisible rift caused in her life by the stranger's arrival was opening noisily at that moment, that the whole building was falling into that black chasm which was advancing with the speed of lightning.

128

"It's dark now," Julia said in a strange tone, and the señora had the impression that the young girl's voice brought together in her house all of the shadows in Ixtepec.

She looked at Felipe Hurtado. His usually amiable face was somber. As she had done the first time she saw him, she became reconciled with the stranger. "Destiny always selects an unforeseen face," she said to herself with resignation.

"I'll help you follow him," she promised, knowing that her fate and that of the young people were now inextricably bound together.

Julia clasped her hands together and took a few steps. Then, without a sound, she ran quickly to the door, opened it, and went out.

Felipe Hurtado ran after her, but the sound of the door slamming stopped him. For a few moments he waited indecisively by the closed door, touched his forehead, took out a cigarette, lighted it, and without saying a word crossed the garden and went into the pavilion.

"Go and tell my niece and nephews that there will be no play today. And not a word about Señorita Julia!" doña Matilde shouted ferociously, and then burst into tears for the second time that afternoon.

FOURTEEN _____

Julia returned to the hotel by a different route. This time she looked for the untraveled streets. She proceeded slowly, walking very close to the houses. She seemed to be very frightened. People passing in the twilight did not recognize her. Dropping behind her were her ghosts: she divested herself of the memory of them, and on the stones in the street were falling for all time her festive Sundays, the illuminated corners of her dances, her empty dresses, her useless lovers, her gestures, her jewels. Feeling that her high heels were a hindrance, she took off her shoes and carefully placed them at the doorway of a house. She walked on in bare feet, in the presence of a future that rose before her eyes like a white wall. Behind the wall was the story that had guided her as a child: "Once upon a time there was a talking bird, a singing fountain, and a tree that bore golden fruit." Julia walked on in the certainty of finding it.

At the door of the hotel, tall, taciturn, obstructing the entrance, Francisco Rosas was waiting. Julia eyed him without recognition.

"Where have you been?" he asked in a low voice.

"Nowhere. I'm going to see something," Julia said with the body and face she had when she was twelve.

130

Rosas saw her childlike tangled mass of hair, her curls falling in her eyes, and her bare feet. He took her by the shoulders.

"What something?" he asked, shaking her vigorously. He felt that he was holding a strange child, and again shook her furiously.

"A tree," Julia replied.

"A tree?" And Francisco Rosas pushed her back and forth with loathing, as if she were the tree that covered his world.

Don Pepe Ocampo, hiding behind a pillar, was spying on them.

"I know what you did, you miserable slut."

Rafaela and Rosa were in their room. Antonia, sitting on the edge of the bed, was answering "yes" and "no" to Justo Corona's cross-examination. Luisa lay on her bed in the dark, not moving a muscle. An astonishing silence reigned in the hotel after Julia went out. No one heard Francisco Rosas and Julia Andrade return to their room.

Doña Matilde released the bolts and latches of the big door and let the dogs out. The servants gathered dejectedly in the kitchen and silently made preparations for Felipe Hurtado's nocturnal journey. The young man was still in the pavilion and did not answer when Tefa called. Night was falling on the garden and the frightened house seemed to be shrinking inward.

Someone knocked at the front door and the servants and the señora hurried to the entrance.

"Who's there?" doña Matilde asked, standing very close to the door like one who is expecting an enemy.

"It's I! Joaquín!" replied the voice from the other side, frightened by her tone. "It's happened," he said to himself.

The servants opened the latches and slid back the bolts.

"Joaquín, something terrible has happened!"

Her husband turned pale. On his walk through Ixtepec he had heard about Julia's visit, and he knew that the town was expecting a disaster.

"It was not meant to have a happy ending," Ixtepec repeated

in unison. The townspeople had drawn their blinds and retired early, and the streets were quiet.

The couple entered the señora's room. Soon afterward, don Joaquín went out to the pavilion. He knocked for a long time but no one answered. He wanted to persuade Felipe Hurtado that he should go away; Cástulo would take him to Tiztla and hide him there until the danger had passed; then he could go wherever he wished. But the guest refused to respond. In the darkness of his room he was deaf to the knocking at his door and the friendly voice that called to him. What was the stranger thinking about in his solitude as he lay so quietly on the bed?

The dogs sensed their masters' fear and nervously kept watch over the garden. Sitting in a circle in the kitchen, the servants spoke in whispers, smoked calmly, and strained to hear the sounds of the night. From time to time they heard the crack, crack of don Joaquín's cautious knocking at the young man's door. Cástulo, with the knapsack of food ready and the wallet stuffed with pesos, waited for the guest to come out so they could be on their way.

"Young Hurtado doesn't seem to be very fond of living."

"How can you expect him to go away? After all, he came for her!" Cástulo replied confidently.

Around ten that night Francisco Rosas, with his jacket unbuttoned, his face and hair covered with dust, walked through the town. He felt the eyes watching him behind every blind.

"There he goes! There he goes!" spread from balcony to balcony.

Francisco Rosas walked on, dragging his boots, not paying attention to the shadows that watched him pass. He crossed the plaza, which was magnified by the silence of that hour, pushed open the swinging door of Pando's cantina, and sat down alone at a table. His eyes were very tired and expressionless. The soldiers did not dare to speak to him; they drank their brandy glumly and avoided looking at him. He crossed his arms on the table and bowed his head. He seemed to be sleeping.

From her balcony, doña Elvira signaled: "There he goes!"

132

Doña Matilde moved away from the window and went to the garden. She found her husband sitting outside of the pavilion door, still calling to Felipe Hurtado.

"It's getting late. He's around here," the señora whispered.

"All we can do is entrust ourselves to God's will."

And the husband and wife returned to their room. They extinguished the oil lamp, leaving the candles burning.

"Poor boy! How good he is!" the señora said, sitting on the edge of a chair.

"Get undressed! He mustn't find us like this. He'd suspect something," her husband ordered.

In nightgown and pyjamas they waited in the darkness, scarcely broken by the candlelight. The play of light on the señora's white nightgown filled it with colors that ranged from orange to green to blue, then changed to red and violently to yellow. The reflection of the lights prolonged time. In the corners grotesque forms appeared, and the odor of giant cockroaches came through the cracks in the door. A viscous dampness permeated the walls and the sheets. Outside, dead leaves fell to the ground with a rustling noise. The coming and going of the insects produced an oppressive sound. The tropical night, consumed by thousands of destructive animals, was being pierced on all sides, and the couple listened in silence to their encroachment.

"I'm afraid. That poor boy! He's so good!"

"Why don't you say, 'He *was* so good'?" her husband said violently.

Around eleven o'clock the unrest of an hour before was replaced by an absurd tranquillity. Perhaps their fear of the General was unreasoning, perhaps he was not so awesome as they imagined and everything would turn out well after all. The clocks marked the minutes in orderly fashion and the night began to advance with its accustomed speed. The sounds that pricked holes in the shadows ceased and the intensity of odors dissolved into soft perfumes. The husband and wife lay in bed and listened as the clock struck twelve.

"God heard our prayers!" they said.

133

In the dark and alone with his thoughts, Felipe Hurtado waited. Doña Matilde tried to imagine him alone in the night.

"He's very manly. He wouldn't agree to leave her. He wanted to share her destiny," said don Joaquín.

The couple tried to imagine the young man. What was he thinking about at that moment? He was probably lost in the memory of Julia, reliving their minutes together. Perhaps he was crying for her.

"Do you think he loves her more than the General does?" the señora asked.

"I don't know. You saw them together—what do you think?"

Doña Matilde did not know what to say, and the two fell silent, embarrassed by their sudden curiosity: they were violating their friend's confidence. But love was a mystery, and had to remain secret. A light sleep clouded their vision and the two slumbered peacefully.

It was after one A.M. when they heard the military band. It was coming down Correo Street, heading straight for the house of don Joaquín Meléndez.

"Here he comes!" doña Matilde shrieked, awaking with a start.

Her husband did not answer. A cold sweat was trickling down the nape of his neck. He closed his eyes and waited.

The townspeople peered through their blinds. The General was on horseback. They heard the animal's hoofs prancing on the cobblestones, the sound cracking over the music. More men on horseback followed. Some random shouts were heard. The procession stopped in front of doña Matilde's bedroom windows. Through the music someone called her husband by his full name and pounded on the door.

"Don Joaquín Meléndez, open up!"

It was the voice of General Francisco Rosas. The señora, paralyzed by terror, did not move. Her husband leaped out of bed and walked up and down in a daze. He had heard the hoofbeats and the music and was speechless, hoping absurdly that it was all a mistake, that it was not his house they wanted. Inside, the dogs barked and ran crazily through the hall. The knocking continued, the window shook noisily. All Ixtepec heard the clamor.

"Open up, don Joaquín!"

Señor Meléndez went to the balcony. His wife tried to stop him, but he pushed her away with a violent movement.

"You'll get the first bullet."

"Coming, General! What brings you here at this hour?" And don Joaquín flung open the shutters with determination. "I thank you for your music, General!" he added, trying to appear cordial and anxiously seeking the General's face in the darkness.

Without dismounting, Francisco Rosas seized the iron bars of the balcony. "I'm looking for a rabbit, Señor Meléndez."

Don Joaquín laughed. "Oh, General! With so many hunters, you'll surely catch it!"

Still clutching the bars, the General swayed precariously as if he were about to fall. He was drunk. "You bet!"

"And which rabbit is it, General?"

Francisco Rosas eyed him scornfully and steadied himself smartly in the saddle. "A very famous one, and it went into your honorable house."

"Well, well! Matilde, bring the bottle of brandy, the General and I are going to have a drink!" Don Joaquín was trying to distract him, thinking that a show of cordiality would disarm the General.

Once again Rosas grabbed the bars, lowering his head. He looked very tired, and seemed about to burst into tears. "Corona! Pass me the Hennessy!"

The Colonel, on horseback, came out of the night to give him the bottle.

Rosas took a drink and handed the bottle to don Joaquín. "Boys, play 'Las Mañanitas' to wake up a pimp!"

The Military Band obeyed the General's order.

> This is the serenade
> King David once did sing,
> And to the pretty girls
> His very words we bring.
> Awake, my love, awake . . .

135

Francisco Rosas, still on his horse, listened to the music, ignoring don Joaquín.

"To your health, General!" Señor Meléndez shouted loudly.

"To yours!" the officer replied. He took the bottle from don Joaquín and drank again. "It's not right to let a woman make you unhappy," Francisco Rosas grumbled as he drained the bottle. Suddenly he ordered, "Put your clothes on! We're going out to get that rabbit!"

"But General, first let's have a little talk."

"Put your clothes on!" the General repeated, bleary-eyed.

Don Joaquín went to his room and gloomily began to dress. Doña Matilde fell into a chair and watched with astonishment as her husband put on his clothing. In the hall the maids were praying audibly. "Souls of the Blessed! Most Holy Mary, help us!" They did not want to light the lamps, and their sighing and weeping could be heard in the darkness. The soap-makers, who slept in the yard, were in the garden of ferns.

"The house has been surrounded by soldiers for several hours," they announced, touched with fear.

Only Felipe Hurtado's room was still, strangely cut off from what was happening in the house. In the street the shouting and the music continued.

The General's voice was heard again. "Tell him to put his clothes on! I don't like to shoot them naked!"

"The rabbit must have a name, General," don Joaquín said coldly, to oblige him to pronounce the name of his rival.

"Hey, Jerónimo! What did you say his name was?" the General yelled to one of his aides.

"Felipe Hurtado, General!" the man answered quickly from the other side of the street. He reined in his horse and came up to don Joaquín's balcony.

Don Joaquín put a pistol in his belt and came to the window. "Another drink, General?"

"Why not?" Rosas replied. He raised the bottle to his lips and then passed it to don Joaquín.

Doña Matilde went to the door of the pavilion and knocked

136

softly. The stranger appeared; in the dark she could feel the emanation of sadness from his eyes. He stood before the señora, who began to cry.

"They've come to get you, son."

The guest disappeared into his room and returned carrying his suitcase. The General's lugubrious voice reached them.

"Look, don Joaquín, I don't want to kill him in your house."

Felipe Hurtado embraced the señora. "Goodbye, doña Matilde, and thank you very much. I'm sorry you've had so much trouble over someone you don't even know." He took a few steps and stopped. "Tell Nicolás to give the play!"

Through their tears the servants watched him go. They were half-dressed, with their hair uncombed and their faces anxious. They would never forgive themselves for having gossiped about him, for having served him so unwillingly. All Ixtepec was distraught over the fate of a stranger who was going away from us as mysteriously as he had come. And it was true that we did not know the identity of that young man who had come on the train from Mexico City. Only then did it occur to us that we had never asked him where he was from or what had brought him here. But it was too late. It was the middle of the night and he was going away.

In the street Francisco Rosas was making his horse caracole. A soldier led another mount by the reins; it was for don Joaquín. They would carry Hurtado between the animals' hoofs. The band was still playing. The night awaited its victim. The stranger said goodbye to the servants, shaking hands with each one. They stared at the floor while tears streamed down their faces.

"Come on! Let's not keep the General waiting," Hurtado called to don Joaquín.

Francisco Rosas forced his horse to a gallop, then halted it at the front door. The others galloped after him. The band, still playing, ran to follow.

Don Joaquín tried to stop Hurtado. "He'll kill us all!" the old man said.

The stranger gave him that certain look of his that spoke of

137

far horizons. Standing at the door, they heard the hostile voices.

The young man slid back the bolts, released the latches, opened the door and went out. Don Joaquín was about to follow, but at that precise moment something that had never happened before occurred: time stopped dead. I don't know whether it stopped, or simply slipped away and was replaced by sleep: a sleep that had never overtaken me before. There was also total silence. Not even the throbbing of my people's pulse could be heard. I really do not know what happened. I was outside of time, suspended in a place without wind, without murmurs, without the sound of leaves or sighing. I came to a place where crickets stand still, in the attitude of chirping and without ever having chirped; where dust does not settle, and roses are petrified in the air beneath a motionless sky. There I was. There we all were. Don Joaquín by the door, with his hand raised, as if he were making that desperate and defiant gesture for all time; his servants beside him, with their tears frozen on their cheeks; doña Matilde crossing herself; the General astride Norteño and Norteño prancing with forefeet lifted, gazing with otherworldly eyes at the happenings of this world; the drums and bugles poised in readiness for playing; Justo Corona, with his hat tilted to one side, holding his riding whip; Pando in his almost empty cantina leaning toward a customer who was picking up some silver coins; the Montúfars spying from behind their balconies, their frightened faces drained of color; and like them, the Moncadas, the Pastranas, the Olveras, everyone. I don't know how long we were lost in that motionless space.

A mule-driver entered the town. He said that it was already getting light in the country, and when he came to the edge of town he encountered the darkness of night. It frightened him to see that the night continued only in Ixtepec. He told us that the night seemed darker when it was surrounded by the morning. In his fear he did not know whether to cross the border between light and darkness. He was still hesitating when he saw a man on horseback with a woman in pink in his arms. The man was wearing dark clothing. The woman was laughing. The mule-driver wished them good day.

"Good night!" Julia shouted.

We knew it was she because of his description of the pink dress, the laughter, the gold beads. They galloped away.

When they emerged from the night they disappeared on the road to Cocula, in the splendor of the rose-colored light of dawn. The mule-driver came into town and told us how all Ixtepec was sleeping round and black, with motionless figures in the streets and on the balconies.

"It was a sea of blackness, with dawn all around it," he said.

We never heard of the lovers again.

PART TWO

ONE _____

After that I returned to silence. Who would speak of Julia Andrade or Felipe Hurtado? Their disappearance left us speechless, and we scarcely greeted one another when we met.

We missed Julia: the serenades were very dark without the splendor of her dresses, her gold necklaces no longer illuminated the trees around the plaza, and the General shot her horse, Cascabel. No trace of her beauty was left to us. "What a life, we might as well be dead!" and we moved through the days that were no longer ours.

And we had to forget Felipe Hurtado, too, to obliterate the mark of his passage through Ixtepec; that was the only way we could save ourselves from greater evils.

"That man was a magician!" don Pepe Ocampo said to himself, and nervously brought his chair to the doorway and propped it against the wall so he could sit and watch the evening and the people passing by. He was angry.

"Get out of my sight!" he said bitterly to the few people who approached him from time to time. What was there to tell them? That Rosa and Rafaela no longer sang? That Luisa and Antonia kept silent too? And that the four women enclosed in their commonplace names avoided an encounter with Francisco Rosas? The insignificance of his secrets filled him with anger. Silently he reconstructed the evening he had spent with the stranger. "He hypnotized me!" he repeated to himself, realizing that he could not remember what Felipe Hurtado had said. As a hotelkeeper in a southern town where only dust falls and only persons of the lowest rank arrive, don Pepe had let the one secret that had touched his life escape. "And to think that I had her right here for so long, and never got a word out of her!"

And he remembered Julia's gestures and smiles one by one. With patience he would solve the mystery. "A miracle was here and I didn't see it," and the evenings, each identical to the one before it, passed in front of his eyes.

"It's better not to visit Matilde for a while. Don't you agree?"

"Yes, Mamá," Conchita replied sadly. She missed the pavilion and the porch at doña Matilde's. The play and the talks had ended, those nights would never be repeated again. General Francisco Rosas had willed that Conchita should be unhappy.

"Something bad is going to happen to them. Rosas will never forgive them for what Hurtado did." Doña Elvira was prophetic at nightfall, leaning out of the window and looking nostalgically at the closed blinds of the Meléndez family across the way.

Doña Matilde closed the pavilion and she and her husband went into seclusion in their home. The only one who came to visit was her brother Martín.

It was said that don Joaquín was very ill, but no one came to inquire about his health. His nephews kept the costumes for the play unfinished, and one morning they went to Tetela without saying goodbye to anyone. It was a long time before Nicolás and Juan returned to Ixtepec.

Francisco Rosas wandered aimlessly through the town. At dawn he came back drunk and the townspeople heard him dragging his boots over the cobblestones of my streets. All that remained of the General were his staggering footsteps crashing against his days. In the mornings the servant girls remarked, "Did you hear him last night? He went to the whorehouse."

Luchi feared his presence; he came in alone, looking saturnine, and fell into a chair. With a glass of brandy in his hand he waited for the night to advance. He was afraid to return to the hotel room where he found an echo of Julia's voice and the trace of her body. Any word that alluded to something that had occurred before the coming of Felipe Hurtado put him on the alert, and with his fist he made tables and glasses fly through the air.

Juan Cariño's presence made him uncomfortable. He felt uneasy with the madman smiling, watching him. Captain Flores, Juan Cariño's friend, tried to talk the old man into leaving.

"Go along now, Mr. President, it's getting late for you."

"The young General shouldn't shout like that. He has no respect for me, and I have no alternative but to strip him of his rank. Mr. General, report to my office tomorrow! Your conduct leaves much to be desired." And Juan Cariño left Luchi's parlor with dignity.

Rosas' aides surrounded him, pretending to be happy. A continual "General!" "General!" was on every solicitous tongue. But he remained very quiet, looking at them with indifference, and stayed alone, to lose himself in his thoughts.

"Surely Señorita Julia didn't give him the infusion, and he will be miserable forever. I hope he won't end up like Juan Urquizo!" Gregoria repeated whenever she saw Rosas in the patios of the Hotel Jardín, and remembered the night when she treated Julia's wounds and watched him sobbing so grievously.

Time passed and we were not able to console ourselves for the loss of Julia. Her beauty increased in our memory. And those eyes that no longer saw us—what vistas were they looking at now? What ears were listening to her laughter, what stones of what streets resounded as she passed, on what night so different from our nights did her dress sparkle? Like Francisco Rosas, we looked for her and carried her and brought her back through imaginary places. Perhaps she, hidden in the night, watched us

145

looking for her. Perhaps she saw her abandoned bench in the plaza beneath the tamarinds, and listened to the military band playing marches for her. Perhaps she hid in the almond trees of the church courtyard and smiled when she saw the women in mourning enter the church and then come out again, looking for the beauty of her bosom. Those who went away from Ixtepec always returned with news of her. One had seen her walking in Mexico City, leaning on Hurtado's arm, laughing as she had done on those nights when Francisco Rosas took her on horseback to Las Cañas. Another told in a low voice how he had seen the glitter of her dress at the fair in Tenango, and how she had disappeared into the crowd when he drew near to greet her.

"Naturally, she was afraid I would tell the General about her whereabouts!"

Others believed she had died, and heard Julia's laughter haunting the streets at night like a phantom.

"Last night we heard her laughter up and down Correo Street until it vanished through the crack in the door of the Meléndez house, agonized in the garden, and then entered the pavilion. There it spent the night laughing at Rosas, at how miserable she had made him."

And we looked at the General, thinking that Hurtado had more power than he did. Francisco Rosas could feel us looking at him, and he moved away as a tiger does before it pounces.

"That poor man!" Ana Moncada dropped her embroidery to spy through the window curtains at Francisco Rosas. He went about now with the shirt of his uniform unbuttoned and his eyes looking inward. "Look, Isabel, there he goes! He's punishing himself!"

The young girl came to the balcony and looked over her mother's shoulder at the General's tall figure. Embedded in his misery, he walked my streets on his way to the cantina to get drunk.

"The poor thing!"

Isabel sat down again and stared ferociously at her mother's impassive face. "I know what you're thinking, that it is just for him to atone for his sin."

Since the night when Julia and Felipe Hurtado disappeared, Isabel paced back and forth through the hall and the rooms of her house, stepping on slippery shadows that obliged her to collapse from chair to chair. She did not want to visit her aunt and uncle: she was afraid she would find the stranger's invisible presence hovering over the garden. Nor did she want to see the pavilion, where the stage was rapidly crumbling to dust. The remains of that world which had appeared magically on the night of the rain, and disappeared the night when Francisco Rosas came to demand his rival, relegated her to a dusty corner. If her brothers had been with her, her life would have been bearable; she would not need to speak, but would only have to begin a sentence, "Nico, I'm very sad . . ."

And behind those words Nicolás would divine the wreckage of the dreams they had invented together. With her parents it was necessary to make explanations, to give reasons that were never satisfactory, and their advice did not help her. They had grown accustomed to ugliness and had invented an unreal world. Behind this apparent world was the real world, the one that she, Juan, and Nicolás had been looking for since childhood.

At night, sitting in the parlor, she did not speak. She watched Félix stop the clocks, and that illusory gesture to escape from the time of each day filled her with pity for her father, a captive in an armchair, reading the newspapers. Her mother, curled up close to the light of an oil lamp, continued to work on her embroidery, taking intermittent sips from the cup of coffee that Félix filled from time to time.

"Politicians have no delicacy."

"Delicacy?"

"Yes. How do they dare to consider themselves indispensable?"

Isabel smiled. Only her mother was capable of saying that Calles had no delicacy, when he was ordering the execution of anyone who seemed to be an obstacle to his remaining in power.

"It's a little more serious than a lack of delicacy." And Martín Moncada continued to read the newspaper.

In those days a new political calamity was beginning; relations between the government and the church were strained. There were conflicts of interest, and the two factions in power were ready to embark on a struggle that would distract the people from the only issue it was necessary to obscure: the distribution of land. The newspapers spoke of the "Christian faith" and "revolutionary rights." The Catholic followers of Porfirio Díaz and the atheistic revolutionaries were digging the grave of agrarian reform together. Less than ten years had passed since the two factions had agreed on the assassination of Emiliano Zapata, Francisco Villa, and Felipe Ángeles, and the Indians still had vivid memories of the revolutionary leaders. The church and the government fabricated a cause to irritate the discontented peasants.

"Religious persecution!"

Martín Moncada read the news in the paper and was depressed. Harassed by misery, the people would enter that fight. And while the peasants and the rural priests prepared for atrocious deaths, the Archbishop played cards with the wives of the atheistic leaders.

"This is very sad!" And Isabel's father violently threw away the paper that spoke of the "progress of Mexico." Its task was to sow confusion and it was achieving that aim.

"What do you think about it?" doña Ana asked in an attempt to rouse her daughter from her stupor.

Isabel did not reply. She listened to the news with fatigue and inattention. What did it matter if unhappiness fell like rain all about her, when she was already so unhappy! Apathetically she said good night.

"Papá, when are my brothers coming?" she asked from the doorway.

"Let them stay where they are!" her mother replied impa-

148

tiently. It seemed to her that Isabel was not interested in anything; she only thought of herself.

"I'm very lonely!" she said bitterly.

Her father looked at her uneasily. His daughter's perennial discontent worried him.

Disheartened, Isabel entered her room, placed the light on her night table, and undressed in silence. She would always be alone. The face that appeared in her dreams was a face that had never looked at her. Melancholically she made certain that her wardrobe and bureau were closed; then she counted the syllables of the last sentence her mother had said: "Let them stay where they are!" Six syllables! And she tried to get to her bed in six long strides. The last one turned of necessity into a leap, and as she fell on the bed she became entangled in the mosquito netting. And this was her way of warding off the darksome misfortunes that surely lay in wait for her in the future. She and her brothers had slept in that room for many years; when they grew older, their mother moved the boys to another room. And now Isabel, alone, was frightened, as she had been when she was a little girl who climbed under the white mosquito netting that floated on the night like a ghost on a dark ocean. The burning lamp was the only lighthouse. She saw herself as a child calling to Nicolás.

"Nico!" Her voice crossed the room and lingered in the corners, where the darkness remained intact in the lamplight.

"Are you afraid, Isabel?" Her brother's voice came protectively from the next bed.

"It's the candles. Do you think my stub is burning out?"

And Nicolás and Isabel descended hand in hand to Dorotea's story. Terrified, they found themselves down in the subterranean vault where men's lives are kept. Millions of candles of different sizes were burning; some were nothing but sputtering wicks. When the black woman who walked up and down among them blew out a candle, its owner on earth died. Nicolás came out of the story with a tremulous voice.

"Your candle is the same size as mine."

149

Doña Ana entered the room. "You're keeping your brother awake!" She drew back Nicolás' canopy, leaned over and gave him a kiss. Then she went to Isabel, who refused the caress; then to Juan. "Pleasant dreams!" Her voice was different. She took a few steps, bent down and blew out the lamp.

The three children were alone in their ships, sailing into the night.

"Nicolás, I don't love Mamá!"

"I know, you never love her at night," the boy replied.

"When will my brothers return?" And Isabel Moncada's head was filled with somber thoughts that blackened the night.

"Do you understand what's going on in Mexico City? What do those government people want?"

"I don't know, Mamá," Conchita replied, thinking of Nicolás Moncada and her days wasted one after another between the walls of her house.

"You see? No one understands anything." Doña Elvira threw the newspapers on the floor and rocked impatiently in her chair. What else could she do? Wills alien to her own were destroying the small pleasures of each day one by one. "The Justinos never end!" she thought, without compunction giving the tyrants her husband's name.

She did not ask for much: to hear her canaries sing, to keep the festal days, to look at the world within her mirror, and to chat with her friends. And she could not: distant enemies were making a crime of each innocent act. The peaceful days and the fiestas would never come again. She looked bitterly at the newspapers strewn on the floor.

"Inés, pick up the papers! This room is a mess!"

Inés came in quietly, her violet dress and black braids impassive. She bent down and handed the newspapers to the señora. Doña Elvira looked for the photographs curiously.

"What a face! What a face! See? He never smiles. He was born to read death sentences!"

150

Inés and Conchita peered over her shoulder at the face of the Dictator, which appeared on several different pages.

"What can you expect of a Turk like Calles? And what about the maimed one?" she added, pointing to the plump face of Álvaro Obregón.

"They'll come to a bad end!" said Inés, feeling sure of herself.

"But before they do, our days will get worse."

"Yes, but they're going to have a bad end anyhow," Inés insisted without altering her expression.

Some time later, the death of Álvaro Obregón, which left him slumped over his plate at a greasy banquet, gave us great joy, even though we were occupied with the most extreme violence.

T W O _____

It was afternoon. The newspaper vendors' shouts announced
that religious worship had been suspended. Their cries crossed
my streets, entered stores, penetrated houses, and put the town
in motion. People came out on the street, formed in knots, and
went to the church courtyard.

"Let's see if they've taken the saints away!"

Under the violet light of afternoon the crowd was growing.

"Let's see who's taking the mother away from whom!"

Enveloped in low-voiced anger, their bare feet tanned like
leather by the stones, their heads uncovered, the poor people
grouped beneath the branches of the almond trees.

"Virgin of Guadalupe, help us get these bastards!"

From time to time a shout was heard, and then there was
silence. While they waited, the men smoked cheap cigarettes and
the women minded their children. What were we waiting for?
I don't know, I only know that my memory is always an interminable wait. The ladies and gentlemen of Ixtepec arrived
and mingled with the Indians, as if for the first time the same
evil was afflicting them both.

152

"What's going on?" was the question that was on everyone's lips. At 7 P.M. the first soldiers appeared; they carried rifles with fixed bayonets. Impassively they took positions to cut off the possible exit of the invaders from the courtyard. A ripple of whispers began to spread; the swell of rancor reached the soldiers, who remained motionless. The warm shadows of the night descended from the tops of the almond trees and covered the courtyard.

Don Roque, the sacristan, pushed his way through the crowd. He was covered with dust and his hair was disheveled. "Go home, all of you!"

The crowd turned a deaf ear to his plea. The courtyard was filled with bonfires, lighted tapers, and prayers. At dawn, people from neighboring towns arrived to enlarge the crowd; a great cloud of dust rose to blend with the questions, the smoke from the blazing fires, the cries of "Get up, mule!", and the smell of food cooked in the open. Groups of drunken men were sleeping in the dust; women wrapped in shawls rested quietly.

The years have passed, and that immense night on which we kept watch at the church appears in my memory with the clarity of a firefly. And like a firefly it eludes my grasp.

The orange streak that announces morning appeared; the light rose through the sky and we were still in the courtyard; we were tired and thirsty but we did not want to let the church fall into the hands of the soldiers. What would we do without it, without its feast days, without its statues that listened patiently to our laments? And would they condemn us to agonize among the stones and to work the dry land? To die like stray dogs, without a whimper, after living a miserable life?

"It's better to die fighting!" a man shouted, throwing his hat into the air.

The others answered his shout with prolonged moans, and all the voices in Ixtepec joined in the chorus, "Sons of bitches!"

Around the church, vendors of cool drinks and of tacos reeking with coriander were present in large numbers. The soldiers, still at their posts, saw out of the corner of a single greedy eye the

153

sweets that were off limits for military discipline. Don Roque announced that before the suspension of worship, the priest would give a blessing to those who requested it and would baptize the innocent who had not received the sacrament. The sacristan's words rang out gravely and the people remained silent. Father Beltrán appeared at the door of the church and patient lines formed, advancing toward the priest on their knees. The day advanced slowly also, dust fell like rain, and the sun beat down violently on the bare heads. The priest officiated amid the ashes; he seemed very old in his cassock of thirty years in the priesthood. Oh, if only God would hear him and would take some of the misery from these unfortunates! He felt that in those moments he was living the innumerable days that were not to be lived.

With the blue band of the Children of Mary on her chest, Charito shouted, "The blood of martyrs will be spilled!"

Her shouts blended with the hawking of the vendors and did not distract the priest from his unexpected task. Standing, imbued with some unknown powers, he saw the whole day pass and did not leave the door of the church. When it grew dark, orders came from the Military Command that we were to leave the church at midnight. We had four hours to bid farewell to a place that had welcomed us since childhood. The people crowded forward: they all wanted to enter the church for the last time. The priest moved away from the door and, very pale, stood at the foot of the high altar.

Under the central nave, in the midst of the throng, Dorotea met Isabel and her mother. Their faces were covered with perspiration and their black veils were wilted.

"We have to leave before twelve," Señora Moncada said.

"I'm going to see the General," Dorotea announced, as a crush of the faithful separated her from her friends.

"I'll go with you!"

Doña Ana pushed her way through the crowd to Dorotea's side and together they went out to the street. Isabel remained alone, waiting for her mother to return. The crowd pushed her

154

back and forth like an aquatic plant swayed by water. Fascinated, she let herself be carried from one side to the other. She felt that a power outside of herself was separating her from the people and carrying her to an unknown place where she was alone.

"That son of a bitch won't see the light of day!"

The threat ran from mouth to mouth; Isabel heard it come and go away again, spinning between the pillars of the nave. Francisco Rosas crossed seas of lightning and below, far below him, were the words uttered in the church. "He isn't afraid of us," the young girl said to herself, and the General's image appeared above the heads of the faithful. Francisco Rosas lived in a world that was different from ours: no one loved him, and he did not love anybody, either; his death would mean nothing, not even to him; he was a sorry fellow. Perhaps, like Isabel and her brothers, he had not found the secret he had been looking for since childhood, the answer that did not exist.

"Isabel, do you think mountains really exist?"

Nicolás' childish voice came to her ears, and from the weeping church she journeyed to the morning when she and her brothers ran away from home and a mule-driver brought them back to their parents very late that night. They had climbed a spiny mountain full of iguanas and cicadas. That was not a mountain! From its rocky ground they saw the real mountains: blue, made of water, very close to the sky and to the light of angels. Seeing their sun-reddened faces and their thirst-swollen tongues, the neighbors remarked, "The Moncadas are bad!"

Perhaps Francisco Rosas was bad because he had looked for that mountain of water without finding it. She felt sorry for the General. She glanced at the people all around her and did not recognize herself in them. What was she doing there? She scarcely believed in God and was unmoved by the fate of the church. She saw her mother coming, pushing her way through the crowd. "Here she comes, all upset, and yet she's always saying bad things about priests."

"The General wouldn't see us!"

155

Her mother's words did not affect her and Dorotea's sad figure left her indifferent. She knew that the old lady considered the church a home and the saints her only family; she spoke of them like friends. "Dorotea is the Virgin's cousin and an intimate friend of St. Francis," Nicolás used to say, laughing.

At that moment her friend's grief caused her to feel a strange enjoyment. If she could have done so, she would have rushed to Francisco Rosas' side. She wanted to be in the world of those who are alone; she did not want shared weeping or celestial friends. Her mother called her several times; she felt someone take her arm and firmly lead her through the multitude. She found herself breathing the perfumed air of the church court-yard, with her mother's face watching her closely. Then they silently crossed my muted streets and went home.

"He's a very strange man. So young . . ."

Isabel did not reply. Doña Ana took off her black veil and looked at herself indifferently in the mirror. Sitting on the edge of the bed, her daughter gave no importance to her words or her gestures. She was miles away, coursing through a future that was just beginning to be delineated in her memory.

"There will be deaths," the señora added.

A silence fell between the two. The ticking of the clock, as punctual as an ant moving along a piece of furniture, was heard. Félix had forgotten to arrest time, and the young girl let herself be carried along by its precise movement to a future she re-membered clearly. Her mother opened the wardrobe to put away her shawl and the smell of mothballs and perfume escaped from its doors. Her father entered the room. He had not gone to the church; before him, Isabel lowered her eyes, feeling guilty. In the distance the bell in the church tower pealed twelve times and the Moncadas looked at one another and waited. A few minutes later the first shots were fired; they sounded like firecrackers.

"There will be deaths," Ana insisted.

The street was filled with running and moaning. They were dispersing the people, who fled in terror before the rain of bullets from the Mausers. Don Martín lighted a cigarette and turned to

156

the wall. It seemed to him that the plaster was splattered with blood.

"Papá, Papá! No one understands me. No one!" Isabel shouted, clinging to him.

"Hush, child," her father said, stroking her hair.

"No one!" Isabel said, contorted by sobs.

"You're very nervous . . ." And doña Ana went to the kitchen to prepare a cup of linden-flower tea for little Isabel.

At 4 A.M. the last invaders left their positions in the courtyard. Under the almond trees there were women whose heads had been shattered by gun-butts and men whose faces were mangled by kicking. Their relatives dragged them away and the triumphant soldiers closed the church doors and put chains and padlocks on the iron grating in the courtyard. Then, excited by the fight, they shot some of the stray dogs that were sniffing around the food left by the Catholics. In the morning the order that was so dear to the leaders had been restored: under the brilliant sun the carcasses of dogs, the bloodstained shawls, the odd assortment of leather sandals lost in the flight, and the broken pots of food were spoils from the battle of the poor. Cordons of soldiers were keeping watch over the havoc.

That day Ixtepec did not open its balconies or its stores. No one walked through my streets and Francisco Rosas stayed in the hotel. In the afternoon Dorotea appeared with her wreaths of flowers. She went along as usual, hurrying and talking to herself. When she reached the courtyard she overlooked the heaps of refuse that obstructed her passage and the presence of troops; with a steady hand she tried to open the iron grating they had secured with a padlock. The soldiers stopped her.

"Hey, lady!"

"Men of God!" the old woman answered.

The soldiers began to laugh, approached her, snatched the flowers and flung them away. As the flowers hit the stones they raised thousands of flies, which buzzed angrily around the carcasses of the dogs. Then the men pretended they were going to

157

impale her on the points of their bayonets, and their coarse laughter exploded ferociously in the empty courtyard. Overcome, Dorotea sat down in the middle of the street and cried. She seemed like one more stone thrown among the heaps of rubbish.

"Go home, Granny," the soldiers urged when they saw her crying. Their words made a hollow sound in the quiet town and Dorotea, sitting in the street, cried until very late that night.

Some silent days followed, and then the useless and bloody riots broke out again. An angry sound invaded me. I was no longer the same with the church closed and the iron grating around it under the surveillance of the soldiers, who squatted on the ground playing cards. I wondered where those people were from, who were capable of such acts. In my long life I had never been deprived of baptisms, weddings, responsories for the dead, rosaries. My corners and my skies were without bells, holy days and hours were abolished, and I regressed to an unknown time. I felt strange without Sundays and without weekdays. A wave of anger flooded my empty streets and skies, that wave which cannot be seen and which advances suddenly, demolishes bridges and walls, destroys lives, and makes generals.

"There's no evil that lasts a hundred years!" "The one who spits at the sky will have it fall on him!" they shouted from the trees and the rooftops. Francisco Rosas heard the shouts and slackened his step. "Look, Francisco, it's lucky for you that I'm so easygoing!" The General, smiling, looked for the face of the one who uttered the threat. It seemed that he had forgotten Julia and now was looking for us instead. If he was afraid, he did not show it, because a few days later he turned the presbytery into the Military Command, and on a certain afternoon he had the church statues burned in a huge bonfire. That was when I saw the Virgin burning, and I also saw her mantle transformed into a long flash of blue. When this happened, the soldiers entered the presbytery and came out again carrying papers that they fearlessly threw into the fire. In the plaza there was a big pile of ashes which gradually blew away.

158

Father Beltrán disappeared. They said he had run away. How had he gone? By the road to Tetela, the road to Cocula? I did not see him leave, nor did I know that he was wandering about through my mountains. It was also rumored that he was being held in Ixtepec and that the army men planned to kill him any night. We preferred to think of him walking down a safe road, far away from Rosas, with his long cassock billowing in the fields of green corn.

"He went to tell about what is happening, and the forces will come to save us." And as we waited, on doors of houses and the presbytery appeared the first signs, bearing the Veil of Veronica with the Face of Christ and a mysterious legend: "Long live Christ the King!" The nightly shootings began also. At daybreak there were dead soldiers in the marketplace; some grasped in their fingers, contracted by death, the lead spoon with which they had eaten their supper of pozole fragrant with oregano. The men of Ixtepec disappeared, and in the mornings we found some of the bodies lying mutilated on the plains that surround me. Still others were lost to us forever or went we knew not where. The use of lanterns to help oneself walk in the dark was forbidden. "Put out the light, damn you!" and a bullet shattered the beam. I began to be afraid of punishment, afraid of my anger. At night we spied on them from our houses.

"Are they going to come?"

No. No one came. No one remembered us. We were only the stone on which repeated blows fell like imperturbable drops of water.

It was Friday. The night stood still, the heavy breathing of the dry mountains around me could be heard, the black cloudless sky had descended until it touched the earth, a somber heat made the outlines of the houses invisible. Correo Street was quiet, no streak of light broke its darkness. Perhaps it was two in the early morning when the sound of someone running echoed in Ixtepec like a drum roll. Other footfalls followed in quick succession, the shoes clattering on the cobbles like the rapid cracking of a whip. Someone was running away and many frantic pursuers followed at close range. The first runner stopped dead. There was the sound of labored breathing; the others stopped also, and then muffled voices were heard.

"Hit him! Hit him!"

A volley of stones clanked on the cobbles and detonated against the shuttered windows, while others rolled along furiously and made sparks fly. Inside of the houses the people were still: some-one was being killed.

"Hit him! Hit him again!"

The voices asked for more stones. A man asked for help.

"Let me in! Help me, blessed Jesus!"

The killer voices fell hoarsely on his. "We'll help you now, you bastard!"

A rain of stones pelted his entreaty. The voice that grasped the bars of doña Matilde's balcony moaned, "Most Holy Mary . . ." One last stone exploded, and it was stilled.

"Let's go!" said the bloodthirsty voices.

"Yes, we'll come and get him later."

"Why later? We have to take him now."

"He'll get blood on us," said a grumbling voice.

"You're right. We'd better wait a while, until he stops bleed-ing."

A door creaked and the voices were silent. They crossed the street, huddled in the doorway of the post office, and watched from there.

Who was that pious man? Carrying a lighted lamp, doña Matilde came out in her nightgown to investigate. She groped her way forward among the shadows, which her light was not strong enough to disperse. "Where are you? Where, my son?"

The assassins broke into a run and the señora, hearing them, stopped. "They're going to go around the block and they'll get me when I come to the corner." She could not move. The steps quick-ly grew fainter and the night returned to silence. Paralyzed by her fear, the señora stared sightlessly at the surrounding dark-ness. She felt the seconds falling on her like enormous ashes.

From across the street the Montúfar women were watching

her through their curtains. They too were mute with fear and, fascinated, they saw doña Matilde raising and lowering the lamp as if she were exorcising the shadows.

"I don't have much time." She tried to walk but the ground sank beneath her feet. Doña Matilde had never realized the enormous distance that separated her balcony and the entrance to her house. When she reached her window she found the silence that is generated in the place where a crime has been committed; the body was not there, the blood was flowing swiftly on the stones. "They took him away." The señora looked questioningly at the bars and the bloodstained wall. At their window the Montúfars were making signs that she did not see. "I hope Nico and Juan get home safely." Ardent eyes were spying on her from the intersection of Alarcón and Correo. The assassins had circled the block and were watching her avidly from the darkness. Doña Matilde spun around, searching; then she retraced her steps, entered her house, and closed the door. Divested of her circle of light, the night returned to shadow. The cluster of assassin eyes moved warily to the scene of the crime.

"Well, what do you know!" said one very low voice.

"What is it?" the grumbling voice asked in a whisper.

"Who knows!" two frightened voices replied.

"It's no good to meddle in God's business," the sad voice said.

"The corpse is gone . . ."

"Let's get out of here!"

And the quiet voices moved away from doña Matilde's house. The night was still again.

Half an hour later, on the other side of Ixtepec, on the road to Tetela, the hoofbeats of four horses could be heard.

"Something's happened."

"Yes. They didn't come. Let's go home," Nicolás said in a whisper.

His brother and two stableboys followed as he took the road to the Moncadas' house. A group of soldiers intercepted them and forced them to stop.

"Who goes there?"

"Friends!" Juan Moncada replied.

"You're not permitted to be on the street at this hour."

"We didn't know. We've come from Tetela," Juan Moncada said.

"Well, you're under arrest."

"Arrest?" Nicolás shouted angrily.

"Yes, just in case you happen to be those fellows who go around hunting for soldiers at night."

Some of the men shouldered their rifles while others seized the reins from the Moncadas' hands. Then they steered them toward what had been the presbytery, now the Military Command. As they crossed the patio of orange trees, a strong smell of alcohol blended with the perfume of the blossoms. They came to the room that had been Father Beltrán's. The previously unalterable order had given way to a clutter of cigarette butts, papers, and obscene scrawls on the whitewashed walls. The nails that had held holy pictures now supported the grim visage of the Supreme Chief of the Revolution, a title which the Dictator had given himself, and the chubby face of Álvaro Obregón.

"And the priest?" Juan Moncada asked.

"He ran away," a soldier replied.

"It's the law now that priests have to be under arrest, that's why he ran away," another man added.

"When will you let us go?" Nicolás asked impatiently.

"As soon as the General comes. He's never late for hangings."

The brothers kept silent and the men began to play cards. The room soon filled with strong tobacco smoke and shouting.

"Three of spades!"

"Queen of diamonds!"

"King of hearts!"

The names of the cards glittered a few seconds in the dirty room. Each king, each queen demolished the stained walls and let the luminaries of the night come in.

"Have a smoke, kid," one of the soldiers offered humbly.

Nicolás smiled and accepted the cigarette.

162

"It'll help you stay awake," the man added as an excuse.

Nicolás lighted the cigarette and the two looked into one another's eyes.

"Things aren't what they should be," the soldier said, lowering his eyes in embarrassment.

They smoked in silence, Nicolás straddling the chair with diffidence, the other seeking out his eyes.

"It's necessary to choose between one's own pleasure and . . . that of others," the man said in a very low voice.

Nicolás smiled at the man's delicacy in using the word "pleasure" instead of the word "life." And the soldier knew that there was no bitterness between the young men and their captors. From the patio of orange trees came voices and footsteps. The soldiers stood up, put away the cards, and smoothed their black hair.

"Where are the conspirators?"

"Here, General."

The door burst open and Francisco Rosas appeared. He stopped and stared fixedly at the brothers. He observed their dirty boots, their trousers, wrinkled by the journey, and their sunburned faces. Their knapsacks were at one side of the room; their pistols, on a table.

"Good evening. Where are you coming from at this hour?"

"From Tetela. We decided to travel at night to avoid the heat," Juan Moncada answered.

The General looked at them for several seconds and then turned to his men. "Don't you see that they're the Moncadas?"

The soldiers remained impassive.

"You can go now," Rosas said, annoyed.

Juan and Nicolás picked up their knapsacks.

"Leave your weapons here," the General ordered, softening his voice to keep from softening his power.

"Good night." And the Moncadas prepared to leave.

"Wait! In your travels, did you happen to meet Abacuc?" Francisco Rosas asked, feigning indifference.

Abacuc was a former Zapatista. When Venustiano Carranza assassinated Zapata, Abacuc kept quiet, laid down his arms, and

163

became a small businessman. He went from town to town, riding on a mule, selling odds and ends, and refused to talk about Carranza's government. Enigmatically, he saw how Obregón assassinated Carranza and seized the power, to surrender it later to Calles. He, Abacuc, went on selling his paper necklaces, gold earrings, and silk scarves while the government leaders assassinated all of the former revolutionaries. When the religious persecution began, Abacuc and his mule loaded with whimsies disappeared from the markets. It was rumored that he had gone to the sierra and that from there he was organizing the revolt of the Cristeros, the Christian militants.

"We haven't seen him, General," Nicolás said very seriously.

"He's getting a lot of followers," Rosas said grudgingly.

"Apparently."

Francisco Rosas raised his hand in farewell. "I'll see you, boys." And Rosas turned his back.

The brothers left the presbytery. Day was breaking when they arrived home.

THREE

In the morning, two pieces of news ran from mouth to mouth. "Rosas is afraid of Abacuc," and "Haven't you heard? Last night they killed don Roque, and now they're looking for his body—it vanished!"

At the Military Command the disappearance of the sacristan's body aroused Francisco Rosas' anger.

"Find it and bring it to me!" he shouted furiously to Colonel Justo Corona.

The Colonel lowered his eyes and bit his lip. At eight o'clock in the morning, followed by a picket of soldiers, he began the search for the capricious corpse. With a sullen face and a handkerchief tied around his neck, he went to Correo Street. When he reached the place where the sacristan had fallen, he inspected the traces of blood on the walls and thoughtfully weighed in his hand the stones that the soldiers had used to break his head.

"This is the spot where he disappeared, Colonel."

"A dead man doesn't disappear!" Justo Corona's voice reached the interior of the houses.

The Montúfar women, who watched the scene from behind their curtains, looked at one another with malice. Apprised of

165

what was happening outside of her window, doña Matilde ran to the kitchen and, without knowing why, began to beat some egg whites. They shouted the news to Dorotea but she, undaunted, went on watering her geraniums.

"Well, maybe not, Colonel, but he disappeared!" the soldier replied firmly.

"You see, Colonel, that what never happens suddenly happened," another man said.

"He must have been alive, then," Corona said thoughtfully.

"He was dead when we left him. Nobody could stand such a stoning."

"We flashed our light, Colonel, we flashed our light in his eyes and they could no longer see . . ."

Justo Corona kicked the loose stones on the street. "Whose door opened?"

"It was very dark, Colonel," the sad voice said.

"But where did the noise come from, approximately?" Corona insisted gruffly.

"From there," a soldier said, pointing to the Meléndez house.

"No, no, from there!" another said, pointing to the corner of Alarcón Street.

"It's not easy to hear at times like that," said the one with the lazy voice.

"A corpse is a corpse!" And Corona looked at his men with distrust.

"It will rot pretty soon, Colonel, and we'll find it from the smell!" the first soldier said to dissipate the suspicions he had read in the Colonel's eyes.

Justo Corona listened without saying a word. Then he went to the corner and from there calculated the distance to Dorotea's door. The entrance to the old lady's house was closer to the scene of the crime than the entrance to the Meléndez house. He searched for signs of blood on the ground. Alarcón Street, at right angles to Correo, had been swept and watered; it was impossible to find any trace there. Corona studied Dorotea's door. "Does the old lady live alone?"

166

"Yes, all alone, Colonel."

"What is she like?" Corona demanded.

"Ugh! Old and ugly!" The soldiers laughed.

"All hunched over!" another added, smiling.

"We already told you she wasn't the one who came out, it was the one over there. And what good did it do her? None! The corpse was already gone."

"You should have seen her, Colonel. She was looking all over the place!"

Justo Corona returned to Correo Street and stared avidly at doña Matilde's door. "She was the meddlesome one, right?"

"We already told you she came out, but she didn't find anything," the soldiers said impatiently.

Corona scratched his chin and remained in the attitude of a man who meditates on a problem without finding any solution. From the house opposite they were spying on him. The Colonel saw the shadows through the light-colored curtains, and ferociously crossed the street and headed for the Montúfars' door. Happily he examined the bronze hand with ringed fingers that served as a knocker, and banged it several times.

"Damn pious women, I'll show them!"

A servant girl came; Corona saw that her lips were trembling.

"Call the señora!" he said, giving her a shove and entering the house. "Come on in, boys!"

His men quickly obeyed. An entrance hall filled with cages and the singing of canaries greeted them. The servant girl started to walk away, and the Colonel impudently followed her down the hall full of azaleas and of parrots and macaws, which shrieked as he passed.

> Parrot, play reveille,
> Because the Colonel ordered it!

Justo Corona made a gesture of displeasure, as if the parrot's song alluded to him. He felt himself growing red with anger. The servant indicated the dining room door, and Corona entered the room with assurance. The widow and her daughter had run

167

hastily from the balcony to the dining room. The table was set for breakfast, but all indications were that they had just sat down. They could not be feigning amazement; they were too pale. The Colonel seemed satisfied by their surprise and stood before them, smiling.

"Good morning, Señora! Good morning, Señorita!"

"Good morning," Conchita murmured, while her mother weakly waved the Colonel to a chair. Conchita bowed her head and tried to control a tremor that invaded her hands. She could not pour the coffee. The Colonel's eyes were riveted on her.

"You're very nervous, Señorita," he said maliciously.

"Nervous?"

There was a silence that the Colonel made it his business to prolong.

"What should I do? Serve him some coffee?" doña Elvira wondered, her hands resting on her lap. From the hall came the unconcerned songs of the canaries and the squawks of the parrots.

"How happy the birds are!" Conchita said in spite of herself.

Her mother looked at her with approval. She would give much to be in their place, singing in a cage, far from the pockmarked glance of that man! The man smiled.

"Not so, Señorita, they are captives that have committed no crime. We only find ourselves in such a situation when we commit a crime—or conceal one." And Justo Corona stared at them fixedly.

The women remained perfectly still.

"For example, you are suspicious and venture to go and sing behind an iron grating . . ."

The señora and her daughter looked at one another with alarm. The mother touched her breast to still the beating of her heart, which could be heard all over the room.

"Sing behind an iron grating?" Conchita asked, defenseless.

"Yes, young lady."

Conchita bowed her head and doña Elvira tried to smile.

"Last night a crime was committed on this street and the

168

assassins hid the corpse. The duty of the authorities is to find the guilty parties and the victim. Imagine what would happen if we could assassinate and bury our enemies at will!"

The women did not reply. So now they had committed the crime? Or was this a trap so that they, in their indignation, would accuse the soldiers? That was what the Moncadas would have done—become eyewitnesses of the events! And that was what they should avoid. The señora looked intensely at her daughter to transmit the thought to her, but Conchita was engrossed in repeating to herself the words they had said to her since she was a child: "A closed mouth gathers no flies!" That sentence, repeated at each instant, marked her childhood, was interposed between her and the world, formed an impassable barrier between her and candies, fruits, reading, friends, and parties. It left her immobilized. She remembered her father and her grandfather speaking about how unbearable women were because they talked so much, and repeating it to her at every moment, putting an end to the games before they began.

"Shhh! Be still, remember that a closed mouth gathers no flies!"

And Conchita remained on this side of the phrase, alone and stupid, while her grandfather and her father went on talking for endless hours about the inferiority of women. She never dared to jump over those six words and formulate what she wanted out of life.

Now the sentence stood like a wall between her and Colonel Corona, who continued to look at her questioningly.

"The innocent must cooperate with the authorities to cast some light on this terrible crime." Corona took out a cigarette and without asking permission began to smoke with pleasure while waiting for the two women to speak.

After the error of mentioning the birds, Conchita was determined to remain silent. She considered conversation very dangerous, and left the responsibility to her mother. Doña Elvira sat up straight in her chair, looked at Corona, and tried to smile. She was searching for a phrase that would not compromise her.

169

"What can two women alone do, Colonel?"

"Tell me what you saw and heard last night," Corona said, feeling that he was now on a surer path.

"We were asleep! Why should we be wandering around the house at that time of night?"

"At that time? Aha! Then you know what time it was?"

"I mean, we go to sleep at seven," the señora replied, turning very pale.

"Women are light sleepers and the man shouted for a long time before he died."

"If we had heard anything, we would tell you."

Justo Corona bit his lip and looked at them with irritation. He knew they were lying. "The corpse was on this street!"

They were silent and hid their eyes from the officer's stern glance.

Corona's voice sounded tragic. "Señora Montúfar, we are going to search your house. I am very sorry to declare you the accomplice to a crime."

"As you wish," the señora said.

Justo Corona turned to the maid who, stupefied, was witnessing the scene.

"Go and tell my men to come here and leave two on guard at the door."

The maid vanished.

"I have orders to find the body and to arrest those who are hiding it," Colonel Justo Corona added solemnly.

Conchita and her mother kept still. The servant returned, accompanied by a group of soldiers. In less than an hour the Montúfars' house was like a strange place. Corona emptied wardrobes, bureaus, drawers of tables, he pulled the mattresses on the floor, he beat the pillows. Then he checked the garden, looked in the storerooms, interrogated the maids. He returned to the side of the señora and her daughter who, livid with rage, heard the devastation without stirring from their chairs. The Colonel saw that they were determined to keep silent, and nodded farewell. When he reached the door, he turned.

170

"Any information you may have on the disappearance of the body, you'd better tell me now to avoid a severe punishment."

In vain he waited for a few seconds. The Montúfars did not move their lips. When he was outside the Colonel gave way to rage. He knew he was gulled and defenseless before the stubbornness of those women. His soldiers walked along dejectedly, pretending not to notice their chief's defeat.

"There's nothing worse than trying to deal with women!"

"Very true, Colonel! Very true!"

"They abuse a man's courtesy," Corona added.

"They're crafty, Colonel."

"Let's go to see this one," Corona said, angrily turning toward doña Matilde's house. And he crossed the street with long strides.

Señora Meléndez had stopped beating the egg whites some time ago and was pacing nervously in the hallway, waiting for the Colonel to arrive. When she heard the loud knocking, she did not wait for her servants but hurried to open the door herself. Corona was surprised to see her.

"Señora! I have the unfortunate mission of searching your house!"

It was better to get right to the point and not lose time or patience talking to her. The señora smiled and let him come in. The soldiers entered the garden and their chief ordered them to search the well and the grounds. Then he asked for the keys to the pavilion where Hurtado had lived. Followed by three of his men, he went through the rooms with doña Matilde leading the way. His steps made a martial sound in the gloomy silence of the house. At the end of the hall, under the arches that led to the kitchen, the servants were waiting expectantly.

The Colonel found the head of the house in bed. "Sick?" he asked attentively.

"Yes, Colonel, fever," said don Joaquín, who had grown very thin since the night on which the soldiers had taken Felipe Hurtado from his house.

With meticulous courtesy Corona searched the room. Don Joaquín made no comment. Doña Matilde stood beside the bed

171

and, without altering her expression, let the soldiers go about their business. The commotion made by the soldiers in the adjacent rooms reached her. Corona wheeled around.

"You went out last night, Señora . . ."

The señora interrupted him. "I heard some soldiers killing a poor man and I went out to help him, but I didn't find him."

"Señora, be careful! Did you say some soldiers?"

"Yes, Señor."

"Señora, don't you know that it is a crime to make unfounded accusations?"

"Yes, Señor, I know, but this is not the case. They *were* soldiers."

"First it is necessary to find the body, and then to accuse the criminal," Corona said bitterly.

"You won't find either one here," doña Matilde replied.

Corona was silent. "This old woman is worse than those two across the street," he said to himself. "I'll find out what she knows, then I'll bring her down a peg or two."

To have something to do, he rummaged in his coat pocket for his pack of cigarettes and lighted one; he had just started to smoke distractedly when he heard doña Matilde's voice.

"Excuse me, but smoke bothers my husband. If you wish to smoke, please leave the room."

Corona quickly put out the cigarette and smiled. "Certainly not!"

The husband and wife did not return his smile. They looked on him as an intruder who occupied a time and a place that did not belong to him. A soldier entered the room.

"Nothing?"

"Nothing, Colonel."

There was no choice but to leave. The señora saw him to the door. Corona made one last attempt.

"And you heard nothing that would tell me who took the body?"

"Nothing! We old people are very hard of hearing," and she leered at him maliciously.

"That insolent old lady is really something!" Justo Corona exclaimed when he was outside again.

The morning was well advanced; the sun beat down on the walls and rooftops. Corona consulted his watch: it was ten-thirty.

"More than two hours looking at junk!" he said sharply.

"Yes, Colonel, what a lot of stuff ladies keep," and the soldiers were about to laugh, but Corona's tense face froze the laughter in their throats.

"Very true, Colonel, those two across the street are easier to handle, nicer . . ."

"What a difference between them!" another said, following the way shown by his companion to distract Corona from his fury.

"Let's go and see the little old lady!" And Corona turned the corner and knocked forcefully at Dorotea's door.

She came to the door with the watering can in her hand. Corona hesitated before the astonished gaze and watery eyes of the old woman.

"Come in! Come in! Make yourselves at home. No one is refused a little shade!"

The men entered the house and Dorotea led them to a corner of the porch where there was a breath of cool air.

"This terrible heat! This terrible heat!" Dorotea repeated as if she were talking to herself, shaking her head incredulously.

The soldiers followed her without saying a word. The house was very different from the others they had visited. Here the whitewash of the walls was blackened by smoke. The bricks were broken and had lost their color. Chickens ran freely inside of the house and pecked at the dirt on the broken flagstones. On the branches of a magnolia tree some worn blouses were drying in the sun. Bunches of paraffin candles hung from the walls beside the clusters of corn and garlic.

The flies were still. A cavelike darkness issued from the doorless rooms. Only the large earthenware jug of water seemed to exist happily in the midst of that dust. Corona and his men did not know what to say. They were in one of those places that are a kind of last station where lonely old men wait for an unknown

173

train with an equally unknown destination, and where everything around them has died.

"I have no place to receive you. The revolutionaries burned my house . . ."

Corona scratched his head and looked at his men in bewilderment. They seemed to say: "Didn't we tell you? Isn't it true that she's an old hag?" Dorotea brought some wicker chairs and offered them to the men.

"Don't bother . . ." Corona quickly snatched the chairs from his hostess's hands; then he himself arranged them in the room and sat down in one.

"Would you care for a glass of water? Or a bunch of flowers? No one is refused a drink of water or a flower."

And ignoring Corona's protests, Dorotea went to the garden to cut roses, jasmine, and tulips.

"Oh, Colonel, how skinny she is! How could she manage to move that heavy corpse?"

"Looks like she's got one foot in the grave herself," another soldier added.

Dorotea returned. Sitting on his low chair, Corona found himself the recipient of a bunch of roses and jasmine. Dorotea passed around glasses of cool water, which the soldiers drank gratefully. The Colonel felt ridiculous to be pursuing that little old lady.

"Señora . . ." he began.

"Señorita. I have never been married," Dorotea corrected.

"Señorita," Corona began again, "don't be afraid. Last night someone died in this neighborhood and the body disappeared. The Command issued orders to search the houses in the section, and as your house is in the affected area, we have to do it."

"Make yourself at home, General, go right ahead," Dorotea replied, waving her hand in a sign of willingness.

Corona gave a signal to his men and they spread through the rooms, the garden, and the yard. The Colonel stayed and chatted with the woman. In a few minutes the first soldiers returned.

"All of the rooms are burned, Colonel. In hers there's only a cot and some little decorations."

174

"There's nothing but stones in the yard," the others said, approaching.

"Then there's no chance . . ." Corona agreed, slapping his legs. He stood up and made a bow that Dorotea rewarded with a smile.

"Retreat!"

Out in the street the Colonel quickened his step. He did not want the neighbors to see his defeat. Dorotea's door opened and she rushed out of the house.

"General! General!"

Corona turned at the call.

"Your flowers, General!" And Dorotea, breathless from her haste, held out the bouquet of roses and jasmine that he had left on his wicker chair.

The officer blushed and took the flowers. "Thank you very much, Señorita." And he left without daring to throw them away. He felt he was being observed by the old woman, who, standing motionless in the middle of the street, watched him walk away with a smile on her face.

In Ixtepec the people remarked jubilantly, "Dorotea covered Corona with flowers like the Holy Child."

"It will turn up!" Rosas declared sententiously when Justo Corona informed him of his defeat. He stood by the window smoking a cigarette, and watched the smoke vanish in the air of the plaza. The tops of the tamarind trees also vanished in the morning light. Nothing in Ixtepec had a body, not even the sacristan, who had died without leaving a trace. The whole town was made of smoke and it was slipping through his fingers.

"It has to turn up!" Rosas insisted, repeating his words obstinately as if they were the only reality in that unreal town, which had finally made him a phantom too.

"Who knows! Who knows!" Corona said doubtfully.

His aide's doubt brought Rosas back to the unreality of his life in Ixtepec: Corona too was disintegrating in that alien light. And he, Francisco Rosas? He was pursued by mouthless shouts and he pursued invisible enemies. He sank in a mirror, he moved through bottomless planes, and all he got was the insult of a tree or the threat of a rooftop. He was blinded by the reflection of silence and a courtesy that granted him the sidewalks and the plaza. That was how they had taken Julia away from him, deceiving him with shouts that no one uttered, showing him images reflected in other worlds. Now they showed her to him in the mistaken dead in the trees and he, Francisco Rosas, confused mornings with nights and ghosts with living people. He knew that he moved about in the reflected light of another town reflected in space. Since her arrival in Ixtepec, Julia led him astray through those timeless passageways. There he lost her, and there he would go on looking for her, even though Ixtepec never gave him the word that corresponded to the deed. He knew it: they were cheating him out of the days, they were changing the order of the dates, the weeks were passing without showing him a Sunday. He was losing his life looking for traces of Julia, and the streets were decomposing into minuscule luminous spots which erased the mark of her step on the sidewalks. A strange order had taken possession of that accursed town.

Justo Corona approached his chief. He too was empty-handed: Ixtepec was slipping away from him like a snake. The two men looked at the plaza spread out like a stone mirror. The people came and went without paying attention to them or their caviling. I knew that behind their innocent faces they were spying on the military men, and laughing at the agility of don Roque's body in having sneaked away from the hands of the assassins. "He always was a sly fellow!" "Oh, I always said it—they'll never get him, not even when he's dead!"

"The pious women won't stand for it if he's not buried in consecrated ground. They'll be coming soon—to ask for permission to bury him." Francisco Rosas said these words to avoid admitting defeat before Corona. The pious women! What did they— or the priests—matter to him? He spoke like that on orders from his superiors.

"Who knows! Who knows! These old ladies are difficult." Justo Corona believed in his words, and if he was sad that morning it was because he had not carried out the orders received from the capital.

Days passed and no one came to the Military Command to request a burial permit for don Roque's body. The General was not surprised. He was accustomed to the deceits of Ixtepec, and doubted that the sacristan had ever lived. He did not know what to say, and wearily paced back and forth in his office.

"These people are up to something!" Justo Corona repeated, anxiously looking out the window in search of an indication that would provide a clue to the whereabouts of don Roque's body. Francisco Rosas listened with deaf ears. He wanted to forget those people and the sacristan. He was searching for something more intangible, he was pursuing the smile of a past that threatened to evanesce like a puff of smoke. And that past was the only reality he had left.

"Yes, Colonel, they're up to something."

He did not want to contradict his deputy or to confess that for him these people did not exist. Justo Corona felt betrayed: his chief was abandoning him, leaving him alone in the fight against the town.

"They're making fun of you again, General, that's what bothers me," he said, making a perfidious allusion to Julia.

Francisco Rosas stopped his circular pacing and stared fixedly at his aide. It was true! Corona was right. Ixtepec's mockery was the source of his unhappiness. He walked to the window with rancor and watched the comings and goings of my people.

"Very true, they're up to something!"

The officers were spying on us, and we were waiting for the coming of Abacuc the Cristero. He was hiding in the sierra and his name ran from town to town. At midnight the men took secret roads and fled from Ixtepec to join the rebels. Abacuc slept during the day and at night he appeared with a holler in the neighboring towns. He killed soldiers, freed prisoners, and set fire to jails and archives. The men welcomed him with answering shouts and ran barefooted after his horse, which again disap-

177

peared into the rude wilderness of the sierra. Some night Ixtepec would hear his cry: "Long live Christ the King!" and that would signal the last night of Francisco Rosas.

"He'll be coming soon now!"

And we laughed, savoring the new conflagration in Ixtepec.

"He's coming—coming!"

And we did not even look at the windows of the Military Command where the army men were spying on us; the General and his aides were our prisoners now.

F O U R

At six on a purple evening an army that was not Abacuc's arrived. Its soldiers encamped on the plaza, lighted bonfires, roasted pigs, and sang old songs about men who had been executed.

> He went from door to door
> Looking for paper and a pen
> So he could write a letter
> To Isabel again.

We watched them with rancor. "Miserable creatures, they don't even have the pleasure of dying for the one they want to die for!" A new general came to inspect the area. In the morning he drove around, sitting very erect, in a motor car which clattered noisily on the cobblestones. The new general had only one eye, a flat face, and lemon-colored skin, he did not lose his calm when dogs barked as he passed or chickens scattered in fright before the cloud of dust his automobile raised. He looked at us fearlessly with his one eye, sweating in his tight, high-necked jacket and his military cap set squarely on his close-cropped head.

He spent the night at the Hotel Jardín talking to General

Rosas, and very early the next morning he went away, followed by his soldiers. He was General Joaquín Amaro and he was going to fight the Cristeros.

"He's a Yaqui Indian! He's a traitor!" we said, frightened: to call him a Yaqui and a traitor was to encompass every evil. The one-eyed general's lopsided glance spoke of punishments and inflamed our spirits, and at night we let out stentorian shrieks that ran from street to street, from section to section, from balcony to balcony.

"Long live Christ the King!"

"Long live Christ the King!" came the answer from a window.

"Long live Christ the King!" came the reply from the darkness of a corner.

"Long live Christ the King!"

The shout was prolonged in the doorways. Shots rang out in pursuit of that cry as it went the rounds of the town. In the shadows the soldiers stalked it, and it rose from all corners of the night. Sometimes it ran ahead of its pursuers, sometimes it pursued them from the rear. They looked for it blindly, advancing, retreating, and their anger grew steadily more intense. Then, during nights and nights, the dance was repeated—the dance of the shout and the soldiers, which zigzagged through my rough and pathless places and my streets.

In the mornings Francisco Rosas pretended not to see the posters stuck on the doors of the Military Command with the Veil of Veronica, the Face of Jesus Christ, and the words "Long live Christ the King!" The General called the soldiers who killed don Roque.

"Are you sure he died?"

"Yes, General, we cracked open his head like a pottery jug."

"I shone the light in his eyes. They were wide open and scared. He was already a goner."

Francisco Rosas remained pensive and secluded himself in his office with Justo Corona.

"Someone is organizing them, that's why I don't think he's really dead."

180

"But the boys swear it," Corona said uncomfortably.

"Well, Ixtepec is making fun of me."

"You'll have to give them a punishment they'll remember."

"Who?"

"The ones who are responsible for the disappearance of the sacristan's body." Justo Corona said these words thinking of doña Matilde.

Rosas did not know what to say. Who were the responsible persons? He did not know. He only knew that since don Roque's disappearance Ixtepec had changed. From the shadows someone was directing those shouts and nocturnal crimes.

"One of those women buried him in her garden or has him alive, and he's the one who is directing this insolent joke. Make another search, Colonel, and if you find freshly dug earth or newly laid bricks, search! The sacristan is there. Bring him to me, just as he is, and also the one who hid him."

For the second time Justo Corona, followed by a picket of soldiers, went to Correo Street. The rumor that he was coming to search doña Matilde's house reached her before he did. The señora gave the alarm to the Montúfars and Dorotea. When Justo Corona appeared, he found the same attitudes in all three houses and no news of don Roque's body. No bricks had been moved in the three houses. The earth in the gardens was untouched and the plants intact. In the yards the stones and grass had not been disturbed for many years. The Colonel returned to the Command in dismay.

"Nothing, General!"

"I can understand the priest's escape, but a dead man doesn't get up and walk away."

"I know, General. But there's nothing in those houses."

The officers were discouraged. From the balcony of Rosas' office they watched doña Carmen passing with her little work basket on her arm and her hair still damp from her bath. The daily visit that the doctor's wife paid to doña Matilde seemed suspicious.

"What are these people up to?"

And they lighted cigarettes and settled down behind the glass of the balcony to spy on the passersby. Next came some servant girls returning from the market, then some small boys chasing each other and shooting, with slingshots, pieces of orange peel that left red marks on their legs. Later Dr. Arrieta's horses and carriage passed. Behind it were two men carrying water. They all seemed to be innocently devoted to their tasks.

"Are the three houses under surveillance?"

"Day and night, General."

The military men found themselves conquered by the silence of Ixtepec. What could they do in the presence of those innocent faces? Of that town, radiant in the morning and dark and shifting as a swamp of sand at night?

"We have to find the informer," Corona suddenly shouted, astonished that such a simple thing had not occurred to him before.

"We have to look for him in the vicinity of the three houses."

A few days later Sergeant Illescas was courting Inés, Señora Montúfar's maid.

The General called Captain Flores to his office.

"Captain, take a walk over to Luchi's house. Find out what they know about the sacristan there."

Captain Flores was going to say something, but he encountered Francisco Rosas' determined glance and Justo Corona's rancorous eyes. Embarrassed by the unimportance of his mission, he left his superior's office without speaking. At night he came to the house of the tarts. He had not been there for several days and the girls received him coolly. The Captain pretended to be in a jovial mood, and turned on the gramophone while ordering drinks for everyone. Luchi sat down beside him. Vainly Flores tried to feel as he had felt before. He was sad: he had never imagined that one day he would have to spy on these women. What a blow to his pride!

"What's the matter?" the patrona asked.

"I don't know, this town has become very dull—I'd like to get out of here!"

Luchi lowered her eyes. Flores looked at her obliquely: he wanted to say that he was tired of shooting peasants, that he did not understand Corona's rancor or Rosas' obduracy, but he was unable to speak. He was their accomplice and had come to find out things that could cost the girl her life.

And why Luchi? What could a poor woman like her know, cut off from the world, cooped up in an evil house? Nothing! The certainty that the woman was in no way connected with the disappearance of the sacristan's body reassured him. He would carry out his orders, and then with a lighter heart he would ask her to dance. He did not know what to say or how to begin, he was a soldier, not a policeman.

"What a lot of talk there is in this town!"

"Yes," she said laconically.

"Have you heard what they're saying about the sacristan?"

"No."

"I wonder what happened to his body."

Luchi's face changed and she looked at the officer with stern eyes. He smiled to minimize the importance of the question that had disturbed her.

"You killed him and now you're trying to scare us."

"Are you sure we killed him?" Flores replied, smiling.

Luchi stood up, went to Juan Cariño's corner, and whispered something in his ear. The madman listened attentively, then rose and approached Flores.

"Young man, I beg you not to upset the order of this house by asking captious questions."

"Mr. President!"

Juan Cariño put his hands on the young man's shoulders and abruptly pushed him down in the chair; then he sat down beside Luchi and stared intently at Flores. The latter felt uneasy under the madman's imperturbable gaze.

"Look at Señorita Luchi. She is very displeased."

"Why?" asked Flores.

"Why? Oh, young fellow, you men have force but you lack reason. And so you want to blame us for your crimes. You want to have a motive for persecuting us."

Taconitos was observing the scene guardedly. Luchi came up to her.

"Get to bed right now!" she ordered angrily.

The girl obeyed without replying and left the room clicking her heels. When she passed the door to Juan Cariño's room, which was closed with a padlock, she murmured bitterly, "Crazy old man!" She kicked open the door of her room and threw herself down on the bed. She heard the gay notes of a Charleston. Her life had become impossible since the night when Juan Cariño had gone on a spree and had not come back until just before dawn.

"Hey, it's 2 A.M. and Mr. President hasn't come back yet," she had said to the patrona that night.

Luchi did not answer.

"But it's after two," she insisted.

"Well, what's it to you?"

Taconitos was curious. Very late, when the customers had gone and she was busy in the living room putting out the lamps, she heard someone scratching at the front door. "Oh, how bashful this one is!" And she blew out the last light and hid behind a chair. She scarcely dared to breathe as she heard the scratching continue. Perhaps Luchi had found a man and was hiding him jealously from her wards. She was overpowered by the strange joy that comes over the curious when they are on the verge of a secret; her heart beat violently and she felt a sharp pain in her chest. She tried to peer through the darkness: Luchi walked across the room and went through the vestibule to the front door. "How well she's kept him hidden from us!"

"This way, Mr. President," Luchi whispered as she entered the room with Juan Cariño, and Taconitos saw them moving through the dark house. Disenchanted, she was about to leave her hiding place when Luchi appeared again; she was carrying a large object under her arm and she walked across the parlor on

184

tiptoe and went through the vestibule and out to the street. "Well! What's she up to?" She heard that Luchi had left the door ajar and decided to wait. An hour went by and then the door opened softly; on the threshold of the room stood Juan Cariño, coming from the street for the second time; calmly, he entered the dark house for the second time. Taconitos was astonished. She was about to go to bed when she heard the front door creaking again and the click of the latch. She waited tremulously and saw Luchi reappear with the same object under her arm.

"You again!" Taconitos said in spite of herself.

"You've been spying on me!" Luchi replied, choking with anger.

"Mr. President is up to something. He came in twice—and he hadn't gone out."

"If you repeat it, I'll break your head open!" Luchi threatened.

Since that night her life had become unbearable; the next day, when all Ixtepec was talking about the disappearance of don Roque's body, she could not take part in the conversation. Luchi did not let her go out or work; when she had a customer, the patrona interfered and made her leave the parlor. And Taconitos, cooped up in her room, brooded.

"Hmmm. Damn it! We can't even talk any more!" and she hid her face in the pillow. She was sure that what was happening in the house never should have happened. Effortlessly she imagined what was going on in the parlor: the madman was observing Flores with angry eyes and keeping him from getting near the girls. "What a miserable life! With no work, pretty soon we'll all die of starvation!"

FIVE _____

From his balcony Francisco Rosas saw them coming, the three women with short, well-brushed hair and powdered faces, wearing their best clothes.

"Corona! Corona! Here they come!" the General yelled, amazed. Was it possible that Ixtepec was coming around?

Justo Corona rushed to the balcony. Doña Carmen Arrieta, doña Ana Moncada, and doña Elvira Montúfar were at that moment crossing the plaza in the direction of the Military Command.

"Look at them, they're coming to ask a favor, General! Be firm with them!"

"They're coming to return the sacristan's body." And Francisco Rosas smiled at the miracle.

The officers felt to see that their gabardine ties were in place, took out their combs and smoothed their hair, and then began to laugh hilariously. They had won!

The ladies were walking timidly across the patio of orange trees; escorted by a soldier, they came to the door of Rosas' office.

He had them come in without wasting an instant. They entered not daring to look him in the eye. The General gallantly offered them a chair and exchanged a look of complicity with his second in command, who, still standing, observed the women impatiently.

"What can I do for you, Señoras?"

The three ladies began to titter. They seemed nervous. Justo Corona took out a cigarette and asked amiably if he could smoke.

"Of course!" the three exclaimed in unison.

The General also lighted a cigarette and goodnaturedly sat down before them. The ladies giggled again and looked at each other in confusion.

"It's amazing how young he is," doña Elvira said to herself.

"What can I do for you?" Rosas insisted affably.

"General, we came to offer you an olive branch!" doña Elvira said pompously, happy to see how young and handsome her adversary was.

The General's yellow eyes looked at her without comprehending the meaning of her words.

"We have to clear the air. We can't live in this violence. We want to offer you our friendship to put an end to this civil war that is so harmful to all of us." The doctor's wife stopped talking; the General's look of astonishment made her forget the rest of her speech.

Doña Ana Moncada came to her rescue. "When one is face to face with an enemy, he's less of an enemy!"

"We've been so selfish with you," doña Elvira continued with a sigh, and at that moment she was sincere; she found General Francisco Rosas very good looking, and was forgetting the bad things he had done to us.

Astounded, Justo Corona hung on every word: he smoked and studied the women without understanding what they were proposing. Francisco Rosas smiled, half-closed his eyes, and waited for the doctor's wife to finish her speech. On the alert, he spied on each of the words uttered by the three friends and tried to discover what was behind their seeming innocence. He would say nothing. Silence did not make him uncomfortable; on the contrary, he moved about in it like a fish in the water. On the other hand, they were chatterers and would soon let the word slip out that told the secret of those old and mendacious faces. Doña Carmen saw that she was treading on dangerous ground and did not hesitate any longer; she launched bravely into a surprise attack.

"We are planning to give a party in your honor, General."

"A party?" Francisco Rosas exclaimed in surprise.

"Yes, General, a party," she repeated calmly. And she innocently explained that a party was the best way to proclaim that hostilities between the town and the military had ended. "Laughter erases tears," she concluded, smiling.

Francisco Rosas accepted the invitation. What else could he do? The ladies set the date for the party and, smiling amiably, left his office. The General turned to Corona.

"What do you think, Colonel?" he asked, still astonished.

"I don't know, but I don't trust women, and the women of Ixtepec even less. Maybe their little party will give them the chance to poison all of us!"

"Yes, it could be a trap." And Francisco Rosas once again wandered uncertainly through the slippery side roads of Ixtepec.

SIX

I too was surprised by the enthusiasm with which my people accepted the idea of the party for General Francisco Rosas. People are so fickle! It seemed that in an instant they all forgot about the closed church and the Virgin transmuted into flames. The posters with the Veil of Veronica and the Face of Jesus Christ no longer appeared on the doors at dawn, and the nocturnal cries of "Long live Christ the King" ceased. My nights returned to calm. The fear magically dissipated by the word "fiesta" changed into a frenzy that only finds a parallel in my memory in the madness that possessed me during the fiestas of the Centenary celebration. I remember those vertiginous days, and in my memory they are identified with the days before the fiesta of doña Carmen B. de Arrieta. That other time, the wealthy people went to Mexico City, and those of us who remained behind waited with melancholy eagerness for the luminous news we received from the capital. We were the exiles from happiness! And although we too celebrated the first century of the Independence, my fireworks and my fancy clothes were overshadowed by the dust raised by the carriages with foreign ambassadors, the brilliant parades, and the skyrockets that set the capital on fire.

Now the party for General Francisco Rosas followed in the luminous wake of the previous parties. Everyone wanted to forget the hangings along the road to Cocula. No one mentioned the dead who had been found on the highways. My people preferred the very short road to the Bengal lights, and the word "fiesta" slipped from their tongues like a beautiful skyrocket.

Juan Cariño was the most exalted of all. He continually tipped his top hat as he greeted the townspeople, and smiled with satisfaction: he was on vacation. The words that floated through the air during those days were his favorite words, and for once he could be mannerly and uncover his head without fear. His hat was emptied of evil words. In his house he spoke brilliantly of the art of the fiesta.

"It is one of the fine arts!" he explained arrogantly to the girls, who listened sadly to the preparations for the fiesta they would not attend.

"The Bengal lights have come!" he announced one afternoon as he placed his useless hat on a dirty little table in the parlor.

The girls smiled melancholically.

"The Bengal lights!" Juan Cariño repeated, trying to lighten by his words the squalor of the house where the tarts lived.

"Oh, good!" said one, not wanting to abandon him in his efforts to produce a miracle for them.

"Do you girls know what Bengal is?"

The women exchanged amazed glances, for it had never occurred to them to ask such a thing. "No, Mr. President."

"Wait a minute: the dictionary, the concerted effort of men's minds, will tell us."

Juan Cariño went to his room and several minutes later came back beaming.

"Bengal! Bengal! Extraordinary blue country in a remote land, inhabited by yellow tigers. That is Bengal, and now its lights have come to illuminate the armistice! The truce!"

The date that everyone awaited forced its way through the

days and arrived as round and perfect as an orange. And like that beautiful golden fruit, it remains in my memory to brighten the darkness that came afterward. The hours fell translucently on the surface of that day, opened a circle, and rushed pell-mell into the house of Carmen B. de Arrieta. Surrounded by luminous waves, with avid eyes and an alert body, Ixtepec waited for the moment of the fiesta. The enchanted house waited with us. The palms decorated with roses sparkled. The tiles shimmered with a waxy luster. Sprays of tulips and jasmine hung on the walls. The large pots of ferns wrapped in orange paper were suns casting green rays. At the rear of the porch a table filled with bottles and glasses tinkled under the servants' touch. The garden opened like a beautiful fan of reflected lights. The fountain, with fresh water, repeated the branches of the acacias adorned with Japanese lanterns, which opened bright paths in the water and on the lawn. Don Pepe Ocampo arranged the tables under the trees and covered them with orange tarlatan as protection against the insects. Maestro Batalla installed his musicians under the orange trees and their violins filled the foliage with the promise of things to come. A solar splendor streamed through the balconies and the door, down to the dark street.

The guests began to arrive, and people gathered outside of the house moved aside to let them pass, calling out their names.

"Here come the Olveras!"

"The Cuevases are arriving!"

And the guests, laughing and talking loudly, passed through the doorway with a fearless air, as if they were about to plunge headlong into a blazing fire. The poor, the "little heaps of rubbish" as Dorotea called them, were satisfied with the generosity of the open balconies, and scrambled to pick up the bits and pieces of the party. "Isabel is wearing red," said one. "Doña Carmen has a fan of white feathers!" said another from a neighboring balcony. At nine o'clock the committee of young ladies who were to go to the door of the Hotel Jardín to bring the General and his aides left the house. We watched them go.

"Here they come with the officers!" And we hurried to the entrance to see the young girls arriving with the men.

"Here they come! Here they come!" We spread apart to give the guest of honor room to pass.

General Francisco Rosas, tall, silent, with his Texas hat pushed back on his head, his boots with a high polish, his trousers and his military shirt of light-colored gabardine, appeared among us, surrounded by the three young girls, and entered the Arrietas' house. We saw him as if for the first time. He was followed by his General Staff: we recognized Justo Corona, Captain Flores, and Captain Pardiñas, who was from Cocula and had very black eyes that looked in all directions like fans. Lieutenant Colonel Cruz was not in the group.

A breath of freshness, a smell of shaving cream, lotion, and mild tobacco entered the fiesta with them. They stood motionless on the threshold, waiting for the hostess, who came out tremulously to greet them. The General slowly took off his hat, outlined a smile that seemed faintly derisive, and bowed respectfully to her. His aides did likewise and the group advanced through the lighted porch, greeting the guests with brief nods. Doña Carmen's guests received the greeting like a favor.

Don Pepe Ocampo ran to talk with Maestro Batalla, who from the bottom of the garden watched in amazement as the group came in. And then the orchestra burst into a flourish.

Memory is treacherous and at times inverts the order of events or brings us to a dark inlet where nothing happens. I do not remember what happened after the officers came. I only see the General standing there, with his weight on one leg; I hear him saying thank you in a low voice, then I see him dancing three times: once with each of the young ladies who went to bring him to the party. I see Isabel's glance very close to his chest, and I see how absorbed she was when Rosas brought her to her place and how, before he left her, he bowed. I see Conchita, who did not grasp the rhythm of the music and made excuses that he accepted graciously. Then Micaela, speaking to her partner's indulgent

192

smile. And I see him alone once again, smoking with his men in that corner of the porch. Beside him the party whirled round and round, bringing couples together and separating them.

The frosty trays circulated translucently; the guests held their cold glasses and kept their sanity intact for an instant as they felt the discipline of the icy coldness in their hands. From the balconies the poor people sang a chorus to the music. Their shouts entered the party in bursts of exultation.

Alone, Isabel took refuge by a pillar and occupied a chair under the sprays of bougainvillea. Absentmindedly she tore off clusters of flowers and chewed on them. Tomás Segovia leaned over her. The girl looked at him sightlessly; the factitious good looks of that small man with curly hair and delicate, effeminate features annoyed her.

"Care to dance, Isabelita?"

"No."

Tomás Segovia did not lose his self-possession at her refusal; he pulled up a chair and contentedly sat down beside his friend. After several moments he looked in one of his pockets for a piece of paper and handed it to Isabel. She took it inquisitively.

"My latest poem. It's dedicated to you."

The young pharmacist still spent his time making verses; his love for poetry had not diminished. Isabel read the poem disinterestedly.

"Oh, is that me?"

"Yes, 'divine creature,' " Segovia said, blinking to give greater emphasis to his words. And then to himself he added sadly, "What's the difference whether I was referring to her or someone else? I'm in love with a person who is insensible to poetry: yes, to Poetry—with a capital *P*."

" 'Like a feather in the confines of oblivion!' " Isabel read, interrupting his thoughts. And the girl uttered a laugh that pierced the party and caused her father to look at her in amazement. Tomás was not offended by his friend's merriment. Her laughter gave him a pretext to elaborate a complicated theory on "the maleficent art of flirtation." Isabel let him talk. Disheartened by the silence of the one he loved, Segovia went away to the shelter of another pillar and observed the girl from that vantage point. He liked "impossible" loves; they gave him "the exquisite pleasure of failure."

Isabel was alone again, with her far from promising thoughts. Her father approached.

"Why don't you dance with Tomás?"

"I don't like poets, they only think of themselves. Who wants to hear him today?"

"That's why you should dance with him, because he talks nonsense. That way you'd stop thinking of what you're thinking of."

Don Martín turned to see if anyone was listening; then he bowed gallantly to his daughter and invited her to dance. The two twirled by the General, who, surrounded by his intimates, continued in his reserved posture. Was it that he did not want to mingle with us, or could not?

He seemed different from everyone. When we saw him so quiet, with that sadness in his eyes, who would have said that he was the organizer of the persecution we were suffering? He must have been very young, perhaps not even thirty. A smile hovered on his lips; he seemed to be smiling at himself. Isabel's mother went up to him.

"I'm a Cuétara. Do you remember the family?" Her surname revealed that she too was from the north.

"Yes, Señora, I remember them."

"They were my brothers," the señora explained.

The General looked at her as if he understood her loss. "They died . . . well, they died before . . ." he said as a kind of condolence.

"Before what?" the señora inquired.

"Before those of us who are here tonight," the General said, and indicated that he considered the conversation closed.

At ten o'clock the guests sat down at the tables that had been placed in the garden. Tomás Segovia, who proposed the toast, gave a speech that was liberally sprinkled with Latin quotations.

194

He directed eloquent praise and meaningful glances at the General.

At last he could talk in a "patrician" language! Rosas listened to the praise with the same indifference he always showed to anything that came from us. Sitting on his left, Isabel looked at the General's hands resting on the tablecloth and was silent, offended by his distant manner. The other officers, scattered at different tables, laughed and joked with their dinner companions.

Justo Corona was the only one who carefully watched, from a distance, his superior's every move; he seemed impatient and frequently looked at his wristwatch. The conversation, animated by the drinking, wound around the trees, the laughter swept through the garden, and Corona, impassive, went on stalking the General.

After dinner the dancing resumed and the General, taciturn, again took up his position in a corner of the porch. Justo Corona joined him and they conversed in low voices. Isabel did not let them out of her sight: she saw Corona make a signal to Pardiñas, who was happily dancing, and she saw the latter leave his partner and approach the other officers. They gathered around the General, who constantly consulted his wristwatch. Isabel turned pale and went to find the hostess.

"I wonder what's going on," she whispered in doña Carmen's ear.

The señora turned with a start and looked in dismay at the men who, apparently about to leave the party, were picking up their hats and searching for her with their eyes.

"What shall we do, my child?" the señora asked fearfully.

"Stop them!" Isabel begged.

Doña Carmen rushed toward the officers to block their way. "Why so early, General?"

"Duty, Señora."

"No, no! Why, you haven't had anything to drink. Come, just one little glass."

General Francisco Rosas surveyed her coldly. The guests stopped dancing and looked in amazement at the group that was

195

struggling to leave and the hostess who was insisting that they stay a while longer. "Are they going now?" the guests asked one another, disenchanted. "Why?"

Ana Moncada, looking strangely pale, went to her husband.

"Be calm! Nothing has happened," he said, feigning serenity.

"I don't know! I don't know!" she answered, trembling.

Isabel looked at her mother and then at the officers; then she pushed her way through the guests and went bravely up to the General. "You can't break up the party!" she said, and held out her arm, inviting him to dance.

Francisco Rosas stared at her in surprise, gave Corona his hat, and put his arm around the young girl's waist. The two twirled in time to the music. Isabel, her cheeks rouged and her eyes riveted on the General, seemed to be roaming through a bloody world. Rosas watched her obliquely, not daring to speak. He became even more serious when he saw that his aides were imitating him and giving in to doña Carmen as she brought them partners.

"Play without any breaks between the numbers, Maestro!" urged don Joaquín, dashing over to the musicians.

Batalla looked at him in consternation, and did as he was told without understanding why. He felt that something very important was at stake and he was grateful to don Joaquín for having made him a part of the secret.

Enthusiastically he played one piece after another and the partners danced without interruption. From their balconies the townspeople uttered joyful outcries to underscore the General's dance with Isabel. The hostess sent them bottles of liquor, which they welcomed with a rain of skyrockets.

Amid the glow of joviality, Sergeant Illescas pushed his way through the crowd and came to the Arrietas' door. With a serious expression he entered the house, followed by a picket of soldiers. Doña Carmen came to meet him. Illescas' solemn Indian face did not change its expression. Without paying any attention to her he went over to the General, who was still dancing with Isabel, stood at attention, and asked to have a word with him. Francisco Rosas stopped dancing, bowed to his partner, and went up to the

196

hostess, followed by Illescas. The fiesta came to a sudden stop. In vain Maestro Batalla went on playing one piece after another without a pause. Doña Carmen accompanied Rosas to another room and the General and Illescas disappeared inside, closing the door after them. The officers silently exchanged guilty glances. The uneasy guests stared at the door through which Francisco Rosas had disappeared.

Señor Moncada poured himself a large glass of brandy and drank it in one gulp. "Did it really happen?" Isabel looked for a chair and fell into it with her arms dangling limply and a vacant look on her face. The music petered out.

"What's going on?" Maestro Batalla asked from the bottom of the garden.

Don Pepe Ocampo ran to talk to him. "A jarabe, Maestro. Play a nice little jarabe!"

And the jarabe filled the treetops, advanced merrily through the porch, and soared rapidly up to the sky.

In the kitchen the servant girls were preparing large pots of coffee. Perspiring, they ran from one side to the other, stirring up the coals; they were happy to be taking part in the most brilliant party Ixtepec had ever had. Suddenly Charito appeared by the fire; she was pale and breathless.

"Gracious! What a scare you gave us, Señorita Chayo!"

The pious woman, wrapped in her black shawl, advanced toward the maids. "Live coals will rain on the accursed ones! Angels will part the flames to protect the just! The earth will open to give way to the infernal monsters, the demons will dance with glee seeing how the earth swallows up the blessed, and Satan, refulgent in flames of sulphur, with his red-hot pitchfork, will view this infernal dance and the world disappearing in a vast pestilential blaze of fire."

"What's the matter, Señorita Chayo?" asked the maids, frightened by the words and attitude of the woman.

"Where is Carmelita? Call Carmelita!"

"Sit down, Señorita Chayo! We're going to give you some cof-

197

fee," the servants said, upset by the woman's sudden arrival, which interrupted the gaiety of the party we had planned so joyously.

Chayito rejected the coffee and refused to sit down. One of the maids went to get the señora. Doña Carmen entered the kitchen; she was worried, and when she saw the woman she became scared.

"Be still, Chayito, you're going to make things worse!" the señora shrieked when the pious woman began the speech again.

"They caught them!" the old lady replied, letting her arms fall in a gesture of helplessness.

"Be quiet! You're mistaken. I don't have time to talk now." And doña Carmen, not wanting to listen, ran out of the kitchen.

Followed by Sergeant Illescas, the General left the room at the very moment when the hostess reappeared on the porch. Doña Carmen, with several ladies trailing her, hurried to meet them. With her arms hanging limply at her sides and her eyes somber, Isabel joined the group. The men did not speak.

"Is something wrong, General?" the señora asked in a firm voice.

"No, Señora."

Doña Carmen smiled.

"Unfortunately, I have to leave," Rosas added, also smiling.

"Leave? You're threatening to leave us again? And the party? It was for you, General!"

Francisco Rosas looked deep into her eyes, partly with admiration, partly with curiosity. "I have to leave," he repeated.

"But—will you be back?" the señora urged, as if she were asking for one last favor.

The General laughed. It was the first time we had seen him laugh; his face was like a child's, and malice shone from his eyes. He stared at the señora and then, as if he had a sudden inspiration, said, "The party is not over, Señora! I'll be back to bring it to a close. Everyone must go on dancing until I return!" And saying this he looked for his intimates; one of them held out his hat; Francisco Rosas took it with determination. He bit his lip and

198

started to walk toward the door, followed by his men, who quickly bowed their heads to us in farewell. Halfway there he stopped, wheeled around, and glanced at us. His eyes rested on Isabel, who was watching him leave incredulously.

The General turned to the Captain. "Flores, you stay here until I come back! See that the music continues and people dance. And that no one leaves until I give the order!" He turned brusquely to Isabel again and gazed at her fixedly. "Only the señorita may return to her home—if she wishes," he said in a very loud voice. Then, raising his voice even more and making a show of calling someone, he yelled, "Music, Maestro!"

The orchestra, overcome by the strangeness of the moment, embarked on a waltz. Mingled with its melancholy melody were the General's footsteps as they reverberated on the tiled porch and the rhythmical steps of the other officers. We watched them leave the party and then, disenchanted, we watched each other. Captain Flores closed the door and seemed embarrassed before the guests, who looked at him apprehensively. The guard brought by Sergeant Illescas remained with him.

"Keep playing, Maestro, the General does not want the party to be interrupted," Flores ordered uncertainly.

The guests kept silent as they listened in surprise to a Charleston.

"Dance, please!" Flores ordered.

No one moved, and Flores' words fell in vain on the motionless groups in their party clothes. Don Joaquín slowly crossed the porch and walked up to Señora Montúfar.

"They are probably searching my house," he whispered in his friend's ear.

"Be quiet, for goodness' sake!" the señora shrieked, fanning herself furiously.

"They must have caught them," don Joaquín insisted.

"For pity's sake, Joaquín, don't make me nervous!" doña Elvira shrieked more loudly than before.

"Don't be afraid, you're in a safe place," doña Carmen said, joining them.

199

"There's no safe place," don Joaquín replied.

The two women exchanged uneasy glances; he was right.

"It's true—but we have to act as if there were," doña Carmen replied.

"I told them over and over again that this was ridiculous, that we should find another solution," he said reproachfully.

"Another solution? Another solution?" Señora Montúfar seemed very offended.

The hostess bowed her head without paying attention to her friend's protestations.

The music disarticulated doña Elvira's words and gestures.

"What a disaster! What a disaster! We must dance!" And doña Carmen left her friends and went to find her husband.

Others followed their lead and danced.

"Remember when we weren't afraid?"

"Afraid? I've always been afraid. Perhaps less afraid now because I have something real to be afraid of. The worst thing is to be afraid of the enemy hidden behind the days," the doctor replied, still dancing, and leaning on the words to forget the fear that was gradually taking possession of his party.

They came close to Isabel, and Dr. Arrieta preferred not to look at her; his wife, on the other hand, winked at the girl, who did not return the wink. Her father, very pale, was with her.

"Everything's gone wrong!" Isabel said out loud.

"Don't jump to conclusions. We still don't know," he replied, trying to believe in his words.

"What more do you want to know? We're prisoners!"

"No, *we're* not. If everything had gone wrong, he certainly wouldn't let *us* leave!"

Isabel looked at him despairingly; her father did not believe what he was saying.

"Let's dance," he said, to drive away an unpleasant thought.

"I'm not going to dance any more, I want to leave," Isabel begged.

Martín Moncada tried to imagine what the world would be

like without that dark day which cast shadows in his memory and left him in an absurd place where he did not even recognize Isabel's voice.

Where did she want to go? He had entered the subterranean world of the ants, complicated by minuscule tunnels where there was not even room for a thought and where memory was layers of earth and roots of trees. Perhaps that was like the memory of the dead: an anthill without ants, only narrow passages through the earth, with no exit to the grass.

"I always knew what was going on. Nicolás knew, too. Since we were children we have been dancing on this day." Isabel's words caused landslides; layers of silent earth erased the subterranean world where Martín Moncada went in pursuit of his memory.

"Don't say such things, my dear."

He remembered where he was, and he remembered Juan and Nicolás. A rain of centuries fell on the party in Ixtepec. And had he unleashed the landslide of the centuries on the bodies of his children? He was one of the enthusiasts of that madness. Now he could not find the memory that had pushed him up to that moment of shattered music. He had walked through blind days. "It would be better if I had not been born." He bowed his head; he did not want to look at Isabel. "It would be better if she had not been born." His children, at his insistence, returned tragically to the unknown fate he took them out of on three different nights that now blended into a single night. In that instant they moved backward to a placeless, spaceless, lightless place. All he had left was the memory of the weight of cathedrals on their bodiless bodies. He lost his other memory and also lost the privilege of the astonishing light.

"I knew it. I knew it," Isabel repeated in her red dress, which weighed and coruscated like a stone in the sunlight. Her eyes fell on Tomás Segovia, sitting beside Conchita, drawing figures in the air to illustrate his words. "People like him don't get burned; they live in the frigid zone," and from the glowing weight of her red dress she tried to imagine Juan and Nicolás. "Let's go!" she urged.

She was incapable of moving and incapable of staying on the lighted porch. Martín Moncada went to find his wife, and the three made their round of farewells. Without knowing why, we said goodbye to them as if they were going away forever. A strange destiny was taking them away from the party; they were the only ones who could leave the house, and yet none of us envied them. The men lowered their heads in a gesture of mourning and the women eyed them anxiously, as one contemplates a known face that will soon be covered with earth.

"You wanted it, my dear," her uncle Joaquín murmured, giving her a kiss.

Isabel did not respond to the caress. Captain Flores opened the door and the Moncadas, very pale, went out into the night. The street was empty. The people, who only an hour before had festooned the balconies, had vanished.

"Dance, please!" Flores urged.

No one listened to him. The astonished guests looked toward the door that had just closed on the Moncadas. Captain Flores let his arms fall without knowing what to say or whom to turn to; he too endured a moment of astonishment. Doña Carmen came up to him cordially and led him by the hand to a group of young ladies.

"Which one of you is going to dance with the Captain?"

The girls blushed. The señora smiled at one and all, and called the servants to bring the trays of drinks, but no one touched them; Señora Arrieta's efforts were useless, the party was at a standstill. Fear hovered behind the music, keeping the branches of the trees and the guests quiet. The silent balconies announced to us the catastrophe that had occurred in Ixtepec.

"I'm very warm!" Conchita sighed sadly as she joined her mother.

"What are you saying! It's not a bit warm! I'm very cold," and Señora Montúfar violently tossed her fan away. It fell noiselessly into the garden.

Conchita blushed and covered her face with her hands, as if

she were going to cry. "Don't do that, Mamá! They'll say you're an eccentric widow."

"It's eccentric to be cold? What evil tongues these people have!" and doña Elvira seemed to be on the verge of one of her fits of anger, which were so well known in Ixtepec.

"I'm also cold, and warm at the same time," don Joaquín said in a monotonous voice.

"Go and dance, dear! Go and dance, because we're all going to die here this very night!" the señora said to her daughter.

"I don't want to dance. It's three o'clock in the morning," Conchita replied, ready to provoke her mother's anger by her disobedience. She was tired and depressed. She did not dare to cry, for if she did they would ask for explanations, and Nicolás Moncada was her secret.

"Three o'clock in the morning? My goodness, three o'clock in the morning and that man hasn't come back yet!" Doña Elvira lapsed into silence, opening astounded eyes.

At Flores' insistence, several couples were dancing like sleep-walkers, while the other guests struck motionless, grotesque poses. A lull had settled on the party.

Groups of soldiers took up positions near the balconies of the doctor's house and peered curiously at the remnants of the interrupted party.

"The soldiers have arrived!" don Joaquín whispered to doña Elvira.

"They're going to shoot us," she said, reddening with anger.

When dawn's first rays illuminated the garden sky, the orchestra played "Las Mañanitas," and doña Carmen ordered that broth and hot coffee be served to refresh the guests, who languished in their chairs. The women were sleepy, and in the greenish light of morning their dresses were ageing rapidly.

The men spoke in low voices and held their coffee cups with unsteady hands. The lack of sleep and the early daylight made them shiver with cold. Only Captain Flores was unchanged as he kept close watch on the door.

In the kitchen Charito no longer spoke or moved. Doña Carmen's prolonged absence caused her to keep silent. It was useless to talk, everything was useless, they were lost. Sitting in a wicker chair with her eyes bloodshot from the lack of sleep, the old lady had an air of stupidity.

"Have some coffee, Señorita Chayo."

The woman accepted the coffee and drank it awkwardly, lost in thoughts which the morning sun had dulled.

"How different this morning is from last night!" one of the maids said.

The others, sitting around the stove and absorbed in their fatigue, did not answer. The radiant comet the house had once been was nothing but ashes now, placed by the sun in an orbit of heat. The remains of the nocturnal fire were changed into a mirror light that made the guests' eyes water.

They took doña Elvira to a room where she could lie down; with frightened, wide-open eyes she waited for the General to return.

"Hasn't that man come back?"

"No, Mamá, he hasn't come back," her daughter answered, tired of hearing the same question over and over again. If her mother had listened to her, they would not be in this situation, but the señora did not allow her to speak and Conchita never had a chance to tell her about the dangerous cracks in doña Elvira's plan to deceive the military men. Conchita, astonished that the adults had accepted her mother's blunder, chose to keep silent. Now doña Elvira, sick with fear, asked continually whether her enemy was back yet. "Why does she want him to return? So she can know the full extent of her madness?" And the young girl looked contemptuously at her mother.

"Hasn't that man come back?"

"No, Mamá, he hasn't come back."

The insistent question jolted Conchita out of the pleasure of being able to think her own thoughts, hidden in the cool shadows of the room. At least she had escaped the unmerciful sun of 2 P.M.

204

and the nauseating spectacle the fiesta had become. She no longer had to look at the tables filled with scraps of food on which the flies freely alighted. Astonished, she had contemplated how the lawn and the porch were strewn with corks, pieces of bread, empty bottles, papers and debris that issued from a secret purveyor of filth. Conchita had been sickened by that invasion of offal. The flower garlands were wilted and the women's clothing wet with perspiration and in a sorry state. Some couples were still dancing under Flores' glance, which had become ferocious. Hidden in that white room she felt safe. She could hear the footsteps of the soldiers patrolling the doctor's house.

Don Joaquín entered the room to find out how his friend was; he walked to the window and looked out warily. The day was well advanced and the street was still empty.

"It seems that everyone has died," he said in a hollow voice.

Doña Elvira kept perfectly still. Her daughter touched her hair, took off the wilted flowers that had adorned her dark head the night before, sadly put the flowers on the night table, and remained melancholically at her mother's side.

"This is a very long day."

"It will never end. We shall have to stay here forever." And the señora turned to her daughter, looking for approval.

"Well, it's getting later, it's two now," Conchita said angrily.

"Since the night when Hurtado went away, I've known that something horrible was going to happen to us," the old man added, still in the same tone of voice.

"I wish we could all lie down!" the señora exclaimed, sitting up tragically in bed.

"That way we would not see what we are going to see," don Joaquín agreed.

"They're smarter than we are! We're blind!" doña Elvira moaned.

"God blinds the one He wants to ruin."

Elsewhere the servants were passing around warmed-over food from the previous evening. The guests felt more like weeping than eating, and stared at their plates despondently. Maestro Batalla threw his plate at a tree and went resolutely up to Captain Flores.

"Mr. Captain, this is an outrage! I have to go home. Look at the faces of my men."

Some of the guests joined the protest. It seemed for a few minutes that everyone was rebelling.

"These are my orders! Orders!" Flores repeated.

Fear made them silent and the orchestra attempted a march, which was interrupted by the fainting of a violinist. The incident caused a commotion; the men rushed to the garden and the women uttered shrieks of horror. The tumult reached the room where doña Elvira was resting.

"The first death has occurred!" the señora yelled.

The garden was ablaze in the dry radiance of 4 P.M. The blanched lawns, the motionless branches, and the smoldering stones were consumed in a stationary bonfire. A monotonous chorus of crickets serenaded its destruction. The sun revolved, sending us its inflexible rays. No trace of humidity, no memory of water came to save us from the set of thirsty reflections. Time did not move forward and the mountains that guard the sun disappeared from the horizon. Collapsed in the chairs, calcined and without hope, we waited. The servants, barefoot and dry-lipped, served bright-colored drinks. We watched them passively.

Tomás Segovia vomited violently and no one went to help him. He went on sitting in the same chair, as if he were on his deathbed, far removed from shame or conformity. Brutally separated from his world of rhymes and syllables, he detached himself from the occurrence, and with his head resting on one shoulder napped for a long time with no concern for his place or his stained clothing. Captain Flores, standing by a pillar, observed him like one who observes a broken doll. Dr. Arrieta walked over to the officer.

"When is this nonsense going to end?" he said, red with anger.

Captain Flores seemed mortified and averted his eyes. "I don't know, I don't know anything, I just have my orders."

"Orders? Orders?"

206

"What do you expect me to do?" Flores whined.

The doctor seemed to be reflecting. Then he looked at the officer with curiosity and offered him a cigarette.

"Nothing!"

And the two men talked about politics by the bright plaster pillar, oblivious of the presence of the others.

The first shadows of dusk found us in inert, dirty groups. Now no none cared about anybody's fate. The town was still dead. Vaguely we had heard the sound of the soldiers as the guards were relieved from time to time. Doña Carmen peered out of the balcony to see the end of the dead day in the dead town.

"Nothing! No one!" And the señora entered the house to order that the lamps be lighted.

The servants came to carry out her wish and circulated among the guests, illuminating their pale faces.

"Maestro, play something gay!" Flores ordered in consternation.

Maestro Batalla did not move or respond to the officer's order.

Don Pepe Ocampo backed up the Captain's request. "Maestro, please . . . for everyone's sake . . ."

The maestro looked at him with rancor and don Pepe felt like a stranger among the civilians. He walked away from the orchestra and tried to straighten his dirty silk shirt and wrinkled tie. He let himself fall into a chair and audibly began a rosary, which no one answered. The only thing left for him at that hostile moment was to invoke God. The night advanced slowly, the water of the fountain was black and without reflected light, the branches of the trees grew until they hid the sky, the insects hovered around the lighted candelabra, and the eyes of the guests, absorbed in their fatigue, seemed not to notice their presence. From time to time they heard the voice of Señora Montúfar asking her question, each time louder than the one before.

"Hasn't that man come back?"

Her question came from a world where actions still counted and hope existed. Disturbed, the guests listened to her shriek, which broke the harmony of the silence. They had given themselves up to despair. Man accepts violence with the same readiness with which he accepts quietude, and the party of Carmen B. de Arrieta had accepted death. The crack, crack of the knocker did not resuscitate them from the chairs they were sprawled on. Perhaps Elvira Montúfar was right and things still happened in the world, but—in what world? And who was interested in these things now? Only Captain Flores, who rushed to open the door.

Followed by his men, Francisco Rosas entered Dr. Arrieta's house for the second time. No one went to greet him, and the wizened eyes saw him pass as if they had not seen him. His coming no longer mattered. The women let him look at them without even lifting a finger to touch their disheveled hair. The men, convinced of the uselessness of any gesture, kept quiet. Astonished, Francisco Rosas contemplated the scene. He and his men were fresh and clean. The same scent of lotion and mild tobacco enveloped them, and only their swollen eyes betrayed their lack of sleep. The General scarcely acknowledged Flores' salute. He seemed indecisive before those shattered people.

Doña Carmen came to greet him. "How late you are, General! But, as you see, we're all here waiting for you, just as you requested." And she formed a smile.

The General looked at her with irony. "I'm sorry, Señora. I wasn't able to come back sooner, as you know."

The doctor joined his wife and greeted the General with a nod.

"Doctor, you will kindly accompany me."

Dr. Arrieta did not answer. His pale face became even paler.

"Your wife, too," Rosas added without looking at doña Carmen.

"Should I bring anything?" she asked innocently.

"Whatever you wish, Señora."

A grave silence greeted his words. Some of the guests stood up and came cautiously to the group formed by the couple and General Francisco Rosas.

"My men are going to search the house."

No one answered. Rosas signaled to Colonel Corona and he, accompanied by four soldiers, went through the rooms. They could be heard shaking wardrobes, moving furniture, emptying drawers. Corona's voice grew gruff as he gave orders. The doctor and his wife heard the soldiers penetrating their intimate domain and a fine sweat appeared on their foreheads.

The General called to don Joaquín, who innocently came running.

"Tell me, Señor, do you plan to join the army?"

"General, what a thing to say! You know me too well to ask such a question, and, besides, at my age . . . If I were younger . . ."

"Seize him!" Rosas interrupted.

Captain Pardiñas took the old man by the shoulders and placed him between the soldiers. Don Joaquín looked at us all with shipwrecked eyes and did something unexpected: he took out his handkerchief and began to cry. Doña Matilde tried to go to her husband but Pardiñas held her back.

"Careful, Señora, the Colonel gave you fair warning. You'll be the loser!"

Don Joaquín moved his head and tried to say something, but his sobs kept him from speaking. We waited for his words.

"I'm crying from shame . . . shame for all of you . . ." he said to the officers through his tears.

Francisco Rosas bit his lip and turned away. "Bring me the pious woman who came in last night a few minutes before Sergeant Illescas."

Doña Carmen looked at the General with loathing: he knew everything, he had tricked them and caught them in their own trap.

Charito appeared at the back of the dark porch. Wrapped in her black rebozo, she advanced in a straight line without concern for the scattered chairs or the guests' glances. Rosas watched her coming, tilted his head and, without taking his eyes off the woman, said to his aide, "Watch out, Pardiñas, she's armed."

As if she had heard, the pious woman let her arms fall and walked up to the General. "Here is the pious woman," she said softly.

The soldiers grasped her by the shoulders and placed her beside don Joaquín.

"You were in last night's disturbance!" Francisco Rosas said, smiling.

The Colonel came out of the rooms he had been searching. He had many papers that were identical to those that had appeared on doors and windows with the legend: "Long live Christ the King!" The soldiers brought rifles and pistols. Doña Carmen and the doctor looked at them in amazement as if they did not know that those posters and those firearms had been kept in their house.

"We found this in the señora's room, General."

"Take the evidence to the Command," Rosas replied dryly. Then, in a different tone, he added, "In the name of the Government of Mexico, Arístides Arrieta, Carmen B. de Arrieta, Joaquín Meléndez, and Rosario Cuéllar are under arrest. Colonel Corona, take them to the military prison!"

The doctor, his wife, Charito, and don Joaquín, with their hands tied behind their backs, were placed in the middle of a picket of soldiers.

Then the General asked for a complete guest list and drew up a document that everyone signed.

"You may go to your homes and stay there until a new order is issued."

No one moved. We were hypnotized. The General wanted to clear the air, and so he shouted to Batalla in a carefree voice, "Music, Maestro!"

Maestro Batalla showed no signs of life.

"Play an Ave Maria."

Batalla approached grumblingly. "But, General, how . . ."

"Oh, so you are a Cristero too?"

Batalla fled to the bottom of the dark garden. "Boys, the Ave Maria."

"Adiós, dear hearts!" shouted General Francisco Rosas. And amid the chords of the Ave Maria he made an about-face and left Dr. Arrieta's house.

The guard leading the prisoners followed him. The guests lowered their eyes, not wanting to look at them.

Through the wide-open door the guests began to slip noise-

210

lessly, wordlessly into the night. The silence and the darkness of my streets greeted them. They encountered no one but the sentinels who were patrolling Ixtepec.

"Who's there?"

"Us . . ."

"Let them pass. It's the guests!"

Doña Matilde came out alone. As she entered the night she remembered how she had looked for the sacristan, and felt that for the second time she was entering the unreal world of crime. She wanted to go quickly, to reach her dwelling and escape from the danger that awaited her among the shadows.

She walked along, stumbling on stones, groping her way through my streets. As she passed the prison walls, she wondered if it was really true that her husband was in there, separated from her forever.

"Joaquín is waiting for me at home," she said to herself to pretend that she was just having a bad dream. "When I wake up I'll be lying in bed between my starched sheets." And what if dying was wanting to awaken and not awakening, ever again? Full of anguish, she reached the door of her house and hammered incessantly with the brass ring, certain that no one would hear her or open the door, which became more and more deaf and impenetrable with each knock. After a while, Tefa half-opened the door.

"Señora!" And the maid burst into tears.

Doña Matilde advanced through the safe paths of her house. She was inside of her known walls, out of the nightmare that had threatened never to end, and she did not notice Estefanía's tears or the disorder in the ransacked rooms. It seemed that a hurricane had visited the house.

"Last night they came . . . They turned everything upside down, and took the Señor's rifles. They wouldn't let us go out at all."

"Let's go and make my bed," doña Matilde interrupted, looking at the mattresses that had been thrown on the floor.

"And the Señor?"

"They took him away."

"They took him away!"

The two women stared at one another. There was someone who took people away, who took them out of their houses to hide them in a dark place. "They took him away" was worse than dying. They chose to be silent. The word that could restore don Joaquín to the order of his house did not exist. The señora let herself fall into a rocking chair, and Estefanía began to arrange the bed, not wanting to look at her mistress.

"We don't know what happened to Dorotea. Last night we heard shots. She hasn't said anything and we haven't budged from here. After the soldiers left we heard shooting in Dorotea's house."

"Call her through the fence," the señora ordered wearily.

Tefa and Cástulo cautiously approached the wall that separated doña Matilde's house from Dorotea's. Leaning against the wall, they strained to hear a sound from the next garden, but a hollow silence prevailed. Above, a dark sky and some orange stars looked down on what was happening in Dorotea's burned house.

Apprehensive because of the silence, Estefanía and Cástulo went to get a ladder, propped it against the wall, and began to climb up to see what was happening on the other side. Cástulo had scarcely poked his head over the top when an alarmed voice shouted, "Who goes there?"

"An honest man!" Cástulo replied, quickly crouching down.

"What do you want?" asked the voice.

"I want to know what happened to Dorotea."

"What do you think! There she is, lying by the door with her face covered with flies!" they cried.

"But, for God's sake, let me come and shroud her."

"We have no orders for that. The only order we have is to arrest anyone who enters this house."

"You shouldn't leave a person's eyes open like that," Cástulo said, peering over the wall.

"Don't get mad, we're going to close her eyes now." Then the same voice, farther away and amplified by the arch of the door, yelled, "It's too late! She's too stiff!"

212

Tefa crossed herself and went to get a sheet to use as a shroud for Dorotea. Cástulo threw it over to the other side.

"There's the shroud! Pray for her!"

"She was a sly old lady. Why did she hide the sacristan?"

"Only God can judge her."

"Very true. Why don't you go and ask permission to bury her? See the General, because she's already started to stink. She's been lying here since 2 A.M.," they replied from the other side of the wall.

Doña Matilde's manservant thanked them for the advice. "May God be with you. Good night."

"Good night to you, Señor," they answered courteously.

Before he told the señora, Cástulo went to the kitchen, followed by Estefanía. "Look in my room for the rolls of paper to make the garlands and the little flags. I'll be back soon, God willing."

The servants stood in a group looking stunned, as if they had not heard his words.

"These days God is not willing for anything . . . and the misfortunes are getting tiresome," murmured Ignacio, who was in charge of the large kettle, as he stood up to do the errand for Cástulo.

The latter left the kitchen and went to the señora's room to give her the news. He entered on tiptoe, afraid that he would frighten her. Doña Matilde did not move from her wicker chair. In a low voice the man announced Dorotea's death and the señora, without any show of surprise, ordered him to go to the Military Command to ask permission to recover her friend's body.

"If you aren't back by dawn, we'll see what we can do for you."

"At this moment, a scorpion's life is worth more than a man's," he replied.

"That's true," Tefa agreed, huddled at her mistress' feet.

Cástulo was afraid to go out into the darkness of the street and to walk through those lonely places. He knew that the house was under surveillance and that the soldiers would give him no quarter. Any word, the slightest movement that aroused suspicion, would mean his life. Blinded by the shadows, he took his first steps into the night.

A hand seized him by the shoulder. "Where are you going?"

"To the Command, Sir."

"Get going!"

With two men following him, he reached the presbytery. He found much activity there: the patio was ablaze with lights and groups of officers came and went, laughing and talking gaily. They took him to an office and put him before two officers sitting at typewriters. Cástulo lowered his eyes without daring to state his request. The soldier who accompanied him explained his case.

"Wait!" they told him gruffly.

"I'd like to know . . ." doña Matilde's servant began.

"Wait, the Colonel is questioning Juan Cariño."

When he heard the madman's name, he wanted to ask a question, but he thought better of it and kept silent.

"Wait, I tell you!" the officer shouted again.

"That's what I'm doing, Sir."

"Well, get out of the way."

Troubled, he looked for a less prominent place; as the room was too small for him to pass unnoticed, he stood close to a wall, in the corner that seemed to be farthest removed from the officers, and waited with lowered eyes, holding his palm hat. The officers acted in his presence with the insolence of the powerful in the presence of the lowly: they told dirty jokes, smoked arrogantly, and talked about the well-known people of Ixtepec. Embarrassed, Cástulo looked at his feet. He could not leave without getting a reply, and he could not help hearing words that mortified him. He felt he was listening to secrets that did not concern him and he tried tactfully not to hear the conversation.

An hour passed and no one called him. The servant sank into a dusty sadness which left him alone in that room filled with voices and smoke. He was less than a stranger, he did not exist, he was no one, and in his capacity of a nobody he stared at his feet in those worn leather sandals, wishing he could disappear. He heard women's footsteps approaching, and raised his eyes in surprise: two of the girls from Luchi's house walked up to the officers sitting at the typewriters.

"We want to talk to the General," they said in a low voice.

"As if he's waiting for you!"

A chorus of laughter greeted the Lieutenant's reply.

"Well, we'd like to talk to someone."

"Wait!"

The women looked for a corner where they could wait, and dejectedly took refuge beside doña Matilde's servant.

SEVEN ─────────────────────────

On the night of doña Carmen's party, no one knocked at the door of Luchi's house and the balconies of the little red parlor remained closed. The girls who gathered in the kitchen had the useless air of rubbish discarded in the wastebasket. On such nights the realization of their ugliness made them bitter. They did not want to look at each other; they resembled each other too much, the same tangled hair and the same obtuse lips. Oppressed by their negligence, they ate their tacos without appetite and made obscene allusions.

"You'll see! You'll see!" Sitting on the floor with her robe open, Taconitos ate her tortilla soberly and said the same words over and over again.

"Be quiet!" the others said impatiently.

"Misfortunes are piling up, one after the other. You'll see!" she repeated.

"We're not going to see anything," Úrsula answered, giving her a shove.

"I tell you you're going to be face to face with misfortune," Taconitos repeated. She moved to the stove and looked at the coals as if she read in them the misfortunes she foretold.

"You're drunk!" Úrsula said.

The others glared at her scornfully and went on eating with bored expressions. At 10 P.M. Luchi came into the kitchen. Taconitos did not move or even deign to look at her: she knew what she was going to hear.

"Fix yourselves up, girls. Just look at your faces!" the patrona ordered, gazing at them with disgust.

The women smoothed their hair; some cleaned their mouths with the backs of their hands, then lapsed into inertia. For whom or for what were they going to fix themselves up?

"Don't you want to receive the blessing?" Luchi asked.

The girls became excited; some stood up, others began to laugh.

"I told you, I told you that misfortunes are piling up," Taconitos repeated without changing her position.

"Voice of doom!"

The woman spit at the live coals, and her saliva emerged in a shower of sparks.

"Come with me," Luchi said without any further explanation.

The tarts followed her to Juan Cariño's room. Luchi went in, closing the door behind her. After a few minutes she came out again.

"You can go in now."

Frightened by her tone of voice, the women entered on tiptoe, and there was Father Beltrán sitting on the edge of the bed, wearing Juan Cariño's morning coat and striped trousers, while Mr. President, standing beside the priest, wore his cassock and seemed quite despondent in his new outfit. The women were dumbfounded. Those who were very devout knelt, while others covered their mouths to keep from laughing at the sight of the two disguised persons. From the door, Taconitos looked over the heads of her friends and exclaimed, "I knew it! Didn't I tell you? I saw him come . . ."

"What are you mumbling about?" Luchi asked angrily.

"I saw him come . . . Juan Cariño came in twice, but the first time it was the padre dressed in Mr. President's clothes. Then Luchi went out with the clothes and took them to Dorotea's house, where Mr. President was waiting. He dressed and came back here, and you brought the padre's cassock wrapped up in a bundle. Don't you remember? It was the night they stoned don Roque. Who knows how long the padre was hiding in Dorotea's house!"

"That's right. There wasn't enough room for both don Roque and me. He was very badly wounded, and I had to leave. If it hadn't been for my friends, I'd have been shot," the priest agreed.

Juan Cariño modestly lowered his eyes and Father Beltrán laughed heartily. The girls did likewise, and Mr. President's room was filled with animated talking and laughter.

"Just think of them looking for you, Father, and all the time you were so well hidden!"

"I couldn't sleep with all their shouting."

"They're scandalous!"

Luchi stood by the door, looking sadly at the priest. "What is a whore's life worth?" she asked herself bitterly, and left the room on tiptoe to walk through the dark house. The voices died away and she found herself alone, moving through the empty rooms. "I always knew they were going to kill me," and she felt that her tongue froze in her mouth. "Perhaps death is knowing that they're going to kill us in the dark. Luz Alfaro, your life isn't worth anything!" She uttered her name out loud to drive away a thought that was taking shape deep within her. If she died that night, only she would know the horror of her death and the horror of her life in the presence of the assassin who was stalking her in the farthest reaches of her memory. She stood by the dark door and sobbed briefly. Then she opened the door and peered at the street; she had to watch for the signal for Father Beltrán's departure. The street was quiet, the shadows of the trees and the walls opposite were motionless. Luchi was tired of waiting. What was she waiting for but that atrocious moment that never came? "Oh God, take away my fear and give me rest now!" At that moment don Roque's tall, corpulent silhouette was outlined against the shadows of the trees, making a signal and then stiffening into immobility. Luchi answered the signal, half-closed

218

the door, and returned to the room. When they saw her, the girls stopped laughing.

"Father, don Roque is waiting. The Moncadas are at Las Cruces."

Her words had a grave sound. Father Beltrán stopped laughing and turned very pale.

"Let's go," Juan Cariño said, taking the priest by the arm.

The padre and the madman went out of the room, followed by Luchi and the women. When they came to the vestibule, the priest turned to the girls.

"Pray for me, and for the souls who are risking their lives for me tonight."

Luchi and Juan Cariño knelt down and the priest blessed them.

"Father, don Roque will go on ahead to lead the way. Stay close to buildings, and come back at the slightest sound."

They all listened respectfully to Luchi's words, and she flung open the door with determination.

"I'll go two minutes after you leave, to protect you from the rear, but there's no danger."

Without further ado, Father Beltrán slipped out into the street. There was not the slightest noise. The frightened women did not breathe; it seemed to them that they had just delivered the priest to his death. Luchi waited for several minutes, crossed herself, and left her house without looking back. Juan Cariño closed the door and sat down on the floor with his ear pressed against the crack, listening to the woman's quick steps as they receded on the cobbles.

"Put out that lamp!" he ordered in a very low voice.

The women blew it out and huddled close to the madman. The night was still, the doorway dark, an infinite sadness descended on the little group crouching in the vestibule.

It was Juan Cariño who broke the silence as he whispered, "Don Roque is opening the path of the shadows, Luchi is guarding him from the rear. In the middle is the padre, as luminous as a burning taper. In half an hour, his holy light will be with the Moncadas, and at dawn, in the sierra, he will illuminate the

219

valley in the hands of Abacuc, the great warrior!" Juan Cariño interrupted his narrative.

Fascinated by his voice, the women had forgotten their fear.

After a few minutes the madman, speaking still more softly, continued. "General Francisco Rosas is dancing, adorned with Bengal lights and music, and no one will hear Luchi when she goes down the street alone, stripped forever of her lofty mission of guardian angel. Here we shall wait for her while Francisco Rosas dances and dances and dances . . ."

At 2 A.M. Juan Cariño and the girls still waited, huddled inside the door of Luchi's house. Sleep had overcome several of them; others, hidden in the darkness, were shaken by fear. Only the madman remained alert, listening attentively to the sounds of the night. "It's not possible, it's not possible," but the horror was indeed becoming more and more possible. Mr. President hid his head in his hands. His mouth was dry and his body drenched with sweat.

"Girls! Girls!" he called in a low voice.

Some of the women raised their heads. "Yes, Mr. President?"

"Listen to this: 'The Saracens came and whipped us, for God helps the good when they outnumber the bad.' "

The girls did not answer.

"Old Hispanic wisdom. The Spaniards too, in spite of being Spaniards, knew something once," the madman concluded. He was making an excuse for having quoted a Spanish source, seeing he was such an adherent of Father Hidalgo.

"What time is it, Mr. President?" asked one of the women who had understood Juan Cariño's despair.

"How can I tell you the time if I can't see the stars from here?" he answered grumpily. He knew that the girl was trying to tell him that the time he was waiting for had long since passed.

Many aggressive footsteps were heard coming down the street in the direction of Luchi's house.

"It isn't Luchi! It isn't Luchi!" the women said, standing up.

"Hide, Mr. President!"

"Shhh!" Juan Cariño replied, and walked away with dignity.

The steps stopped in front of the house and many fists pounded violently on the door. The women kept silent and the knocking became so forceful that it threatened to break down the door.

"Open up in the name of the law!"

"Damn sons of bitches!" the women replied.

The latches gave way before the pressure of the Mauser butts and Justo Corona entered Luchi's house in triumph. He pushed the women aside with one hand and, guided by his lantern, went into the little parlor. The circle of light fell on the figure of Juan Cariño sitting with the dignity of an official personage. The Colonel was astonished; then he began to laugh hilariously, without taking the light off the figure of Mr. President stuffed into Father Beltrán's cassock. The soldiers gazed at the madman with amusement.

"Light the lamps!" Corona ordered, still laughing.

The tarts obeyed, and placed lighted lamps on all the tables.

"Three of you search the house!" Corona ordered his soldiers without removing his eyes from Juan Cariño, who was still pale and motionless.

"Who brought the priest here?" he asked after several minutes.

The women and Juan Cariño were silent.

"Where did Beltrán come from?" Corona repeated, raising his voice.

"Colonel, kindly do not shout in my presence," the madman said, drawing himself up ridiculously in the cassock.

"I've had enough of this nonsense! Take him to the Command!" Justo Corona ordered.

The soldiers roughly manacled Mr. President and then pushed him rudely out of his house.

"You'll all talk!" Corona said before leaving.

The women lowered their heads. The house had been turned upside down and they did nothing to restore order to the ransacked rooms. Frightened, they went to the kitchen.

"Do you think they'll release Mr. President?"

"I think they're going to shoot him," Taconitos replied, huddled by the burned-out stove.

"What time will Luchi come back?" asked a very young girl.

"I don't think she'll ever come back," Taconitos said.

The girls waited in vain for their patrona to return. At 11 A.M. one of them peeked through the door and encountered the bored faces of the soldiers who were watching the house.

"Do you know what's happened to Luchi?" she asked timidly.

"She's lying at Las Cruces," they replied bluntly.

The day passed and no one came to the house to give them any hope. Dirty and frightened, they stayed in the kitchen, crying. Night fell, and when it was very late they decided to go to the Military Command and ask for Luchi's body. Two of them volunteered to carry out the precarious mission. A soldier escorted them from their house to the officers' presence. In the office they met Cástulo.

"What time is it, Señor?" asked the braver of the two.

"I guess it's after two," doña Matilde's servant replied.

And the women and the man went on waiting.

EIGHT _____

"I swear I'm not going to the fiesta!" Lieutenant Colonel Cruz said, smiling.

Lying on the bed, Rafaela and Rosa looked at him with rancor. They could hear the sound of the rockets at doña Carmen's party.

"Don't you believe me? Look me in the eye!" And Cruz leaned over them, staring at them fixedly.

The twins replied with a frown, and he caressed the waists and thighs of his loved ones as a connoisseur caresses the rumps of two mares.

"What could I find at the fiesta that I don't have with you?" he asked as his hand moved from one sister to the other.

"Insults!" Rosa said.

"Insults?" the man exclaimed.

"Yes, insults to us," Rafaela said, pushing the man's hand away with disgust.

"Who can insult my pleasure?"

"They! The respectable girls who haven't invited us."

"The respectable girls? You don't know what they're like!" Cruz said scornfully, while his hand ran up and down the bodies of the sisters to dispel their anger.

The girls grew calmer, closed their eyes, and inhaled with delight the fruity odor that invaded the room. A voice from the hall called to the Lieutenant Colonel. He extricated himself from the sisters, who had remained quiet, and left the room on tiptoe. The moment he was gone, Rafaela sat up in bed and looked incredulously toward the door through which their lover had just passed. Angrily she heard the jovial voices of the men who were gathering to go to doña Carmen's party.

"Ready, Colonel? The young ladies are here," called the voice of General Francisco Rosas.

A few seconds later the girls heard the sound of shiny boots walking down the hall, reaching the door, and disappearing in the street.

"He's going to pay for this!"

"He thinks everything can be settled in bed!" Rosa said.

And the sisters, quivering with rage, looked around, trying to find their revenge. Luisa and Antonia entered without knocking.

"What's wrong?" Luisa asked, seeing the disturbed faces of the twins.

"We're going north!"

"You're leaving? When?"

"Right now," the sisters said.

"Don't leave me alone!" Antonia begged.

Luisa also seemed worried. The sisters bounded out of bed. Their decision made them energetic.

"Eat!" Rafaela said, holding out a basket overflowing with fruit. Then she collapsed into a chair and said seriously, "Let's see if this teaches Cruz to be more of a man!"

"Yes, you shouldn't insult your pleasure!" Rosa added.

"I wish you could have seen him before he went to the party, lying there," and Rafaela pointed to the bed.

"We let him get excited so he wouldn't suspect anything. You have to take them up very high, and then drop them . . ."

224

"Then you're really going?" Antonia asked incredulously.

"Of course we're going!" And the sisters took their dresses and heaped them up on the bed.

Luisa thoughtfully smoked a cigarette while she looked at them, worried. Then she stood up and announced hoarsely, "I'm going, too."

"Let's all four of us go, and when they come back from their party we'll be gone!" And the sisters began to laugh as they imagined the officers' surprise when they returned and found the empty rooms.

"We have time. Let's take the horses while they're dancing, and tomorrow let them look for us."

"It's time for a change of towns and men."

"I'd certainly like to hear some different words for a change!" Rosa shrieked.

"Go and get your things ready," Rafaela urged, pushing Luisa and Antonia out of the room.

When the sisters were alone they lay on the bed and began to cry. It frightened them to travel, to leave the hotel and look for another town and another man.

Antonia entered her room. She could not find the light, and tried to imagine in the dark what would happen if she ran away that night with the twins. She would have to go through sleeping towns, greet the mule-drivers who traverse the shadows of the plains with machete in hand, cross the sierra full of snakes. At dawn she would arrive in Tierra Colorada; then she would cross the river in a scow and be stared at by the men who rowed it, and on the other side she would continue her trip to the sea. But the sea would still be far away, for they had brought her far into the interior of the country. She covered her face with her hands and sobbed: she was not capable of making the trip alone. At night the sierra is austere and does not let fugitives pass, it throws rocks in the roads, and souls in torment pass by, howling on the black crests of the mountains. She seemed to hear the hoofbeats of her horse, to feel herself as cold as a dead woman lost in the mountains. "I'll go where they go, and from there I'll send word to

Papá so he can come and get me!" And she waited for the others to call. "Oh, to get away from the smell of this room once and for all!"

Luisa opened her wardrobe and looked at her dresses. Her life passed before her in the form of streets that crossed and rushed impetuously toward her. She saw balconies and closed doors. Where would she go? She passed through her sisters' houses with their rows of children, nursemaids, and husbands in dark suits. She entered her aunts' houses with their French-style balustrades, their mirrors and seashells. "If you're good, Luisita, you can listen to the ocean in the seashell before you leave," they told her in the parlor of her Aunt Mercedes, and she, sitting on a gilt chair, ate crumbly cookies and stared at her feet as they hung down without reaching the floor. Her Aunt Mercedes wore black satin shoes, let herself be served by an elderly servant, caressed a gray cat, and cast occasional glances at a little gold watch dangling from a pearl chain that fell in the black creases of her dress. Her Aunt Mercedes loved her. It had been quite some time ago that she had read of her death in the newspapers. She tried to imagine her house with its brocade draperies. Aunt Mercedes was her grandmother's sister and had always lived alone, surrounded by porcelains and servants. "What would she think if she could see me in this town?" It seemed to her that from the fold of an invisible curtain her aunt's voice came to her: "Go away, dear, go!" She selected two dresses and made them into a small bundle. She did not want to take anything of her past as a . . . she paused before saying the word "whore" to herself. Silently, guided by her childhood manners, she left her room with respect and knocked at Antonia's door. She had not given a thought to her husband or her children—so far away! Her friend came to the door, empty-handed.

"Aren't you coming?"

"Yes, I'm coming."

"Without bringing anything?"

"That's right. Everything in this room smells," Antonia said, frowning with disgust.

They found the sisters' room in disorder, with shoes, bottles, and clothes scattered on the floor.

"Be ready in a minute!" Rafaela said from astride a bundle she was tieing up energetically.

"And how are you going to carry this?" Luisa asked, indicating the bundles and suitcases on the floor.

"We're not going to leave him any of the stuff he gave us. Is he going to return the pleasure we gave him?"

"In two or three trips," Rafaela answered.

"You can't. Once we've left here, we won't be able to come back," Luisa said seriously.

"Let's leave everything, then!" Rafaela said bravely.

"No, I'm taking my green dress! What would I wear in Culiacán?" Rosa shrieked, and she quickly began to undo the bundles.

"You're going to ruin everything just for a crazy notion!" Luisa said angrily.

"Do you know what a 'crazy notion' is? No, you don't," Rosa moaned.

"A 'crazy notion' is a rose growing in a dungheap, the most precious, unexpected thing you can imagine," Rafaela explained, rummaging through the dresses and skirts. Her hand touched her sister's green dress and she held it up triumphantly to her friends.

"Come on, let's go!"

They put out the light and peered out through the door. A curious silence prevailed in the hotel with the men away. Leonardo and Marcial, two old soldiers, were patrolling the gardens. Each carried a lighted lamp. The girls watched them, and when their lights moved toward the reservoirs, they ran quickly to the front door, barefooted and holding their shoes. Stifling their laughter, they waited for a few seconds, unlocked the door, and stole out to the street. In the distance they heard the rockets and violins from doña Carmen's party. They walked cautiously to the stable. Fausto, Francisco Rosas' groom, was drunk and he greeted them exuberantly.

"A little ride? Of course, Señoritas, I'll saddle your horses right away!"

The man seemed not to realize the time or the strangeness of their request. The girls began to laugh hilariously and Fausto became serious.

"Every head is a world in itself."

Rafaela felt sure they were not deceiving him: he knew that they were going to run away. His calm thoughts reached her: "They must have their reasons."

"Fausto, wouldn't you like to have a new hat?" And the girl held out several gold coins.

"Why should I, Señorita Rafaela, if the beauties are leaving?"

The girls stopped laughing, saddened by his words.

"We in Ixtepec are very grateful to have had you with us so long," Fausto said, patting the rump of Rafaela's gray horse.

She kept the money: she did not want to offend him.

"We were very happy in Ixtepec," Rosa replied, returning the compliment.

"This is the first time that Señorita Antonia has visited me. Señorita Luisa doesn't know how to ride, either," Fausto said, looking at Antonia's blond locks and pale face and then at Luisa's blue eyes.

"Yes, Faustito, but as you see, everything comes to him who waits. Saddle Abajeño!"

"The pleasure is ending," Fausto said, going to the back of the stable to get Abajeño, Colonel Justo Corona's horse. His steps faded away on the ordure and his voice rang out gravely under the stone arch.

Luisa lit a cigarette. She was nervous. She would go on Rafaela's horse and then on Rosa's, and the thought of being dependent on the sisters unnerved her. She tried to forget the cold sensation that was rising from the pit of her stomach. "The pleasure is ending." Where would they go now? They would be the mistresses of someone. Rafaela tried to see the face concealed by the word "someone." Other towns and other uniforms, disembodied and without prestige, awaited her. The officers had become absurd since they had been spending their time hanging peasants

228

and polishing their boots. "And they get paid for that? As if they were mailmen!" She felt she had been made a fool of. It was better to go away. "My next lover will not receive a salary!" she said to herself in disgust. She had seen Cruz's pay check, and the sum was not adequate to cover his expenses. "He's a thief!" and she was dumbfounded. It was amazing what came to her as Fausto saddled the horses. But—how did Cruz steal? When? She heard his cannibalistic laughter and saw his avid hands jingling gold coins. She felt sad. Cruz had deceived her. He had made himself pass for someone he was not.

"Hey, Fausto's taking a long time," her sister said, jolting her out of her meditations.

It was true, Fausto was not making any noise and the horses were still.

"Fausto! Fausto!" Rafaela called apprehensively.

"What is it?" Luisa asked, alarmed.

"I don't know, he doesn't answer . . ."

The girls went into the stable. It was not possible that he had betrayed them. He had seemed so happy to see them, so friendly.

"Fausto! Faustito!" Rafaela called again.

No one answered. Francisco Rosas' groom had gone without a sound, sneaking away like a snake.

"That rat!"

"Let's go!" Antonia urged.

"Do you want them to grab us at the edge of town?"

"Remember Julia!" Rosa replied glumly.

When they went to the street, they saw groups of women and children running along close to the buildings. What was happening? They passed doña Lola Goríbar's house and saw her lighted windows with the curious faces of the señora and her son Rodolfito peering out. Their house was the only one that seemed calm in the midst of that strange spectacle of people running away as they were on that dark night, perhaps because it was the only house where there was a chapel and the rosary was prayed regularly. The Goríbar family's wealth and hidden power increased as Ixtepec grew poorer. Touched with fear, the girls came to the hotel door they had left ajar, pushed it gently, and went in, locking it behind them.

Two shadows were crouching there, waiting for them.

"The officers will be told of this," said one of the shadows, moving toward them.

Rafaela broke away from the watchmen and went to her room. The others did likewise with an air of dignity, carrying their shoes.

"We have to tell," Leonardo told them, indicating that he had authority over them.

Then the two soldiers uttered coarse epithets, secured the locks, and continued their silent rounds throughout the hotel garden.

The girls restored order to the sisters' room. They were afraid and did not want to leave any traces of their attempt to flee.

"Did you see how the people were running?"

"Yes. Something terrible must have happened."

And they looked at the walls of the room where they were prisoners. They could not escape from their lovers. The longing for freedom, which a few moments before had perplexed them, now became intolerable, and the Hotel Jardín filled them with terror. In the street the hurried steps had stopped and the town returned to silence. Ixtepec was a prisoner and as terrified as they were. In the garden, the lanterns of Marcial and Leonardo continued to move back and forth; in the streets, the lanterns of the soldiers also moved about, looking for the culprits.

Someone knocked at the front door. Rosa blew out the lamp and the four girls rushed to the hall to see who it was. The knocking was repeated violently. The girls saw Leonardo's light moving toward the door. A few moments later the tall silhouette of Francisco Rosas appeared in the corridor.

"He has a woman with him!" Rafaela whispered.

The General moved through the hall of the Hotel Jardín, accompanied by a woman in a red dress. Leonardo's light made the sheen of her dress and the crown of her black curls visible. The couple stopped at Rosas' door. He took the light from

230

Leonardo's hands and, still accompanied by the unknown lady, entered the room that had been Julia's.

"Did you see?"

"Yes," Luisa whispered.

"It was Isabel Moncada."

"It certainly was," Luisa replied; groping her way, she collapsed into a chair.

Rafaela went out in the hall to catch Leonardo. "Was that Isabel Moncada?"

The man nodded and disappeared down the dark hall.

"Something terrible has happened!"

The girls huddled together on one bed and spoke in low voices. They did not dare to separate or to sleep. In their fear they stayed awake all night long, and the light of dawn surprised them in the same attitude. In the morning they saw Leonardo passing with the breakfast tray. A while later Francisco Rosas, shaved and smelling of cologne, left the hotel. Rafaela knocked at the door of Julia's room. There was no answer.

"She won't come to the door," she told her friends.

"Something terrible has happened!" Luisa repeated.

None of the officers had returned to the Hotel Jardín.

NINE

"Martín, I want to know what has become of my children!"

Ana Moncada listened to herself repeating these words. Her mother had said the same thing in a house with high ceilings and mahogany doors. A smell of burning firewood and a frigid wind coming in through the cracks of the window mingled in her memory with the room where a candle blinked. The Revolution had finished her house in the north. And now, who was finishing her house in the south? "I want to know what has become of my children," said her mother's letters. The news of her brothers' deaths had come to Ana in the dates written in the handwriting of Sabina, her youngest sister.

"Martín, I want to know what has become of my children!" she repeated, looking at her husband and her room with bewilderment. She could not explain why the smell of snow and firewood seemed to haunt her.

Could she be living the hours of a made-up future? She rose from her bed and went to the balcony. She opened the shutters, wanting to feel the frosty air from the Sierra of Chihuahua, and encountered instead the hot, cloud-spotted night of Ixtepec. The horror of the landscape forced her to her bed, sobbing. Her husband let her weep. The to-and-fro motion of Martín's rocking chair repeated Isabel's name over and over again.

"She's bad! She's bad!" Ana Moncada shouted, feeling that she herself was guilty for her daughter's evil conduct. She looked apprehensively at her bed and heard herself saying, "Coming?" That was the word Rosas had used when he called Isabel, and her daughter went away with him in the darkness.

After Nicolás was born, she, Ana, had called to her husband each night, "Coming?" She remembered those nights; she had softened her voice as Francisco Rosas had done, and called to Martín, "Coming?" And, like a sleepwalker, her husband had come to her bed, bewitched by that unknown Ana, and together they saw the dawn come.

"How lively and pretty she is! You can see that she was conceived with pleasure!" she heard the midwife say as she bathed the newborn Isabel. "When girls are made like that, they come out like this," the woman added.

From her bed, Ana blushed. Martín looked at her with desire. Everyone would know of their lust, thanks to the beauty of their daughter. She bit her lip with anger. Isabel had come into the world to denounce her. She swore to amend her ways, and did, but Isabel continued to resemble those nights. No one could take away the stigma. Her husband consoled himself for her change of behavior by taking refuge in their daughter. He saw her as if she were made of the best and the worst of themselves, as if the girl were the depository of all their secrets. That was why he sometimes feared her and was sad. "This girl knows us better than we know ourselves," and he did not know how to treat her or what to say to her. Embarrassed, he lowered his eyes when he was with her.

The pale bunch of everlasting flowers, the photographs framed in red velvet, the porcelain candelabra, and the closed sewing basket were indifferent to the rocking of Martín Moncada's chair. The candlelight gave fleeting reflections to Ana Moncada's white dress as she lay on the bed weeping. Her husband remained inflexible to his wife's tears. In their party clothes they seemed

233

like ageing actors who had no parts to play while a tragedy was being enacted on the stage. They were waiting for their cue, and during the wait their costumes and their faces were getting wrinkled and dusty.

The ticking clock, supported by two naked angels, had marked the end of a night, the course of a day, and the return of the second night, and the waiting and the evil that grieved them were invariable and intact.

A new rhythm ruled the house: the air was hollow, the inaudible movement of the spiders blended with the impassive ticking on the bureau. An immobile presence left the furniture quiet and the expressions in the portraits dead.

In the parlor the console tables remained in suspense and the fearless mirrors divested themselves of their images. The Moncadas' house would never again escape from this enchantment. This was the beginning of the time without pianos and without voices. In the kitchen the servants kept silent watch over the silence.

At three-thirty in the morning someone knocked at the front door. The dull sound echoed in the patio and the rooms. Several minutes passed, and Félix appeared in his master's room, accompanied by Cástulo.

"Señor, Cástulo's here," Félix murmured without daring to enter the room.

Martín Moncada did not move from the rocking chair; his wife did not raise her head from the pillow.

"Señor, Cástulo's here. He has come from the Command."

The señora sat up in bed, while her husband went on rocking.

"I've come to say . . ." Cástulo began awkwardly, not knowing what to do with his hat. "I've come to tell you . . . that at four o'clock they will give the bodies . . ."

Martín Moncada showed no expression. The señora looked at him with wide-open eyes.

"What bodies?" she asked innocently.

"Dorotea's, Luchi's and . . . Master Juan's . . ." Cástulo explained, lowering his eyes.

234

"Master Juan's body?" the mother repeated.

"Yes, Señora, it's there . . . I just saw it," and Cástulo brushed away a tear.

"And they aren't going to give us Master Nicolás'?" Ana Moncada asked.

"He got out alive . . . He's under arrest . . ." Cástulo replied, happy to give some good news.

"Let's go," the father said, standing up.

And followed by the servants he left the house and went to the Military Command.

At dawn doña Matilde's servants recovered Dorotea's body. On the dusty bricks by her door there was a dark stain. The officers gave permission to take the body but not to stay with it in Dorotea's house. Cástulo, helped by Tefa, wrapped the body in a sheet and carried it to the house of Charito's sisters. There they shrouded it and put some little Mexican flags in her hands. When the sun was high the flies alighted on the dead woman's face and Cástulo, with a larger flag, drove them away while he responded to the hastily-said prayers. They had been ordered to take the body to the cemetery before 9 A.M.

Four soldiers went on living in the dead woman's house. The trapdoor was open in one of the burned rooms, just as Corona had left it. That was where don Roque had lived from the moment when Father Beltrán had brought him there badly wounded, when their first attempt to escape had failed and the Moncadas waited for them in vain on the road to Tetela. The priest had waited for him that night, hiding behind Dorotea's door, and had heard his shouts; when the soldiers walked around the block, he took advantage of doña Matilde's presence and brought the sacristan into the house.

The bandages and medicines Dr. Arrieta had used to treat his wounds were still behind the trapdoor. Now the soldiers were searching through the mountains for the sacristan, who had escaped again. "He'll be caught soon. The mountain is dry and he won't find anything there but iguanas and snakes."

235

The little procession that accompanied Dorotea to the cemetery met Luchi's cortege. The girls hurried along with a serious air; they wanted everything to end quickly; with the sunlight, the young girl's death had become more terrible than they imagined it during the two nights they had waited for her to return. The blue sky, the green branches, and the mist rising from the earth were at variance with the thirst of Luchi's body imprisoned in a coffin lined with cheap, shiny silk. The girls wanted to get rid of the loathsome presence of their patrona, and secretly thanked the officers for the order to bury her before nine.

On the way back from the cemetery, two of the women took the road to Las Cruces. They wanted to say a prayer at the spot where their friend had died. Now that they were unburdened of her presence, they were overcome with pity for the dead woman. They climbed the hill full of stones and thorns. The sun was very high when they met two soldiers who were keeping watch at a lonely place.

"Was it here?" one of the women asked, her mouth dry from the heat and the dust.

The men laughed cynically. One of them cut a blade of grass and chewed on it before answering.

"On this very spot," he said, taking quick, secret glances at the women.

"Here we catch them like little birds," his companion said.

"Someone squealed," one of the tarts replied with rancor.

"I'd say so." And the man went on chewing the grass, disdainfully showing his white teeth.

"We hid among the tall cactuses at 5 P.M. Around ten that night we saw the Moncadas arrive. They were coming from Tetela and brought horses for the priest and don Roque. Then we saw Señorita Chayo coming with baskets of food. After that, the sacristan, followed by the priest and Luchi. As they were mounting their horses, Lieutenant Colonel Cruz gave us the order to stop them. In the shooting that followed, two fell and the sacristan escaped . . ." The soldier interrupted his account.

The tarts sat down on some rocks and stared dry-eyed at the

place where Luchi and Juan Moncada had died. The high round sky was still. The singing of the cicadas was heard, and nothing gave any indication that a tragedy had occurred.

"This is where Luchi died!" the soldier said, kicking a brambly spot.

"And this is where Juan Moncada died!" the other said, pointing to a place farther away.

"We don't know who squealed. We only know that someone did," said the soldier who was chewing on the grass, looking avidly at the women.

His companion offered them cigarettes and they accepted them indifferently. The men exchanged glances and approached the women with evasive eyes.

"Cut it out!" one of the women said, violently pushing away the man's hand, which insolently fell on her breast.

"Are you going to pretend to be a lady?" the soldier exclaimed, looking at her with sudden rage.

"What if I am?" and the woman stood up, looking bored, and walked away, wiggling her hips.

Her friend did likewise, and the two went down the hill, tottering unsteadily on their high heels.

The two enraged men remained above, watching them go away on the stony terrain. In the distance they heard the mocking laughter of the women.

"Damn whores!" the soldier cried, angrily spitting out the grass he had been chewing.

Plagued by the heat, pale, and with his shirt dirty, Martín Moncada walked rapidly through my streets. He was followed by his servants and by some of his sister Matilde's servants. "I've just buried Juan. I've just buried Juanito," he repeated to himself at every step, as if he were trying to convince himself that the task he had just performed was real. My pink and white houses were melting in the radiant morning light and Martín looked at them sightlessly, as if they were only a mass of bright dust that disappeared in the hot morning air. He himself was a

237

mass of debris and his feet walked along independently from the rest of his body. "I've just buried Juan. I've just buried Juanito." His son's surprised face came to him, sinking slowly into the black earth, as a leaf sinks in water. The certainty that the cemetery earth was of a poor quality and the memory of the black coffin drained his body of all sensation.

It was not he, Martín Moncada, who walked the streets of Ixtepec. He had lost the memory of himself, and he was an unknown personage who was losing the members of his body in the demolished corners of a town in ruins.

"Here, Señor..."

Félix took his master by the arm and gently led him into his house. After him the door solemnly closed, closed forever. Never again would we see him on my streets.

At the exact moment when the Moncadas' door closed, General Francisco Rosas began to interrogate the prisoners.

The sun entered his office cheerfully, illuminating the chalices and missals found in Dorotea's house. In the next room were the weapons and the Cristero posters found in the houses of the guests. Francisco Rosas, in his light-colored gabardine uniform, smoked absentmindedly while Corona arranged the papers on his desk and the typist sharpened the pencils. He was worried. The victory had not given him the expected joy. Isabel's presence in his room had ruined his success. Francisco Rosas walked to the balcony, looked at the plaza, and let his eyes rest on the hotel across from the Military Command. "There she is," he said to himself bitterly. Why had she gone with him? When he had called her at the door and brought her to his room, knowing that Juan was dead and Nicolás in the garrison jail, he thought of total victory over Ixtepec. He did not even know what she was like, that girl who walked beside him at midnight. When he entered his room and looked at her closely, her obstinate eyes and red dress annoyed him. He liked docile women, enveloped in light colors. Julia's pink silhouette came between him and the young girl who stared at him spitefully, reading his thoughts. His first, confused impulse had been to say, "Go, go home," but he had restrained himself. He wanted to know and to make known to Ixtepec that all that counted in Ixtepec was the will of General Francisco Rosas. Hadn't they all been laughing at him for months? They had all been Felipe Hurtado's accomplices. He picked up a bottle of brandy and drank generously; then he turned to Isabel, who waited silently, standing in the middle of the room. "Now they will know that I share my bed with the one who hurts them the most," he said to himself.

"Undress!" he ordered without looking at her.

Isabel obeyed without replying and Rosas, intimidated, put out the light; in bed he found himself with a strange body that did his bidding without saying a word. The morning light found him abandoned. At his side, Isabel slept or pretended to sleep. Rosas slipped out of bed and shaved, trying not to make any noise. He wanted to get out of the room, which asphyxiated him. When Leonardo appeared with the hot coffee, the General raised a finger to his lips to indicate silence, drank the coffee quickly, and left the room. The morning air, scented with magnolias, comforted him. He did not return to the hotel all day long. At night, his aide went to get him a change of clothing and brought it to his office; he changed there. He was in a bad mood. He had to wash at the well because there was no bathroom in the presbytery. "Those backward priests!" he said to himself while the icy well-water ran over his shoulders. Afterward, feeling better, he went with his aides to close doña Carmen's party. He got back to the hotel very late, and there he encountered Isabel's obstinate eyes. He had tried to imagine that it was not she who waited for him but the other one, and disconsolately he put out the light and went to bed. The young girl did the same and the room was filled with lianas and fleshy leaves. There was no space for him, or for his past; he was choking. "She takes up the whole room," he said to himself, and at that moment he realized that he had made an irreparable mistake.

Colonel Corona and the typist were awaiting his orders. Rosas kept looking at the hotel. "There she is!" he repeated to himself vehemently. "When I return, I'll tell her to go, and if she refuses, I'll personally take her out to the street. An outcast!" The word made him smile. He imagined how alarmed the townspeople's faces would be at this new scandal, and Isabel's obstinate eyes returned to his memory. She was not the one who could take Julia's place. The name of his mistress transported him to a vanilla-scented past. He felt the softness of Julia's skin acutely on his fingertips, and heard her voice calling him. Frightened by the memory, he turned to Corona.

"Bring in the first of those fools!" he said, and promised himself angrily, "As soon as I'm back at the hotel, I'll get her out of there."

The arrested men came before him one by one. When Father Beltrán's turn came, the General smiled. The sight of the priest wearing the madman's morning coat and striped trousers cheered him.

"Yes, Señor, you will be given clean underwear, but you will go on wearing these clothes. It's a test."

The priest did not answer. Flushed with anger, he signed the deposition and left Rosas' office without saying goodbye.

Juan Cariño came in. Treating him with deference, Francisco Rosas stood and listened to him as if he really were the President of the Republic. The madman seemed satisfied, but when he heard that he would have to attend the trial wearing the priest's cassock, he exploded with anger. "Is the General unaware that since 1857 there has been separation of church and state?"

"No, Señor, I am not unaware of that," the General replied humbly.

"Then how do you dare to make this fortuitous change of investiture permanent? I protest this new outrage!" And Juan Cariño ordered the typist to state his protest and the bad faith of the usurper Francisco Rosas.

The madman left the office, and Rosas stopped laughing when he saw that Nicolás Moncada was next. In the young man's presence the General was thoughtful: Nicolás looked too much like his sister.

240

"I have to go. Corona, you continue the interrogation," he said, standing up, and went out not knowing where to go.

He walked around the plaza several times and then returned to the Military Command. One of his aides went to the hotel to get his meal, and Francisco Rosas ate in a room that was isolated from the coming and going of the soldiers. Corona came in to have coffee with his chief.

"What did he say?" Rosas asked; he was worried, and avoided mentioning Isabel's brother by name.

"Everything!" Corona said, satisfied.

"Does he know what happened to his brother and sister?"

"I think so, but he's quite the little man."

"All women are whores!" the angry Rosas said sententiously. Corona agreed with his chief.

"All of them!" And he took a long draw on his cigar.

T E N

In the afternoon the stores opened and the people went out to inspect the town, happy to be in the sun and to encounter their friends again. At night Ixtepec was seething with rumors, which reached the neighboring towns in the phrase, "There's a revolt in Ixtepec!" The mule-drivers did not come to town on Saturday, and we spent an empty Sunday. The people clustered around the hotel to peer through the windows at Isabel, the thankless daughter, but she hid behind closed blinds. The prisoners were still incommunicado in the Military Command, and we passed their door many times in vain: the soldiers refused to give us any news of them. On Monday, proclamations were posted, accusing the prisoners of sedition, treason to the fatherland, and murder; they were signed by the well-known names of the General, the municipal President, and a personage with a harsh name: Effective suffrage, no re-election.

Thus we returned to the dark days. The game of death was played painstakingly: the townspeople and the military did nothing but plot deaths and intrigues. I watched them come and go sadly. If only I could have taken them on a stroll through my memory so they could see the generations now dead: nothing was left of *their* tears and sorrows. Absorbed in themselves, they did not realize that one lifetime is not long enough to discover the infinite flavors of mint, the lights of a night, or the multitude of colors that colors are made of. One generation follows another, and each repeats the acts of the one before it. Only an instant before dying, they discover that it was possible to dream and to create the world their own way, to awaken then and begin a new creation. And they also discover that there was a time when they could possess the motionless journey of the trees and the navigation of the stars, and they remember the ciphered language of the animals and the cities opened in the air by the birds. For several seconds they return to the hours that guard their childhood and the smell of grass, but it is already late and they have to say goodbye, and they discover that in a corner their life is waiting for them, and their eyes open to the dark panorama of their disputes and their crimes, and they go away astonished at the creation they made of their years. And other generations come to repeat their same gestures and their same astonishment at the end. And thus I shall go on seeing the generations, throughout the centuries, until the day when I am not even a mound of dust, and the men who pass this way will not even remember that I was Ixtepec.

Doña Carmen's party broke the enchantment of the Hotel Jardín forever and we were no longer enamored of its inhabitants. Isabel had entered the heart of the enigma. She was there to conquer the strangers, as vulnerable as any one of us, or to decide our downfall. Her name erased the memory of Julia, and her figure hidden behind the blinds became the only enigma of Ixtepec. The group of officers and their mistresses had been intact before, but now it was broken. The bored soldiers spoke scornfully of their chiefs and their women.

"Why are they so fond of those ugly dames?"

And they watched coldly as the young girls came and went. The mistresses were no longer to be envied. Isabel's invisible presence made the others seem insignificant, changed them into supernumeraries in a drama they did not want to take part in. They knew that *she* was there, and that took away their desire to

243

fix their hair; they went about looking sloppy, with pale lips and glassy eyes.

"How sinful! How sinful!" they kept saying.

Why was Isabel with the General, knowing the fate of her brothers? The girl frightened them. Apprehensively they avoided an encounter with her. Isabel spoke to no one. Shut up in her room, she walked down the hall only at dusk, to lock herself in the bathroom. The servants heard the water of the shower and, when she came out, the mistresses spied on her from a distance. The girl was aware that she was being observed, and studiously avoided any contact with the inhabitants of the hotel. She ate alone and somberly waited for the coming of Francisco Rosas. The General returned at dawn and found her awake, sitting in a chair as if she were there on a visit, paler and paler in her red dress. The girl and the color of her dress annoyed him, but it never occurred to him to give her gifts as he had done to Julia, and the party dress Isabel wore when she came to the hotel was the only one he saw her in.

Grieved by the girl's loneliness, Gregoria was the first to approach her. She spoke in the tender language of old servants, which Isabel knew so well, and thus a friendship was established between the old woman and Francisco Rosas' new mistress. Isabel asked her to do little errands, such as buying certain articles of underclothing she needed urgently. When it grew dark, Gregoria entered her room with the modest packages and the news of Ixtepec, accompanied her to the bath, dried her back, brushed her hair, and spoke to her with affection. Isabel accepted her help passively and listened to her with resignation.

"What does she say?" Rafaela asked the servant.

"Nothing, she has no remorse."

"Does she know about the death of her brother Juan?"

"Yes, I told her and she was very still."

"The worst of it is that the General doesn't love her."

"The only one he loves is the dead Julia," Gregoria said sententiously.

And it was true. Isabel's presence made Julia's absence intolerable. Her airy shadow vanished, driven away by the voice and the body of the new mistress. At night, before he entered his room, Rosas promised himself, "Now I'll tell her to go." Then, in her presence, a kind of embarrassed pity kept him from putting her out in the street. Infuriated by what he called his "weakness," he reluctantly blew out the light and got into bed without speaking to her. He misjudged her. How could a respectable girl share his bed after what had happened to her family? Francisco Rosas tried to find out what went on inside of Isabel, but he did not understand the oppressed forehead or the somber eyes of his new mistress. Nor did he understand the halting conversations he held with her. "I shall never be sorry enough for having called to her at the door."

"Go to sleep! Go to sleep!" he repeated at night when he found her sitting and watching the dancing shadows cast by the lamp-light.

Without saying a word, Isabel undressed and got into bed to stare fixedly at the ceiling.

"What are you brooding about?" Rosas asked one night, frightened by Isabel's eyes. "It's bad to think . . . very bad," he added.

He did not want to think. Why should he? All of his thoughts led him to the effort he had to make at night to share a bed that was encompassed by shadows.

"I'm not thinking. I hear sand trickling inside of my head, and it's covering me up."

"You're worse than Antonia. You scare me," the impatient man replied, and prepared to take off his boots while glancing furtively at the young girl, who seemed, in truth, to be covered with sand.

"Tell me something," Isabel asked, turning her eyes to him.

"I can't," Rosas said, remembering the interview with Nicolás earlier that day; Isabel and her brother both looked at him with the same eyes. "I don't want to be looked at by those eyes any longer." It was not fair that he should be subjected to the same eyes both day and night. He blew out the lamp. He did not want to be seen in his nakedness by those eyes that observed him from an unknown vantage point. He got into bed and felt strange between the sheets. He tried to move away from Isabel's body.

"There is a wall covering my house and my brothers . . ."

"Sleep," Rosas begged, frightened by the word "brothers."

Through the grille on the door the night looked deep and very clear. The stars shone in solitary splendor; Francisco Rosas gazed at them nostalgically, remembering the time when they came down to his bed and ran up and down Julia's body, as luminous and cold as a brook. Isabel gazed at them, too. In other times they had lulled her to sleep in her house. She tried to imagine her other house, her other life, her other sleep, and she encountered her forgotten memory.

"Francisco, we have two memories. I used to live in both of them, and now I only live in the one that gives me the memory of what is going to happen. Nicolás is also in the memory of the future."

Francisco Rosas sat up violently in bed; he did not want to hear the sound of Nicolás' name or his sister's foolish words. He was a man of a single memory, that of Julia, and the Moncadas were trying to take him away from her and drown him in the darkness of his life before he knew her. He had fallen into a trap, and he was sorry for himself, feeling that fate was hounding him.

"Go to sleep," he ordered again, in a very low voice.

Dawn found them still awake. When he brought their breakfast, Leonardo saw that they were pale and remote, spinning in different orbits. He left the tray on the table and then, as had become his custom, he went to see Rafaela.

"They didn't sleep all night."

"Were they brooding?"

"Yes, running away," Leonardo said.

Rafaela went back to her room thoughtfully and looked coldly at Lieutenant Colonel Cruz. Her sister Rosa was still sleeping.

"You see, my loves? You see I didn't deceive you? I didn't go to the party. I went to get the priest and the Moncada boys, who

246

were getting away from us," Cruz had announced to his mistresses when he returned to the hotel the day after doña Carmen's party. "Aren't you going to congratulate me?" he asked, seeing that the sisters kept silent.

"No, it would have been better if you had gone to the party," Rosa replied.

"What!" Cruz yelled.

"And danced instead of chasing after a poor priest."

Cruz laughed. He did not understand women, but he knew that laughter was the best way to handle the rages and vagaries of his mistresses. The girls always capitulated to pleasure, but this time they glared at him with eyes that froze the laughter in his throat.

"Come, my loves," and he held out his hand to caress them.

"Don't touch us, you troublemaker." And the sisters moved to the other side of the room, leaving Cruz with an empty gesture.

"Don't be obstinate. I'm very tired," the officer groaned.

The girls did not answer.

Seeing their angry eyes, he said submissively, "I'm going to bathe now," and left the room. He had not slept, and he felt stupefied by the lack of sleep and the excitement of pursuing Father Beltrán and the Moncada brothers. "I'll make them happy later," he said to himself, feeling the bracing effect of the cold water, and he smiled maliciously as he thought how happy he would make them. He could not complain, after all; his life was filled with delights: sensuous days and kindly nights. He dried himself quickly: he wanted to be close to his girls again. But the girls were still out of sorts, and the days passed without the Lieutenant Colonel's being able to make them smile. Then his life became melancholy, his nights sad and lonely.

Without consulting him, the twins began to sleep in one bed, obliging him to sleep alone in the other. Sadly he watched them kneel and pray for a long time before they turned out the light. "How pretty they are," and his eyes caressed their bodies in their scanty nightgowns.

247

"This is the work of priests, making two women miserable when they were born to be loved," he said to them one night when his empty bed was becoming particularly unbearable.

"Sacrilegious . . ."

The Lieutenant Colonel approached the girls with an air of humility: it was too cruel to see them half naked and not be able to touch them.

"Let me give you a little love," he begged.

"No, life will never be the same again."

"Tell me what it is you want; I always satisfied your wishes," he begged again.

The sisters interrupted their prayers, sat down on the bed, and looked at him gravely. Cruz felt relieved to see that they were willing to talk to him. He would listen attentively, and then he would sleep with them. He looked at their cinnamon-colored skin and felt that all of his sadness would vanish as soon as his fingers could run up and down their bodies at will.

"What do we want? We want you to release Father Beltrán."

"Release him?" Cruz screeched, taken aback.

"Yes, and let him escape. Then everything will be the same again."

"Don't ask me for that, my girls," Cruz begged.

"All right, then, go to your own bed," Rafaela ordered.

"I can't sleep, let me give you a little love," he said in anguish.

Rosa stretched like a cat and slid down under the sheet; her sister followed her example, and the two locked in a close embrace, ready to sleep. He was outside of that paradise of entwined bodies and returned dejectedly to his bed, where he heard the sisters' even breathing. Melancholically he buried his head in the pillow. He was in a hostile world, a world that was alien to him and had a will and desires that were different from his own. He closed his eyes and tried to imagine what someone else was like, what Rosa and Rafaela were like. "I don't even know if their pleasure is the same as mine," he said to himself sadly when the morning light was beginning to shine through the cracks in the

248

door. As Rafaela had promised, his life would never be the same as before.

Accompanied by her son Rodolfito, doña Lola Goríbar came to the Moncadas' door to express sympathy for Juan's death. The strange light, the solitude, and the silence that surrounded the most uproarious house in Ixtepec surprised her. She felt oppressed and indecisive; she knocked with the brass ring, and as she waited she smoothed the folds of her mourning cloak and Rodolfo's black suit. She would never cease to congratulate herself for having declined the invitation of Carmen B. de Arrieta. Her instinct had told her that there was something dangerous about the party for the General. "Don't trust them, don't trust them," she had told her son, and together they spied from behind their curtains on the disaster that had come after the music and the fireworks.

"Didn't I tell you?" she said as she waited on the sidewalk in front of the silent door, which bore witness to the magnitude of the catastrophe.

"They're crazy," her son replied, apprehensive because a secret seemed to be hidden behind the Moncadas' walls and door.

From the opposite sidewalk, curious bystanders were watching them in amazement. No sound came from the house. "Why did we come?" the Goríbars wondered. The house with its closed windows and motionless walls seemed dangerous. It was only a few hours since they had buried Juan, and it was still too early to foresee the implications of the adventure that the Moncadas and their friends had gambled on. The señora turned to her son.

"Let's go. They aren't going to open the door."

It would be more prudent to leave the neighborhood; Rodolfito agreed. The way the street looked and the height of the house unnerved him. He took his mother's arm, on the point of leaving, when the door silently opened a crack, as if it were fearful of letting its secret escape, and Félix's solemn head appeared.

"The Moncadas are not at home to anyone."

Rodolfito and his mother, thwarted, gazed at their mourning clothes. What a waste of time it had been for them to spend hours deliberating on whether or not to present their condolences!

"Excuse me," Félix said, ignoring the funereal splendor of the Goríbars, and closed the door. The servant's gesture seemed like an insult.

"They're embarrassed because of Isabel," the señora said.

The townspeople watched her walk away, leaning on her son's arm, without having witnessed from within the downfall of the Moncada family, which for her, as she proclaimed many times, was the disgrace of Ixtepec.

A whole week passed and the house continued to be motionless and closed. The servants went to the market, where they found new stalls and fresh fruit, and continued in their imperturbable silence. The people approached to greet them but they walked away disdainfully, not wanting to share their invariable secret. It was useless for friends to knock with the brass ring; the reply that came through the half-opened door was always the same: "The Moncadas are not at home to anyone." Doña Matilde, who never visited the house, communicated with her brother through the servants.

Shut up in her house, she waited for order to be restored so Joaquín and the children would come home again, not accepting what was happening in her family. "They are away on a trip," she said to herself over and over again, until she convinced herself that Joaquín was visiting Mexico City with his niece and nephews. In the evenings she fervently studied the newspapers to see the attractions advertised there, and imagined what movies and restaurants they were going to in the capital.

On the other hand, doña Elvira patiently took it for granted that the Moncadas' door should be closed to her friendly words: "I am to blame for everything." She had lost her good humor, and her mirror reflected the image of tragedy in the dark circles that had formed under her eyes.

"Poor Isabel!" she whispered in the ear of the servant girl who blocked the way to her friends' house.

"Yes, the poor little girl. It's all Julia's fault!"

"I always knew that that woman would bring us nothing but trouble," the señora replied with new hope, seeing that the maid was willing to converse with her.

"I have to go now," the woman interrupted brusquely.

"Tell Ana she can count on me."

"Oh! If you could only see her!" the woman whispered, closing the door softly.

The maid's remarks left her dumbfounded. She wondered what was happening to Ana. She walked away quickly, followed by some of the curious, who tried to read in her face the news that escaped through the crack in the Moncadas' door. She glared at them angrily; she would not tell them a thing, their curiosity annoyed her; and besides, she was depressed and in no mood to speak to those hungry-eyed people who followed her surreptitiously. "We never know who will betray us." Someone must have told Rosas what the party was hiding, and the informer's words had caused our troubles. She walked faster. She had to visit Carmen's children, who were alone now, in the care of the servants. "Oh, if I could find the traitor, I'd kill him with my own two hands." She flushed with anger. She was the only person who had come out of the adventure unscathed. Her friends might doubt her loyalty. The fear of knowing she was innocent, and yet feeling guilty before the others, kept her awake at night. "I have to find the traitor!" Engrossed in her thoughts, she passed several friends without seeing them.

"How strange children are. You should see, they don't even remember Carmen!"

The señora picked up her table napkin with its embroidered initials and looked across the table at her daughter, who seemed not to be listening. After her walk through the town she felt relieved to be home again, far from the glances and remarks of the curious. The return to the pleasure of her birds and plants consoled her for the calamitous outing.

"I said, children are very strange." And then, seeing Conchita's bored face, she said to herself, "She's not in a good mood."

The señora waited for Inés to bring the food. The walk had stimulated her appetite. It was shameful to be hungry when her friends were in jail and poor Juan dead before his nineteenth birthday. But she was like that: she liked to eat! She gazed at the radiant sun illuminating her crystal and her silver pitchers, and felt comforted by the beauty of the dining room. "It must be God's will that it affected the Moncadas." Inés came in with the tray, her lilac dress, bare feet, and black braids floating in the golden light of 1 P.M. The señora caught the Indian girl's large eyes and gave her a grateful smile.

Conchita stared at her plate while she was being served. The maid lowered her eyes and quickly left the room.

"Mamá, Inés is the sweetheart of Sergeant Illescas, Corona's aide."

"What did you say?" doña Elvira screeched, dropping her fork.

"That Inés is Sergeant Illescas' sweetheart," Conchita repeated, stressing the syllables.

The señora heard her daughter's words and looked at her, stunned; the balconies darkened and the silver pitcher on the table glittered dangerously: she was sure they had poisoned the water.

"Do you know what that means?" the girl asked, looking sternly at her mother. "Of course, *I* know," she added cruelly, nibbling one of the radishes that garnished her plate as her mother remained immobilized by terror. "Don't look any farther, the mystery is solved!" the daughter insisted after a long silence.

The señora raised her eyes and was about to say something terrible, but at that moment the beautiful Inés appeared again, reverently carrying the shiny tray as if it contained the heart of a sacrificial victim. Doña Elvira covered her face with her hands and Conchita impassively let the girl serve her.

252

"We've been betrayed," the señora said when Inés had disappeared through the door.

"We can't throw her out," Conchita replied laconically.

"No. Can't you imagine what the reprisals would be? These Indians are treacherous!"

"Shhh!" her daughter said, lifting a finger to her lips.

The señora obeyed, and a rush of misshapen fears almost caused her to lose consciousness. There was no doubt, the betrayal had originated in her house, and she was incapable of clearing her honor and avenging her friends. There was the accursed one, going in and out of the kitchen and laughing at her misery. Although she had obtained permission to visit Carmen in jail, she could not go to see her now. How would she tell her that the betrayal had come from her house?

"We talk too much! Too much!" she yelled, exasperated.

She remembered clearly the conversations with her daughter and how freely she had explained the details of the "plan" without taking care to see who was listening.

"How right your father was. How very right! A closed mouth gathers no flies." And doña Elvira, exhausted, retired to her room.

On Thursday she did not go to the prison to visit her friend: one of her servants took a message saying that the señora was ill. Elvira Montúfar was suffering from an attack of terror.

"Widow's complaints!" the servants said, smirking.

"She's afraid," Inés said, getting ready to meet her lover, Sergeant Illescas.

ELEVEN _____

Where do dates come from, and where do they go? They travel for a whole year and, with the precision of an arrow, pierce the appointed day, show us a past now present in space, dazzle us, and burn out. They emerge punctually from an invisible time, and in an instant we recover the fragment of a gesture, the tower of a forgotten city, the words of heroes dissected in books, or the astonishment of the morning of our baptism when they gave us a name.

To enter the nearby space we had forgotten, we merely have to utter the magic of a number. In my memory, October first will be forever the day when the trial of the guests began. When I say it I am no longer sitting on this apparent stone, I am below, slowly entering the plaza, following my people, who began gathering there very early to learn the fate of the accused. The sentencing took place inside the Military Command and yet we followed, step by step, the words and gestures that took place behind closed doors. The General passed us, looking at the tree-tops; at this moment I can smell the freshness of his cologne and see his empty glance at leaves and branches. We remained under his motionless shadow, which repeated the same crime over and

254

over again with the painstaking precision of a maniac. In his immobile time the trees did not change their leaves, the stars were fixed, the verbs "to come" and "to go" were the same; Francisco Rosas stopped the amorous current that makes and unmakes words and deeds and kept us in his circular hell. The Moncadas had wanted to run away to find the coming and going of the stars and the tides, the luminous time that spins around the sun, the space where distances are within the reach of one's hand; they had wanted to escape from the single, bloody day of Ixtepec; but Rosas abolished the door that leads us to the memory of space, and rancorously he blamed them for the motionless shadows he had heaped on us. The General only knew of the existence of a few streets, and by dint of his believing in them, they became unreal to him and he only touched them when he pursued the shadows he found on their corners. We paid him for his fixed world with crimes.

"He has just slept with the sister," the women murmured bitterly.

"Long live Nicolás Moncada!" someone shouted.

"Long live Nicolás Moncada!" many voices answered.

Francisco Rosas smiled as he listened to the shouting. He entered the presbytery and a cordon of soldiers surrounded the building. Then more soldiers arrived with briefcases and worried faces.

"There go the lawyers!" yelled a mocking voice, and we echoed it with laughter.

Lawyers! Who do they think they're going to judge? We waited for the answer we already knew: traitors to the fatherland. What treason and what fatherland? In those days the fatherland bore the double name of Calles-Obregón. Every six years the fatherland changed its name; we, the people who wait in the plaza, know it, and that is why the lawyers made us laugh so hard that morning.

The women selling food and cool drinks arrived; we munch on snacks, and the patriotic leaders execute us.

Behind the iron grating of his hotel window don Pepe Ocampo

watched what was taking place in the plaza. Some men approached his balcony.

"Tell Isabel that her brother's on trial!"

The hotelkeeper looked at them scornfully and continued to strain his eyes to see the distant facade of the presbytery.

"Doesn't she care about what happens to her brother?" A man grasped the iron bars, and glared sardonically at don Pepe.

"You pimp!" many voices shouted.

When he heard the offensive shouts, don Pepe hurried into the hotel and ordered his servants to close all of the balconies. The hotel was cut off from the tumult in the street and was no longer a target for insults.

"Let's climb the tamarind trees and go into the hotel through the roof and get Isabel so she can plead for her brother's life!"

"Come on!" dozens of voices chorused.

"Long live Nicolás Moncada!"

With the agility of cats the men climbed the trees to get to the roof and drop down to the hotel patio; others tried to force open the doors. Then there was a clamor that spread through the whole town. From the Military Command came the order, which no one obeyed, to leave the plaza. The barracks doors opened to make way for the cavalry. The people scattered, shouting, before the thrust of the riders; palm hats were crushed on the cobblestones and some of the women's shawls were caught between the horses' hoofs.

In the radiant space of a morning the trial of Father Beltrán and his friends changed into the cause of Nicolás Moncada. The young man made us forget the church and the others who were on trial. The priest, Joaquín, Juan Cariño, Charito, the doctor and his wife took on the quality of extras in the Moncada family's tragedy. The eyes of Ixtepec were riveted on Nicolás, and his words and his gestures miraculously passed through the walls of the presbytery and reached the plaza, where they went from mouth to mouth. We knew that the young man refused the meal that Francisco Rosas had ordered brought from the hotel for those who were on trial, and that he did not accept the clean clothing offered by the soldiers. At night he washed his only shirt in a pail brought by one of his guards.

"Long live Nicolás Moncada!" shouted my streets and my roofs. The shout was multiplied, as the shout of "Long live Christ the King" had been multiplied before, and it was heard in the tribunal. At night, curled up on his cot, Nicolás listened to it melancholically as he searched for the words and gestures he would use before his judges the next day. He knew he was in a blind alley that led only to death.

"We'll leave Ixtepec, we'll leave," he and his brother and sister had said to each other since they were children. Juan was the first to find the way out; when Nicolás approached to look at him he was lying on his back, looking for all time at the stars. "Get going, you son of a bitch!" he heard them say as they pulled him away from his brother. "When I go, it'll be face down so I won't take with me anything of this town that has betrayed us." And he was not able to cry; astonished by his brother's escape, he did not even notice when the soldiers tied his hands behind his back. "We'll go away from Ixtepec." The three of them had wanted to run away, to return later and let some fresh air into the town, which was closed like a macerating vat for corpses. The iron grating of the cell clanked shut and he remained standing, asking where Juan was.

Why did it have to be Juanito? In an instant he let go of Nicolás' hand and Isabel's and fled. "Here you pay for illusion with your life," Felipe Hurtado's voice said to him from the night, whose warmth came in with the soldiers' sweat. He saw the day come, and before he went to make his first statement the guards told him that Isabel had slept with General Francisco Rosas. "She should die for this!" The presence of Rosas kept him from weeping. He did not see Justo Corona's face asking him questions. "From the blood of the innocent will spring fountains that cleanse the sins of the evil." Dorotea's voice repeated a tale from his childhood, and in Rosas' office the obtuse voice of Corona turned into meaningless words. And the fountain of blood shed on the stones at Las Cruces, and the fountain spilled in the doorway—whom had they purified? Certainly not Isabel, shut up in the Hotel Jardín. His anger changed into fatigue and his life was reduced to a single old, worn-out day. His sister's betrayal catapulted him to that shabby day, and in its ruins he had to act as if he lived in the full-blown days of his judges. He forced himself to view the General coldly, and tried to learn what had happened in his life and in that of his brother and sister; the evening they went to Tetela, to return to Ixtepec a few days later to rescue Father Beltrán and don Roque, the three were sad. Listlessly they rested under the shadow of Rome and Carthage and talked together for the last time.

"Do you care whether the priest lives or dies?"

"No," they replied.

"The one who should save him is his friend Rodolfito. Then the padre can go on blessing the lands he steals."

The boys laughed at their sister's vehemence.

"Silly! It's the way to get out of here!"

Now the "way out" was brutally barred by his cell in the Ixtepec jail. But then, under the trees by their house, they believed they could return to break the curse of Francisco Rosas, and that was what they told one another. Pensively they threw little stones at the narrow columns of ants that hurried by, carrying the leaves they stole from the acacias in the garden.

"The Franciscos are thieves!"

And on that last afternoon the three laughed, hearing Nicolás baptize the ants with the General's first name.

"Do you think we'll be successful?" he asked under the shadow of Carthage.

"Get away from Carthage, come over to Rome!" Juan shouted, crossing his fingers superstitiously and touching the bark of the victory tree to drive away the bad luck of his sister's tree.

Under the branches of Rome they spoke with rancor of Ixtepec and remembered the words and the plump face of doña Elvira: "Sometimes the signal is given by the simple."

"If anything goes wrong, Rodolfito will make a deal," they said prophetically.

In the prison nights, that afternoon and the words they had spoken came to him in fragments. "If anything goes wrong . . ." As he heard the phrase, it was impregnated with the smells and sensations of a remote past. His past was no longer his past, the Nicolás who spoke those words was a personage detached from the Nicolás who remembered them in his jail cell. There was no continuity between the two; the other one had a life of his own, different from his; he had remained in a space separated from the space of the Nicolás who remembered him with the elusive precision of dreams. Like Isabel, he did not remember with exactitude the shape of his house or the days he had spent in it; now his house was only a heap of forgotten ruins in a dusty town with no history. His past was this cell in Ixtepec and the continual presence of the sentinels. He remembered his future, and his future was death in a field in Ixtepec. Isabel's betrayal abolished the miraculous death. They would no longer move toward the mystery. And Juan? Now he knew that Juan had died as he would die: alone, without Isabel, his hair, his eyes, and his feet would die in a motionless horror; from within he would look on his body as it became worm-infested like the swollen bodies of the dead they had found lying on the plains of Ixtepec when they were children. He had not escaped crime, he had not escaped death in the town. Obstinately he tried to imagine what Isabel would do to be with them in that future, as close as the door of his cell. "She can't stay here, she can't leave us here," and he saw the fields of his childhood, filled with corpses. "We'll go away from Ixtepec, we'll go away!"

"Young fellow, you're not sleeping," said one of the soldiers who had heard him sobbing at midnight.

"You're crazy, I sleep very well," Nicolás exclaimed, feigning surprise. His own weakness seemed unpardonable and he enclosed himself in a dry pride.

Before his judges he tried to hide his fatigue and the horror of finding himself so alone in a room that spied on his words and gestures. "Yes, Señores, I am a Cristero, and I wanted to join the rebels from Jalisco. My dead brother and I bought the weapons."

259

His confessions made us shudder. "He's giving them the ammunition to kill him with." His decision irritated his judges. They wanted to justify their sentence by oppressing him with evidence, they wanted him to defend himself so they could prove his guilt and put him to death as a criminal, but Nicolás wanted to die by his own hand.

"No one instigated us. Isabel, Juan, and I made the plan and carried it out voluntarily, without advice from anyone."

When he heard the name of Isabel, spoken as if it belonged to the accused, Corona bit his lip and turned to see if Francisco Rosas was in the tribunal. He was relieved to see that he was not.

"He's making fun of them. Abacuc is going to come to Ixtepec," we said to one another, convinced that the army we awaited would soon be coming to save us. Some thought that Nicolás' words meant that salvation would come to us from Isabel. The girl had not gone to the hotel to betray us. She was there like the avenging goddess of justice, waiting for the propitious moment.

"Don't yell at her any more! She's there because she has to be!"

"Ever since she was a little girl she was very brave!"

And we viewed Francisco Rosas with envy. He went on walking across the plaza, ignoring the townspeople who gathered under the tamarinds to shout in favor of the brother of his mistress. He did not attend the trial; he remained in a nearby room, playing cards and talking with some of his aides, while others brought news of what was happening in the tribunal. When they repeated that the young man insisted on pleading guilty, he interrupted his game and nervously approached the window to look at the Moncada supporters who were filling the plaza. He seemed very depressed. The wills of the brother and sister were leading him to a strange place: he felt incapable of judging Nicolás and of sleeping with his sister, but it was too late for him to turn back now. What could he do? Frightened, he came back to the hotel room very late. Isabel's red dress shone beneath her dark eyes by the oil lamp.

260

"Turn out the light!"

His voice had deserted him. He no longer found the traces of his past. The Moncadas had taken his Julia. In the darkness he pulled off his boots and hesitated before getting into the bed where he found only the fear of himself. He was lost, treading on unknown nights and days, guided by the shadows that the brothers and sister had cast over him.

TWELVE ————————————

On October fifth they said in Ixtepec: "Today they are reading the sentences. Today Abacuc is coming. Today Isabel will do something." The day grew under the light of these phrases, the sky became round and the sun shone perfectly. Jubilant because of the radiant sun, we went to wait in the plaza and to hover near the hotel balconies. We saw how the officers left very early and walked hurriedly to the presbytery. They seemed terrified. We talked about them confidently as we ate jícamas and peanuts. The day that unfurled on the valley seemed like a Sunday, full of pink shirts and coconut candy. We filled the benches in the plaza, formed groups and stretched out lazily in the peaceful morning air. On the tops of the tamarinds the hours ran along effortlessly and the shadows swirled around the trees. At noon the peanuts had made us thirsty and feet began to grow impatient, waiting for Abacuc. We looked toward the front door and the closed windows of the Hotel Jardín, and Isabel's name was charged with violence. Around two in the afternoon the phrases and the anger were melting in the heat and it had stopped being Sunday.

"Father Beltrán condemned to death!"

262

The sentence fell on the plaza with the meaningless fury of a rock crashing down on a hut. We looked at each other with fright, and searched for the place the sun had occupied. "It doesn't matter, it's still early." We strained our ears to hear the gallop of Abacuc's horse. All we heard was silence. The sierra was far away, perhaps the heat was making them travel slowly, but they would come. They could not abandon us on that most unhappy day.

"Dr. Arístides Arrieta condemned to death!"

Again we waited, without words and without threats, for the gallop that was so many years late in arriving.

"Joaquín Meléndez condemned to death!"

And if Isabel was betraying us? If our people did not arrive? And who were our people, if we were nothing but orphans whom no one heard? We had been waiting for so many years that we no longer had any other memory.

"Nicolás Moncada condemned to death!"

So Nicolás was to die, too? We turned to look at the windows of the Hotel Jardín, motionless and alien. The hotel, with its pink walls and black iron grating, seemed very far away. It was a stranger in the streets of Ixtepec. It had turned into an enemy a long time ago and its presence was an insult to our sorrows. Inside it was Isabel, another stranger. The women began to cry; the men, with their hands in their pockets, stamped on the dirt and looked at the sky to conceal their anguish.

"Rosario Cuéllar, five years of prison!"

"Carmen B. de Arrieta, free on bail!"

"Juan Cariño, free because he is not in possession of his faculties!"

It had all ended in accordance with the strangers' will and we did not leave the plaza. We went on waiting.

The sun blazed behind my mountains and the birds that live in the tamarinds began their nocturnal chirping. On any day in my past or my future there are always the same lights, the same birds, and the same anger. The years come and the years go and I, Ixtepec, still wait.

The officers left the presbytery, took out their handkerchiefs indifferently, wiped the sweat from their faces, and went calmly to the hotel. Who cared about our anger or our tears? Certainly not they, who moved as peacefully as if they were alone. In silence the purple skirts and pink shirts melted into the orange shadows of the night.

If memory restored all of my instants, I would tell now how we left the plaza, and how dust fell on Agustina's hot bread, and how that evening there was no one who would eat it.

And I would also tell about the funereal light of that night and the shapes of its violet trees, but I do not remember. Perhaps the plaza was empty forever, and only Andrés, the barber, went on dancing with his wife, holding her so close that she wept in time to the music, and we watched that embrace with amazement. But October fifth was not a Sunday or a Thursday, and there was no serenade nor did Andrés dance with his wife. There was only lassitude and the name of Nicolás Moncada, which grew softer and softer. We wanted to forget him, to know nothing of him or his brother and sister. It frightened us to remember and to know that that very afternoon we had solemnly abjured living within the sight of his eyes. Now, as I sit on this apparent stone, I wonder time and time again: What has become of his eyes? What did the earth become when it devoured our eyes reflected in his?

After that afternoon there came a morning that is here in my memory now, shining alone and standing out from all of my mornings. The sun is so low that I still do not see it and the coolness of the night populates the gardens and the plazas. An hour later someone crosses my streets to go to death and the world is frozen like a postcard scene. The people say hello to one another again, but the word is empty, the tables are abashed, and only the last words of the one who went away to die are said and repeated, and each time they are repeated they become more strange and no one is able to decipher them.

At dawn of the day appointed for the execution the towns-people came out to the plaza and the streets to wait for the funeral procession. It was said that at 4 A.M. they would take the prisoners to the cemetery, the place chosen for the execution. The plaza was quiet, the almond trees in the church courtyard motionless; the people were silent, looking at the ground, which was beginning to turn slightly pink. Now everything had been said.

In his room Francisco Rosas, naked to the waist, stood before the mirror. A strange face looked at him from the glass. The General ran his shaving brush over the mirror's surface to divide the image in half, but instead of becoming deformed and disappearing like a face reflected in water, it went on looking at him impassively. The mirror reflected an unknown image of himself: his yellow eyes were oil stains that looked at him from a vegetable world; the lamplight made him arise from a dark corner at the bottom of which the plaster shone undaunted. Nervously he lathered his cheeks to disguise the face that looked at him, and concentrated all of his efforts on shaving.

From the bed Isabel, half naked, watched him. "Why are you getting up so early?"

He was startled. The girl's words took him out of the cadaverous world of the mirror. He cut his upper lip, and the lather turned pink, like strawberry ice cream. The grotesque face in the mirror stared at him.

"What questions you ask!" he replied, furious.

"Is it true that it's going to happen?" Isabel's words entered the mirror like insults.

"You know. You knew," the man replied brutally.

Isabel kept quiet. Rosas turned back to the mirror to finish shaving, then dressed very slowly, tied his tie carefully, selected two handkerchiefs and moistened them with cologne, and put them absentmindedly in the back pocket of his trousers.

The girl followed his movements, fascinated. Francisco Rosas' tall shadow ran along the walls, imitating his gestures; the coming and going of his boots on the tiled floor echoed on the ceiling. No sounds came from the street. It was not yet light.

"I'm not to blame."

The steps stopped for an instant and the man turned to look at her. "Neither am I."

"I'm not the only one who is guilty," she said.

"And what am I guilty of? Calling you that night at the door? You had already offered yourself. Don't tell me you're innocent. You knew what you wanted and you brought me to your hell. Do you hear me? To your hell!" And Francisco Rosas, livid and menacing, went up to the girl with his fist raised, ready to beat her face to a pulp.

Isabel's eyes, alien to his anger, stopped him. "I want to see Nicolás. He knows that I didn't invent these deaths."

"Shut up! I don't want to hear the Moncadas mentioned again. Never again! When you danced with me you knew everything."

"You had already killed Juan when you called to me." Isabel jumped up and put her voice close to Francisco Rosas' face.

The General slumped into a chair and held his head. It was true that he knew it, and that was the only reason he had called her to come with him. Why had he done it? He would never know.

Isabel came close to him and leaned toward his ear. "I want Nicolás," she said in a very low voice.

Francisco Rosas raised his eyes and looked at her face, which was like that of a young boy.

"I want Nicolás," Isabel's face repeated, more and more like the face of her brother.

They heard the footsteps of the aides approaching their chief's room, ready to go to the execution. Francisco Rosas heard them coming and it frightened him that the girl could hear them. He stood up, moved the screen from in front of the door, and closed it. Isabel rushed to get her red gown and began to dress. The General held her by the shoulders.

"Isabel, listen. Yes, I knew that your brother Juan was dead."

The girl looked at him. She shivered as if she were very cold.

"Yes, I knew it," Rosas insisted.

"That was why you called me. I always knew you would do it."

266

"No," he said, dismayed. He released his hold on the girl and took refuge in a corner of the room. Behind him he heard the crash of Isabel's fury as she opened bureau drawers and rummaged through the clothing, throwing shirts, bottles, and ties on the floor while she looked for something she could not find.

"What are you looking for?" he asked, frightened.

"I don't know. I don't know what I'm looking for," she said with a bottle in her hand, realizing that she was not looking for anything.

The General came close to her, took the bottle away, and then let it fall on the floor. "Don't look any more, there's nothing. You don't know it yet, but there's absolutely nothing."

"Nothing?"

"Nothing," Rosas repeated with conviction.

"Nothing," Isabel repeated, looking at her half-buttoned red dress.

The General felt relieved. "Nothing—seven letters that mean nothing," and nothing was to be out of that room, out of that life, not to walk through the same day again for so many years: peace.

"Then give me Nicolás."

"You should have asked me sooner," Rosas moaned, feeling that there was still something and that he would go on bouncing from day to day like a stone thrown into a bottomless pit. "Sooner," he repeated, embracing Isabel as if he were clutching at any plant he could reach to break his fall. Suffocated by the embrace, she went on trembling for a long time as she huddled close to her lover's chest.

In the hall the officers avoided each other's eyes; they would have preferred not to have heard the broken voice of their chief or Isabel's distraught voice. Don Pepe Ocampo came up to them solicitously.

"They're bringing you hot coffee now."

The officers did not answer; they looked gravely at the floor and adjusted their belts. Captain Flores took a bottle of brandy out of his trouser pocket and passed it to his friends, and each took a drink.

267

"This is a must."

"Yes, you have to have it to go on living," he said without seeing them. The morning had found him in disgrace. Each day that passed he felt more miserable. Like Francisco Rosas, he awaited the nothing that persisted in disguising itself as corpses, card games, songs and shouts. The company of his friends no longer consoled him. At that moment the shadows in the hall helped to hide his tears. He turned his back on his friends and saw Luisa in her blue robe standing at the door of her room. He walked over to her meekly.

"Don't expect anything after today," Luisa said, and slammed the door.

Flores stood in front of the closed door for a few moments. He did not know what to say or what pose to take. He did not expect anything. Embarrassed, he returned to the officers.

"Captain, you shouldn't allow such behavior. Women are supposed to obey."

The officers smiled: Justo Corona had always said the same thing—until today, the fifth of October, the day when they were going to execute a priest and a twenty-year-old boy who was the brother of their general's mistress.

"He's had bad luck with the one he lost and bad luck with the one he found," Pardiñas remarked, alluding to Francisco Rosas' delay.

"Cruz's twins have revolted, too. He hasn't come out yet. Go and call him, Pardiñas, it's getting late," Justo Corona said, looking at his wristwatch by the light of the lamp.

Pardiñas approached Cruz's door and knocked loudly; he heard the Lieutenant Colonel's panic-stricken voice.

"Who's there?"

"It's 4 A.M., Lieutenant Colonel."

"Coming," Cruz replied.

Inside the room, Rosa and Rafaela were praying softly; Cruz, dressed and shaved, was standing before them trying to obtain their pardon.

"What do you want me to do? I can't defy my orders. Do you

want them to shoot me? Listen, is that what you want? Yes, you want to see me shot, my belly ripped open by bullets! And is that why you pretended you loved me? The only thing you've wanted is to see me dead. Girls, listen! I'm a man who loves life. I'm very different from a priest. What is a priest good for? He doesn't love women or life. For him it's all the same whether he lives or dies —and now that we're killing him he'll go to heaven. But I have no other life or other heaven than the one you give me."

The girls, kneeling, continued to pray.

"All right, I'm going," Cruz said, walking to the door.

He waited for a few moments and then, seeing that his friends did not change their position, pounded his fist on the wall. "You want to see me wallowing in my own blood, but you're not going to!" And he went out, slamming the door.

THIRTEEN ─────────────────────

A very fine orange-colored streak rose from the dark horizon;
the flowers that open at night closed, and their perfumes remained in the air for several moments before disappearing. The
blue garden began to emerge from its purple shadows. Another
morning passed unnoticed for the men who drank coffee before
going to organize more deaths. Cruz joined the group. Don Pepe
offered him a cup of steaming coffee. The Lieutenant Colonel
accepted it and looked at his friends, trying to smile.

"What's going on?" he asked, pointing to the door of Rosas'
room.

"They're fighting to find peace," Flores said.

The General caressed Isabel's curls and forehead; then he
gently broke away from her, arranged himself a little, and went
out into the hall, shaking. His men stared at the floor. He glanced
at them and pointed to the cups of coffee they were holding.

"Where's that fellow?" he asked scornfully.

"He was right here. He brought the coffee."

Flores was about to go to find the hotelkeeper, but Rosas
grabbed the pitcher of coffee and poured himself a cup.

270

"It's cold!" he said angrily, and emptied it on the plants in the garden.

Don Pepe, appearing with his habitual smile, said, "General!"

"Lock the door securely so they won't be able to get in," Rosas said without looking at him. He moved toward the lamp and looked at his watch; it was 4:11 A.M.

He began to walk with long strides. As he left the door and caught sight of the groups of silent townspeople, he turned to his men. "What a life!" he exclaimed.

The people scarcely looked in his direction. He had won, and nothing but sadness inundated the subdued town. He realized that we were in the street to witness our defeat. He quickened his pace. For the first time he was advancing through a different world; the smoke had cleared and the trees, the houses, and even the air took on visible form.

He felt that he carried on his shoulders all of the weight of the world, and a very ancient weariness made the distance from the hotel to the presbytery interminable.

When Rosas crossed the barricades of soldiers who were guarding the Military Command, some knots of vindictive men and women walked over to Isabel's balconies to call her by name, to shout that she was an ungrateful daughter, and to insult her; with angry voices they described what was happening in the street.

"Now they've reached the presbytery!" And they pounded on the door of the balcony, but the balcony remained closed to the words of Ixtepec.

In the Military Command Francisco Rosas listened to his own voice giving absurd orders. Father Beltrán and Dr. Arrieta would go in the first platoon, led by Captain Flores. Flores stepped forward and stood at attention before his chief.

"Take a heavy guard," Francisco Rosas added laconically.

Nicolás Moncada and don Joaquín would go in the second platoon, led by Captain Pardiñas. Julio Pardiñas looked at the General without blinking. "Damn, it had to be me!" he said to himself unhappily and tried not to show his disappointment.

Rosas called him aside. "Make sure that when we reach the cemetery, Moncada won't be there!"

The Captain stared at him without understanding, but he found it more prudent not to ask questions.

"Before you cross the river, get rid of any curious bystanders and dismiss most of the guards," Rosas added without changing his tone of voice. He did not like to give explanations to his subordinates.

"But . . ." Pardiñas began.

"No buts, Captain. The Lieutenant Colonel will give you another prisoner." Francisco Rosas took out his cigarettes; he offered one to the officer and took another; he blew out a cloud of smoke and looked at his watch. "Cruz has gone to the municipal jail to get him now. As soon as his aide comes to tell you that he and the prisoner have left, we'll go." He rested his leg on the embrasure of the window and contemplated the quiet plaza. The blessing of a new day awakened the birds, opened the treetops, and outlined the houses in a soft light. The General felt peaceful.

"I understand, General, we must give pleasure if they give it to us." Julio Pardiñas gave him a sidelong glance. His words did not take the General out of that ineffable moment. The officer felt troubled. Suddenly Rosas' idea made him happy and he looked at him with admiration.

He would carry out the order to execute four condemned men and save Isabel's brother. He would be above reproach, as would the General. He wanted to say something kind, and he thought of Isabel. "And they say that the one we love is the one who does not love us."

The allusion to Julia broke the moment of peace. Francisco Rosas turned to look at him, threw away his cigarette, and adjusted his trousers with both hands.

"When we forget, it's because life has ended, Captain."

In what wasted dawns did Julia float now? She had escaped forever from the dawns of Ixtepec. He saw her in that instant traveling through the skies of other plazas, and his body felt as heavy as if he were going to be executed that October fifth in the cemetery of Ixtepec.

Several minutes passed in silence, and Julio Pardiñas was sorry for the words that had brought Julia to the balcony of the presbytery. "He'll never get over her," he said to himself, and wished that the wait with Francisco Rosas would soon end.

Cruz's aide arrived, breathless. "General, they're already on the way with the chosen one, who is a . . ."

Francisco Rosas interrupted him violently. "It doesn't matter who he is! Have the first platoon get ready to leave. And you and your prisoners will leave ten minutes later," he added, looking at Captain Pardiñas with annoyance.

The halls and the patio of orange trees were filled with comings and goings, peremptory orders, shouts and footsteps. The death of others is a rite that demands absolute precision. The prestige of authority resides in order and the deployment of useless forces. Even the lowest-ranking soldiers had a solemn and impenetrable face that day. Immobile, with their rifles raised and bayonets fixed, they awaited the arrival of the prisoners.

General Francisco Rosas left the Military Command, followed by a small group of aides. He headed for the cemetery on horseback. The people saw him go and the news went from mouth to mouth, from street to street.

"Rosas has left for the cemetery!" they shouted in front of Isabel's balconies.

The girl did not hear the shouts that came from the street. Instead, she advanced through a space where the nights and days were illusory. Outside of time, with her back to the light, she was changing into other Isabels, who assumed unexpected forms. The room in the Hotel Jardín and the objects that furnished it belonged to a time from which she had departed without changing her position. They were only the vestiges of an abolished past. All that existed was a future outside of time, where she moved toward a predictable end.

The excited outcries from the street entered the rooms of the other mistresses. Antonia, driven out by the shouting, rushed to the hall, where she encountered Luisa, who was on her way to the twins' room. Sitting on the floor, the sisters looked up in astonishment to see their friends. Luisa fell on the unmade bed and rubbed her hand on her opaque hair. Her eyes were the same dirty blue as her rumpled robe. Antonia lay down beside her and hid her face between the sheets.

"He's already gone to the cemetery," Rosa repeated incredulously. Then, were there no miracles? Had their prayers been ineffectual? "Perhaps it may still rain fire before the shots ring out."

"I want to go to Papá," Antonia moaned.

"And the other one?"

"Shut up in her room."

"Poor Isabel!" shrieked Antonia, the girl from the coast.

"Poor, you say? She ought to get out of here, he doesn't love her."

"Then why did he bring her here?" the twins asked innocently.

"To do evil! He's bad. Bad!" Antonia screamed, possessed by a sudden fury.

"Of course, to do evil . . ."

"Bad! We're like him, and tonight life will begin again as before," Luisa said sententiously.

"You're wrong, it will never be the same as before," Rafaela replied.

FOURTEEN ─────────────────

In the patio of the Military Command they were lining up the prisoners. The first platoon was organized to go out to the street. Father Beltrán, wearing Juan Cariño's morning coat and striped trousers, occupied his place between the soldiers. As a sergeant tied his hands behind his back, the priest stood quietly, offering no resistance. Dirty and wan, Dr. Arrieta stared at the priest's hands, which had begun to turn dark red. The same sergeant came toward him and quickly tied his hands and placed him next to the priest.

Justo Corona yelled some incomprehensible orders that reverberated in the patio and the first platoon began its march, passing under the orange trees and on to the street, where the light was still muted.

We greeted the sight in silence. "Now they're taking them away . . ." The eyes that saw them leave would not see them come back from that journey of no return. Embarrassed, we lowered our eyes and listened to the rhythmical sound of the military boots that walked monotonously on the cobbles of the plaza.

They veered to the left and went down Correo Street, looking for the shortest route to the cemetery. The trees were grave, with quiet boughs. The shouts gradually spread: "They've taken away the priest and the doctor!"

Luisa caressed the medal she wore around her neck. It was a useless gesture: the medal would not take her out of the imminent night that was now inside of the hotel.

"Clean my boots! They're stained with the priest's blood."

Luisa obeyed her lover's order without flinching and polished Flores' boots until they shone like mirrors. She would always accept the abjection to which she had been reduced. "No one falls; this present is my past and my future; it is I myself; I am still the same instant." Again she caressed the medal of the Divine Face and let it slip down on her breast, where it had been since the day of her first communion, so much like the day she was living that it seemed to be the same day.

When the first platoon went down Correo Street, Colonel Justo Corona appeared on horseback, followed by a group of his men. The Colonel was trying to appear indifferent but his distorted face and the stiffness of his shoulders revealed his emotion. It was too late for us to try to free the condemned, and nevertheless Justo Corona rode up and down on the lookout for danger, glancing furtively at the half-open balconies and the curtains drawn in mute farewell to the victims. A few minutes later the second platoon, with don Joaquín and Nicolás, went out into the imperfectly delineated Ixtepec morning. A large guard followed it. Don Joaquín, manacled, found it difficult to follow the pace of the younger men and seemed worried about keeping step, as if he did not want to make a bad showing on his last journey through Ixtepec. His face was tired but it seemed that the jail had rejuvenated him; there was something childlike in his manner. As he went out to the street with his hands tied behind his back, Nicolás looked at us with a broad circular glance, half surprise, half joy; then he turned away and walked on, keeping step.

276

"Goodbye, Nicolás!" they shouted from the balconies as the young man in shirtsleeves passed.

The goodbyes jolted him out of his surprise; startled, he turned and regaled the people with a flashing smile. When he passed his Aunt Matilde's house, he lowered his eyes; he and his sister and brother playing in "England" remained there forever. He remembered its green woods and red-coated hunters. "They will still be just as green on this dry morning." He heard the words of the play in the melded voices of Hurtado and Isabel; only his sister lived outside of his memory, grasping his hand day and night. "We can't stay here!" Below, watching them, were his mother and his aunt, sitting on two identical chairs; far from them his father was stopping the clocks, and despite his gesture the minutes advanced swiftly on the road that led to the cemetery: "We'll go away from Ixtepec."

Don Joaquín did not want to see the closed windows of his house. "I lived there." Everything was a dream, a beautiful, disciplined dream where each bottle and each gesture fitted inside of an exact minute. The disorder of that morning troubled him and he turned to look at his nephew, who also looked at him. How strange that the two, who belonged to different generations, would die at the same time! It was better not to talk to one another.

The morning advanced delicately. The cows coming out to pasture encountered the condemned men. The dogs also came to meet the soldiers leading the prisoners, and barked angrily for a time at the soldiers' boots. Don Joaquín looked at them gratefully: "I hope someone will take care of them!" and watched them sniffing in the rubbish heaps for something to eat. No one had lighted a fire in the houses. The people stared at the funeral procession; some women followed Nicolás' platoon, while others accompanied the priest and the doctor from a distance. The Moncadas' house was as silent as it is now as I watch it from this height; its windows were already closed, preserving for all time the strange air of that morning, the morning of the execution.

Nicolás and his uncle came to the edge of the town and Captain Pardiñas dispersed the women who were following the procession. Only the soldiers and the prisoners took the road to the cemetery.

This was the place where Julio Pardiñas was to permit Nicolás Moncada to escape. The officer turned frequently to look at the young man, who, unaware of his imminent freedom, walked along in the certainty that he would soon die. Cruz's aide was waiting under a pepper tree with the prisoner from the municipal jail. In the distance Pardiñas saw the two men smoking under the tree. On the other side of the river, several hundred yards away, were the white walls of the cemetery; behind them, on the hill, shone the small blue crosses on the yellow earth.

"There goes Nicolás!"

The shout restored form to the shadows in which Isabel was wasting away. The young girl stood up and moved close to the window to hear the sounds that rose from the plaza. The same shout persisted in repeating itself and falling on her like a shower of pebbles. She did not understand.

They had taken Nicolás to the cemetery!

A strange voice clinging to the cracks in the blinds entered her ears as if it were trying to tell her a great secret. She moved away from the window and once again did not recognize the room: she was in a motionless paradise where the earth and the sky were of stone. The door burst open.

"Go and plead for your brother's life!" Rafaela ordered.

Some women with eyes of stone were looking at her. Isabel did not answer; she had never met them. She remembered serenades and young girls spinning to the music like the tails of comets. She had not joined that clamor of jewels and small talk. The strange girl approached, buttoned her dress, and looked for her misplaced shoes in the heap of clothing on the floor.

"Rosa, go and get Gregoria."

Rosa went out to find the old woman. The eyes of the mistresses waited as if they were frozen, outside of time, like the little hands of the clock that Félix stopped. The servant woman came in.

"Accompany Isabel to the cemetery to plead for her brother's life."

"He promised it to me," Isabel remembered.

"He lied!"

They took her by the arm and led her to the closed front door of the hotel. The women talked to don Pepe Ocampo, unlocked the door, opened it, and pushed her out into the street. She found herself in the plaza, surrounded by dark knots of people who moved like a misshapen animal. Gregoria took her hand. "They've taken your brother to the cemetery," the mouths said, coming so close that they dampened her face with saliva. "Ungrateful daughter, your parents are weeping over your disgrace." And the dark eyes shone for an instant near her own, illuminated by the light of dreams. She could not move: she swayed back and forth as she had done that night in the church when she looked for Francisco Rosas and was separated from her own people.

"Let her through."

Rocked by the hatred, Isabel lost her direction and the minutes collapsed in the coming and going of steps and voices.

"Let her through," Gregoria implored.

When they reached Correo Street, the servant woman's braids were undone and tears were rolling down Isabel's cheeks.

"I hope we'll get there in time, my dear!"

Before them the street descended rapidly to the edge of town. The light of dawn became sharper, turning into a narrow sword. They began to run, and their steps were repeated on the cobbles and the abutments as if a thousand runners pursued them. Behind their curtains the townspeople smiled. "It's little Isabel, poor thing," Cástulo sighed; he was spying from the roof of her Aunt Matilde's house. Cástulo was the only one who wanted Isabel to obtain the life of her brother; all Ixtepec wanted her to pay for her sins.

They came to the river. At that season the water was very deep, and Nicolás' sister forded it on foot and came out on the other side with her red dress dripping wet. Gregoria, soaked, watched the river take her shawl away.

"Don't cry, dear. God will make us arrive in time."

In the cemetery the execution was taking place. The General, standing very close to the open graves, witnessed the deaths.

Captain Flores approached to give the *coup de grace* to Father Beltrán and the priest's blood spurted out on the starched collar of Juan Cariño's shirt. The first light of morning illuminated the priest's face, which had become strangely frozen. "Young men, you lack reason; that is why you commit crimes." Mr. President's words lived on in the bloody morning coat. Flores tried not to look at him. How confused everything was! Why did that strange face have to die with the words and the suit of his friend?

Don Joaquín, with lowered eyes, looked at his shoes, which sank in the soft earth that would soon fall on his body. "How strange to be beneath the ground; I have always walked above it." Why were they going to hide him so soon, and with his shoes on? The sun rose punctually and, instead of seeing it reflected on the walls of his room, he was standing up, wearing his black party shoes. "I haven't even taken off my clothes yet," he said to himself with amazement. That day the time and the events were out of joint. "This letter is for my wife," a familiar voice said, and the words bounced from tomb to tomb, filling the morning with the voice of Arístides Arrieta. The words were silenced by a discharge that was more sonorous than the previous one. Don Joaquín saw that his shoes were sinking deeper into the earth of that ceremony and that the light advanced softly to illuminate the end of the most brilliant fiesta Ixtepec had ever had.

"General, I wasn't invited! I'm just a horse thief!"

The order of doña Carmen's party was broken by the intrusive words of the stranger, who stood by the open grave intended for Nicolás Moncada, proclaiming that he was an uninvited guest. A discharge and a *coup de grace* silenced the stranger's protests. Order was restored, and don Joaquín knew that his turn had come and that the door of doña Carmen's house would be closed to him forever. "I hope they accept animals in heaven!"—and he remembered the sad fate of Ixtepec's stray dogs.

"Who will take care of them now?" And he thought intensely of heaven, trying to imagine the faces of the angels he would see momentarily. But he did not have time: lying on the blood-soaked earth, his eyes were still searching for the faces of the angels, protectors of dogs, when Pardiñas came to give him the *coup de grace*.

Then there was an astonishing silence. The cemetery smelled of gunpowder; the soldiers were silent in the presence of the dead, who bled profusely and, with their blood, broke the harmony of the blue crosses and white headstones. The broken heads and chests lived an intense and disorderly life, and the blue and white cemetery seemed to reproach them for their presence. The soldiers looked at each other uncomfortably. Why had they killed these people? They had committed a stupid act. Francisco Rosas bit his lip.

"That's everyone, isn't it?" he asked, summoning strength before ordering the burial of the victims.

"There's one more! Me!" someone shouted from a cemetery path.

Francisco Rosas turned irritably: he had recognized the voice. Nicolás Moncada, very pale, walked toward him in a straight line. Disconsolate because of the young man's presence, the General looked for the officers and saw their faces, now tired of blood. "He did not accept my pardon." He turned pale and slapped his thighs with the palms of his hands.

"Oh! Captain Pardiñas sent word that you had escaped," he said after a few seconds.

Nicolás remained silent: Rosas made a vague gesture and Pardiñas approached the young man. Behind his back the General heard the shot.

Fascinated, the officers watched as Nicolás' white shirt, stretched out in the morning air, filled with blood. They heard someone running, and Lieutenant Colonel Cruz's aide appeared behind the tombs. He was sweating and breathless.

"He wouldn't come with us, General. He got away from me and headed for the cemetery as fast as he could go," the man said without taking his eyes from Nicolás' body.

Francisco Rosas pounded his fist on one of the stone crosses and, without saying a word, bit his lip.

"I'd say he probably didn't like life very much," the man added, frightened by the General's fury.

"The one who doesn't like it is you, you son of a bitch!" Cruz shouted, infuriated.

Francisco Rosas looked at his hand, surprised at the pain produced by the blow. He thought he was going to cry, and pounded the stone cross more forcibly than before. His men forgot the dead to glare savagely at the soldier who had let Nicolás escape. Rosas glanced briefly at the young man lying on the earth and then turned away. Why did he always kill what he loved? His life had always been a lie; he was condemned to walk alone, forsaken by fortune. He felt miserable, and thought bitterly of Nicolás, who was watching his defeat with the glassy eyes of death. The Moncadas had shown him the world of camaraderie, and when he entered it, confidently, they snatched it away from him, leaving him alone again, back in the nothingness of his days. They had deceived him, and he had played fairly. "Never again will I pardon anyone," he said to himself with regret, and remembered Isabel's words of deceit and her brother's proud face. But something inside of him was broken; he felt that from then on, his orgies would have no place for women, only alcohol.

His career as a Mexican general had just collapsed in the blood of a twenty-year-old boy. What did Nicolás believe in? Something that he had caught a glimpse of that morning. His whole life rushed over the silent tombs of Ixtepec; a succession of shouts and shots had left him paralyzed; Isabel and Julia were shattered in the din of the execution, his sierra nights and his garrison days were broken into smithereens. He saw himself standing aimlessly in that cemetery reeking of powder, hearing a bird singing on one of the tombs. There were five corpses stretched out at his feet, and Nicolás was looking at his back. "And now what, Francisco

Rosas?" he said to himself, afraid of bursting into tears before his subordinates, who respectfully kept silent and stared at the ground. But Francisco Rosas, who did not want anyone's pity, began to walk down the cemetery path. He never thought that the death of that foolish boy would affect him like that.

"He had his whole life ahead of him—what a shame!" and he wanted to flee from the cemetery where he too had just died. He restrained himself from running. "Too bad about the horse thief," he said to himself in order to forget Nicolás' eyes.

He could never again look into the eyes of Isabel. "I wasn't invited, General." And who had invited *him* to Ixtepec? He was a person who had been executed too—by fate. He found his horse and took off at a gallop through the open country. He wanted to go away from Ixtepec, not to know anything more of the Moncadas ever again. And he rode willy-nilly through the radiant morning, which rose from the earth full of lights and smells, so remote from his sorrow. Colonel Justo Corona followed him at a full gallop.

From a distance, Isabel and Gregoria saw them pass. With her eyes the young girl followed her lover's horse as it raced away under the golden light of October.

"He's running away," and she slumped down on a stone.

The strange girl in the Hotel Jardín who had buttoned her dress was right: he had lied to her.

"Yes, dear, he's running away."

Gregoria sat down beside Isabel and wept with the forbearance of those who are acquainted with grief and accept it. She became engrossed in her weeping, not looking at Isabel, who was lost in a tearless solitude. She wept not only for the Moncadas: one misfortune had followed another in her life, and rarely had Gregoria had the time to commemorate them and to cry over them.

FIFTEEN ───────────────

The sun rose vigorously and the countryside was filled with the song of cicadas and the hissing of snakes. It was late when the soldiers returned to town after burying the dead. On the road they encountered the two women sitting on the stones; recognizing Isabel, they hastily went away. Gregoria went after them. She wanted to know what had happened at the cemetery. She came back to Isabel and the young girl frightened her: she looked so strange in her red dress, sitting in an empty field. The old woman did not dare to tell her what the soldiers had said. She stared at Isabel for a long time. What was that last guest at the fiesta of Ixtepec thinking, clad in red silk? All that remained of the night illuminated by Bengal lights was the red dress drying in the sun.

"Do you love him very much, my dear?" she asked, terrified.

Isabel did not answer. Gregoria uneasily patted her knee: she wanted to break the spell of that morning, identical in appearance to all other mornings.

"It's a sin, my dear." And Gregoria looked toward the cemetery where Juan and Nicolás lay buried. "Child, you don't have a home any more."

284

No word could touch Isabel; she was possessed by the devil.

"You can't go back to the hotel, either."

The old woman had the impression that Isabel did not hear her. She wanted to get up and leave that place which deafened her with its silence. "Let's go to the shrine, child. There the Virgin will take Rosas out of your body."

Her words revolved in the world without any sound from Isabel. The future did not exist and the past was gradually disappearing. She looked at the glazed sky and the countryside, imperturbable and identical to it: round, limited by mountains as permanent as that round day, which was limited by two identical nights. Isabel was in the center of the day like a rock in the middle of the countryside. From her heart stones sprang forth; they ran through her body and made it immovable. "To the marble statues, one, two, three!" The words of the childish game reverberated in her memory, and echoed like a bell ringing. She and her brothers froze when they said those words, until someone they had secretly chosen passed by, touched them, and broke the enchantment. Now no one would come to break the spell that had been cast on her; and her brothers would be frozen forever. "To the marble statues, one, two, three!" With the repetition of the magic words the day was frozen, too, like a statue of light. Gregoria was speaking to her from an airy, glancing world she no longer shared. She looked at her without blinking.

"We must go now, child."

The old woman stood up and took Isabel's arm. The girl let herself be led, and the two women took the road to the shrine where I am now, the vantage point from which I contemplate myself. From here I see them circling the town, because Gregoria did not want to walk through it: it frightened her to know that they would see Isabel and that Isabel would see them. And so they went around me, walking on the slopes of the hills that guard me. Around 5 P.M. they sat down under a pepper tree; the heat made them seek its shade. Gregoria remembered that Enedino Montiel Barona lived near there. He was the wisest and most courteous of my people. Now his hut is only a heap of rubble, and

285

it has been a long time since his doves died and since Gregoria left Isabel under the pepper tree while she went to ask him for help. Enedino, like the good poor man that he was, gave her what he had: a handful of tortillas, a little salt, and a jug of cool water. Isabel drank the water and Gregoria put salt on the tortillas and ate them discreetly.

At that time no one had yet asked about them. In Ixtepec the day passed oppressed by misfortunes and each one bowed his head, waiting for the end of those hours that seemed not to want to leave my corners.

"And will the Virgin be able to take away this morning?"

"With God's help, but you mustn't think of Francisco Rosas, my child, not once! You must keep your thoughts on the Virgin, and when we come to her feet she will remember us, and when we go down the hill, that man will have gone away forever from your thoughts. The Virgin will keep him away with her own hands."

Isabel listened attentively and watched how she chewed her tortilla. The name of Rosas was scarcely familiar to her; her past was fleeing from her memory; all that remained was that morning formed of astonishing coincidences, reduced to Gregoria eating her tortilla.

They rose and continued on their way. At 7 P.M., as the two were climbing the hill I am looking at now, Gregoria prayed in a very loud voice and suddenly her words took on the form of blue cones, smiling lizards, and enormous pieces of paper that danced before Isabel's eyes.

"He killed Nicolás. He lied to me. Rosas deceived me."

Gregoria said that the child Isabel turned to look at her with terrified eyes. She had blood on her knees, the red dress was in tatters, and there was gray dust on her curls. The sun was sinking and its last orange splendor extracted dark reflections from the red silk. The girl stood up and began to run down the hill.

"Although God may condemn me, I want to see Francisco Rosas again!"

Her voice shook the hill and reached the doors of Ixtepec.

286

Lightning came out of her eyes, a tempest of black curls covered her body, and a whirlwind of dust rose and made the locks of hair invisible. In her rush to find her lover, Isabel Moncada got lost. After looking for her for a long time, Gregoria found her lying far down the hill, transformed into a stone. Terror-stricken, she crossed herself. Something told her that the Señorita Isabel did not want to be saved: she was too smitten with General Francisco Rosas. Gregoria approached the accursed stone and addressed God, begging mercy. She spent the whole night pushing the stone up the hill to leave it at the feet of the Virgin, next to the other sinners who lie here; she brought it here as evidence that man loves his sins. Then she went down to Ixtepec to tell what had happened.

After midnight Juan Cariño left the jail and walked across town. He did not want to accept freedom until he knew that no one walked my streets. He did not want them to see him wearing the cassock; it seemed to be an affront to his dead friends. The crack-crack of the knocker startled the tarts. They had already forgotten his existence, and in their fear they called out without opening the door, "Who is it?"

"One who was," the madman replied, accepting his future condition as a ghost.

SIXTEEN _____

The weeks and the months passed, and like Juan Cariño we never became our old selves again. Francisco Rosas also stopped being what he was; drunken and unshaved, he no longer searched for anybody. One afternoon he went away on a troop train with his soldiers and his aides and we never heard of him again. Other officers came to give land to Rodolfito and to repeat the hangings in a different silence in the branches of the same trees, but no one, ever again, invented a fiesta to redeem men from execution. There are times when strangers do not understand my fatigue or my dust, perhaps because now there is no one to mention the name of the Moncadas. The stone, the memory of my suffering, and the end of the fiesta of Carmen B. de Arrieta are here. Gregoria put this inscription on it. Her words are burned-out fireworks.

"I am Isabel Moncada, the daughter of Martín Moncada and Ana Cuétara de Moncada, born in the town of Ixtepec on December 1, 1907. I turned into stone on October 5, 1927, before the startled eyes of Gregoria Juárez. I caused the unhappiness of my parents and the death of my brothers Juan and Nicolás. When I

288

came to ask the Virgin to cure me of my love for General Francisco Rosas, who killed my brothers, I repented and preferred the love of the man who ruined me and ruined my family. Here I shall be, alone with my love, as a memory of the future, forever and ever."